A Warrior's Legacy

Orestes

J. E. Bell

A Warrior's Legacy: Orestes

330 Publications LLC
3609 Mattingly Road
Buckner, KY 40010-8803

Second Edition
Printed in the United States of America

CONTENTS

Part I: Warrior Peak

Part II: Serenity Valley

Part III: Tyrclopia

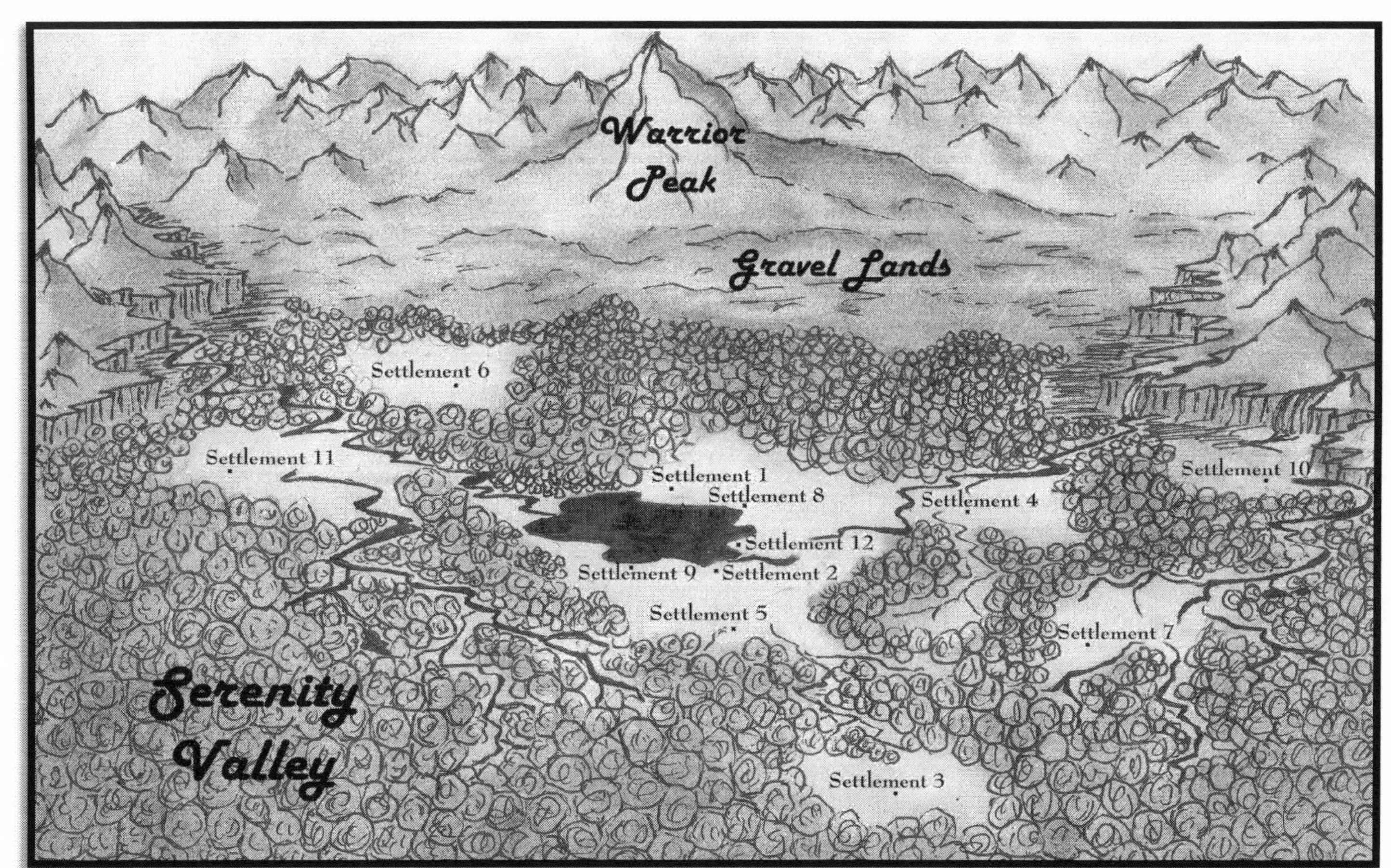
Warrior Peak
Gravel Lands
Settlement 6
Settlement 11
Settlement 1
Settlement 8
Settlement 10
Settlement 4
Settlement 12
Settlement 9
Settlement 2
Settlement 5
Settlement 7
Serenity Valley
Settlement 3

PART I: WARRIOR PEAK

Chapter One
The Intruder

Year 313

I WAS IN THE TOWER the day that the intruder came to the Facility.

I was only five years old at the time, but I still should have suspected that something was amiss. Trainees were rarely kept inside for longer than it took to wait out a sandstorm or recover from a particularly bad injury. At the time, however, it made little difference to me whether I was inside or outside our jagged tower planted in the heart of one of the desert's great dunes. For when we were outside, my fellow trainees and I were pelted constantly by tiny grains of sand that banded together to become harsher fists than those of our trainers. Our bodies were never free of sand and grit, so much so that we couldn't recognize each other's faces without that familiar outer layer and so that our bodies felt cold without that coarse blanket. Inside the tower offered little more comfort. We were confined to our dark, solitary rooms where we lived in our own filth and blood and where, after a while, we longed to face the elements outside instead.

Some preferred the security of the tower's uneven stone walls because the trainers didn't harass them here. But the other trainees didn't have a guard outside their doors, and none of them had to endure visits from Dirth. Those two things were reserved for me.

Dirth's footsteps were the same that day as they were every other time he came. There was no mistaking his gait—hulking and deliberate, accompanied by the gentle singing of metal on metal as countless weapons bounced against his every limb. My heartbeat fell in line with his stride as the footsteps moved down the stone corridor and warned every other living being to scramble against the wall. When my guard muttered his salute, I jumped to my feet and straightened my shredded tunic. It was always better to start out standing.

He actually grinned at me when he entered this time. He was dressed in his typical hodgepodge of ripped and frayed cloaks, no more elegant than the rest of his army, mostly in colors of brown and tan. Although he covered as much of his skin as he could, there was no hiding his blotched face, as erratically colored as his clothing, and the dirty, straw-like hair that hung to his shoulders.

Though trembling, I stood my ground even as he came toe to toe with me. At eight feet tall, he towered over me, and I stared straight ahead at his thigh as I waited to see what abuse awaited me. I heard the air whistle as his arm swooped down and grabbed what was left of my tunic. My jaw clenched to stem the oncoming vomit as he lifted me to his eye level as easily as if I were a piece of cloth.

"You are a stubborn one," Dirth laughed.

His jagged teeth glinted in the brown hues of sunlight that squeezed through the tiny window behind me. Never having been tall enough to reach it, I was tempted to glance through my window now, but I knew better than to break eye contact.

"I would expect nothing less, of course," he continued, "but I wonder, do you know why I'm here, Orestes?"

Orestes. I hated the word because he was the only one who used it, but I loved it because it was mine. I was Orestes, and he was Dirth. No one else in the Facility had his own word.

"No," I said. In vain I tried to keep my body still and my voice from betraying the terror behind it. Dirth and his army thrived on fear.

His patchy face stretched more tightly against his skull as his smile widened. "Stubborn but not clever. Well, Orestes, I'll tell you a secret. There is an intruder in our desert, and he's coming to the tower."

I said nothing. What could I do about an intruder? I was only five then and still small; I had eight years before I was even allowed to compete for a chance to join the army. And once a trainee turned into an army member, he could kill any intruder three times over singlehandedly.

"I haven't decided what I will allow the intruder to do here, but in case he tries to follow in Zachaes's footsteps, I want to remind you of a few things, pathetic though you still are." His left hand slipped into the layers of ragged cloaks piled onto his body. From them he drew a glass vial no bigger than one of his claw-like fingers. "Do you know what this is?" he asked. He shook the vial before my eyes so that the red liquid inside swirled hypnotically.

"Serum," I murmured.

"Right, serum—what separates you from me. Do you want to be like me, Orestes?"

Although I knew the serum was what could one day change me into an army member, the thought of looking like Dirth—towering, disproportionate, angular, and clawed at every tip—was suddenly too horrible to bear. Still, "yes" seemed to be the right answer, so I forced myself to say it.

Dirth cackled. "Little fool. No matter what happens today, you are under my control, under Lernuc's control. You will never do anything he won't be pleased by. Kill me, kill Humans, kill Morroks—prove your power the only way you know how, and we will have won." With the tip of one of his yellow nails, he uncorked the vial. "So that you remember where you come from—what you are."

Before I could react, he had dropped me to the ground and pinned me there with his arm. While I was still dazed, he shoved two of his fingers into my mouth, prying it open. I thought my cheeks would rip from the strain and my tongue burst from the foul taste. Then he tipped the vial and drained its contents into my mouth. The liquid burned the back of my tongue and inflamed the roots of my teeth.

Petrified but with a sudden burst of courage, I freed one hand, grabbed Dirth's fingers, and squeezed them together until I could close my mouth enough to spit the substance into his face before it invaded my throat. Undeterred, he shoved the vial further into my mouth, but I bit down as hard as I could, breaking the glass and drawing blood from his fingers. He recoiled with a growl as I doubled over, spitting out blood, glass, and that horrible liquid. The last I knew of Dirth was his pointed boot piercing into my stomach and the door slamming behind him so hard that the stone floor trembled.

I didn't know how long I lay there coughing and massaging my aching stomach. Before I even tried to sit up again, there were more footsteps outside my door. A whimper escaped me as I forced my body up to its knees. The door opened again long enough for two bundled babies to be dropped inside near the threshold. Their wails drowned out even the slam of my door as the guard resumed his place in front of it.

At first, the noise didn't bother me as much as the fact that they were in my room at all. Babies were always kept together on the first floor until they were big enough to walk around and get their own food. Then they each got their own room, just as I had mine. No one ever shared, least of all with me.

After watching the babies for several minutes, I decided no one was coming back for them. I thought it best to move them from right in front of the door in case Dirth or my guard stepped on them when they walked in. When I picked up the first one, I was surprised at how heavy it was; none of the babies on the first floor were this fat. I dropped them a few feet away from the door, which only made them cry more. Now the sound was starting to wear on me. Tears were a sign of weakness, but they wouldn't know that for a few more years. Figuring it wasn't a good idea to cover their mouths, I instead shoved my fingers into my own ears and retreated as far away from them as I could.

Hours passed. Besides the babies, all I could think about was the intruder Dirth had mentioned. Where was he? Dirth had said that he wasn't from the desert. I knew that there was a land somewhere outside the desert, but all we heard about it was that it was where new trainees came, usually when they were babies. But why would an intruder come here all on his own? I had never heard of such a thing. A fleeting image of a creature greater and uglier than the members of Dirth's army flashed through my mind. I wasn't sure if it comforted or frightened me.

Suddenly there were murmurs in the corridor; someone was in the tower who shouldn't have been. Another event out of place. No one could enter or leave our dune unless we let them.

Thankfully the babies had stopped crying. I listened eagerly for further disturbances inside, but none came for several minutes. There seemed to be something happening outside, but I couldn't reach my window to check. The shouts and clangs from without almost made me miss the sounds in my own corridor.

A single set of footsteps, light and quick, was coming toward us. Silently willing the babies to keep quiet, I padded across the room to the door and pressed my ear against it. My guard was reacting to the footsteps as well; I could hear him unsheathing his sword and moving toward the sound.

Suddenly two swords clanged together. A younger voice joined my guard's grunts as a duel began, right outside my room. In less than a minute, there was an almighty crash as something slammed against the other side of the door with such force that I leaped backward, nursing my ear. The babies started to cry again.

After a few moments of silence, something smashed against the door's lock, and the door swung forward. There stood a lanky boy with my guard dead and bleeding at his feet. He was about of age to join the army, but he was bigger and healthier than any thirteen-year-old I had ever seen, and like the babies, his clothes were clean and free of holes. He held a sword that was nearly half his height, and despite the blood dripping from his blade, I did not fear him.

He cast me one curious glance before crouching over the babies. Although he seemed reluctant to do so, he sheathed his sword and picked up one in each arm. He straightened up and made it as far as the doorway before he paused and looked back at me.

"Do you want to come?"

It was a simple question, but I had never been asked what I wanted before, not until today—not until Dirth had asked if I wanted to be like him. If I stayed, I would most surely become like Dirth—if not now, then certainly when I turned thirteen and had to take the serum with the rest. But if I went with the boy, maybe I wouldn't have to join the army. Surely this must be the intruder, the one from outside the desert. He must have been going back to where he came from, and this was my one chance to see what was beyond the desert.

"Yes," I said. I winced as I straightened up and felt Dirth's blow again, but I was determined to show the intruder that I was strong enough to go.

"I can't carry you, so you'll have to keep up," the boy said. He hoisted the babies more securely on each side and set off down the hall. I climbed over my dead guard and scurried after him.

As we hastened down the many winding stairs of the tower, it became clear that the noises I had heard outside were those of a battle taking place in the dune. When we reached the first floor, we found it free of army members. They were all outside, shooting arrows at the top of one side of the dune, where several dark-skinned people stood shooting back at them.

The boy ignored the battle and hurried to the other side of the dune, where the army members weren't paying attention. With great difficulty, he started the steep climb upward without the use of his arms. I got down on my hands and knees to follow him.

At the top of the hill waited a four-legged animal that stood taller than the boy. It was covered in short, brown hair, and its face was long with eyes bulging out to the sides rather than facing straight ahead. A long tail swished behind it, and a leather pallet was thrown across its broad back. The boy seemed unconcerned by the creature's odd appearance as he grabbed the rope tied around its face and looked over his shoulder at the dune.

"If I get on first, can you lift the twins up to me?" he asked me.

I had no idea what "twins" were, but I assumed he meant the babies, so I nodded. Leaving the babies in the sand, the boy clambered onto the beast, pulling himself by its longer hairs, until he sat with one leg on either side of its back. He reached down as far as he could without falling off, so to do my part, I picked up the first baby and held him over my head so the boy could grab him with ease. The second one was a bit more difficult because one of the boy's arms was busy with the first baby, but we managed it, in spite of both babies' incessant wailing.

Then there came a terrible moment in which I was sure the boy was going to leave without me. I hadn't been afraid up until this point, but now I began to imagine what fate awaited me if Dirth found me outside the dune. He would make me go back to my little room and put more than one guard outside it, and the next time he wanted me to take the serum, there would be no refusing him.

But no sooner had that image invaded my mind than the boy's arm came down again, this time for me. I grabbed ahold and jumped as he yanked me upward, far enough for me to pull at his clothes and the animal's hair and position myself to sit behind him.

The moment I was settled, the boy dug his heel into the animal's side, and it took off at a faster run than even the long-legged army members could have done. I screamed and threw my arms around the boy's waist to keep from falling off.

After a few minutes, I settled into the rhythm of the animal's jostling movements and chanced a look back at the tower. Only its black tip was visible poking from over the top of the dune. I tried to remember all of what Dirth had told me and wondered if he had meant for this to happen. But no matter what his threats meant, no matter who Lernuc was, no matter what the serum did, Dirth had given me at least one memory that wouldn't haunt me: my word—Orestes.

*

I looked on in amazement as the sand disappeared from under the four-legged animal's feet and was replaced by thousands of tiny green blades. The air also emptied of whipping grit, and the sky burst into a bright blue and the sun a bright yellow. I had never seen colors so brilliant.

Just as the last grains of sand disappeared, we came upon a man whose face was hidden by a cloak. On his chest was a picture of a sword framed by what looked to me like a large, solid triangular dune. The man held up his hand for us to stop, and the boy tugged on the ropes attached to the animal's head so it slowed to a halt in front of him.

"I was instructed to take the boy," the man said.

"Which one?" the boy asked. He held up the babies and glanced back at me.

"Him," he replied, pointing at me.

The boy looked back at me again. "Instructed by whom?"

"He will be safe. Don't you recognize this symbol?" He pointed at his chest.

"You must go back to defend your village. The Morroks will be angered by your actions. They value these boys highly, and it is important that we keep them safe, especially the one behind you."

The boy glanced back at me yet again, this time with a frown and a cocked eyebrow. I didn't want to go with the man, but the boy and I seemed to have no choice.

Before the boy could say anything, the man spoke again. "You're wasting precious time. Don't make me take him by force."

"You should go with him," the boy said to me, too softly for the man to hear. "But if he tries to take you back to the Morroks, you fight like hell to get away."

I nodded, wondering what Morroks were and why I had heard them mentioned so many times that day. Before I could say anything back to the boy, I felt the man seize me around the waist and lift me off the animal. He didn't put me down but instead pinned me to his side as if I were a bundle of spears and set off at a run.

Although I had agreed to go, I resisted his hold with all my might. Despite my struggle and my various threats and insults, the man said nothing but only gripped me harder. Once we were far away from the boy, he stopped and set me down. No one else was within sight. I considered running, but I didn't even know what the ground was made of outside the desert, much less where a safe place to hide would be.

"Okay, boy, you and I need to get a few things settled before we continue," the man began. He threw back his hood and crouched down so that we were at eye level. I balked at his appearance. I had never seen anyone like him. He looked like a big trainee; he was taller and broader than my rescuer, but his face was wrinkled and his hair gray. Still, he was nowhere near Dirth's size, and his skin and body weren't distorted like the army members.

Unsure of what he meant, I said, "I could kill you."

"No, I don't believe you can," he said. When I opened my mouth to tell him how sorry he would be, he added, "Not yet, anyway. Listen, I have no desire to harm you. I am taking you to Warrior Peak. It is my home, and I will see to it that you will be safe and grow up normally. I will not treat you like the Morroks did, but in order for me to do that, you have to stop acting like one."

"What's a Morrok?" I asked, my curiosity overriding my better judgment for a moment.

The man gritted his teeth and looked away. "Those monsters that were holding you prisoner."

"I was *not* a prisoner. Those stupid babies might've been, but I wasn't."

The man chuckled. "Whatever you say, son. But if you come with me and listen to what I say, I promise you that we will train you to be strong enough to fight the Morroks or anyone you wish."

I considered his words for a moment. This new world was becoming increasingly overwhelming, but I didn't seem to have a choice but to go with him. "Okay," I said when he didn't continue.

"Very good," the man replied, reaching for my hand. Thinking he was going to pick me up again, I snatched it away and called him a few nasty names. He persisted, though, and ended up holding me in place with one hand and shaking my hand with his other. "My name is Alec. What is yours?"

I thought for a moment, wondering if he meant my word. Then, for the first time in my life, I said, "My name is Orestes."

Chapter Two
Ten Years Later

Year 323

"YOU LOOK LIKE A COUPLE OF GIRLS prancing around each other like that."

Several appreciative chuckles from the other students accompanied Conrad's remark. The two "girls" in question reacted very differently; the young sergeant lowered his sword as he tried not to grin, but the old major brandished his blade at Conrad in substitution of an angry fist.

"Boy, you don't understand the first thing about evasion," Major growled. "You lumber around these training grounds outmuscling everyone who crosses your path, but what's going to happen when you finally run into someone bigger than you, huh?"

"I don't know," Conrad replied, not meeting Major's glare, "but I know dodging doesn't win you a fight."

There were murmurs of agreement among the other students. This was why I liked training with the older boys; they didn't cower before shouting teachers but instead questioned lessons that didn't make sense to them, like now. I, however, knew exactly what Major meant about evasion. Although I was beginning to rival my senior classmates in height, I was far from catching up with their muscles, and against giants such as Conrad, I had no chance in a contest of strength.

Before Major could counter again, I jumped to my feet and dusted off my hands. I moved to the front of the group with the two officers and relieved the sergeant of his training sword. "Dodging can earn you plenty," I said. "Try me."

A low "ooh," mingled with a few laughs, twisted through the group of boys. Although I had joined their class weeks ago, not many of them had seen me fight yet except for casual spars outside of class. Both in and out of class, students practiced their swordplay on the dirt training grounds, which was a fenced-in rectangle surrounded tightly by the military school's many wooden buildings. Several other classes like ours were taking place in different corners of the grounds, and after dinner, most everyone would be back for games and duels not under our instructors' watchful eye.

I had purposefully kept quiet in my new class because almost all the other students were older and bigger than I was. I had needed some time to size them all up so that, when a moment like this came, I knew I could win.

Conrad, indignant at being corrected by a skinny fifteen-year-old but unable to decline a challenge, rose slowly to his feet and accepted a sword from the major. Everyone scooted away to give us a wide berth. Conrad and I faced each other and nodded to let the other know we were ready. Deciding to take the initiative, I darted forward and jabbed at Conrad's side. He blocked, but before he could parry properly, I withdrew my sword and slid away toward his other side. Disgruntled, Conrad whipped around and swung heavily at me. The power behind the strike made it too difficult for me to hold the blades locked for long, so rather than trying to throw him off, I slackened my push and hopped out of the way so that his sword crashed down into the dirt. Taking advantage of his overbalance, I threw all my weight behind thrusting my shoulder into his ribs. Unfortunately, he was already moving and absorbed much of the blow as he staggered upright.

I couldn't help but smirk as the others' laughter provoked Conrad's face into an ugly snarl. His temper was quite contained, however, as he struck more quickly, trying to control my movements by forcing me to block blow after blow. To his frustration, this tactic also failed when I leaped backward, out of his range. Again I pounced toward his side, jabbing and skipping away before he could strike back. After a few minutes of this, I felt I had made my point and commenced with the finale. Throwing myself to the ground, I rolled twice, wrapped my arms around Conrad's knees, and found the right pressure point to bring him sprawling down to my level—all before he realized where I had gone.

Even Major chuckled as Conrad tried to untangle himself, kicking me without remorse along the way. Unperturbed, I scrambled to my feet and resumed my seat as everyone clustered together again.

"Perfect example. Well done, Orestes," Major said. "That's about all I have to say today. Go eat. And Conrad, take these blades to the blacksmith; it seems you chipped them."

Ignoring the other boys' comments as they moved toward the dining hall, I headed off Conrad as he approached the officers. "Hey," I said, "thanks for not taking my head off back there."

"We were using dull blades, stupid."

"Which would've made it all the more painful for me," I said. "Listen, why don't I take the swords? I can obviously move more quickly."

His face reddened, but then he caught my smirk. Mouth twitching ever so slightly, he replied, "You'd better take them because I'll flatten you if you don't."

I laughed as he trudged toward the dining hall with the others. I, on the other hand, set off straight to the blacksmith forge. The military school was a self-contained cluster of buildings, including everything from barracks and tailors to stocks of food and weapons. It was also the largest structure of Warrior Peak; because the city was built on the face of a mountain, the incline made it difficult to have large pockets of settlements. Below the military school level, all the houses, shops, and offices were spread haphazardly to the foot of the mountain, but above it sat only the Elder's cave and the General's level, both of which were rarely seen by anyone except the Elder and War Council generals themselves.

Warrior Peak was the only inhabitable mountain in a great range that stretched as far east and west as the eye could see. The other mountains were so steep and craggy that only a house or two might fit on their cliffs, which made them inhospitable for a people group as large as the Warriors, who numbered in the hundreds of thousands. Even we were confined to a limited space on the southern face of our mountain; the eastern and western sides became as rugged as the rest of the range to the point that our defensive outer wall only partially covered the foot because the jagged cliffs rendered any additional protection unnecessary.

When I reached the school's blacksmith forge, I was pleased to find my friend Aldis working alone inside. Like most Warriors, her hair was brown, though age had added an occasional streak of gray. Her complexion, however, was light, like mine. Generally Warriors had ruddy and tan skin that came from working and training outdoors most of their lives, but Aldis and I shared a naturally whiter tone. With my blond hair and fair skin, I never stood a chance of blending in with the other Warriors, and it was comforting, in a way, to know that Aldis couldn't either.

Before I could greet her, Aldis threw up her hands defensively. "I haven't had time to think of another story since your last visit."

"Oh, you need to be more organized than that," I said as I tossed the dull blades on a table littered with similar weapons. The entire forge was full of old equipment, from the weapons to the bellows; it was rarely used to produce new blades and indeed seemed more like an annex for weapon storage. New blacksmith forges had been built in recent years, but Aldis, content with repairing old blades, had remained faithfully at hers every day for as long as I could remember.

Aldis scoffed. "Well, if you boys wouldn't keep chipping my swords, then perhaps I'd have time for more leisurely activities."

"As if you've been slaving away all day!" I said. "It could be the middle of winter in here! I don't see one drop of sweat on you. There's not even a fire going. Or are you rubbing sticks together to melt metal nowadays?"

Aldis laughed and waved me onto a stool across from her. I absentmindedly selected a small hammer and balanced it in my hands as she spoke.

"So how is your new fighting class treating you?" she asked.

"Fairly well. I fought one of the biggest kids today. He must have been eighteen and more than two hundred fifty pounds."

"You're going to have to learn how to beat those types consistently if you ever want to win the tournament."

At the end of every year, all the male students competed in a sparring tournament that took place at the foot of the mountain. Many officers watched the highest levels of competition for superior students about to enter into their ranks upon graduation. I had never made it far enough for anyone except my mother to watch me fight.

"I'll be as big as any of them one day, don't worry. I'm just biding my time for now," I said. "So you really don't have a story?"

"I'm afraid not, unless you want to hear an old one again."

"No, I'll just come back when you've learned how to use your time a little more wisely." I dropped the hammer and darted out the door, fearful of the several blades, however dull, piled within Aldis's grasp.

Listening to Aldis's stories was my favorite way to end a long day of sparring or enduring the training officers shouting at us. Like every other boy in Warrior Peak, I lived at the military school, but I was always aware of how different I was from the rest of them. All Warrior children started their training at five years old, and although I had been five when I came to Warrior Peak, my adoptive parents, Fallon and Glynis, felt that I was too violent to be among other children at first. The first couple years of my life at Warrior Peak had therefore been spent mostly in my parents' house, one level below the military school. It was during that time that they taught me that it was wrong to cause other Humans pain and then how to form relationships with others (friendship among Morrok trainees was brutally discouraged).

And so I started military school at seven years old. It had been humiliating to sit through classes with five-year-olds who were learning to hold dull daggers properly when I had been wielding sharp swords since I could ball my fists. In addition, I was a foreigner and therefore an anomaly at Warrior Peak because no Human outside the mountain knew of our existence. However, from the first time I had stumbled into her forge, Aldis had always encouraged me as I moved up quickly through the fighting classes, losing friends my age and trying to gain older ones along the way. When reality became too heavy, she told me fantastic stories about other lands with clever but imperfect heroes who nonetheless seemed to deserve their victory in the end. Most of her stories involved Morroks, but I liked the characters so much that I didn't mind remembering the tower and Dirth while I listened. Very few Warriors had ever heard of the Morroks (and if they had, they barely believed in their existence), so it was a relief to know someone else who understood their power.

When I left Aldis's, I crossed the short distance to the dining hall, where the usual din suffocated whatever solace I had left. A few people hailed me, but I chose to sit with my friend Ritter. He was three years older than I and was an exceptional fighter despite his deceptively thin and unimpressive appearance. He was the son of my father's close friend Cyrus, and so he and I had grown up together and now carried on our fathers' lasting bond. Besides my parents and the General, Ritter and his father were the only people at Warrior Peak who knew about my past at the Morrok Facility, which cemented our bond all the more. Although Ritter wasn't very clever beyond knowing how to wield a sword, he was so outgoing and friendly that he was always surrounded by a group of friends.

"Hey," I said as I pulled food from the middle of the long table. The pickings were already sparse after the first rush of hungry students.

"Hey, Orestes. I wouldn't get too comfortable. Your uncle's been looking for you."

He said this offhandedly so as not to draw the attention of those seated around us, but I knew what "your uncle" meant. I suppressed a groan and started eating as quickly as I could. My "uncle" was no less than Alec, the General of all Warrior Peak, and the man who had taken me from the Morrok Facility ten years ago. As General, he was second only to the Elder, who lived at the top of the mountain and spoke to no one except the General once or twice a year. Although people sometimes doubted the Elder's existence, his word was law; a direct command from him was rare but always well-placed. Besides those few times, the General exercised ultimate authority over the land.

After a hasty good-bye to Ritter and his friends, I left the dining hall and hugged the northern edge of the military school compound, looking for the narrow alley that led up to the General's level. All the students knew the path existed, but rumors and tales of the General and Elder's security kept most of them at bay. The cockiest among us said that they would have no problem climbing the ladders to pay a visit to one of the generals, but when pressed, they always found an excuse not to.

That was why I was surprised to stumble into a girl darting out from between the old armory and the tailor that formed the alley. She rounded the corner without glancing up and barreled directly into me. More surprised than hurt, I staggered backward as she fell to the ground. Chuckling, I covered the distance between us and offered to help her up. She ignored my hand and jumped to her feet, beating the dust off her clothes. Although tall, she looked to be no more than thirteen or fourteen.

"Are you all right?" I asked.

"Of course, I love getting knocked over," she said, flicking her short blonde hair behind her ears irritably.

"Well, sorry about that—um, what's your name?"

"Is knowing someone's name really that important?" she asked. I had the distinct impression that she was mocking me, or at least talking down to me somehow. Nevertheless intrigued by her question, I started to reply, only to have her take off again, as fast as she had come, toward the military school's southern gate.

Shaking my head, I hurried up the old, rickety ladder toward the General's level. Since the General had brought me to Warrior Peak, he had kept up with me regularly, although I knew my surrogate father Fallon, who was the General's cousin, also reported my progress to him. I still had no idea why perhaps the most powerful man on either side of the mountain had personally taken me from the Morrok Facility, and I doubted he would ever tell me. Our visits were always an annoying ordeal because he treated me like an avalanche ready to fall, as if he expected the Morrok in me to attack everything in my path.

A guard met me outside the hallowed General's cavern. There was no physical barrier surrounding the level, because many more guards than the one before me watched the cave entrance day and night. Only years of explaining my identity and receiving confirmation from the General himself had taught these guards not to attack me on sight. The only visible one nodded at me as I entered the cave.

At first glance, one would not guess that the cave was inhabited, but after a closer look, the nine meticulously carved tunnels branching off the mouth betrayed their owners' presence. Seven of the tunnels belonged to the general of each of Warrior Peak's divisions: Militia, Army, Intelligence, Training, Inventory, Domestic Affairs, and the now-deserted office of the Laconic Warriors. Although I didn't know why, no one talked much about the Laconic Warriors, except in hushed, furtive tones. I knew that Fallon and the General were descended from them, and this fact seemed to darken their otherwise gleaming military reputations. The General himself lived in the eighth tunnel of the General's cavern, and the ninth was where the generals met and stored vital records.

Squashing the ever-present temptation to peek inside the last room, I veered off to its immediate right and soon came upon the General's door, where I straightened my hair and uniform before knocking. He appeared within moments and ushered me inside.

Besides a few additional wrinkles and completely grayed hair, General Alec bore much of the same severity as he had when we had first met outside the Morrok desert in the north. His home, however, did not reflect that he was the second most powerful man in the world. A permanent bachelor, he left his rooms in constant disarray with papers and half-eaten food piled on every spare piece of furniture. True to his military training, however, his uniform and weapons, I knew, were spotless and stored in the back rooms somewhere. Despite his premature signs of age, the General was young to have earned such a rank. He was just under fifty, but the dignity of his age was lost at the moment to his ink-stained hands and face.

"As always, I appreciate your silence as to what you see here," the General said gruffly as he wiped off his hands and nodded at me to sit at a littered table across from him. This comment had become a ritual between us, but I was never quite sure if he meant it as a joke or not. Either way, I said nothing in response to him and told no one about the interior of his home. Our meetings were supposed to be somewhat of a secret anyway, though I didn't know why.

"So, I hear you have moved fighting classes again?" he said.

"Yes, sir," I replied. I should have known that this was the reason for the meeting. Every time I was presented with a new fighting challenge, the General spent an hour cautioning me not to become frustrated and to stop if the battle felt too heated. There had been only a few incidents in the past in which I had continued fighting when the teachers said to stop, but that didn't mean he had to treat me like an untamed animal. Besides, the thought of backing down from a fight turned my stomach, but I always smiled and said "yes sir" until he seemed satisfied.

"Have you dueled many of your classmates? Any success?" he asked. He sounded genuinely interested, like any distant relative might have been, but I had seen how the General treated other people. The pleasant rumbling tone he used now could turn into a vicious roar at the slightest bit of annoyance, even when he was dealing with Fallon, his only living family member with whom he was very close. Yet the General was pleasant with me for some reason, although I often wished he would yell so that I could yell back and tell him how stupid he was for putting us through these conversations.

"No, sir, I haven't fought much. Just watched," I said.

"Not a bad idea. Gives you time to strategize. I wish I'd learned that when I was your age."

"Yes, sir."

"Have you been reporting regularly to Fallon?"

"Yes, sir."

"And he thinks you're doing well?"

"Yes, sir."

"And he thinks you moving to a new class is safe?"

"Yes, sir."

"He's talked to you about it?"

I sighed. "No, sir."

"Then how do you know what he thinks?"

"He hasn't said anything to the contrary, sir."

"Very well," the General said. He dropped his gaze from me and pulled a nearby paper toward him. That was the first signal that I was close to freedom.

After keeping me in suspense for several minutes, the General glanced up again and said, "You are dismissed, but remember, keep a cool head no matter how intense the fight. Frustration and anger will get you nowhere."

"Thank you, sir," I replied, and, trying not to move too quickly, I rose from my seat and exited the General's home.

Amazed by how lucky I was to have such a short visit, I decided that I could take the long way back to school without anyone missing me. When I emerged from the General's cave, I turned left and wandered along the unsettled face of the mountain. I knew that if I continued, I would eventually end up on the other side of the mountain, the fabled and mysterious "north" that so many in Warrior Peak were ignorant of. However, with my parents in the Intelligence division, I was not so naïve. To the north of the mountain range was Tyrclopia, where Dirth and the Morroks were. Glynis, who dealt with our limited activity in the north, told me that the Tyrclopians were Humans, just like we were, but they were oblivious to what lay on the other side of the mountains.

Fallon, on the other hand, worked with our people south of the mountain range. At the foot of Warrior Peak was a rocky desert called the Gravel Lands, and beyond that was a wild, vast forest called Serenity Valley. Warrior Peak had been sending groups of settlers to the forest for generations, not only to explore the land, but also to use its resources; very few trees grew on the mountains nearest us, so all of Warrior Peak's buildings were made from Serenity Valley timber. The land itself was reportedly large beyond comprehension, and yet no one had ever found signs of natives besides the several types of animals and plants.

My daydreaming about Serenity Valley nearly caused me to overlook the crumpled body. It wasn't facing me, so I had almost drawn level with it before I realized there was a person lying on his or her side at the foot of a large cliff that loomed overhead. Horrified, I froze, my eyes darting from the cliff above to the body lying not ten feet from me. The top of the cliff was unmistakably on the Elder's level. Had someone tried to intrude? What if there had been an attack? No doubt the Elder's numerous guards could handle any trouble. But as I found my muscles again and began to approach the body, I realized that it was no more than an old woman, judging by the gray-streaked hair covering her pale face.

I stopped again. One of the only people on the Peak with light skin. It couldn't be. I had been with her less than an hour ago.

But as I crouched next to the cold, stiff body, there was no mistaking her thin frame and pale skin. Aldis's eyes were closed and her face slack, and the rest of her body seemed to have collapsed from all the broken bones. There was also a wound in her side that was still bleeding. I tore my gaze from her to look up the cliff. Could the fall alone have killed her?

The thought passed quickly as tears of disbelief stung at my eyes. I couldn't bear to touch her oddly angled form, but I couldn't move away from it either. I hadn't seen a dead body since I was five years old. But those had been bodies of children—killed by other children's hands as they fought for the serum, Dirth's serum.

Had I drunk any serum that day before I was rescued from the tower? Would even a drop make me like those children, even though I was free?

I jumped up and covered my eyes. I didn't want to think of that, not now, not without Aldis's stories to comfort and distract me.

My vision slid in and out of focus as I gazed desperately down at Aldis's body. There was nothing I could do. She was gone.

I had to tell someone. Yes, someone had to know about this. The General. I had just come from the General's.

With great effort, I turned from the body and stumbled back toward the General's cave, trying in vain to master my emotions as memory after horrible memory plagued my mind.

Chapter Three
Man from the Other Side of the Mountain

THE BURIAL WAS QUIET and uncrowded. The fact that there was a burial at all—not a cremation as most people had—surprised me; but even more surprising was that many of the attendees were high-ranking officers. They said very little but merely looked on solemnly and murmured greetings to Fallon as they left. Soon only Fallon, Glynis, myself, and a woman who had dark, almost black skin stood around the freshly filled-in grave. Glynis hugged me yet again and whispered for me to be home for dinner. Then she and Fallon departed, leaving me alone with the other woman. I had a suspicion as to her identity, but I didn't care to speak to her, or anyone really.

At my request, Fallon had spoken to some of the Elder's guards who had been on duty at the time of Aldis's death, and they claimed not to know what happened. They recalled permitting her to visit the Elders' graveyard, and that was the last anyone had seen Aldis alive.

Her death certificate said she had died from the fall. Still, I couldn't understand how Aldis could have been so careless. How could she have fallen from a cliff? Although very few people had ever been there to bear witness, the Elders' graveyard was said to be rather unsettled—just a patch of flat land off to the side of the mountain. Aldis should have known better than to travel on such risky land. She was getting on in years, but she was strong enough to temper and mend swords. How could rocks have been her undoing?

The dark-skinned woman moved for the first time as the sun began to sink behind us. She, like Aldis, was old but sturdy. If she was who I thought she was, her name was Lexa; Aldis had always called Lexa her sister even though they weren't blood related. I almost didn't notice her leaving until she spoke.

"Orestes, correct?"

"Yes," I said, my voice croaking after days of not speaking.

"You were the only reason she continued to work in the forge for so long. You made her feel young, like she was before we came here and lost so much. She said you reminded her of a boy we once knew, and now that I see you, I agree."

She paused, and I turned my hollow gaze to her. This had to be Lexa. But why was she telling me this now when Aldis never had?

"The stories she told you were all true," Lexa said. "Zachaes, Xander, Jade, Acules—they were all real people, and she and I lived among them. Aldis was a strong woman. Don't ever think of her as less than that."

When Lexa had faded out of sight, I continued my vigil by Aldis's grave, wondering if she had ever planned to tell me that she had once fought among those who killed Morroks.

*

That night Ritter and his father, Cyrus, joined Fallon, Glynis, and me for dinner. This was a ritual that had become less and less frequent over the years, but there was still something enjoyable about eating in a house rather than in the school dining hall or the General's cave. Every house in Warrior Peak was made of wood and had much the same design—a large front room for social meetings and meals and a few small rooms behind for sleeping. Compared to the General's cave, our house was much more welcoming; it was much brighter thanks to the windows puncturing the walls every few feet, and Glynis actually cleaned and decorated with paintings and comfortable coverings for the furniture.

In addition to the comfort of being at home, I was also grateful for the distraction that Ritter and Cyrus provided. I wasn't expected to speak, because none of us could ever get a word in over Fallon and Cyrus. They both worked with the Serenity Valley settlers to the south and always found them a fascinating topic of conversation.

"Did you read the report from Settlement Four—Christopher's village?" Fallon was asking as Glynis piled yet more food on Ritter's and my plates. Glynis had always taken it upon herself to coddle Ritter as much as she did me because his mother had died when he was young.

"About them traveling south? Yes, I read it. Says some of his men found an ocean."

"An ocean?" Ritter repeated. "A real one with waves and everything?"

"I see they've been drilling you in geography," Cyrus said wryly. "Yes, it seems that an ocean forms the southern border of Serenity Valley, at least for a good stretch. Report says the men didn't stray too far east or west so they wouldn't get lost."

"I would love to see an ocean," Glynis said. "I don't blame Ritter for being excited. All we have around here are a few puny streams. In Tyrclopia there are lakes and rivers and all kinds of little tributaries. Before the northern forest colony disappeared, they reported an ocean bordering the north of Tyrclopia too."

"We need a damn *map*," Fallon said, pounding the table. "I'm tired of guessing and approximating. No matter how many times I remind those cursed messengers to measure their travels, they don't do it."

"Now, Fallon, those 'cursed messengers' give the better part of their lives to traveling through the forest and collecting reports from the settlements," Glynis chided.

"I bet that jumpy kid will remember to keep track of his group's travel times," Cyrus said. "What is his name? It's his first time going into the forest."

Fallon leaned back and squinted at the ceiling. "He's a sergeant—very eager. Nearly wet himself when I said I thought he was ready to go."

"Wait just a moment," Glynis said. "Colonel Fallon doesn't remember a name? Honey, first rule of good leadership is—"

"—to know your men as individuals," I finished for her. "Fallon, I believe to be an individual, you must have your own name."

"Todd, damn it," Fallon said. "His name is Todd. There, you bunch of pompous smart alecks."

We all laughed as Fallon became intensely interested in the last few scraps of food on his plate. With his jaw set in defiance like it was now, Fallon reminded me of the General, whose face was also worn from years of stress and hard work. Many people said that Fallon should have been a War Council general by now—head of his division and living in one of the caves next to the General. But Fallon had turned down any promotions so he could continue heading the efforts to colonize and explore Serenity Valley. He could recall from memory almost every man, woman, and child he had recruited to move to one of the twelve settlements, and nothing excited him more than receiving news and letters from the forest Warriors.

Glynis couldn't have been more different from Fallon. She too had her fair share of both gray and wrinkles, but she wore them on a full figure and a face stuck in a permanent smile. Whereas Fallon could have been mistaken for the General himself, Glynis hardly seemed to fit her role as a major of the Intelligence division. I had never seen her give an order to a subordinate, and I wasn't sure I wanted to in case she ever lost her amiable countenance.

After everyone had finished eating, Cyrus stood and stretched. "Well, Glynis, the meal was delightful as always. I have to be going now, though. I owe Fallon here some reports for tomorrow."

"I need to get back to school before curfew," Ritter added. "Are you coming back yet, Orestes?"

"I don't think so, not today," I said. I glanced at Fallon, but he didn't object.

"All right, but the girls are going to be disappointed. They haven't had anyone to giggle about for two days already."

"What?" I asked, searching his face for sarcasm.

"I'm serious. You know there's always a flock of them watching us practice in the evenings, and they—"

"No, I don't know that."

"Well, there is, and because you're there every single day, you give them a lot to swoon over. Hell, Charlotte talks more about your looks than mine."

"No, she doesn't," I said. Charlotte was a tall, dark-haired girl with whom Ritter had been flirting with the past few weeks.

"Think what you will, but I'm just saying—they're going to be sad."

Although no one laughed aloud, I refused to meet anyone's gaze as we showed Cyrus and Ritter to the door. I was ready to continue my protests to

Fallon and Glynis until I heard Cyrus ask "Who's Charlotte?" as he and Ritter disappeared into the darkness. Imagining Ritter's stuttering response almost made the whole conversation worth the embarrassment.

Silence followed our friends' departure as the three of us cleared away the food and utensils. After a few minutes of work, I cleared my throat. "Fallon?"

"Yes?"

"I was wondering—how high up do you have to be for a fall to kill you? I mean definitely kill you."

Both Fallon and Glynis stopped their cleaning. Glynis's eyes darted between the two of us, but Fallon ignored her as he considered me.

"Although it really depends on how the body lands, I would say thirty feet would probably do it, and that cliff's about thirty feet."

Ignoring his reference to Aldis, I said, "But you could survive a thirty-foot fall?"

"I suppose so, but you'd be pretty hurt no matter how you landed."

"But if your neck doesn't break, there's a good chance you could survive."

"Orestes," Glynis said, "Aldis is dead. I know you wish it were different, and I do too; but speculation about that cliff isn't going to bring her back."

"Her neck wasn't broken!" I burst. "I saw her body. She had tons of broken bones, but she had a wound in her side too. What if the fall wasn't what killed her? What if something happened to her before she—"

"Enough," Fallon interrupted. "Anything could've happened. She could've hit a sharp rock as she fell, she could've injured herself before she even made it to the graveyard—anything's possible. If you continue with the what-ifs, her death will never become easier for you. I'm sorry, son, but you need to let it go and start to move on."

Stung but determined not to let it show, I finished my share of the cleaning without a word and then retreated to my room. My room didn't have much in it besides a bed and a chest of clothes. I also had a pile of partially made swords strewn across my bed. Although blacksmithing skills were not required for military school, Aldis had allowed me to try my hand at sword-making, and I had kept all my failed attempts to study what I had done wrong. I had hardly begun my routine of polishing them when Glynis followed me into my room and closed the door behind her.

She sat on the edge of my bed that wasn't covered with half-made blades and misshapen hilts, but several of them slid toward her anyway because of the sag she created. "Honey, you have to forgive Fallon. He's seen a lot of deaths—lots of people disappear on a mission for him and never come back. You know that Intelligence is a dangerous division. Sometimes he forgets what it's like to be young."

"I'm young, but I'm not innocent, Glynis," I said.

She stopped rearranging the swords and looked away, her gaze unfocused. "No, I suppose not."

"Listen, I'm not in denial about Aldis. She's gone and I'm sad, but there's still something not right about this. You know the stories she told me? They all really happened, and I don't see how a woman like that could just fall off a cliff."

Glynis looked back at me, pity in her eyes. "She was a great woman, honey, but accidents happen. Not all heroes are destined for a heroic death. I don't want you to get worked up over something that may not be."

After that, I maintained a stony silence, convinced that I was right. Glynis gave up eventually and bade me good night. Long after she and Fallon had settled in their room, I stayed awake, idly cleaning my failures and planning my stunt for the next day.

*

The next day when I was sure Fallon and Glynis were safely at work, I left the house, taking care to be unarmed. I had told Glynis that I would spend the day exploring the lower levels where there were more shops, and I would be true to my word, at least for a while. Besides, it wouldn't hurt to have an alibi, just in case.

I received a few strange looks as I wandered along the paths and down the mountain. I wasn't wearing the army-issued school uniform, and any teenager tramping around while school was in session was a rare sight. Military school was technically optional, but being a civilian was not an easy path in Warrior

Peak society. Even people who had no talent for or interest in fighting still usually went through school so they could join one of the divisions. The only truly dangerous divisions were Militia and Intelligence, but the others offered a wide variety of positions that didn't involve swordplay. Military school was more than worth the invested time because a carpenter belonging to the Army often earned far more than a civilian carpenter ever would, even if the civilian was better at his craft and the Army officer never had to don his uniform in battle.

The shopkeepers on the lower levels were more than willing to help me spend my money. I nodded and commented appropriately as men and women alike displayed everything from diamond-studded daggers to tiny tin figurines and colorful hairpieces.

Around midday, I decided I had wasted enough time. I walked up the levels again as casually as I could, though I felt unbalanced without a sword or dagger hanging by my side. When I reached the training level, I made a wide circle around the school so as not to draw any attention to myself. Before I mounted the first uneven stair toward the General's level, I stopped to dry my sweaty hands and calm my breathing. I was fairly sure I could talk my way through the General's guards, but the Elder's would be much more difficult. The more I thought about it, the less likely it seemed that my plan would succeed; I just hoped that if I failed, I would fail quietly without wreaking too much havoc.

"What are you doing here?" a guard demanded of me the moment I reached the General's level. "The General did not say you were coming."

I let a few moments pass as I frowned and did my best to look puzzled. "I—I don't know, sir. I thought—I mean, Colonel Fallon—my father—he said that I was to come up here. I'm sure it was today. Maybe I wasn't supposed to come until later? Is the General holding council, or . . . ?"

The guard considered me for a moment. Beneath his helmet, I could tell he was young to be a guard on the General's level. His lack of experience was lucky for me. I wasn't sure if the General always announced my visits, and hopefully he didn't know either.

"Very well," the young guard said, "but if you disturb him, it will be on your head, not mine."

"Thank you, sir," I said. Then, when I was sure his back was to me, I proceeded toward the only way to the Elder's level: a rather shabby, precarious-looking ladder to the left of the General's cave. Conscious of the concealed guards around the entrance, I hoped against hope that they assumed the front guard had given me clearance to continue up to the Elder.

They either believed that or pitied me for going up without permission, but regardless of the reason, I was able to climb the ladder without interference. When I reached the top, however, I hadn't even pulled my second leg up on solid ground before my face was in the dirt and my arms were twisted painfully behind me.

"What are you doing here?" a voice above me barked. Although I heard no additional footsteps and was pinned facedown on the ground, I could sense shadows falling over me, blocking the sunlight.

"Graveyard," I gasped, finding it hard both to breathe and hold back tears of pain at the same time.

"Speak up!" the same voice growled.

"Elders' graveyard," I said. "Pay respects . . . to a friend. . . . I'm unarmed."

Hands move swiftly up and down my body, checking for weapons.

"Stand," someone demanded.

The guard holding me did not let go of my hands but released some pressure so I could struggle to my feet. Four muscular men, each garbed in camouflage that concealed almost his entire body, stood around me in a tight circle, no pity in their eyes.

"Are you a citizen of Warrior Peak?" one of them asked.

"Yes, sir."

"Are you a student?"

"Yes, sir."

"Why aren't you at school?"

"A friend of mine died the other day."

"Are you sure this isn't just a stunt? Seeing if you can catch a glimpse of the Elder?"

Terrified as I was, I could barely resist the urge to laugh. Every once and a while, a few kids who had nothing better to do would dare each other to get as close as they could to the Elder without getting caught. To my knowledge, no one had ever made it past the General's level.

"With all due respect, sir," I said, "only idiots who think they're too good to spend their spare time training make dares like that."

The guard's eyes widened. He probably hadn't expected more than a "no sir."

"State your name," he said.

"Orestes son of Fallon."

A few of the guards murmured to each other. Fallon must have been more well-known than I thought. Maybe I had a chance.

"And you say you want to go to the graveyard to pay respects to a friend."

"Yes, sir."

"Boy, there is no one in that graveyard you were alive to know."

"The friend I spoke of—she died there a few days ago, sir, and I just wanted to see for myself—that is, I wanted to see what she saw right before she . . ."

The guard who had been speaking cocked his eyebrows and looked at each of his partners. A few of them murmured to one another again.

My hands had lost all feeling by the time my questioner had made up his mind. I was almost ready to abandon the whole scheme when he said, "Proceed, but be sure that we will know if you go anywhere else."

I was too shocked to move as my holder released me and the guards faded back into their hiding positions. I was probably one of the few men to come to the Elder's level without permission and not be thrown in the mines for a long time because of it. Feeling lightheaded, I turned to my right and continued along the face of the mountain, completely forgetting to sneak a peek at the Elder's cave.

The journey across the face of the mountain was a tough one. Unlike the lower sections of the Peak, the upper part was steep and uncivilized. There were no ladders or staircases, however crude, to help me along. What had been a short walk along the General's level now became a trying hike with no end in sight.

I didn't realize I had reached my destination until I tripped over a miniscule headstone. After scrambling to my feet, I gazed around the large, unimpressive ledge peppered with dry grass. The oldest headstones were just small marble rocks protruding a few inches from the grass, but the farther I explored, the taller and more elaborate the graves became. Some were just large square slabs, but others were great columns that had huge bases and elaborate carvings. Each marker was engraved with a man's name, the dates of his birth and death, the length of his time as Elder, and a description of him, ranging from "the Benevolent" to "the Slayer."

I found myself lost in wondering about the men who had ruled the stronghold of Warrior Peak hundreds of years ago. I recognized some names from history lessons at school, but the titles were strange to me. How could they even earn such titles as "the Slayer"? As far as I knew, Warrior Peak had been officially at war only twice in its long history. I thought about Alec, who, as the General, would become the Elder when the current Elder gave way to old age. It was hard to imagine that a man I knew personally would ever join ranks with the legends like the men buried under me.

After a few minutes of investigating, I found the cliff from which I believed Aldis had fallen. Cautiously, I craned my neck to see over the edge. The drop was frightening but not impossible to survive. I was sure of it. Any footsteps or signs of struggle in the dirt from four days ago were long gone, but I searched for ways that Aldis could have tripped and then perhaps tried to stop herself. The cliff was remarkably clean of any big rocks, and there were no grooves or cracks in the earth. Surely Aldis couldn't have been so clumsy. She had always been so precise in her movements; I had seen her make molds for metal with the most meticulous designs. No, it just wasn't like her to be so careless, I concluded as I retreated from the edge of the cliff toward the face of the mountain. It just didn't fit.

Although unsatisfied, I wasn't sure what else I could do there. Before I made up my mind to leave, however, I heard a repeated thudding from somewhere up the mountain. I turned my head in enough time to see a heavy object barreling toward me, kicking up clouds of dust on its way. I tried in vain to leap away, but the object smashed into my side with enough force to send me flying. My breath deserted me as I slammed into the ground quite a distance from where I started.

I kept my eyes shut as I tried to gather my wits. The grass that surrounded the Elders' graves brushed against my face as I struggled to get my wind back, so I knew I hadn't fallen from the cliff that had taken Aldis. When I was sure nothing was broken, I pushed myself to my feet to investigate what had knocked into me.

A cloud of dust still hung along the object's path, and I lost what little breath I had collected to a gasp as the figure of another Human emerged through the veil. Cursing myself for coming unarmed, I backed away and almost tripped on another tombstone, but the man who came out of the dust seemed uninterested in fighting me.

"You saved me from quite a fall there. Are you all right?" he asked breathlessly. His dark, unmarked vest and pants matched the unkempt brown hair that hung around his ears. Like me, his skin was not naturally tan and ruddy like most Warrior Peak citizens, and although young, he was not without his scars.

"I'm fine," I said. I didn't know what to make of him. He had obviously fallen from up the mountain, from even higher than the Elder's, but neither his clothes nor his many weapons bore the symbol of Warrior Peak. Despite all this, I knew I had met him before but hadn't learned his name. I never forgot names or faces. They were marks of individuality that had been too precious to me when I was young.

"Who *are* you?" I asked.

"Acules," he said. He had begun glancing anxiously around the cliff. "Is this—am I in . . . ?"

I cocked an eyebrow at him. Acules was the name of a character in many of Aldis's stories, but it would be too coincidental for the real Acules to show up just after she died.

I knew I should have been running to the Elder's guards to report an intruder, but as I sized him up, I had the distinct impression that I would never be able to match him in a duel, which intrigued me. He wasn't particularly muscular, his sword and dagger were somewhat plain, and he seemed to be only in his early twenties; but even the way he casually rested his hand on his sword hilt made me feel as if I was standing in the presence of a great warrior.

"Is this Warrior Peak?" he asked when I only continued to stare.

"Yes," I said.

"Great. I'm looking for a man named Xander. Do you know him?"

Xander! He was in nearly all of Aldis's stories.

"Where are you from?" I asked.

"Tyrclopia," he said. "But what about Xander? Or maybe his wife, Lexa, or his brother's wife, Aldis? Have you heard of them?"

So Aldis was from Tyrclopia! That made perfect sense. She and her companions had fought Morroks, and Glynis always said that the only Morrok base was in Tyrclopia. I had believed Lexa when she said the stories were true, but only now did it seem to be possible. Acules, Zachaes, and Xander were all real and from Tyrclopia.

"Well?"

"I believe Xander is dead," I said, recalling Aldis's tale of the man leading an army into the Morrok Facility and never returning. "Aldis died just recently, but Lexa still lives."

He looked away and blinked several times before he was composed again. "Fine. Do you know where Lexa is?"

I was struck yet again by how little I knew about Aldis's life. I knew the histories of her family members backward and forward, but I hardly knew where she and Lexa lived. "I can take you close enough to ask around," I said.

"Great, I love playing the vagrant. Lead the way."

I had taken two steps in the direction of the Elder's before I stopped. "Are you a Warrior?"

He seemed taken aback by the question. "I—I guess I am."

"Not warrior as in fighter; Warrior as in citizen of Warrior Peak."

"Oh. Then no."

"I thought not. We'd better not go this way then. The Elder's guards would slit a citizen's throat if he came too near the Elder's cave, and since no one in Tyrclopia is supposed to know about Warrior Peak, there's no telling what they'd do." I paused for effect, but his expression remained one of passive curiosity. "Anyway, ready for a climb?"

*

After a rough journey down an unsettled side of the mountain past the Elder, General, and training levels, Acules and I were able to walk through the lower levels in relative peace. On the way, I explained the hierarchy that prevented us from going down the easy way, which then launched me into a verbal tour of the entire mountain. Acules was fascinated and asked surprisingly intelligent questions about the finer points of our defense measures and training programs.

When we were nearly to the foot of the mountain, I had to stop to get my bearings as darkness obscured the familiarity I had with the area. "Whenever I walked her home, this is about where Aldis always said she could make it herself," I told Acules, "and she went to that clump of huts. Hers might be the one a bit off on its own there, but I'm not sure. You can ask around."

Acules nodded. "Did you know her well?"

"Yes. She was really . . . great, just . . . great," I said, failing to find the right word for her.

"I know what you mean," Acules said, his eyes glazing over. I was tempted to ask him how he knew her, but he spoke again. "Well, thank you again. What was your name?"

"Orestes," I said.

"Thanks, Orestes. Maybe we'll meet again sometime."

"Sure," I replied politely, though my mind was reeling, "sometime soon."

Chapter Four
Matching Daggers

"I CAN'T BELIEVE you snuck someone in."

"I didn't *sneak him in.*"

"You idiot, what do you call helping him skirt around all the guards into the middle of the city? You snuck him in. They could throw you in the mines for . . . damn, I don't even know what the penalty is for that."

I was back at school and talking with Ritter in the dining hall to keep the conversation concealed in the usual flurry of activity. Instinct had warned me not to tell Fallon about Acules, but Ritter's words were making the situation seem much worse.

"You don't understand. He knew what he was doing. No one in Tyrclopia is supposed to know about Warrior Peak, but he knew where he was and who he was looking for. That has to mean something."

"Mean something? Orestes, you are so stupid. How many foreigners do we get around here? Even if he's the nicest man in the world, you know the General would have to know about it immediately. And it's a lie to say he knew what he was doing over here. He fell down the mountain! He didn't know enough about this place not to kill himself the moment he set foot on our side of the Peak."

"Well, then he wouldn't make a good candidate for some sort of spy or assassin, would he?"

"Or he's a really good actor."

I had nothing to say to that. Ritter didn't look happy about having the last word, but under his worry, I sensed a bit of incredulous admiration. No matter what he said, though, I knew Acules was trustworthy. He seemed so familiar to me, but now I was concerned that other people wouldn't find him so harmless. Not only would I be sent to the mines for threatening the security of the entire mountain, but Acules would be labeled as an armed intruder and wouldn't be safe until he escaped to Tyrclopia again.

"Listen, it's up to you," Ritter said after a long silence, "but you should at least say something to Fallon." I opened my mouth to protest, but he waved me off. "Anyway, how do you feel about the tournament? It's only a week away."

"I have a lot of ground to make up after being out," I replied, grateful for the change of subject. "Fallon didn't have time to spar with me at home. How about you?"

"I'm about as good as I'm going to get, but I've got another year left in case that's not good enough. Want to go a few rounds?"

"Sure."

We stood and wove our way out of the dining hall and to the training grounds. As we chose our dull swords from a pile outside Aldis's forge, I couldn't help but notice groups of girls along the fences around the training grounds. Because it was the evening, they weren't in uniform anymore, which they were allowed to do because they didn't live on the training level. However, they seemed quite uninterested in watching any of the boys practice; they sat in the dirt, leaning against the fence and talking to one another and sparing only an occasional glance for the boys fighting in the middle.

For the next hour or so, Ritter and I dueled, more for the exercise than to refine our technique. He and I knew each other's styles so well by now that it was impossible to trick the other. He always beat me—that is, disarmed me and held his fake blade to my neck—but not as easily as he used to. Between sets, we sat with the girls and talked to them as we caught our breath. After a while, it became clear that Ritter was more concerned with them than me, and I was about to abandon him for another opponent when I saw a peculiarly tall figure among the students.

Acules seemed to have been passing through the training level but stopped midway through the training grounds to watch the couple dozen boys and few girls sparring. Without a word, I leaped to my feet and left my group to hurry over to him. Ritter didn't noticed.

"Acules!" I called as I came closer.

"Hello, Orestes," he said.

"Are you all right? No one's caught you, have they?"

"What? Caught—? Oh, no, no. Lexa vouched for me. I just came from meeting the General and the Elder."

"*What?*" I shouted so that several people turned to look.

Acules laughed. "That's about how Lexa said I should've reacted when I received my summons. I didn't even know what a privilege it was except from what you told me on the way to Lexa's. But now I understand. He knows, really *knows* . . . well, everything."

I wasn't sure what he meant, but the glazed expression that overtook him reminded me of how I had felt at the Elders' graveyard.

"Anyway," Acules said, shaking his head as if to throw off his thoughts, "I saw you fighting. If you don't mind me saying, you're not very good."

I scoffed. "I train with kids older and bigger than I am. Not many students are allowed to skip classes like that. And I don't know if you saw, but I was just fighting Ritter. He's eighteen and one of the best—"

"No, you misunderstand me. You're not good for you—by your standards. Compared to these other kids—sure, you do fine, but you could be so much better."

I wasn't sure whether he was trying to challenge or insult me. I thought I was doing quite well, as did all my instructors. Acules couldn't possibly know my standards, and it wasn't his place to say anything about them. All the same, under the resentment that bubbled to the surface lay the intrigue that I had felt when I first met him—the intrigue that had driven me to break probably countless laws without thought.

"What do you say to practicing with me sometime?" Acules asked.

"Sure," I said, trying not to sound too eager. "It's getting too dark now, but you can come up here anytime. These are the biggest training grounds on the Peak, so it's open to everyone even though it's usually crowded with students."

Acules nodded. "Also, Lexa wanted me to invite you to dinner if I ran into you, as thanks for connecting me to her. How's tomorrow?"

"Sure," I said again. "Which house did it end up being?"

"I'll let you ask around," Acules called over his shoulder as he disappeared into the growing darkness.

*

The next evening, I bolted to my house after losing several long minutes to talking my way out of school for the second time in a week. Male students were technically not allowed to leave the military school level unless summoned by their parents, but I found more and more that the officers secretly didn't care what we did as long as we came to class, were back by curfew, and didn't cause trouble in the times between.

I didn't receive a warm greeting when I reached home. The General had obviously told Fallon about Acules, and over Glynis's lecture about "responsibility" was Fallon's tirade, which I retained little of besides the fact that I was an "impetuous fool." However, once they had both exhausted themselves, they were glad to hear that I was having dinner with Acules and possibly training with him later. Acules was evidently an influential leader in Tyrclopia and was one of the country's best fighters. These facts only enraged my curiosity about Aldis's past again, but I shrugged off the speculation as I changed out of my uniform and into my own loose shirt and pants.

As I was leaving my room, I happened to glance at my pile of half-finished swords. Among them was a small, unfamiliar leather handle. Curious, I tugged it out of the clump and found a full dagger blade attached to it. On the whole, the dagger was plain and unimpressive, measuring less than a foot and a half including the handle, but it was made of strong metal. Upon closer inspection, I realized that it was one of the weapons that Acules had had on him the day I met him. There was no telling how it had found its way into my room, but, conscious of my lateness, I tied it quickly to my belt and rushed out of the house.

I found the correct house on the third try. The other two I unwittingly visited seemed exasperated with people searching for Lexa. When I knocked on the third door, it was Acules who answered, also looking exasperated, and I could hear hysterical laughter from within the house.

"Come on in. Lexa's already opened the liquor," he said. He retreated back inside, leaving me to close the door behind us.

"I am *not* drunk," Lexa said, abruptly cutting off her giggling. "Sit down wherever you like, Orestes. Acules will get the food in a minute."

I took my pick of one of the few plain chairs circled around a low table. The front room in which we sat was remarkably bare; it had no decoration or unnecessary furniture. Like my house, it had its share of windows, but they were small and narrow and not particularly inviting. Although it was still daylight, several candles had already been lit and were scattered around the room.

"She sure knows how to treat guests, huh?" Acules said. "I answer the door, I prepare dinner, and all I get in return is harassment over my wife."

At the last statement, Lexa again burst into laughter not unlike some of the younger girls who sat around the training grounds.

"What joke did I miss?" I asked Acules.

"Lexa finds it highly amusing that I married Jade," Acules answered loudly as Lexa's volume increased upon hearing the name. "Lexa knew her before she, Xander, and Aldis left Tyrclopia. Jade and I were only thirteen at the time, and I guess Lexa never imagined us together."

"Well, I hardly thought—" But what Lexa hardly thought was never clear as she couldn't stop another wave of mirth from overtaking her.

"You know, you're going to start making me feel bad," Acules whined as he rounded to face her.

At this, I joined Lexa in her laughter. I had, of course, heard stories about Jade, and it surprised me that she had married anyone, much less Acules. Jade had been fiercely independent in her childhood, and although she had accepted Aldis and Lexa's offer of a home off the streets, Aldis had always described her as a spunky fighter who had a quick temper.

The rest of the night passed in much the same way. We ate with our plates in our laps and talked and laughed, mostly at one another's expense. Acules seemed unnerved by my extensive knowledge of Tyrclopia and Aldis's friends until Lexa explained our storytelling ritual.

"So you had no idea that all of it really happened?" Acules asked.

"No, I didn't. I didn't even know it was Tyrclopia she was talking about.

She never gave the land a name, though she seems to have described everyone and everything else pretty accurately."

"So what'd she say about me?" Acules asked.

"Quite a bit," I replied. "She said you were a great fighter even though you were really young. Actually, she told me once that you killed three Morroks at once when you were only thirteen, but I never really believed that one."

"Well, I helped," Acules said, "but I'm sure she exaggerated. It was the first real battle I was ever in, but I shouldn't have been outside at all. Zachaes did most of the work, trying to protect me, before he . . ."

Acules and Lexa both bowed their heads.

"Who was he exactly?" I asked. "Aldis never said much about him—just that he was Xander's brother."

"He was Aldis's husband," Lexa said. "Didn't she tell you anything about her own family?"

"No," I said, surprised. "She never talked about anything personal. I mean, she told me all the amazing things that Zachaes did, but I never would've guessed he was her husband. Is that why you left Tyrclopia? Because of Zachaes dying?"

Lexa and Acules glanced at each other before Lexa answered, though she would not look me in the eye as she spoke.

"Yes and no. I had just given birth to my sons, and Acules was about thirteen when—well, something terrible happened, and we thought my boys had been killed, and my husband . . . you know, as brave as Aldis made Xander sound in her stories, my husband was actually a—well, a cautious man, and we'd been told years ago that if disaster struck, Warrior Peak was a safe place for us to go. So when Zachaes was killed, Xander rushed Aldis and me here."

She drew a breath and glanced at Acules again, who gave a small, encouraging smile.

"It wasn't until you brought Acules to me that I knew he was alive, and my boys as well. I can't tell you what a joy it has been, and I only wish Xander and Aldis . . ."

She trailed off, her eyes shining with tears. I was suddenly embarrassed for having brought up such a topic of conversation.

Perhaps Acules sensed my feelings because he stood up and said, "Come on, Orestes. I promised I would train with you."

Ignoring the fact that night had fallen, I murmured a thanks and a good-bye to Lexa as Acules collected two dull swords from one of the back rooms. We set off into the cool night, not speaking to each other. Assuming Acules knew his way around this level better than I did, I followed him blindly. We were well away from any houses when he seemed satisfied and stopped. He handed me one of the training swords and unstrapped his real one to lay it on the ground close by. The moon was fairly bright, but I had never fought in the dark before.

Acules gave me little time to ponder this. I was able to block all of one blow before he had twisted the sword from my grip and knocked me on my back. I sprang to my feet and scrambled to retrieve my weapon. It was scarcely back in my hands before he rushed at me again.

The strength and precision of his strikes were unlike any I had ever encountered. Time after time, he batted away my pathetic attempts at countering and shoved me to the ground. The thought of complaining or quitting never crossed my mind as I rose to my feet again and again, trying desperately to find a way at least to match Acules, never mind beat him.

All my efforts were in vain. I lost count of the number of times I fell, but by the time Acules abruptly dropped his weapon and helped me to my feet, we were both sweating and breathing heavily, I more so than he. I leaned against a large rock as he collected his sharp blade.

"That was good," Acules panted. "You held your ground. We'll build up your muscles so you can keep it."

We spent several minutes half standing, half leaning as we waited for our breathing to return to normal.

After a while, Acules said, "Lexa told me you were the one to find her body."

"Yes," I replied, "and you know, something just wasn't right about it. It was as if she got hurt *before* she fell. She had scratches on her that couldn't have come from rocks, and there was a wound in her side that I can't think of an explanation for."

I couldn't see Acules's expression in the darkness, but he had stopped even tapping his fingers on his sword hilt. It was a relief to find someone who might take me seriously, even if he didn't have anything to say about it.

"If that school has a curfew for you, you've broken it," Acules said after a long stretch of silence.

"It's okay, I know every way to sneak in," I replied as I pushed myself upright. It was only then that my body began to scream with pain from our long spar.

We walked back to the settled part of the mountain, and just before we parted, I remembered the dagger I had found. "I think this is yours," I said as I untied the little blade and handed it to him.

Acules examined it in the moonlight. Then he reached for his own belt and drew out an identical dagger.

"Oh," I said. It suddenly seemed foolish to think it possible for his dagger to end up in my room. "I found this one in my room, and I remembered yours was pretty plain looking, so I guess I just thought—"

"Look at the base of the blades," Acules interrupted. He handed me both daggers. I brought them close to my face to see in the darkness. In addition to being the same length and being made of the same metal with the same leather-covered hilt (Acules's more worn from use), each blade had a small but elaborate cursive letter *L* etched in it at its thickest part.

I looked up at Acules. "*L?*"

"I have no idea," Acules said as he took back his copy and sheathed it. He handed me the other one. "As far as I'm concerned, I think you should keep that thing—I mean really keep it with you. I can't tell you how many times mine has come in handy. Good night, Orestes."

"Good night, Acules."

Chapter Five
A Message Fit for One

Year 324

A QUIET YEAR PASSED in which little around me changed but little about me didn't change. With Acules still at Warrior Peak, I trained constantly with him at school, near Lexa's, near my house, on the steps between levels, anywhere we could. I outgrew in height all the women I knew and began to rival Fallon and Ritter. My muscles finally began to show and build upon themselves. I baffled my classmates and instructors. At the end-of-year tournament of 323, I lost in the second round because I had been so sore from training with Acules, but in spite of the embarrassment, I had no regrets.

And now, less than a year later, I dominated the second-best fighting class among boys three and four years older than I was, and such skill was winning me friends and popularity unlike I had ever known among Humans. I was beginning to understand the difference between the standard Acules set for me and the standard school set for me; Acules wouldn't be satisfied until I could dispose of every student and teacher no matter their age or size, and he even suggested that I should be able at least to scare him in our duels. I was close to neither, but I was beginning to feel that anything was possible.

As the boys' end-of-year tournament approached again, Ritter and I started practicing at the foot of the mountain to reacquaint ourselves with the size of the low fenced-in rings. There were at least fifty rings scattered around the entrance to the desert to allow several matches to take place at once. When we were younger, we had marveled at the fact that we were standing in the Gravel Lands, but after growing up with Fallon, I was more interested in what lay beyond the Gravel Lands: the huge forest of Serenity Valley. The closer I came to graduating, the more I thought about one day exploring the country I had heard so much about as a child.

About two weeks before our tournament, Ritter and I had to yield our practice space to the girls for their end-of-year tournament. Now that I knew more of my peers, I was excited to attend an event that involved all the thousands of girls of Warrior Peak. I spent the day not thinking about training and instead joined a group of boys who ran from ring to ring watching friends' and matches.

Ritter and I were there primarily to watch his latest sweetheart, Anna. About midway through the afternoon, she lost to a girl at least two years her junior. The single-elimination tournament had dwindled down from thousands to the top sixty-four, so she was disappointed to have gotten so far only to lose to a younger girl. Anna held herself together long enough to shake hands and walk out of the dueling ring, but then the tears began to flow—something new to my tournament experience. A group of friends huddled around her and ushered her to the makeshift tiers of seats set up along the city's outer wall. The tiers were long benches made of melted-down scrap metal and had to be put up and taken down every year because they created a staircase straight up the city wall surrounding the base of the mountain.

With Anna out of the tournament, I was thinking about slipping away to find Acules, but a match close to where we sat caught my eye. It involved two girls of similar size and build, both using swords. One of the girls was about my age, and she had the most peculiar style, almost lazy. She stood in the middle of the ring, her sword dangling against her hip, almost as if she had no interest in fighting. But whenever her opponent approached her, she moved so deliberately and precisely that I thought she might have memorized the other girl's strikes beforehand. Unfortunately the psychic girl was using a sword that was way too big for her, and so her opponent eventually twisted it out of her hands. With a shrug, the girl left her sword on the ground, shook her opponent's hand, grabbed her bag from the edge of the ring, and started to walk toward the tiers.

I watched her until she climbed past me to sit on the top row of seats. Up close, she was pretty but not made up; she shook her hair out of its tie to reveal a mane of dark brown hair that hung around her shoulders. I couldn't believe that anyone had allowed her to use a broadsword; she wasn't particularly tall and certainly didn't have the muscle to handle one. What intrigued me the most, though, was the fact that once she sat down, she opened her bag and spread out several papers, a quill, and an inkwell with no regard for the tournament going on before her. I abandoned my group and made my way up to her.

"Hi, I'm Orestes."

As I settled on the row below her, she glanced up, but she didn't stop writing when she spoke. "I'm Levina."

"What are all these papers? They look boring," I said. Although I didn't want to take the effort to read them, a cursory glance revealed them to contain several lists of people's names.

"They're census records from the year 211. The paper is getting old and frayed, so the Census department is paying me to make a fresh copy of them."

"I'm surprised they allow you to take their precious papers out of their sight. I visited one of the Inventory buildings once with my father, and they almost attacked me when I started to unroll some old scroll. I don't even know what it was."

She grinned down at her paper. "I don't doubt it. My grandfather has been friends with the head of the Census department for years, and he's been giving me this dull work since I could write. I have a pretty good record of caring for these documents, so they're a bit more flexible with me."

"Ah, nepotism. I have no such luck with parents in Intelligence. I don't know a damn thing more than the average civilian."

She actually laughed at this.

"I doubt I could help them with their work at all anyway," I continued. "I can't read or write well."

Levina stopped writing to look at me. Our faces were very close as she remained leaning over her papers. Her eyes were brown. "You can speak well, though. I can't tell you how many people think they can 'read good.'"

I grinned. "My father always taught me to give at least an illusion of intelligence but also to be able to relate to different people on their own level. You don't seem like the type of person I should merely 'talk good' around."

Flushing a little, she went back to copying. "Sounds like your father's breeding you to be an officer."

"Something like that."

A few moments of silence passed as I turned to watch the match going on below us. Ritter, Anna, and the other boys had left the tiers for a closer look.

Turning back, I said, "You know, I was watching you earlier—your last match. Have you ever tried using a smaller sword?"

"Yes, I've tried everything," she sighed. "I've used thin blades and tried swords of weaker, lighter metal, but nothing seems to work."

"No, not a lighter sword—a smaller one, like a short sword or even a dirk. You don't get the same range, but they're much easier to control."

"I'll think about that, but there's not much point. I've never had a knack for fighting."

"You made it to the top sixty-four, and you're only, what—"

"Sixteen."

"See? You've got a unique style. I bet you'd do goo—ah, well—if you had the right weapon."

I was rapidly growing fond of her smile as it spread across her face again.

"I'll think about it," she repeated.

Satisfied with leaving on that note, I stood and stretched. "I need to round up my friends. We should be training."

Levina straightened and gazed up at me. "Oh yes, good luck in your tournament. Do you have many years left?"

"Plenty of time to go for the win. I'm only sixteen too."

"Really?" she said. "You don't look sixteen."

"You don't sound sixteen."

There was an awkward pause that ended only when I flashed her one more grin and said, "Bye, Levina."

"Bye."

None of my friends were interested in leaving the tournament. There were now sixteen girls left, and although I knew most of them, I didn't feel obligated to watch them. Instead, I reentered Warrior Peak, thinking that I might run into Acules and train with him.

I had no such luck, however, as I walked up level after level and finally reached the abandoned military school. I was about to enter Aldis's old blacksmith forge to practice my skills because Acules was horrified that I couldn't make my own weapons ("How do you expect to fight with something someone else made? It's supposed to be *your sword*."), but then I saw a young man stumbling through the training grounds toward the exit. He appeared to have come from the General's level.

"Hey, are you all right?" I called. As I neared him, I saw that he wore the unique uniform of the Warriors who lived in Serenity Valley—a sword sheathed in a tree rather than a sword in a mountain. His skin was unusually pale and his brown hair unusually long—both of which were marks of spending several months under the thick canopy of Serenity Valley's forest.

"Yes, I need—I need to f-find Fallon—Colonel Fallon. The General wouldn't s-see me—I d-don't know what to do. N-no one will ever—ever b-believe me."

I seized his upper arm and directed him again toward the exit. "I'm Fallon's son. I'm not sure where he is right now, but we'll find him."

"Th-thank you."

I rushed him down to the next level, catching him by the arm every time we changed direction or his legs failed him. I had never seen anyone, much less a full-grown man, so shaken. I found myself predicting how much he weighed in case he fainted and I had to carry him.

Luckily he was still standing when we reached my house. My yell for Fallon was almost out of my mouth before I saw him sitting at the paper-laden dinner table in the corner of the front room. He sprang up the moment the door banged open, and he crossed the room in five swift strides to grab the man's other side. I opened my mouth to explain, but Fallon was already screaming as we led the man to a couch.

"Todd, what the hell were you thinking? I expected you back two months ago, but not one word! Did you get lost? Going to Serenity Valley is the most dangerous mission a Warrior can do, and I thought I could trust all of you to handle yourselves! We've had too many groups disappear for you not to follow procedures. Where the hell is everyone else?"

Fallon seemed to want an answer to this question because he paused and stared down at Todd as he lorded over him on the couch. The man didn't seem to be able to speak. From my position sitting next to Todd, I glanced up, expecting Fallon to start in on him again, but he kept calm as we both waited for Todd to speak.

"The others are gone," he said finally. He stared down at the floor and shook more with every word. "We spent a little longer at a few of the villages, but we figured you wouldn't be too upset if we were a couple weeks late. Then we ran into some hitches—supplies disappearing, like a bag of rations or someone's favorite dagger or even a tent once. But it wasn't that big of a deal, you know? We knew how to deal with that sort of thing. But I think—I think we came out of the trees at the wrong place. We'd planned on crossing the desert a bit to the east, where it's not as arid—more chance of an oasis, you know. But—but we came out directly south of the Peak. It was awful. We thought we were going to die just from the travel."

Todd let out a dry sob as he choked on his last words. I glanced at Fallon, who did not return my gaze. His eyes were still boring into the top of Todd's head, though there was no anger in his stare now.

"But we didn't die then," Todd continued. "We made it halfway through the desert. We thought we were going to make it. Then we started seeing traces of settlements—footprints, scraps of food, and the like. We started hallucinating—thought we saw skinny little children darting around, like unhealthy skinny and almost naked except for dirty, shredded tunics. Then one night—we hadn't slept in a while, and we were up again—one night, they came. Not the kids. Monsters, dozens of them. They were—they were huge and pale and pointy. Even their hands were like claws. But we were Warriors. We fought. And every one of us died . . . except me."

The couch abruptly stopped trembling. Todd seemed too horrified to move for the next part. Eyes wide with horror, he raised his gaze to Fallon. "And you know what? It's not even like I escaped. They let me go. When they were done slaughtering the rest of us, they surrounded me. I could hardly lift my sword so I could at least pretend to die honorably. But one of them said—terrible, scratchy voice—said, 'Let this one go. It's time the Humans know we rule both sides of the mountain.' I swear, Colonel, I think they were Morroks."

I had remained fairly calm up until then, but at the word *Morroks,* I rose, strode outside, and vomited. From the moment Todd had mentioned the children, I had known what he was talking about, but a desperate hope had kept me from thinking of that word. Morroks on this side of the mountain, in the Gravel Lands. Morroks within a few days' walk. How could no one have known about this? Not one of the dozens of scouts and spies under my parents' command had found evidence of Morroks. How long had they been there? Was there an entire Facility separating us from Serenity Valley?

Then something fell into place. Lexa had said that she, Aldis, *and* Xander had left Tyrclopia to come to Warrior Peak. And yet Aldis had told me that Xander died leading an attack on a Morrok Facility. I had always assumed she meant the Tyrclopian Facility, the one in which I spent the first five years of my life. Xander had gone to a Facility south of us! But he had died years ago. How could Todd's ambush come as a surprise?

I wiped my mouth and marched down the mountain, too agitated to return hails from friends leaving the girls' tournament. I passed Lexa's level completely when I came to it and had to double back to her house. After knocking once, I threw open the door. Lexa was sitting alone in the front room playing some game with little round marbles. I crossed the room and gripped the edges of the table to lean toward her.

"Is it true that Xander was killed by Morroks?"

Lexa stared wide-eyed at me and opened and closed her mouth several times before speaking. "Yes, that's what we presume. He led an army into the Gravel Lands to search for the Morroks, but then the army just . . . disappeared."

"Why didn't anyone do anything about it? Everyone thinks the Morroks are only in Tyrclopia. Hell, only a few Warriors know what a Morrok is. Did no one go looking for Xander? How could they ignore it?"

Lexa sighed and set down her marbles. She beckoned me to sit, and I did so without taking my eyes off her.

"It's complicated, Orestes. This happened in the year 314, the year after we came here from Tyrclopia. Xander was interested in what lay to the south of Warrior Peak, and in his explorations, he found signs of a Morrok Facility in the Gravel Lands.

"As you know, in Tyrclopia we knew much about the Morroks and how they operated, thanks to Zachaes. So Xander went to the leaders of Warrior Peak to tell them all he knew and what he suspected about the Gravel Lands. I think they believed him for the most part, but they wanted to take their time dealing with it.

"But Xander knew the Morroks didn't work like that; the more time you give them to build up their army, the more indestructible they became. I've told you before that he was a cautious man, but after Zachaes's death and what we thought happened to our sons, he looked at this as his chance to redeem himself for all the times he thought he should've acted. He started preaching in the streets, warning people about the dangers of Morroks and trying to get them roused to action. Some—mostly younger people who didn't have families of their own—listened and started training with him, but most people he just unsettled. Many of the top-ranking officers thought he was trying to stir up the people against them in some way, and they wanted him gone.

"So when Xander announced that he was taking his followers to the desert to start the resistance, they thought it was all for the best. If they found nothing and came back, all would be well. If they found something and came back, it would help with their planning. If they didn't come back, the leaders could do as they like and write off Xander as an eccentric foreigner. So when they didn't come back, people forgot about them and the Morroks."

"That's outrageous!" I said. "How could they not listen to him? These are the Morroks we're talking about!"

"That's just it. It's like you were saying—hardly anyone here understands the danger of the Morroks. It's been hundreds of years since Warrior Peak has seen them. People have become too relaxed. They don't understand the horrors—how one of them can kill three men at once, how they have no feelings or no emotions, how they steal ch—"

"Okay, I get it," I said, standing up. "Thanks for the information, Lexa. I've got to go."

"Why did you want to know all this?" she called as I slammed her door behind me.

Crowds of people were beginning to return from the girls' tournament, but I couldn't stand to be around them. They had no idea . . . none. . . .

I retraced my steps as quickly as I could and darted into my house. Todd was gone, and Fallon had taken his place on the couch. He made no comment about my sweaty face or jerky movements but instead pointed to the seat across from him. I sat and tried to calm down as I faced him.

"First, I need you to tell me every detail you remember about the Morrok Facility in Tyrclopia," he said. "Then I need you to tell me if you think you can handle a journey into the desert, where you might have to fight and kill those you used to live among."

His gaze was benevolent, but I was too shocked to speak for several minutes. Memories hurtled like an avalanche into the forefront of my mind. Then I began to speak, recounting every nightmare I had ever experienced. Each word cost me as much as a small cut or bruise during a training duel, but as they added up, the pain became nearly unbearable. Every detail that resurfaced reminded me that, no matter how hard I tried to forget them, the Morroks would always be with me, just as Dirth had promised.

Chapter Six
Investigating a Stronghold

FOR THE SECOND YEAR IN A ROW, I disappeared from school in the days leading up to the end-of-year tournament. Again, the sacrifice was worth it to me. A mere two days after Todd's reappearance, Fallon already had a plan in motion that the Intelligence division general approved only because the General was Fallon's cousin. No matter how much Glynis protested, Ritter and I would accompany our fathers, two of their closest friends in Intelligence (Jacob and Holt), and Acules into the desert to investigate a possible Morrok stronghold. It was Fallon's idea to invite Acules along because of what he had learned about him from the General and because of my raving about his experience and skill.

These seven men huddled into my house near midnight that second day after the girls' tournament. Only two candles lit the space, flickering with each heavy breath from the many faces surrounding them.

"Based on my readings and eyewitness accounts provided by Acules and Todd, I know enough to tell you that we will not survive an entanglement with a group of Morroks of equal or greater number," Fallon said. "Acules tells me that fighting a Morrok is drastically different from fighting a Human and that there is no way to practice except to experience it firsthand. They are taller than any of us, some greater than eight feet, and they use weapons of proportional size. We will be hard pressed to match their strength. Therefore, if I order you to run, you sure as hell better run, or you will die. Do no throw away your lives for foolish pride. Agreed?"

He gazed at each man in turn as we nodded. He continued, "I tell you all these things because I do not intend for us to return until we find hard evidence for or against the existence of Morroks south of the mountain range. This means that either we scour the entire area south of Warrior Peak and find nothing, or we see a Morrok. I believe it will be the latter."

Fallon paused again, letting the thought sink in. I was glad it was too dark for the other men to see me shift uncomfortably in my seat.

"However," Fallon said, "that should not concern us for a day or two. For now, I want to remind all of you that our presence is not to be detected from the time we exit this house until the time we reenter it. The only people who know of our mission are our wives and the War Council. Are there any final questions before we depart?"

No one spoke.

"Very well. The guards are supposed to be opening the gates for us at about midnight, but only for a few minutes. Let's go."

We all stood and gathered our small survival packs and our respective weapons. Then, once the candles were blown out, we filed one by one out of the house, moving as silently as possible.

In school, we were trained to travel with a great deal of gear, but carrying all of it for a purpose felt strange and unnatural. I would have been much happier just having a good broadsword strapped to my back, but instead, I was loaded down by chain mail armor. My survival pack was wedged between myself and a small circular shield strung loosely to me. Secured to the left side of my waist and often clanking against the bottom of the shield was one of Fallon's old swords that I had sharpened for the trip, and to the right of my weighty belt, close to my hand, was the dagger whose brother stayed likewise close to Acules. True to his suggestion, I had made a habit of carrying it with me at all times, although I had not yet used it.

The few people we passed on the way down the mountain said nothing but hurried out of our way as we jogged along. Such a scene wasn't all that common, but the rest of the population knew better than to ask questions or get too worried; if something were wrong, one of the War Council generals would tell us. At least, that was what I had believed before I heard Xander's story.

When we reached the single great set of thick wooden doors leading out of Warrior Peak, the guards did not acknowledge us, but we saw that they had left one door ajar. Once we were all outside, the door was heaved closed, and we were left with nothing but the bleak scenery before us.

It felt like we should have taken a moment to stand and ponder what lay before us, but Fallon hardly swept a glance over the stretch of land before he hitched his equipment more securely on his shoulders and trudged southward. Ritter and his father, Cyrus, started off immediately after him, followed by Jacob and Holt, and finally Acules and me bringing up the rear.

As we passed the deserted tournament rings, Acules let out a hollow laugh. "Do you realize how ludicrous it is that the day the Morroks revealed themselves in the Gravel Lands, there were thousands of Warrior Peak's finest exposed in their territory armed with nothing but toy swords?"

"What, you mean the girls' tournament? I didn't know you even knew about it."

"Knew about it? I was there, of course."

Now I laughed. "Really?"

"Yes, it was great. Did you see the last match? One of the longest duels I've ever seen. They had amazing endurance."

"I didn't think you'd be interested in that kind of thing."

"Well, I've found that we value our female fighters in Tyrclopia more than you do at Warrior Peak. I guess having so many male warriors pushes your women off to the side."

"We *are* stronger," I said.

Acules laughed again. "Sure, in most cases, but that doesn't mean we're better. When we were kids, Jade used to beat the hell out of me when I made her mad. Women just fight differently. You can learn a lot from watching them."

I didn't say anything more but couldn't help but smirk to myself. Although a superb fighter and a good friend, Acules was an odd man to admit that a woman had ever beat him and to suggest that I should watch girls for strategy tips. I had never raised a sword against a girl, and strategy wasn't exactly why I looked at the opposite sex.

We traveled throughout the night at different paces to keep our strength up. Nothing changed from mile to mile. We breathed the same stale, cool air as we passed rock after boring rock. The only parallel I could draw between the desert where I had spent the first five years of my life and the one I traveled through now was the total lack of water. Any rivers that spilled down from the mountain range had dried up after an hour's jogging, and I found myself counting the minutes until the next break so I could wet my throat.

The situation did not improve as the sun came up. My armor quickly became suffocating, and no amount of pulling it away from my body would help. The older men's faces were red, but they said nothing of their suffering. It had never occurred to me before now what veterans Fallon and his friends were at real missions. Nowadays they mostly organized and issued orders, but in their younger years, they had been the spies and scouts who had investigated the land on dangerous adventures. For the first time, I saw a glimpse of what bound these four men together so that they ate dinner at each other's homes years after they stopped working together directly.

Sometime after noon, Fallon halted and peered up at the sky. "It's about time for the heat of the day," he said. "The sun will be unbearable for a few hours, so let's stop and set up shelter."

Before he had finished speaking, the older men had already slung off their packs and begun work on the shelter. It was nothing more than a long, low canvas that had no walls but would nevertheless protect us from the sun.

We took our simple meals and drank our warm water without complaint as we huddled under the canvas. We cast off our shirts, boots, and armor in an effort to cool down. Although the flat terrain allowed us to see miles in every direction, every half hour or so, two of us walked a wide perimeter around the camp to ensure we were alone.

There seemed to be no signs of life around us until Acules returned from his patrol with Ritter. "This could be coincidence," he said, "but I found an area with several small, flat rocks all spaced about three feet apart."

Everyone else cocked their eyebrows, but I forgot to breathe for a moment. "Headrests for when we sleep," I whispered. The others swiveled around to stare at me as I cringed against the memories. Don't panic, not now. . . .

Acules held my gaze for a long moment before speaking. "He's right. At some point, there were Morrok trainees in this area, and the Morroks never let them stray too far from camp. If they haven't already, the Morroks will soon learn of our presence, and we will have lost perhaps our only advantage."

I blinked several times, trying to collect myself as Fallon weighed Acules's subtle advice.

"I want to see them," he said finally. "Even just one. We will head toward the supposed trainees' area and continue from there. Remember my orders: Be ready to run."

In less than five minutes, we were fully dressed and packed again as if we had never stopped our journey. Following Acules and Ritter, we padded toward the rocks they had found. True to their training, the Morrok children had left no traces of themselves, so it was impossible for us to tell how long ago they had been there or how many there were.

"Look!" Ritter shouted. We all started at the sound and followed his finger.

In the distance, silhouetted by the distant mountains, were four steadily growing figures taller than any man. The others reached for their weapons, but my arms had gone numb. Eleven years later and I couldn't face them. . . .

"All right, we've seen them," Fallon said. "Those four must be silenced, and we must escape this desert immediately afterward before they find the bodies. Acules, can you handle one on your own?"

"At least," Acules said.

"Very well. Jacob and Holt, take another, Cyrus and Ritter, the third, and Orestes and I will fight the last."

No one objected. Fallon strode forward as easily as he had when he left our house. The rest of us followed, me fumbling for my sword and shield with unsteady hands.

When the Morroks realized that we weren't one of them, they began to jog to close the gap between us. One peeled off, running toward the east. Like a wolf on his prey, Acules bolted after it to engage it before it could alert others to our presence.

The two groups clashed the moment we met. I was last to arrive, and even as I raised my sword, I knew I was defeated. The Morroks were just as horrible as ever. They still towered over me, each of them at least seven and a half feet tall. Their claw-like hands gripped swords to match their gigantic sizes, but even the huge weapons weren't as horrific as the faces. The cruel, bright sun revealed disproportionate and inhuman features; multicolored skin seemed stretched across their faces, giving them the appearance of a skull with hair hanging limply around it like dead grass. The noses and mouths were sharp and pointed, as if sprung from the page of a bad sketch.

But their eyes were the worst. Sunken in and hollow, the only sign of life behind them were red pupils, angry and alive, terrible and tragic at the same time. These were the eyes that had followed me my whole life, and now that I saw them again, I was suddenly five years old and wanting desperately to curl up and hope they would only kick me and move on. My hands felt empty and my back bare but for the shreds of a tunic that I had worn since before I could remember. There was nothing I could do to stop them—no amount of hatred or willpower could help me—because I was nothing more than a tiny boy who came up only to their thighs, naked and exposed and living from day to day on a hope of escape that would never be fulfilled.

One of the Morroks shoved past Fallon and came at me. I stood where I was because there was no point in running. They always caught us, and the punishment for running was always far more painful.

The Morrok hurled a knife at me as it came. I bit back a scream as the small blade grazed my right shoulder, just inches from my neck. My hand involuntarily released my sword, and I dropped my shield to grab at the wound.

All too soon the Morrok was upon me, its sword raised high over its head. I automatically reached for a sword around my waist, but my hand closed instead around my dagger handle. In the moments it took for the Morrok's sword to begin its downward strike, I grabbed the dagger with my left hand, lunged at the Morrok, and plunged the blade between its ribs. I didn't stay to see how far it went in but darted away from the Morrok's body, clutching my bleeding shoulder.

The Morrok ripped out the dagger and tossed it aside, but before it could turn its great weapon on me again, Acules appeared by my side, his own broadsword bloodstained and poised in front of him.

The ensuing duel was unlike any I had ever seen. Although I had dueled Acules dozens of times, I had never seen him fight to his fullest ability. His feet and his sword moved constantly, and he never faltered in his choices—whether to block or dodge, whether to stab or give ground. He moved too quickly and precisely for the Morrok to keep up with him, and no matter how much weaker he was physically, it was only a matter of time before the giant fell. But what really sent my mind reeling was the fact that—if I wasn't mistaken—I saw a flicker of fear in the Morrok's red eyes just before it died.

All four Morroks were down within a few minutes with only minor injuries on our side. Acules tore a few strips from his tunic and tied my arm tightly to still the bleeding, and then he helped me gather my useless weapons. He barely spoke and glanced repeatedly in the direction from which the Morroks had first come. When Fallon saw that we were all intact, he finally gave the order to run, and we did not hesitate to obey.

The heat of the desert didn't bother me anymore. I knew I should have felt ashamed. All those years of hating the Morroks—denying my memories of them, but hating them all the same—and I had not been able to move in their presence. No matter how much I had learned about being Human over the last ten years, I couldn't forget the rules of the Facility. I couldn't forget when the army members were three times my height and when the backs of their hands left welts for days at a time. I couldn't forget the consequences for a trainee who dared lift a hand against an army member or, even more perilous, tried to dodge their blows. And worst of all, I couldn't forget that those Morroks we had just killed had been, perhaps not all that long ago, trainees like me.

It was nearly evening before we stopped to rest. We didn't bother setting up the canvas, so I was able to sit safely apart from the other men. They probably assumed I was ashamed of performing badly in my first real battle. I turned my back to them and tried to drown out their worried voices as they contemplated just how many Morroks could be lurking in the desert.

After a few minutes, Acules plopped down in the dirt next to me. His face was gritty and worn as if he hadn't slept in days, but he did not have a single cut or bruise to show for his part in the battle.

Before he could speak, I waved him back toward the other men. "I know what you're going to say. You're going to tell me I have nothing to be ashamed of, and you may even have some anecdote about your first battle. But I don't need to hear any of that."

"You'll want to hear what I have to say."

"Acules, I don't give a damn about that battle. Just leave me alone."

"No, *I* don't give a damn about the battle, but you do, and I understand why a hell of a lot better than anyone else you're ever going to meet, so you're going to listen to me."

I finally looked him in the eye. He was gazing at me more intently than I had ever seen him outside of dueling, almost as if he was afraid of my reaction. Just as he opened his mouth, Fallon called for us to start moving again, so we stood and fell into pace a small distance away from the others.

"Well?" I said.

He sighed. "I should've—I should've told you sooner. I realized who you were very shortly after meeting you, but I guess I was just curious to see if you could guess about me." He laughed, but the laughter didn't last long. "I'm the one who took you from the Facility all those years ago."

He paused and glanced at me with the same anxious expression, so unlike himself. I couldn't think of what to say. Images of that day flickered through my mind's eye, and I wondered why I hadn't made this connection this when I had recognized Acules's face in the Elders' graveyard the first day we met. He was the right age, and I knew Aldis and Lexa's family was the only threat against the Morroks in Tyrclopia; no one else in the country would have survived invading the Facility.

"The whole situation was just the blunder of a stupid thirteen-year-old," Acules continued. "I thought I could handle the Morroks like Zachaes did, and when Matthew and Jonathan—Xander and Lexa's sons—were captured, I followed the Morroks to the desert without telling anyone what was happening. I thought I could rescue them by myself. And, being the idiot that I was, I traipsed into the Facility all on my own. It turns out Dirth—"

As I heard the name spoken aloud for the first time in years, a long, unbidden string of curses burst out of my mouth before I could stop them.

"—yes, him—turns out he was toying with me for one reason or another, and after talking to me for a while, he let me walk out. But he didn't count on me finding Matthew and Jonathan, and when I saw you in the cell with them, I couldn't leave you. We were lucky that the Nomads distracted the Morroks so well, or else I can't imagine how we would've gotten out. And at the time, I had no idea it was the General I handed you over to when we got outside the desert. I only did it because I recognized the symbol on his cloak—the sword with the mountain—"

"That's Warrior Peak's symbol," I said.

"I know that now, but at the time, I'd never even heard of Warrior Peak. Listen, I'm not telling you this because I want you to thank me or anything; it was all just good coincidence—well, turning out to be destiny, I should say—but I just wanted to tell you so you could understand that almost the very same thing happened to me.

"I was born in that same Facility, but Aldis's husband, Zachaes, saved me just like I saved you. Aldis and Zachaes raised me like their own son, and when I was thirteen, I saw the Morroks murder Zachaes right in front of me, so it's been easy for me to hate them all these years. But I wanted you to know that I understand. I've had some of your nightmares. But when it comes to this—when it comes to fighting them—remember that the kids you grew up with aren't there anymore. They are all dead. The Morroks are soulless and heartless, and we have to put a stop to them if we want to save more kids like us. Orestes, we—you and I—have the best chance of doing that because we know how the Morroks work. We will never underestimate them. I know you hate yourself for ever being like them, but if you need the motivation to fight, that's it. Save yourself and me and all the others by getting rid of those monsters."

Neither of us spoke a word for the rest of the trip, and even though I felt like Acules was keeping something else from me, I had never been so at peace with myself. It didn't matter that the other men treated me like an invalid until we arrived home or that Fallon tried to pity me by not telling Glynis about the mission in front of me. For once, I understood why I was here and that my past wasn't an accident. I had never imagined that my history as a Morrok could be advantageous or that it wasn't weak to have my nightmares. But more than anything, I was glad not to be alone in the world, even if knowing Acules was purely coincidence.

Chapter Seven
A Catalyst for War

ALTHOUGH WE HAD BEEN ABSENT for only a few days, it seemed like everyone I ran into was curious about where Ritter and I had been and why my shoulder was bandaged. We didn't even try to come up with excuses or stories; we just told people it was none of their business. Ritter had hardly spoken to me since we got back but instead threw himself back into training for the end-of-year tournament. Because he was graduating from military school this year, it was his last chance to win, and I was confident that he would. I, on the other hand, was strongly advised not to use my right arm for a few weeks. The healer said that the cut wasn't very deep but that moving would make it worse, so it was best left alone for a while. I decided to heed the advice and practiced halfheartedly with my left hand. There was always next year.

I had taken up a new hobby of flirting with Levina, the pretty girl I had met at the girls' end-of-year tournament. Now that I knew who she was, she seemed to pop up everywhere around school. We didn't talk much, but whenever we passed each other, I asked her how she was doing, and then she fed me a long, obscure word for which I had to ask around for the rest of the day to learn the meaning. It was a clever way for her to make me think about her until our next meeting, but I had a feeling she was thinking about me too by the way she smiled from the time she spotted me to the time she gave me my word of the day.

One such occasion was the morning of the boys' end-of-year tournament. Although I wasn't fighting, I was among the dawn rush to breakfast. It was harder than I thought it would be to talk about the tournament, knowing I wasn't going to be a part of it. A few times I considered entering anyway and using just my left hand, but I knew that in the heat of dueling, I would default to my right and possibly reopen the wound. Although Acules insisted that I shouldn't have one strong hand but two equal ones, I didn't want to risk permanently damaging my right until I learned to use my left just as well.

I dragged my feet as the rest of the boys hurried down to the Gravel Lands to squeeze in some last-second stretching before the crowds began to come. Girls were beginning to stream into the dining hall, chattering animatedly about which boys they were going to watch and how well they thought each would do. Several of the older ones, who cared about more than the entrants' looks, mentioned Ritter as the favorite. Pleased, I started to make my way outside, but then I saw Levina enter.

"Hi, Levina, how are you?" I asked in one breath. The two girls who had walked in with her giggled and left her to sit down. I ignored them and tugged Levina out of the doorway so we wouldn't be crushed by the traffic.

"I would have to say that I'm feeling buoyant right now," she said after a moment's thought.

"No, you already gave me that one," I said.

"I did? Then what does it mean?"

"Really, really happy."

"Fine, I'll come up with something else for you next time."

"Oh, no," I said, catching her arm again as she began to walk away. "I demand a word."

"Demand, do you? Since when can you demand something from me?"

"Levina, you're my only hope for an education outside of sparring."

"That's an awful lot of pressure to put on someone you barely know."

"Barely know?" I said. "I know what kind of day you've had for the past two weeks. We're great friends."

She shook her head. "Don't be stupid. We're not really friends."

"Fine, if I'm not your friend, what does it take to be your friend?"

"Well, it's not that you can't be *my* friend. Just in general, you have to have more than a 'hi, how are you' relationship to call it a friendship."

"And again, I ask what it takes."

"Well—you have to—" She stopped and pulled at her hair and readjusted her bag as she kept her eyes fixed on my shoulder. I could hardly contain my grin. "Friends talk—I mean, really talk, like confide in each other—"

"Great. A couple weeks ago when I was gone from school, I was actually on a mission with my father. That's where I got this beauty"—I lifted my tunic sleeve to reveal the full bandage on my shoulder—"which is keeping me from fighting in the tournament today. I haven't told that to anyone else. Next?"

Apparently repulsed by my injury, she shifted her gaze to my chin as her grooming became more irritated. "Friends spend time together—eating, studying, attending events—"

"Even better. We can watch the tournament together. Unless you have a date with the census of 212?" I asked, poking the bag hanging from her shoulder.

I had never enjoyed seeing someone so flustered. Finally, after a futile attempt to catch her friends' eyes, she said, "I'll go with you, but *don't* bore me with all the technicalities. That's all my grandfather ever does when we go to these things together."

"I can guarantee nothing."

After Levina had sufficiently rolled her eyes, we set off down the mountain and were soon lost in the horde of people all trying to squeeze out of the narrow front gate into the Gravel Lands. Even more so than the girls' tournament, the boys' was a staple social event that emptied nearly the entire Peak every year. It was the beginning of the new year's celebrations that would start the next day, including feasts, plays, music, and tournaments for adults. The first day of a new year marked one of the few times that everyone threw open their front doors and celebrated together regardless of rank or division. Because Fallon was such an important man, he rarely had to leave the house to see anyone in his department, but Ritter and I never stayed on any one level for more than twenty minutes at a time. We made it our goal to obtain a free sample of everything being given away on the mountain that day, and we were usually quite successful.

By the time Levina and I arrived in the desert, the boys were milling around in the center rings waiting for their first matches, and thousands of adults and girls were around the edges of the rings and on the several makeshift tiers. When several men from the Training division appeared laden with parchment containing brackets, ring assignments, and a list of all our names, the crowd quieted and allowed them to pass through to the center ring. All the boys stood in attention as the general of the Training division stepped forward. He was as ancient as any of the War Council generals and carried himself with the pride he deserved, but he dressed as simply as the children standing around him in their military training uniforms. "The tournament," he croaked, "has officially begun."

There was a short roar of applause followed by the chaos of assigning the boys their first matches and the families of the boys trying to locate their respective rings. I enjoyed every moment of it, but each time I hailed a friend getting ready for a match, I inwardly cursed my injured arm. With all of Acules's training, I would have done so well this year.

Levina helped to distract me from too much self-pity. Between us, we knew almost everyone from age thirteen up, so we spent the day trying to angle ourselves to watch several matches at once. We were never very successful, but it was fun debating who we thought would win each match, though we agreed that Ritter would be the champion. By midmorning, we started placing bets whenever we disagreed, and by midday, I owed Levina four pages of copying censuses and a day of slaving at her household chores, and she owed me two sword polishes (though she didn't seem to understand how many I had), a day of assisting me in the forge, and an open-ended promise to help me read better. Because I knew she would never ask me to help her fight better, I was biding my time to make that one of my rewards for betting correctly.

As the afternoon wore on, the competition whittled down enough that many of the rings farthest away from the mountain were no longer in use. Levina and I were on the edge of one such ring as we watched Conrad—a huge boy I had fought only once in class and who was perhaps Ritter's biggest competition—duel a stocky sixteen-year-old. No bets were placed on this match, because we agreed that Conrad had it won before he lifted his sword. However, the spar had dragged on so long that all the matches around it had finished, and the area was all but abandoned as the other matches were compacted into the inner rings.

Conrad's frustration was getting the better of him as he failed to strike one of his infamous heavy-handed blows on the younger boy. His opponent recognized Conrad's fraying emotions and began taunting him. Conrad's anger mounted, and he began swinging wildly as if he desired more to silence the boy than to win the match. The younger boy took advantage of his sloppiness and dealt a well-placed blow to Conrad's sword hand. Conrad howled and dropped his sword, and before he could retrieve it, the other boy brought his sword to Conrad's neck, thereby winning the match. There was scattered applause from the few people who had stayed for the whole match. After Conrad grudgingly shook the younger boy's hand, everyone but he, Levina, and I wandered to the distant occupied rings.

Conrad seemed close to tears as he threw down his dull sword and stripped off his gauntlets. Levina looked as if she wanted to say something to him, but I held up a hand for silence as he shuffled past us more deeply into the desert.

"Let him walk around for a while, and then he'll find sympathy from pretty girls who didn't see the match and who will believe him when he tells them how the other kid cheated and how he was robbed of his glory."

"I didn't realize you boys took this tournament so seriously."

"Well, it's harder for him because it's his last year, but yes, it's really important to all of us."

"It's killing you not to be in there, isn't it?" Levina asked as she shifted her gaze from Conrad's back to me.

I didn't meet her eyes but murmured, "Yes."

"I don't understand you," she said. Before I could ask what she meant, she continued as if I had said something offensive, her tone rising with each word. "You pretend that you don't realize everyone knows you and wouldn't mind pitying you all day. I know plenty of girls who would sit with you on the tiers and fawn all over you, and I lost count of how many boys said they'd trade places with you in a second if they could. Your father's more well-known than most of the division generals. That Tyrclopian Acules does nothing but train with you when he could be lounging about with the General himself. And you—everyone's known there's something special or peculiar about you since you came here, with your blond hair and light skin, and now—"

"Now what?" I snapped. I wondered if she had wanted to say this all day, if not longer. "This is coming from a girl who this morning didn't even consider me to be her friend, and now you're telling me that I want attention for every unwarranted praise people give me? Yes, I know people know me, but it's because I know them. I *want* to know them so they don't have false impressions of me. I'm *not* one of those kids who strut around and think they're better than everyone because Daddy's title's going to get them a high position the second they graduate. If that's all you think of me, then I wish you'd stop wasting my time because I know I'm better than that."

"I was going to say," Levina continued, undaunted, "that now you've made a name for yourself because of your fighting skills and the way you are with people. What I don't understand is the fact that after you meet someone, you say hi and move on, but you continue to flirt with me even though I come from no impressive stock and haven't given you a fraction of the attention other girls do. Are you trying to make fun of me? Is this some bet you have going?"

"Damn, you are presumptuous!"

"Don't curse in front of me."

"Well, how do you know who I do and don't flirt with?"

"It's 'with whom,' not 'who with,' but have I not made my point already? I know girls who will brag if you do just say hi, but with me, you . . ."

I was about to fill in her silence, but then I noticed that her gaze was back to Conrad. I twisted to follow her line of sight but saw nothing.

"What are you—"

"He fell," she said, her face suddenly pale. "I could hardly make out his shape, but he definitely fell. And I think I saw—no, it couldn't have been."

My stomach seized as I twisted around to look. I saw nothing but Conrad's prone figure. "What did you see? Levina, you have to tell me."

"I thought I saw someone else—someone tall—but it moved too quickly to be anything but a shadow. Conrad must have fainted or something. Let's go—

he can't stay out there like that!"

"You're right, but you're not coming with me to investigate. Find Ritter and tell him to come here now."

She opened her mouth to argue, but I said, "Levina, please."

She nodded and sprinted toward the distant crowd.

My heart beat faster than it had at any point during my argument with Levina. Acules's words from two weeks ago haunted me. "Do you realize how ludicrous it is that the day the Morroks revealed themselves in the Gravel Lands, there were thousands of Warrior Peak's finest exposed in their territory armed with nothing but toy swords?" Fallon had said after the mission that the Morroks might retaliate, but I hadn't thought anything of it. But what if Conrad had strayed just a bit too far?

My suspicions were confirmed when I found the body. Although there was no sign of the monsters themselves, the arrow that had buried itself perfectly through Conrad's chest was so large that only a Morrok-sized bow could have shot it. I couldn't bring myself to look at his face but instead stood over the body with my dagger drawn. Every shadow, every gust of wind, every distant shout made me suspect that a Morrok archer was about to bear down on me. The expanse of the desert made it impossible for me to feel at all secure. I kept turning and repositioning, determined to relieve the feeling that at any moment an arrow would strike me in the back.

After some time, I glanced down at the arrow penetrating Conrad's lifeless form. Attached to the stem was a tiny scroll. Again trying not to look at my former classmate's face, I tugged the paper off and unrolled it. It read: "Son of Lernuc, you cannot hide." Chilled, I tucked the paper into my tunic and glanced up in time to see Ritter and Levina approaching at last.

Levina let out a small scream when she saw what had happened to make Conrad fall. Ritter and I ignored her as we crouched next to Conrad.

"Morrok?" Ritter said as he ran his finger along the arrow.

"Definitely. We need to tell Fallon and Cyrus before anyone else finds out about this. None of the other officers would understand."

"All right, but you two probably ought to go somewhere where Fallon can find you because you're the only witnesses. I'll find our fathers and Jacob and Holt and bring them here."

"No, you need to go back to the tournament," I said. "It'll look suspicious if you disappear in the middle of it, and you could be disqualified if—"

"This is more important," Ritter said, though his voice cracked as he spoke. "Come on, you need to get the girl out of here. There could be more out there."

I nodded and grabbed one of Levina's hands away from her face. The three of us sprinted the length of the empty rings, but when we came closer to the crowd, we sauntered through as if we had just been picnicking out in the desert. Ritter broke away from us, heading for the tiers, and Levina and I proceeded through the crowd, ignoring calls from friends and nearly knocking over a blonde girl I had met once on the way to the General's cave, until we were safe within the walls of the mountain.

Levina seemed too shocked to speak as I led her up the many levels to my house. Once inside, we wordlessly began to pay off the debts we owed each other from our bets earlier that day. We sat on the floor in the front room, I with a quill and a stack of papers and she with my pile of misshapen swords. After several minutes of silence, we began to criticize each other's work (she missed several spots in her polishing and I made too many mistakes in my writing) until we swapped and called it even.

Nearly an hour later, we heard shouts outside. We both rushed to the windows just as all the members of the War Council hurried past. Most of them, like the officers of the Training division, were dressed in old cadet uniforms, and I would have laughed aloud at the absurdity of our leaders masquerading as students if not for the way that they huddled together as if fearing for their lives.

I walked back to sit with my pile of half-finished swords. "Fallon will be a while longer. I'm sure he won't leave until every single person is back inside the Peak."

Levina lingered by the window. "Ritter said it was a Morrok that did it," she said. "Is that true? How did you two even think to suspect Morroks? They haven't been on this side of the mountain in centuries, and most people don't even know what they are, not really."

"And you do?" I asked.

"Yes," she said as she joined me on the floor again. "The Inventory division stores historical records and transcripts of every War Council meeting ever held. I've snuck into those records for years, and there are detailed descriptions of Morroks—what they look like, how they operate, where they might have come from. It's like something from a nightmare. I only half believed they existed until now."

I felt an overwhelming connection to Levina just then. Finally someone else who had an idea of the horrors. "Well, they do exist, and it seems that they have some sort of gathering or stronghold in the Gravel Lands. Fallon and others before him have been trying to get the War Council to act on it, and now I think they finally will. This attack was way too close to the Peak."

Levina bit her lip as she dropped her gaze down to the census spread out before her. "Orestes, I'm sorry about earlier. I really do like you, and everything else just seems silly now." She paused. "Do you think we're in danger?"

"No, not immediate danger. No one's ever breached Warrior Peak, and it won't happen now. However, I think the Army's going to be mobilized for the first time in decades, and that will change everything. We won't be alone in our knowledge of the Morroks, which is a relief, but I'm not sure how our society's going to handle actually living out our military credo. And I really like you too."

She smiled and went back to her copying.

Another few hours passed, and we heard more and more people, ignorant of Conrad's fate, return home celebrating whomever had won the tournament. The moment Fallon and Glynis arrived at the house, Glynis embraced us both and gushed about our safety and our bravery. After she calmed down and Levina had been properly introduced, we sat around the dining table to exchange stories.

Fallon told us that once he, Cyrus, Jacob, and Holt had seen the body and confirmed our suspicions that it was the work of Morroks, he had alerted the War Council discreetly during the final matches of the tournament. They too wished to see the body, but they allowed the tournament to finish so as not to cause panic. Although the General had believed our report about finding Morroks in the desert a few weeks ago, Fallon thought that a direct attack like this would spur the War Council to action.

"At least the boy's death wasn't in vain," he concluded.

Glynis scoffed, but Fallon headed off her moral reprimand by inviting me to tell him our account of the day's events.

The others listened mutely as I recounted exactly what we had seen, from Conrad losing the match to Levina and I leaving the tournament. Finally, I extracted the paper I had found and handed it to Fallon. "This was the message attached to the arrow."

"'Son of Lernuc, you cannot hide,'" he read.

Glynis clutched his arm. "Fallon, what does that mean?"

"A long time ago, the Morroks were called the sons of Lernuc," Levina said. We all raised an eyebrow at her, and she grinned sheepishly. "If that helps at all. I think Lernuc might've been their first leader or founder or something."

"Well, no matter what this threat means," Fallon said as he pocketed the paper, "we will soon be at war. Alec has to speak to the War Council and the Elder first, but he told me it was unavoidable. Most of the population is still ignorant, but the outer gates are already on lockdown now that the tournament is over. Not even my men going to Serenity Valley are allowed to leave until it's lifted."

Levina perked up when Fallon mentioned Serenity Valley but didn't comment. We spent the rest of the evening discussing what the future may hold. We were occasionally interrupted by Fallon's friends and Acules, who had thought our absence from the new year's festivities conspicuous. Levina discovered that Lexa lived near her, and so when night fell, Acules volunteered to walk her home. Soon after they left, Glynis yawned and retreated to bed, and Fallon headed to the General's level to see if the War Council had made any decisions.

I cleared the front room of my stubby swords and polish, and as I extinguished the candles, I thought about the message on the arrow. It sounded more like a warning than a threat to me. Lernuc. I had heard the name before today.

It wasn't until I was halfway asleep that I remembered Dirth's words from the last time we met in that stone tower. *No matter what happens today, you are under my control, under Lernuc's control. You will never do anything he won't be pleased by. Kill me, kill Humans, kill Morroks—prove your power the only way you know how, and we will have won.*

I was the son of Lernuc.

Chapter Eight
Xander's Legacy

Year 325

THE YEAR 325 WAS one of the most turbulent of Warrior Peak's history. The entire Army—which included the vast majority of the population—was ordered to dust off their uniforms and assemble in the various training fields, where their skills were tested for the first time since graduating from military school. This proved to be a struggle for many older officers who had grown fat and clumsy with the weapons of their youth. Fallon said that the General was furious about this and so ordered weekly training sessions for every member of the Army until he was satisfied with everyone's proficiency. The training grounds were therefore filled night and day with adults being subjected to the trials and orders of the Training division officers. Most of us students spent our evenings watching our teachers instruct our parents, which infuriated the adults but amused us to no end.

But the Army wasn't the only division gearing up for battle. The Inventory division was in a frenzy issuing weapons, uniforms, and supplies in addition to its new job of keeping track of each adult's individual training progress. Even Domestic Affairs saw a rise in activity as Warrior Peak's crime rate soared when more people started drinking away their increased stress and as an unnaturally large number of young couples married and needed housing to start their lives together.

The biggest tolls, however, were taken by the Intelligence and Militia divisions. Fallon and Glynis, along with many others, suddenly spent all their time organizing wartime spies rather than working on their projects in Serenity Valley and Tyrclopia. Both my parents were sick with fear not only because of the increase in fatalities among their spies, but also because they had no idea what was happening in their respective countries. The Militia saw even more deaths as they rushed to confront any group of Morroks that came within a few miles of the mountain range. Any of these skirmishes that reached public ear caused a renewed ripple of unease throughout the Peak and had those living on the lower levels near the gates begging to move their families to higher ground.

I too was doing everything I could to prepare for my next meeting with the Morroks. Because several of the Training officers were busy with the adults, it was easy for me to leave school to train with Acules, which I considered a much better investment of my time. I continued to grow physically as well, until few men stood taller than I did and few objects outweighed my ability to lift them. Although I never officially bested Acules, I came closer every day and left him just as exhausted as I was every night after our duels.

Because Ritter had graduated and was in Intelligence with our fathers, there was little I missed about school other than Levina. In the past months, we had become close friends, visiting each other's houses and spending time with each other's families when we weren't in school. I was humbled by Levina's grandparents, who, though they were both civilians, were very kind and brave people who were helping with the war effort by collecting and delivering supplies to the city gates—a place most people avoided nowadays. Levina likewise adored my parents. Although she—like many—was in constant awe of Fallon, she sometimes visited Glynis even if I wasn't there.

With each passing day, I knew that I cared for Levina in a way that I doubted any woman would ever rival. She was a constant source of relief, enjoyment, and encouragement after a long day of training, and when we were apart, I frequently worried about her safety, especially with her house being so close to the bottom level. Still, I couldn't bring myself to act on any of those feelings, because every time I thought about being close to her, I remembered the violence with which physical affection and personal attachment was repulsed at the Facility. If the Morroks sensed a hint of friendship between two trainees, they were immediately set to duel each other until blood was drawn on both sides, sometimes more than once. It had taken years of Ritter's unyielding persistence for me to feel safe calling him my friend, and the closer I got to Levina, the more I felt that old sense of terrified resistance in the pit of my stomach.

Yet through all the chaos of my own life and society in general, there was still the old excitement of the end-of-year tournament. I couldn't help but want to do well after the last two years of missed opportunities. Acules had no doubts about me winning, but I wasn't ready to be as cocky.

"You haven't been in school so much that you just don't remember how mediocre these kids are compared to you," he said one day while we took a break from dueling. We had abandoned using practice swords nearly a year ago because Acules insisted that fighting with the threat of a bruise wasn't enough to learn how to fight in life-threatening situations.

"Maybe, maybe not," I said, "but I sure as hell hope that my classmates are better than mediocre if they have to fight Morroks someday."

"Mediocre compared to *you*," Acules said. "I said compared to *you*. If those kids went to war against my militia in Tyrclopia, I'd be embarrassed, to say the least."

"But Aldis always spoke as if your people fared well enough with Morroks," I said. Even two years after her death, Aldis was still my most trusted source about Tyrclopia, even over Acules, Lexa, and Glynis.

"Yes, my family does, but the rest of them are really just a bunch of farmers and tradesmen."

"Do you ever worry about your family?" I asked. "And your militia? Won't they be suffering without you? You've been here nearly two years."

Acules froze as if I had struck him. When he stood abruptly and walked away, I realized I had pried too much. Although Acules referred to his family as often as anyone would, he never spoke as if he missed them, and I had begun to think he wasn't attached to them in the same way Fallon and Glynis were attached to each other and to me.

"I think about them every hour of every day," he murmured so that I could barely hear. "In fact, I don't think I'm going to stay here much longer. When I came, I sensed I had a job to do, but I've been thinking about my sons more and more, especially Asgerd. He was only a baby when I left, and now I'm sure he's walking and talking."

I grimaced at the thought of ever having a son who didn't know who I was the first few years of his life. I did my best to keep my face neutral as Acules turned back to me and sat down.

"You said you thought you had a job here," I said, "but you've spent most of your time training with me. Now we're in the middle of a war—a war you could very well tip the balance of—and you're leaving."

"I've done my part in telling the officers how to teach your people to fight Morroks. But maybe my real job was just to train you," Acules said. "I told you two years ago that you have different standards of fighting well, and you're just now starting to fulfill them. I didn't understand at the time, but I know now that it's important that I rescued you from the Facility all those years ago. You should be the one to tip the balance of this war, not me."

"Why is it important that you rescued me?" I demanded. "We know now that it was the General you gave me to. What was he doing there in the middle of the Tyrclopian desert? It doesn't make sense! Why did Dirth even put Lexa's sons in my cell? You wouldn't have ever found me if it hadn't been for that. Damn it, Acules, you know! You talk to me as if you can see my future."

"I know you're frustrated, but it's not for me to tell you these things, so stop harassing me," Acules growled. "Look, I've made promises that I have to keep, so don't try to pry anything out of me. I'm just trying to fulfill my duty to you. Take it or leave it."

We sat in a huffy silence. Like the dull training swords, we had long ago given up on practicing on a training field; we instead opted to duel on one of the far sides of the mountain, away from Warrior Peak but not so far that we were on Tyrclopia's side. We were about to resume training when we heard footsteps running toward us. Both of us relaxed when we saw it was Levina.

"Orestes!" she called as she sprinted closer. When she arrived, she collapsed against me. Tears streaked down her face. Acules and I exchanged alarmed glances as I pushed her gently upright.

"What happened? Was there an attack?" I asked. Levina, unlike most people, knew better than to panic over a small battle miles from the Peak.

"No," she said. "I was just at your house, and Fallon said that the General's cutting off Serenity Valley!"

"What do you mean?" I asked. I couldn't imagine why this would drive Levina of all people to tears. In fact, I had never seen her cry before now.

"He's cutting them off! Fallon's been pushing the General to send extra supplies and men down there to warn them about the Morroks, but the General says we need everyone here. I hate him, Orestes! How could he do this? Those are all citizens of Warrior Peak in the forest! I hate him!"

"Levina, you have to calm down," I said, unnerved by her behavior. "Come on, let's go back to my house and talk to Fallon. I'm sure he won't stand for this."

"Don't you understand?" she said. "Haven't you been listening to what Fallon's said these past few months? The General's sick of Fallon. He's under an enormous amount of pressure, and every time Fallon gives him advice, he thinks he's trying to take over his job! All the other War Council generals are starting to make Fallon out to be another Xander—stirring up trouble where he doesn't belong. You aren't at school anymore; you don't hear what the kids say. Their parents are dragging Fallon's name through the mud, and you're not there to stick up for him! We're at the General's mercy, and hundreds of Warriors in the forest are going to die for it."

I released Levina and stomped away, trying not to scream myself. How could the General abandon all those people? And why shouldn't Fallon give him advice? Fallon would have made a better General than Alec; he would never let the entire population turn against his cousin solely because he was advocating for our forest brothers. Fallon had spent his whole career recruiting people to colonize the forest, reassuring them of their service to Warrior Peak and promising their safety. We couldn't leave them to fend for themselves. I hated the General too.

"Orestes, I think you'd better talk to Fallon," Acules said. "I'm sure he already has a plan."

I stopped pacing and took a deep breath. "You're right." I turned back and grabbed Levina's hand. "You coming?" I shot at Acules.

He waved us off. "No, this is your territory. Good luck."

My territory. My job to tip the balance of the war. The thought of fighting without Acules brought a tightness to my chest that made it difficult to run as Levina picked up the pace to my house. I held her hand more tightly and forced myself to keep going, one step at a time.

*

Cyrus, Holt, and Jacob were already assembled in the front room when Levina and I arrived. Fallon beckoned us to shut the door and draw the curtains over the windows before we sat down. Glynis hurried to light some candles as we joined the men in a tight circle of chairs.

"Did Levina tell you?" Fallon asked me.

I nodded, not trusting myself to speak in case Fallon still took offense to someone insulting his cousin.

"Very well. Now as all of you know, Alec and I grew up as brothers, as we had no one else to lean on with all the trouble our families suffered for being the only remnants of the Laconic Warriors." There were nods of understanding all around, adults from evident experience and Levina probably from her historical readings. I couldn't remember exactly who the Laconic Warriors were, but I had heard many people express surprise over such successful men as Alec and Fallon being connected to the Laconics.

Fallon continued, "Alec and I have disagreed on almost every political issue, but in the past, those challenges only increased our respect for one another. We brought our family name back from disgrace and have always supported each other. Alec has found himself unable to do that for me now.

"Therefore, I have decided to take matters into my own hands. All of us know what a strong division Intelligence has become because we helped to train almost every member of it. I know most of my men and women personally. I have met their families and have eaten with several of them. I have made every effort to be there for every tragedy and every success. I trust them with my life, and now I shall trust them with my division. I am going to leave Warrior Peak, and I want all of you to come with me."

At this, the men, usually so controlled and disciplined, exclaimed and began firing off questions on top of each other until they were yelling to be heard. Glynis stared at Fallon as if he were a stranger who had just threatened her children. Levina's eyes were filled with tears again. I nudged her to try to find out what was wrong, but she ignored me as she too stared unblinkingly at Fallon. He allowed the outrage to continue for a few minutes before holding up a hand for silence.

"As I know the people of our division, I also know and care for all my men and women in Serenity Valley. In the past, I have asked my subordinates to leave their friends and families so I could communicate with the forest Warriors, and now it is time for me to do the same. Since the first attack a year ago, I have spoken with Acules several times, and he agrees that the Morroks will—if they haven't already—turn their attention to Serenity Valley. The country is so enormous and the settlements so spread out that the Morroks know as well as we do that the Warriors there will never be able to resist them if they choose to conquer the area. With Serenity Valley's unlimited resources, the Morroks will be able to build a war machine with which our walls cannot contend. I fear they may have already done this. They have amassed at the foot of our own mountain without our knowledge, and so I believe anything is possible. We must warn every forest settlement so they can prepare themselves and eventually mobilize so we can attack the Morroks in the Gravel Lands from both fronts."

Silence followed this sentiment. I couldn't believe the War Council wasn't taking such logic seriously. They should have been ordering half the Army to complete such a task, not forcing one man to try to accomplish it in secret. I hated the General.

"What you say is true, my friend," Holt said finally, "but the mission you speak of will take years to complete. There are twelve settlements in Serenity Valley, and they are spaced well apart from each other. We have no map, and it takes your veterans nearly a year to cover four, maybe five settlements. We would be cut off from Warrior Peak and any news of the war. And assuming your suspicions are true, what if we take this risk only to find the villages overrun by Morroks?"

"Holt is right," Cyrus said. "No disrespect, Fallon, but not many men are going to follow you. If Serenity Valley is already conquered or will be conquered during our journey, we will be a small group unable to resist any Morrok presence. We all fought them in the desert. You know we'd be slaughtered."

Levina was weeping softly by now, and I was torn between trying to figure out what was bothering her and trying to catch every word the men were saying. Either way, she ignored all my glances and attempts to get her attention. I compromised by putting an arm around her but not looking away from Fallon as he spoke again.

"I don't deny any of your concerns, and I have already considered them. I am prepared to take the risk that the Morroks haven't already conquered the Valley because we have seen no evidence of that advantage—no imposing wooden structures, no great ladders to breach our walls. As for them invading the forest while we travel—I stress again how large the forest is and how unlikely it is that we will encounter a group large enough to defeat us. I hope that your wives and Cyrus's son will also accompany us so that we will not be apart from those dearest to us for such a long time. In addition, I value them all as fighters and friends. There are also two other members of our division who I believe could be valuable to our mission. If all those I wish to come would consent, we will have a group of twelve."

"Twelve?" Jacob said. "You, Glynis, and Orestes, myself and Cara, Holt and Abby, Cyrus and Ritter, and your two additions—that makes eleven."

"And Levina here, if her grandparents allow her. This is perhaps more important to her than to any of us."

Levina buried her face in her hands as everyone swiveled around to stare at her as if they hadn't realized she was sitting there until now. She was crying harder than ever. I glared at them until they all looked away.

Fallon raised his hands again for attention. "I realize that this is a lot to ask, even of my dearest friends. Go home and discuss this with your families while I visit my two other prospects. We will not be leaving for at least two months, but I request a response in about ten days' time, if possible, as I need time to start gathering supplies. Good-bye, my friends, and thank you for listening to an old man's ravings."

The three men rose and gave a shaky farewell as they left. Glynis opened the shades, but somehow the daylight felt out of place now. Glynis herself was more agitated than I had ever seen her, and when Fallon moved to rest his hands on her shoulders, she jerked away. Levina and I sat frozen as Fallon tried to touch Glynis again.

"My dear, we have already discussed the possibility—"

"Yes, the *possibility*," she snapped. "How dare you uproot our lives without talking to me? I've put up with a lot from you in the past, but never—*never*—did I think you would do this to me. I've supported you in every decision you've made, good or bad, defended you from every criticism, and defied my own family by even *speaking* to you. How *dare* you open this door to your friends the same time as your wife? I've had enough, Fallon."

"But you must agree that this is what we should do. You've said it yourself."

"That's not the issue at hand, and you know it," she said. Without another word, she strode across the room and disappeared to her own, slamming the door behind her.

Fallon watched her go, his whole body slack as if his strength had disappeared with her. Levina and I dared not look at him. Several moments passed in which even breathing too loudly felt intrusive.

"Levina," Fallon said finally, causing her to jump, "I'm sorry if I caused you any pain. I've known who you were ever since your parents left for the forest, though I don't think you were old enough to remember meeting me before they left. You are under no obligation to accompany us, but I thought that you had a right to know what we were doing and that you should have an opportunity to participate if you wished. Even if you weren't personally connected to the forest Warriors, I would still value what you would bring to our mission. You are a smart girl and have read more about the Morroks, the Peak, and the forest than any of us. I hope you can help us."

Without looking at either of us, he crossed the room and left through the front door.

"You never told me your parents were in the forest," I said. "I thought they were dead!"

"They might as well be, to me at least," Levina said as her tears returned. "They left when I was four. My father didn't want me. He thought having a little girl along would hamper his new life in the forest. My grandparents—my mother's parents—hate him and make no secret of it. I think they would've kept me even if he wanted me to come."

"Then why do you care to go on this mission? Why do you care what's happening to them in the forest?"

"Because I believe in this cause," Levina said passionately. "I can't believe the General would ignore this. I think Fallon's right; sometimes you just have to take matters into your own hands." Her voice dropped. "Besides, they are still my parents, and I want some peace with myself."

I sensed the daily pain behind those words, but I didn't know what to say to comfort her. Although I knew I should have had more to say, I finally blurted, "They just didn't know you yet."

She nodded and stood abruptly. I started to follow her to the door, but she told me she wanted to be alone. I watched her pace down the path toward her house and cursed myself for my lack of sensibility.

With Levina gone, my parents arguing, and Acules easing himself out of my life, I wasn't sure what to do with myself. As I thought of Acules, I realized I still had not constructed my own sword. He asked me about it nearly every day and had even taken a few days off training to show me how to create a masterpiece like his. I had always understood the technique, but actually putting it into practice was another matter entirely.

I darted back to my room and rummaged through my belongings until I found some coins for supplies. Acules was right. I couldn't go into the forest without a sword made by me for me. I couldn't control much else around me, but at least I would steer my own hand.

Chapter Nine
The Laconic Warriors

MOST OF THE TWELVE did not need the full ten days to think about Fallon's offer. Cyrus and Ritter both told Fallon the next day that they were willing to follow him into the heart of the Facility if that was where the mission ended. Jacob and his wife, Cara, visited two days later to confirm their support, and Holt and his wife, Abby, held out a day more only so Abby could ensure that she could transfer from Militia to Intelligence at a moment's notice when we were ready to leave.

Fallon's other two prospects each agreed almost on the spot. One was Todd, the young sergeant and lone survivor of the last mission to Serenity Valley, who I had met after the end-of-year tournament two years before. Fallon said he was a "jumpy kid" but had a flawless memory—in other words, our closest equivalent to a map. The other prospect was Joanne, a middle-aged woman who would have been as close to Fallon as Cyrus was if not for her gender. She had worked directly under him since she entered Intelligence, and ever since her husband had gone missing on a spy mission for him, Fallon, in the spirit of a protective older brother, had seen that she was taken care of in every aspect of life.

I gathered these updates during my frequent visits home between my experiments in Aldis's old blacksmith shop and my continued training with Acules. I told Fallon I was willing to drop out of school right then, considering that I hardly went anymore and was going to quit anyway when we left for Serenity Valley. But for some reason, he was adamant for me not only to participate in the end-of-year tournament, but also to win it. Fallon had never put pressure on me to do well in the tournament, and I couldn't figure out why he was picking such a hectic time to start.

So I continued to train, though I told myself I was really preparing for fighting Morroks, not my classmates. And after several dozen refining practices, I began to create the swords I pictured in my head. Acules gave me invaluable pieces of advice between duels, and between that and years of observing Aldis, my products became as sophisticated as any blacksmith's. However, in all my hours holed up in the forge and training with Acules, I saw very little of Levina. I didn't realize I missed her so much until I absentmindedly began to produce short swords that I thought would fit her fighting style perfectly.

The day I completed her sword was also the day before the end-of-year tournament. It was unusually warm for that time of the year, and the added heat of the forge was almost unbearable. I was admiring my work when Levina herself burst through the door. Unused to interruptions, I jumped off my stool and squinted against the sunlight that flooded in after her. She looked agitated, but before she could say anything, I shoved the sword into her hands.

"What's this?" she asked.

"Your sword. I told you a year ago that you need to use something like this, but you never tried it."

She hefted the sword and turned it skeptically in her hands. The blade was straight and simple and the hilt comfortable and unadorned. I wanted to tell her all the finer points of its construction but waited for her to ask.

Smirking, she looked back up at me. "You worked really hard on this, didn't you?"

"Yes."

"And you put a lot of thought into such a gift?"

"Yes."

"And you expected me to fall over in gratitude for it?"

I hesitated, sensing a trap. "Maybe you could stay standing up."

She laughed aloud and hugged me, sweat, grime, and all, even though she usually wouldn't even speak to me until I washed after working in the forge. "It's beautiful, Orestes. Thank you."

Relieved, I dragged over another stool for her to sit on. "So have your grandparents given their answer? The ten days are almost up."

"I know," Levina said. She looked away as she ran her finger along the flat of her new sword blade. "I think they'll let me, but even if they don't, I'll go anyway. I'd just rather have their approval."

"Why do they hesitate?"

She scoffed. "They don't understand. They think I want to go in hopes of seeing my parents, and they don't want me to waste my time."

"You know Fallon will talk to them. Just say the word."

"No, he has enough to do. I'm actually doing him a favor by finding you."

"Oh?"

"Yes," she said. Her face twisted in irritation again. "Apparently the General wants to have dinner with you this evening."

My eyes widened. "Dinner? He hasn't called me for one of his stupid checkups in more than a year. Why would he now?"

"Don't ask me, but Fallon wants you to go so you can tell him everything that Fallon would tell him if he were speaking to him."

I laughed. "I don't know about that, but I have a few things I'd like to say to him. I have to go to clean up, but I'll tell you about it tomorrow."

She nodded and waved me off. I went outside and left her admiring her new sword.

I strode across the training grounds of the school, only returning greetings rather than giving them. I noticed that there were fewer friendly faces among the students. Between not spending as much time at school and being attached to Fallon's degenerating reputation, I had lost touch with many of the acquaintances I had built over the last couple years. With so many other pressing matters, I hardly counted this as a sacrifice, but I still missed knowing everyone around me.

"Hey, Orestes!" someone shouted just as I was exiting the training grounds. The greeting had a hint of challenge in it.

I turned on the spot to face a boy named Samuel, who was a few years older than I was. He was in the fighting class below me and was a few inches shorter but very muscular. A few other boys in his class were flanking him.

Samuel strode forward until we were nearly toe to toe. "Are you too good for us now too?"

I took a few deep breaths and tried to remind myself that he was just repeating whatever rumors his father had fed him. "Too? Who else is too good for you?"

"Your father. Too good to listen to the General, too good to work together for the greater good. You both strut around here without any regard for the rules or what people above you order. The General ought to take care of Fallon before going for the Morroks. Your whole damn family does nothing but stir up trouble. At least the General moved on from the usurping Laconic Warriors, but Fallon won't be content until he's killed the Elder with his bare h—"

With my newly calloused blacksmith fist, I punched him across the jaw. His friends cried out as Samuel stumbled back into them, flailing to maintain his balance. I glared at each of them for a few moments before I turned to leave, trusting that they would know better than to follow. I *hated* the General.

*

My anger had waned and was redirected by the time evening arrived. When I went home to change clothes, Fallon pestered me with a hundred things he wanted me to say to the General until, much to both of our surprise, I bellowed at him to stop. The rest of my time at home was spent in silence, which was really not uncommon these days because Glynis was still barely speaking to Fallon. The unseasonably warm weather seemed to have everyone on edge.

The training grounds were deserted as I made my way through the school toward the General's level. I could hear the noise of the distant dining hall and was struck again by how detached I felt from my peers. I should have been in there chattering about my chances in the tournament the next day. I should have been practicing on these grounds day and night in hopes of a great victory. Instead, I barely remembered why I wanted to compete in the tournament, and that night, I would be dining with the General of our country, who I would rather see step down from office than hand me a tournament medal.

I happened to glance back just before I mounted the ladder leading up to the General's level. Entering the training grounds was Acules, who, like me, was dressed in a finer tunic than he normally wore. Before he saw me, I pressed myself against the side of a nearby building. He seemed lost in thought as he wandered toward the same ladder, and I regretted that I had no more than my dagger to ambush him with.

As he drew level with me, I let out a yell and pounced on him, my dagger poised at his throat. Acules knocked my hand away with the same force I had seen him use on a Morrok. Undeterred, I launched myself at him again, but he had already drawn his great sword from its sheath and met my dagger like a bear to a fly.

We continued sparring for several minutes, and I was surprised that my little dagger was able to hold up in the fight. Acules held back nothing, but even with my inferior weapon, I kept up with him blow for blow until finally I began to fear for my fingers and took an opportunity to kick him in a very vulnerable spot.

A few curses escaped him as Acules tried to master himself. He bit his lip and began to raise his sword again, but I laughed as he could do no more than stumble toward me.

"What would you have done if you'd been fighting a woman?" he grunted as he sheathed his sword.

"I won. No need to be bitter."

"You did not win, you little cheat."

"But you must admit that I'm getting better."

"Yes, I'll admit that but nothing more."

I grinned but stopped as I studied him more closely. He had all his weapons strapped to his belt and had discarded a small bag when we began to fight. That was everything he had brought with him to Warrior Peak two years before.

"Are you leaving?" I asked.

He tried to smile. "Trust me, I'm becoming more of a hindrance than a help here."

A few moments passed as I tried to accept what was happening. Acules had told me that he wanted to go home, and I was about to leave the Peak too, so it shouldn't have mattered if he was the first to go.

"But I won't have anyone else to duel," I said. "You're the only one who can beat me. Ritter can't even touch me anymore."

"Don't worry, you'll learn as the need arises. When you do, you'll realize that I was a terrible teacher anyway."

"Will you ever come back?"

He glanced up to the sky and sighed. "Your destiny lies on this side of the mountain and mine on the other. I can't tell you if our paths will cross again, but I hope they do, even if it's years from now. Until then, let's both trust that the other is doing everything he can to stop the Morroks."

I nodded and tried to smile too. As with Levina a few days before, I should have had more to say, but as it was, I couldn't even make my mouth say "goodbye." Acules didn't seem to expect anything else but merely clapped me on the shoulder and continued on his way up the mountain.

I gave him a few minutes' head start before I raced up the face of the mountain, conscious of how late I was. When I reached the next level, the one visible guard scrutinized me from the moment I appeared on the level to the moment I entered the General's cave. They apparently hadn't forgotten my visit to the Elder's level two years ago.

The General's cave seemed more dismal than usual. None of the torches along the walls were lit, and there was no sign of life in it, save for a worn path to the central meeting room. I felt my way through the short passage and rapped on the General's door.

Five minutes and five red knuckles later, the disheveled General appeared at his door. The once proud leader of Warrior Peak now stood slightly hunched, as if he had been leaning over a desk for hours. His beard was eccentrically long and unkempt, and the bags under his eyes were as dark as the unlit cavern behind me. Even his usually polished uniform suffered from ink stains and wrinkles. A sword was strapped to his waist.

"Come in. Don't step on anything," he rasped.

I nearly laughed at the instruction. There seemed to be more papers in his front room than in the whole of the Inventory division. Some were stacked with quills penetrating every few layers, and others were scattered in loose circles as if the General had sat on the floor and arranged them around him. Through the sea of black-spotted white were weapons and uniforms I recognized as regular Army-distributed equipment. Half-eaten food and filthy clothes were swept into dusty corners.

"I have a spot for you here; just move—no, you don't touch—I'll move . . ." The General shifted a stack of paper to reveal a sliver of table surface. I stood by, unmoving, as he struggled to unbury a chair and find new homes for the papers. Finally, after several minutes of cursing, there were two chairs facing each other across a partially cleared table. The General shoved a plate of fruit and bread toward me. It seemed even the General was suffering from a lack of meat, as most of the regular hunters had been working with the Army or the Militia.

When the General didn't take anything for several minutes, I reached for the bread. "Sir, if you don't mind me asking, why don't you have cooks and maidservants helping you?"

"I have not relied on another person to care for me since I moved out of my parents' house when I was nineteen years old. There is no reason for me to begin now."

"Yes, sir," I said. A ripple of anger attempted to rise in my mind but failed. The normal awe of being in the company of one so powerful was still with me, but another odd attitude was taking precedence. With an unpleasant jolt, I realized it was pity.

"After more than a year of no contact, you must be wondering why I asked you here," he said.

"A little, sir."

"Well, it is for purely selfish reasons, Orestes."

My eyes widened. He hadn't called me by my name since I was five years old.

"I know what Fallon's planning to do, and I'm letting him do it because he's taking only about a dozen of my people away. High-ranking people, but alas, he is my cousin. However, I don't want you to be among them."

Now anger overtook awe and pity. My hands curled into balls as I rose to my feet and began to protest vehemently. But even with his tired, sunken eyes, the General glared at me until I relented and sat back, silent, though I kept my fists clenched until I had lost feeling in my fingers.

"And I could keep you here if I wanted to. You damn well better realize that."

"Yes, sir," I growled.

"But I won't," he continued, "because I need you on my side."

"*You* need *me*, sir?"

"Yes, I do, although I don't know why," he said, the shadow of a twitch crossing his eyelid. "The Elder himself has ordered me to keep you informed as to why we are acting as we are."

"*Why?*" As ludicrous as it was to contradict the General, I only half believed that the Elder would speak about me personally, much less lend me top-ranked information.

"I told you I don't know," the General barked, his bloodshot eyes widening. "Same damn reason I had to go to Tyrclopia to get you, I suppose."

My second "why" was halfway out of my mouth before I decided it was best not to upset the General when he was already at his wits' end. Instead, I waited for him to continue.

"Anyway," he said, "to give you an overview, we are drawing all our forces back to the Peak as subtly as possible so as not to arouse suspicion. The Morroks obviously know that we are aware of their existence because they sent that sergeant back to us a year ago to tell us. You were the one to find the sergeant, were you not?"

"Yes, his name is Todd. He works for my father."

"Yes, so you already know that. Nevertheless, we are choosing not to act at the moment. We are still gathering information—trying to figure out their numbers and exactly what we're up against. As you know, we have training programs going on so that when we are ready to engage them, every man and woman will be prepared."

"What if it's not our choice to engage?" I said, unable to stop myself. "The Morroks don't work like that. They're not opposed to sneaking in here one night and killing us in our sleep. You can't count on them knocking on your door and saying 'We're ready to duke it out on neutral territory.' Most of them can't even talk very well; they only know how to follow orders."

"Don't be ridiculous," the General said. "They could never breach Warrior Peak. Therefore, we control the war."

"You're a fool if you think we're in control. They'll crush us if they have even half our numbers. And they don't even go for hand-to-hand combat if they can help it. They were teaching us how to break into a house when we were four years old!"

The General stood and paced around the room, massaging his temples. I felt sick and unclean. I had successfully kept from talking about the Morroks in detail for an entire year even though it was the sole topic of conversation around the Peak. The sounds of the desert now penetrated my mind, and it took all my willpower to shut out the memories that came along with my verbal admission to having been part of the Morroks.

"I did not bring you here to critique what the War Council has decided," the General finally said. "Fallon has done enough of that. He fashions himself a humanitarian, but he doesn't understand what it's like to think of the safety of hundreds of thousands of people. Sure, he's got his twelve villages in Serenity Valley with a population of a few hundred each, but do you understand, boy, that I have to depend on these walls? These damn walls! If I could solve everything by being a wall myself, I'd do it, damn it. If I had to die, I'd do it. The Elder wanted me to talk nicely with you, but to hell with it. I'm doing everything I can to keep our children from getting kidnapped by those monsters, and if a teenager—a teenager who knows the same information that some men have worked their whole lives to know—doesn't approve of my methods, then to hell with me too! I'm done fighting Fallon."

I had unconsciously scooted away from the General and stopped only when my chair hit the wall. I didn't dare move while he stalked around, fuming as he snatched papers off piles and put them back without reading them. Despite the rage he was in, I finally remembered what a good person the General really was. I remembered the first time I met him and how he had called me by name and shaken my five-year-old hand as if I were his equal. I remembered how he had called the Morroks "those monsters" and his complete disdain for them. The power struggle was not against the rest of us and the General; it was solely between the General and Fallon, and I couldn't pick a side anymore.

"What do you mean by children getting kidnapped?" I asked in a low voice.

The General stopped moving, though he was still breathing heavily. He now adopted the anxious expression that he donned whenever he asked me how my new fighting class was going. "Don't you know? That's how the Morroks build their army. Although they produce a child nearly every time they mate, they rarely do so because there aren't many women among them and pregnancy would prevent females from fighting. Plus, mating would encourage too much affection among them, and their children are born pure, normal Humans, so there is no advantage there. No, the Morroks steal their enemies' children. They build up their military by taking away from ours. So essentially, Morroks are you and I without love and compassion. The serum takes care of those."

I shifted uncomfortably in my seat. What if I had swallowed some of the serum that Dirth had tried to force down my throat the day I left the tower? Was that enough to allow the Morroks' evil to have a permanent hold, however small, on me?

"So . . . my parents—my real parents," I said, wanting to change the subject, "are some people in Tyrclopia who didn't have a good enough lock on my door?"

The General collapsed back in his chair. "I—I can't really . . . it's not for me to . . . well, I didn't expect you to ask me that." He paused. "No, your parents are not Tyrclopians, but you'll have to hear the rest from the Elder if he ever chooses to speak to you. Don't ask me any more about it."

We sat in silence for a long time. It was probably completely dark outside by now. The General absentmindedly picked at his food, not looking at anything else. I followed his lead even though I wasn't hungry. I tried to think of subtle ways to draw more information out of him about the Morroks or my parents, but there was no good way to go about it. Instead, I tucked away this information with all the veiled clues that Acules and Fallon had given me over the years. After a while, I decided to switch topics altogether.

"I don't know if you meant for this to happen, sir," I said, "but Fallon has started to get a bad name among many people."

"My conflict with the man is personal and nothing more. The other War Council generals may be running away with our bad blood, but I have said nothing against him myself." He sighed. "Still, the fault comes back to me, but there's not much I can do to stop gossip. The women of the Peak outnumber us."

I grinned. "Well, no matter who started the incrimination, it's trickled down to the military students, and I had some idiot today say something to the effect that Fallon wanted to kill the Elder like the Laconic Warriors. So I was wondering—who were the Laconic Warriors?"

The General cocked an eyebrow. "First, is the 'idiot' still alive?"

I stuttered over my "uh" for a few moments before answering. Trivial as it was, I didn't want to admit to the General that I had broken a school rule. "Well, I didn't see him move his jaw again before I left, but I only hit him with my fist, so . . ."

The General actually laughed. "You showed amazing self-control then."

I smiled nervously.

"Anyway," he said, growing serious, "I'm surprised that Fallon's never told you. Actually, maybe I'm not surprised; it's not something we like to remember." He scratched his chin thoughtfully. "The Laconic Warriors nearly started a civil war within Warrior Peak. They started out as a sort of accelerated program within the military school. The kids just came to a couple extra dueling classes. Nothing too special. They didn't even have a name for it back then." He paused, his eyes becoming unfocused as if he were trying to remember something. "Then it became a different program, still within the school. The kids slept in their own barracks, their trainers had to undergo special tests before they could teach them, and they created all sorts of 'secret society' rules, the most prominent of which became a vow of silence throughout the last part of their training—hence the name *Laconic Warriors.*

"Of course, as with all intimate groups, the members wanted to stay in contact with one another even after they were graduated. So the Laconic Warriors began to meet regularly outside school. They did all kinds of things—raised money for widows and orphans, pooled resources for business, and even began to host their own tournaments. All the while, the training to become a Laconic Warrior became stricter and stricter until some parents became wary of the effects the practices were having on their children."

The General took a long draught from his goblet. "That's about the time when the first rifts began between the Laconics and the actual military. Sure, the Laconic Warriors were still part of the military, and many were very high-ranking officials. You have to understand that they were producing the best fighters and sharpest minds in our society, but because they were all linked, they became a dangerously powerful sect. They were in every division, and if they decided they didn't like something, it was usually changed, even if the War Council didn't entirely approve. The General of the time finally had to step in because their unofficial political power was beginning to threaten his authority. The prominent members of the Laconic Warriors were insulted, saying that they did everything for the good of the Peak and that it wasn't their fault if that didn't fall in line with the General's opinion."

I had to contain my grin at the irony of the last statement. He might as well have been telling his and Fallon's story.

"But the General reached a compromise with them. He agreed that the Laconic Warriors had such a great program and influence that they should have the representation of a division, and so an eighth member was added to the War Council. This was the Laconic Warriors' dream. Every single one of their students graduated and went on to their very own division just like they would enter as a private into Intelligence or the like. However, the Laconic division had no defined task like the rest; instead, they did a little of everything so that they were like their own miniature Warrior Peak. No one saw the signs of danger.

"This was about the time when my and Fallon's grandfather and his brother were born. Our grandfather's name was Caden, and his older brother was named James. The boys showed talent from an early age, but their parents didn't want them to have anything to do with the new division. However, by that time, the Laconics had become—as you can guess—very *persuasive,* and both brothers were compelled to enter the program."

"Sounds like the Morroks," I said.

"Yes, it does," the General replied. "Too much like the Morroks, in fact. But no one spoke up, and so James and Caden grew up with the Laconics like many others before them. But right before the brothers graduated, the Laconic Warriors did something unthinkable: They moved."

"Moved?"

"Left Warrior Peak. They took every member willing—and to be sure, most were—and they built a city on the mountain directly east of Warrior Peak. If people hadn't been concerned before, they were then, James and Caden among them. James completed military school by winning the end-of-year tournament over only Caden and his fellow Laconics. Then he moved to the Laconic community for fear of what they'd say, or perhaps do, if he didn't. In the few years before Caden graduated, James wrote to him frequently, reporting all the amassing of weapons and continued training the Laconic Warriors were doing. Then his letters stopped."

The General paused to take another drink, and I realized I was leaning forward anxiously and almost covering the food tray. As casually as possible, I slouched back into my chair.

The General continued, "Caden didn't trust what he heard, and so he visited the Laconic Warriors, which wasn't at all suspicious at the time. He stayed with James for a few weeks, and they agreed something bad was about to happen. Through some perilous investigation, they were able to discern that the Laconic Warriors were planning to break away from Warrior Peak completely, by force if necessary.

"The problem was that even though the Laconics had superior skill, they didn't have the numbers that Warrior Peak did. So, like the Morroks, they were planning to, um, *compel* just about every child into their program, which was conveniently going to be moved to the Laconic community in the near future. The General had created a monster, but no one could tell him so because most of the Laconics were too absorbed in the scheme, and the few who weren't were too afraid to step out against them.

"James and Caden were different, though. I don't think you and I can really appreciate how difficult it was for them, but somehow the two of them escaped the Laconic community with some sort of documented proof of their plans. Grandpa always claimed that the General fainted when they told him, but I still doubt that a General could show such a sign of weakness."

I smirked. "What, you get some supernatural guard against emotion when you're promoted?"

"Absolutely right," the General said seriously. "Anyway, the General had not forgotten the political strife the Laconics had already created, and so he believed the boys and sent them back to act as spies, Caden in the military school and James in the community. Tensions were mounting in the leadership of both sides, and everything broke down when the War Council general who represented the Laconic Warriors at the Peak realized that the other Laconic leaders had met once without him. Somehow, the leaks in Laconic security were traced back to James, and the Laconics executed him before Caden or the General of Warrior Peak even realized there was a problem.

"Caden broke all pretenses after that. He was too humble to tell Fallon and me the details, but we heard his tales from many others. For with James's execution, the Laconics' intentions were no longer secret, and in anticipation of a war, the Warrior Peak Army was called up—a rare occurrence, as you well know.

"Caden saved many lives with his actions following the death of his brother. He saw to it that all the Laconic students were returned to their parents before they were forced to move to the Laconic community; meanwhile, the Laconic trainers fled to the eastern mountain. Then Caden himself went to the community, denouncing his brother and swearing loyalty to the Laconic Warriors. Grandpa never told us what he had to do to prove to them that he was on their side, but Fallon and I have always suspected that he had to draw his own blood or something equally barbaric. Even the General thought he had betrayed Warrior Peak, but in truth, Caden had taken spying to a whole new level: assassination.

"There was a single battle between Warrior Peak and the Laconic Warriors. This is another horror that I don't think anyone alive now can truly imagine. Humans were killing Humans. Yes, we kill Morroks, which were once Humans, but that is nothing like one Human killing another. One battle was more than enough to devastate Warrior Peak, and if it hadn't been for Caden, there would've been many more battles.

"In the midst of the melee, Caden found the leaders of the Laconic Warriors. They were all fighting in a cluster, so the moment Caden struck one, the rest would realize his betrayal and kill him. But by some miracle, Caden was able to strike down three of them and then escape, for a while at least.

"The battle disintegrated after that, but Warrior Peak was unable to save Caden from the Laconics. He was captured, and his trial and execution were meant to be an example to the rest of the Laconic Warriors. The remaining leaders were planning to torture and kill him publicly. This is the vaguest part of the story because Grandpa never told us about it, and the rest of the witnesses disappeared. But apparently, when Caden was brought out for his trial, he gave some sort of desperate speech denouncing the Laconic Warriors and comparing them, as you did, to the Morroks. Those holding him nearly killed him in their attempts to silence him, but his words worked. The Laconics rose up against their own leaders, and I think they killed them, though Grandpa only remembered parts of the day because he was struggling to stay conscious.

"The rest is really anticlimactic. Every Laconic Warrior literally disappeared. Realizing the gravity of their betrayal and afraid to face whatever consequences they might meet at Warrior Peak, the Laconics fled—maybe to Tyrclopia, maybe further down the mountains, maybe to Serenity Valley. No one knows. Only Caden returned, though he never could blend back into society. For some years, he refused to tell what had occurred, and so people labeled him as a traitor and treated him as an outcast. So the boy who said that Fallon was a traitor like the rest of the Laconic Warriors is a product of years of disgrace our family has had to overcome because Caden was too pained to speak of his past."

"I don't blame him," I said.

"No, I suppose you wouldn't," the General said. "However, it's very late now, and I hadn't planned on spending so much time on this meeting. I probably won't see you again before you leave, so good luck to you at the tournament tomorrow, and be careful in the forest. I can't give you much advice about it, because I'm ignorant of the area, but I can remind you to heed your training if and when you meet Morroks."

I stood up. "Thank you, sir. And good luck to you too."

"Thank you, Orestes. You are dismissed."

Chapter Ten
The End-of-Year Tournament

Unable to sleep, I walked around for a while after leaving the General. I had the overwhelming urge to run, to fight, to forge, to do anything that didn't involve thinking about the Morroks. What if my parents really weren't Tyrclopians? What if they were Morroks? I had never allowed myself to hold out hope that I would find my birth parents, but I would rather have gone on believing that I fell out of the sky than suspect that I had truly come from the Morroks. Then I really would always be under Dirth's control. I was a son of Lernuc no matter where I went, and I really couldn't hide, not forever, not if that was where I came from, no matter what the General said about the nature of good and evil.

Without paying attention to how I got there, I finally settled in Aldis's old blacksmith shop. I barred the door, lit a few candles, and fired up the forge. While I was waiting for the heat to grow, I remembered that the end-of-year tournament started in a few hours' time. I couldn't make myself rest for it, though. I didn't care to. Nothing was the same anymore. The tournament wouldn't take place in the Gravel Lands because of the war. Instead, the matches were scattered over the dozens of training grounds throughout the Peak, and only a limited number of people were allowed to attend. We were told to leave the grounds between matches and go home if we lost to allow for more space. There would be no running from ring to ring, cheering on friends and consoling the losers. There would be no crowd filling tiers and tiers of seats, glad that the year of anticipation hadn't been in vain.

Yet even if everything had been normal, I didn't know how much I would care. Acules and Fallon had ruined what should have been the first year of me having a chance at victory. Because of Acules and his training, I would win without question, and because of Fallon and his defiance, no one would care.

And because of the Morroks, I would never get to experience this joy again.

*

It was around dawn when I began to hear voices outside on the training grounds. I wiped a layer of sweat off my face and unbarred the door in case Levina was among them. I hadn't slept all night, but I had finally started on the perfect sword. It was far from being finished, but my vision had become defined enough that I could make a mold of the right length and shape. There was no time to make any more significant progress that day, so I began to lay out the tools to cool.

Not too long after I unlocked the door, Levina let herself in. She immediately gathered her hair off her neck and started to fan herself.

"I went to your house, and Fallon said you never came home last night. He's really angry. He wanted a report on what the General said."

"Good morning to you too," I mumbled without looking at her as I searched for the shirt I had discarded hours ago.

"So what *did* he say?"

"Nothing really." I picked up a piece of smoke-filled cloth that had once been clothing. I doubted that Levina would go back to my house to retrieve me a change of clothes so I could avoid Fallon.

"He had to have said something important or else you wouldn't have holed yourself up in here."

"He's not a bad man," I said. "He told me about some of the war plans—nothing we didn't already know—and he told me the story about the Laconic Warriors. It was amazing. I know you probably could've told me all the facts, but he got it straight from Caden, the man who stopped the war."

Levina grinned and came to sit near me. "You're just a sucker for a good war story, that's all. But I'm still angry that he would leave the foresters to fend for themselves."

"I'm not happy about it either, but all we can do is keep moving forward with Fallon's plan."

"Did you sleep at all last night?" she asked. She leaned toward me as I continued to rummage among the tools. Our faces were suddenly very close.

I turned away so she wouldn't see my bloodshot eyes. "A little."

"Are you going to be all right? It's going to be a long day, and Fallon really wants you to do well."

"Why is that, do you think?" I asked.

"Well, it's your last one, and you're having to drop out of school, which will set you back whenever we return from Serenity Valley. Maybe he just wants you to enjoy yourself."

"Maybe."

"Come on, let's get you changed and see where your first match is. Don't worry about anything else. We'll have fun today, I promise."

*

The first few rounds of the tournament were predictably boring and one-sided for everyone. Because the tournament encompassed every male student, there were some cases of nineteen-year-olds fighting petrified five-year-olds. A debate ensued every year as to whether or not the tournament should be split up according to age, but tradition always prevailed. The most anyone could expect of a child under ten was for him not to run out of the ring screaming.

I tried not to scare my first two opponents, who both looked younger than nine, but in both cases, once we had exchanged a few blows, they just stood still and let me take their dull swords from their hands. The sparse spectators clapped briefly before the Training officers chased the poor boys out of the rings to make room for the next match.

My next few opponents were a little older and a little more interesting; they repeated their training drills beautifully for the few moments before I used one of Acules's tricks, which left them baffled. As the day wore on, I realized how dull classroom learning was in that way; only the oldest students had learned to develop styles independent from their teachers, who, despite their students being divided according to talent, had to accommodate students of all levels of ability in their classes.

It was a little after midafternoon before I consistently met students who were comparable at least to my age. I found yet again that I had little in common with them anymore. Of course I still knew their names, but I hadn't practiced with them, eaten meals with them, or even slept in the same barracks with them for months. Between matches, I had only Levina to talk to for more than a few seconds at a time. I hadn't seen Fallon, his friends, or Ritter all day.

"Top eight," Levina said when I joined her after winning a five-minute spar with a seventeen-year-old. We were near the foot of the mountain, but even the heightened fear of the desert hadn't kept the new year's crowd at bay. Although the Training division had asked that only the immediate family of the opponents come to each match, no one had heeded this, and so the streets were packed with people trying to squeeze their way from one match to the next.

As Levina and I made our way up the mountain for the next round, people pressed together on the narrow paths, and after Levina had her toes pinched twice, I was ready to start elbowing people out of the way. Sensing my frustration, Levina pulled us out of the crowd, and we started to climb up an unsettled part of the mountain.

"How is it that you've been able to come to all my matches even when there's only been room for family?" I asked.

"Let's just say it's amazing how all your opponents seem to have a beautiful seventeen-year-old sister," Levina said.

"Beautiful, huh?"

She reached up and pinched my cheek. "You'd better be nicer to me; I have a new short sword ready to use, you know."

"Then maybe you could take my spot in the tournament."

"A year ago you were near tears because you couldn't compete. What's wrong with you?"

"Nothing. Let's hurry up." I grabbed her hand and lengthened my stride.

Fallon and Glynis had already left the house by the time we arrived looking for them. Personally relieved, I led the way through the increasing crowd into the heart of the military school training grounds, where the seven other competitors stood in a loose cluster surrounded by their respective supporters.

After we had joined them, Levina tugged my arm down toward her until her mouth was right next to my ear so I could hear her over the crowd. My skin tingled as I felt her breath against me. "Listen, before Fallon sees you, I should probably tell you something. When you win—"

"If."

"—*if* you win, when they have you make your speech, Fallon wants you to mention . . . well, us."

"You and me?" I asked, bewildered.

"No, no, Serenity Valley—our mission and all. And he said it wouldn't hurt if you talked about your, um, real parents, whatever that means."

I drew myself up to my full height and scrutinized her for any trace of falsity. Surely Fallon wouldn't want me to talk about the Morroks. Only he, Glynis, Cyrus, Ritter, and the General knew about my history as a Morrok trainee, and he had warned me since I was a child not to tell anyone else. It would frighten people. No one would understand. No one understood how the Morroks worked, and if they knew I had been a part of them in any way, they would want me gone. And even if they took the time to understand, Fallon knew how painful it was for me to talk about the Morroks just to him, much less announce my shame to all of Warrior Peak.

"Damn him," I said.

"Orestes, what's wrong?" She tried to catch my eye as I scanned the crowd for Fallon.

"Nothing. I'm not making any damn speech. Find him and tell him that. What a hypocrite. What an unbelievable hypocrite."

"Orestes—"

A training officer appeared at our side. "Miss, we're about to begin. Please clear the rings." A group of the Training division's top members had gathered with us in the middle of the training grounds, and everyone except the competitors was squeezing into the spaces between the buildings and the low fence surrounding the grounds.

Levina frowned at me and squeezed my hand. "Good luck," she said as she turned toward the crowd.

I barely heard the officers announce the finalists' names and who would be fighting whom. After some applause and further shuffling among the crowd, we were stationed in the four corners of the training grounds. My opponent was an eighteen-year-old named Nathan with whom I had always gotten along. He gave no sign of recognition as we faced each other. I hardly noticed as I spotted Fallon at the front of the crowd. He met my glare with a set jaw. Glynis stood beside him, smiling and waving at me. I wondered if she knew what he wanted me to do.

Nathan struck abruptly, and I barely avoided receiving a deep bruise on my upper arm. The other three matches were already underway. The din of the crowd drowned out the knocking of dull swords and the grunts of the competitors. Nathan struck again, and this time I met him. I moved automatically, unable to make myself concentrate. My gaze kept falling over the heads of the crowd to Aldis's old blacksmith shop, where my half-finished sword lay. I wanted to be in there more than anywhere at that moment, not fighting a kid I barely knew anymore or balancing the subtle political battles of old men.

As I looked at the forge, I saw a large body moving away from the training grounds toward the General's level. At first I thought it was a trick of the eye—just my imagination running away with thoughts of the Morroks. But my body told me more than my mind. My stomach clenched, and a chill spread through my limbs as I saw the giant silhouette fade back around the corner of the blacksmith shop. The crowd had its eyes fixed on us, and Nathan had his back to it; no one would have seen it except me.

Without pausing to consider, I untangled my blade from Nathan's and raced at the fence. The front row of the crowd gasped and pulled back as I leaped the barrier and pushed my way through them without a word. No one followed me.

The Morrok had left the grounds of the military school by the time I dove into the alley between Aldis's blacksmith shop and a classroom. It saw me immediately and began to run. This Morrok was no different than any other. The top of its head nearly grazed the overhanging roof of a nearby building, and the contrasts in its sallow, discolored skin shown clearly in the oppressive sunlight. I was all too aware of the bluntness of the training sword in my hand, but I knew it would have to work.

With its long legs and powerful muscles, the Morrok outstripped me easily until we had long left behind the noise of the tournament and were standing on an unsettled patch of the mountain with no signs of life within eyesight. It was there that the Morrok stopped and waited for me to meet it with my inferior weapon.

Even after a full day of dueling, my muscles did not feel loose enough to meet the power behind the Morrok's every movement. It fought with surprising agility for one of its size, partly because it was using a one-handed sword. Nearly all my memories were of Morroks holding two-handed swords, axes, or maces larger than my whole body, but this Morrok, needing the stealth required to sneak into Warrior Peak, carried a small sword that still made my tired arms quake on impact.

As the fight continued, the panic of finding an intruder subsided, and a numb obedience to my instincts rose in its place. It was just like dueling Acules. I didn't have time to think about the Morrok and everything it represented; I didn't have time to see myself in its training and movements. The only thoughts that came to mind were dodge, block, strike, parry, and a new, rather unsettling command: kill.

Over the clang of metal, I noticed a strange croaking sound. I withdrew my sword and skipped back a few steps. The Morrok didn't follow, but the croaking continued as the Morrok's hoarse, unsteady voice became audible: "Leave here, or they will die."

The sweat on my arms and neck seemed to freeze over in an instant. I swallowed, trying to soothe my dry throat. "Listen, I don't know how you got in, but I assure you that no more of you will breach these walls. No one here will die."

"We killed Aldis, we killed Conrad, we kill all. We know all. These walls mean nothing. Leave here, or they all die. Levina first."

"How do you know her name?" I shouted, gripping my sword more tightly. I felt like I was going to vomit.

The Morrok's blotchy face stretched into a smile. "Son of Lernuc, you cannot hide."

Before my mind could weigh the validity of its threats, my body was charging at the Morrok, my sword forgotten and my dagger drawn. All I wanted was to silence it, no matter the means. The Morrok poised its sword in front of itself, but I, all caution abandoned, swatted the flat of its blade with my bare hand and launched myself full body onto the Morrok. As we overbalanced, its claws began to dig into my neck, but it couldn't push me away before I stabbed it in the heart.

As the Morrok gasped and moaned beneath me, Dirth's words from twelve years before resounded more strongly than ever. *Kill me, kill Humans, kill Morroks—prove your power the only way you know how, and we will have won.*

Dirth would certainly be pleased now. But what could I do? Acules had said that I could tip the balance of this war, so if I did nothing, the Morroks would win. But if I continued to kill, Dirth would still win. I drove my dagger more deeply into the Morrok beneath me.

Son of Lernuc, you cannot hide.

I was a son of Lernuc. I was a Morrok. I thought that my understanding of the Morroks was supposed to be some tactical advantage, but in reality, the understanding seemed to go both ways. Although I was in Warrior Peak, a supposedly impenetrable fortress, they had still found me and had known how to threaten me—had known even Levina's name. I stabbed the Morrok again.

Leave here, or they will die.

Leave Warrior Peak. I already was going to leave by my own will. But why did they want me to? Was I again playing into their hands when I thought I was working against them?

"Orestes, stop it! Stop it!"

Glynis's shrieks pulled me back to the present moment. I pushed myself off the dead Morrok as she, Fallon, Levina, and half a dozen officers finished jogging toward me. They stopped a few feet short of the battleground as if not wanting to come near the Morrok. As I bent to retrieve my dagger, I noticed that my hands looked as if they had been red from birth. I straightened again and met each gaze of horror with defiance until I finally settled on Levina.

Then the blood splattered all over my torso was suddenly vile, the dagger in my hand monstrous, and every thought of the past moments despicable. She averted her eyes and walked away.

"Orestes, were there any others? Did he say anything before he died?" Fallon demanded.

"*It*," I said, "didn't say anything, but I doubt there are more."

"The General will probably order a complete lockdown," one of the older officers said. I vaguely recognized him as War Council general of the Training division. He too avoided my direct gaze. "Colonel, if you would stay with the body, I will stop the tournament and send everyone to their homes so the Inventory division can do the head count. And Major," he said, turning to Glynis and lowering his voice, "until we call him for questioning, keep this boy out of sight if it's the last thing you do."

*

Glynis knew as well as I did that, once I had cleaned up and burned my bloody clothes, I was going to sneak out of the house. Night had fallen, and every citizen, from the highest-ranking officers to the lowest-paid civilian, was locked safely into his or her respective home. Only two dozen officers from the Inventory division combed the streets, stopping at each home and making sure that everyone was there who was supposed to be and that there were no additional intruders or spies in our midst. The moment they left our house, I retreated to my room and barred the door. Then, with a few practiced moves, I slipped out the window and propped it open with only a thin stick.

It was nothing short of eerie to dart around completely deserted streets. Over the years, I had seen the Peak at all hours, and never were the streets devoid of all activity and life. The General had threatened extensive time in the mines to anyone caught outside his or her home tonight, but more than his treats, it was fear of the Morroks that kept everyone inside. No one could fathom the possibility of Morroks gaining entrance to our city by themselves, and so talk of spies became rampant within minutes of the public hearing the news. But who would betray us to monsters? There was no gain for a spy, no possibility of protection for him if Warrior Peak fell to the Morroks. But

Warrior Peak would never fall. No one would dare give breath to the notion.

If anyone saw me, there was a chance I would be shot on sight, whether by one of the paranoid fathers peeking out his window or by one of the armed Inventory officers looking for a Morrok in every shifty figure darting between houses. But I knew my shortcuts and was more cautious than would have been necessary even if there had been hundreds of patrollers on every level.

Soon I was standing outside Levina's house, my hands sweating and stomach clenching more than they ever had while I had fought the Morrok. The look of disgust she had given me when she saw me standing over the Morrok was already haunting me, and I had to make sure she wasn't going to stop seeing me because of it. I couldn't handle the thought, especially not after all that had happened today.

Levina's windows didn't have wooden shutters like mine but only thick curtains, which were drawn closed when I reached that side of the house. I climbed through the opening and untangled myself from the fabric without making much noise.

Levina sat fully dressed and hunched over her desk, pen in hand and a small candle flickering dangerously close to her long hair. She gasped and looked around at the shifting curtains, but when she saw who it was, she turned back to her work. Noting that her bedroom door was locked, I stayed where I was, unsure of what to say but intensely aware of how fretful her silence made me. For a few moments, I tried to content myself in looking around her uncluttered room. Besides a few piles of carefully stack paper, she had only a bed and the desk for furniture along with a large trunk full of clothes. The sword I had given her the day before was already on display, hanging on two pegs on the wall near her bed.

I finally strode over to her desk, where she was blowing on the new ink. She had been writing in a small, black leather-bound book. I crouched next to her and blew on the thick pages with her. The last few sentences she had written read, "I knew something must have been wrong. Orestes would never run from a fight, no matter how small. So Fallon, Glynis, and I followed him."

"What will you say about the next part?" I asked, glancing up at her.

"That you had killed a Morrok, that we were all shocked that it had gotten into the Peak, that we had to go on lockdown. You've had the same life for the last few hours; you should know what I'm going to write."

I expected her to move away or turn her back to me again, but she just sat there, staring blankly at the wall.

"You won't—you won't say anything about what the Morrok looked like, what I . . . ?"

"I started this diary the day Conrad was killed. It is a log I will keep until this war is over. What details I deem important or what feelings I choose to put to paper are hardly your concern."

We sat in silence for a long time, she in the chair and me squatting beside her, each of us staring at a different spot on the desk. I tried to take her hand, but she pulled it deliberately out of reach. I wasn't sure why I felt so miserable or why she was so upset. An apology was on the tip of my tongue, but it would have served only to calm my own conscious. I wasn't sorry for killing the Morrok, and I didn't know why I should have been. But the fact remained that Levina wouldn't look me in the eye.

"Levina, please," I said finally, "what's wrong?"

She shook her head. "I knew you wouldn't understand."

"That's why I'm asking. Humor me."

"It's not exactly comforting to see your best friend kill a monster."

"Best friend?" I laughed. "Do you think I'd come and check on Ritter if I thought he was a little upset?"

"That's not the point! Best friend, beau, whatever you are—and I'm not a little upset! You killed someone!"

"Levina, where the hell do you think you are?" I sprang to my feet and paced a few steps away from her before rounding back. "Why do you think we train with swords and maces from the time we're five years old? This is *Warrior Peak*! What do you think your grandfather would do if he saw a Morrok? What do you think any of us would do? I didn't kill someone! I killed some*thing*. Don't insult me, and don't flatter them."

"Fine," she said, likewise jumping out of her chair. "Fine, you didn't kill someone. You *mutilated* something. Orestes, you scare me. You get in these moods. . . . You just get so angry, and I don't know what to do, and then if you don't lock yourself in that blacksmith shop, something like this happens."

"Something like what? When do I kill things because I'm mad?"

"Well, maybe not kill, but you don't see yourself when you're fighting. I watch you duel Acules; it's so intense, as if you're out for his blood, anyone's blood. It's just not normal, not—not—"

"Not Human?" I said. All throughout my childhood, the General had worried that I would lose control in my fighting classes, and now he was being proven right. I hadn't thought I fought differently than other men, but then again, the Morroks didn't fight so differently either; the real difference was in their eyes—angry and unrestrained—and that, perhaps, was what I could not see in myself.

Levina's eyes widened at my accusation. "No, of course not. I would never say anything like that." She crossed the short distance between us, and I couldn't help but be distracted by her nearness. "I just don't understand why you get like that. You were out of control today, and it was so frightening. Do you even realize what you're doing when you fight?"

I couldn't bring myself to tell her everything. If Levina thought so little of me when I fought like a Morrok, what would she think if she knew I once was one? Or at least was going to be one. Maybe even came from one. The truth was that I had known exactly what I was doing, and I hadn't cared to stop. That Morrok had confessed to being part of Aldis and Conrad's murders, and it had threatened Levina's life. It represented everything I didn't want to be, and I had wanted it gone—if not figuratively, then at least physically.

"No, I didn't really know what I was doing, not completely," I lied. "I just lost control of my emotions, that's all. That's how I let out my anger—fighting and exercising and moving. I'm sorry I scared you. I don't want you to be afraid of me. I would never hurt Humans, no matter how mad I get, and I certainly would never hurt you."

Levina took one last step toward me so that our bodies were completely aligned, foot to foot, hip to hip, shoulder to shoulder. She snaked her arms under mine and embraced me as she apologized again and again. After a few agonizing moments of her rubbing my back and feeling her warm breath on my neck, I couldn't resist any longer and lifted her chin toward me to kiss her.

The kiss didn't last long before Levina pulled back to look at me. A thrilling mix of embarrassment and pleasure enveloped us as we grinned shyly at each other. Our reverie didn't last long, however, as pounding from the other side of the house startled us out of our silence.

"That's the front door," Levina said. "The Inventory men must be here to check us. You have to go. Now." She squirmed away from me and extinguished the candle on her desk.

"Wait, answer me this," I whispered, following her as she scurried to her clothes trunk. "Have your grandparents said whether or not you can go to Serenity Valley?"

I couldn't see her face in the darkness, but her rifling through the clothes became more violent. "They said no," she said, "but I don't care. Tell Fallon that they're okay with it; I'll make sure they never talk otherwise. Just give me half an hour's notice before we leave, and I can collect my things and sneak out. That's all I need, half an hour."

"Levina—"

"Orestes, don't you dare argue with me." She stopped her search to hold my gaze. "I believe in what we're going to do, and I'm old enough to stand up for what I believe in. The General may be a good man, but the fact remains that he's left hundreds of people stranded without warning of what might happen, and somebody has to do something about it. We're going to make a difference; I can feel it in my bones, and there's no way I'm going to be left behind. Now go; I need to change into my nightgown."

The pounding was now on Levina's bedroom door. I kissed her again, quickly, and then dashed to the window. As I crept through the cool night air, I heard Levina snap, "For goodness' sake, hold on; I'm not decent!" and didn't try to repress my smile. I never would have been able to make it through months of tramping around Serenity Valley without hearing that lovely voice.

PART II: SERENITY VALLEY

Chapter Eleven
Settlement Six

Year 326

ALTHOUGH I HAD BEEN IMAGINING what Serenity Valley would be like—the size of the land, how tall the trees were, what the leaves smelled like—since I was a child, my daydreams were a mere shadow compared to the reality of being under the great forest's canopy. Serenity Valley's trees were so thick that it took six of us joining hands to surround some of the mightiest trunks, and they stood far too tall for us to measure. In fact, most of the time, we could not see the tops of the trees from the forest floor, because a thick layer of branches and vines intertwined about three-fourths of the way up to form a canopy that suspended in the air between the tree trunks. Although the canopy blocked out much of the sunlight even during the day, the shade was a relief after our long weeks of traveling through the desert.

Even if I hadn't been enamored with the forest before we left Warrior Peak, our days in the Gravel Lands were more than sufficient to make me grateful for every moment we breathed in the forest's cool air. Because the Morroks controlled the Gravel Lands directly south of Warrior Peak, we had been forced to travel west through the desert, hugging the mountain range and unable to find any relief from the desert's heat and lack of any life other than our group. In addition to carrying our own weapons, tents, and clothing, we had been weighted down with enough food and water to last us for our forty-five-day trek through the desert. Now the forest's plentiful resources lightened our load as well as our sense of relief and security.

We did not come across a single Morrok in the Gravel Lands, but we had feared an attack every day of our journey so that deep sleep was hard to come by, even after a long day of marching under the beating sun. Even though the dark, thick trees lent themselves to the possibility of a surprise Morrok ambush much more than the flat, open desert, Fallon was confident that there were no Morroks in the forest because none of the settlements had ever reported a Morrok attack or sighting in more than thirty years of his working in the Intelligence division.

Although the canopy provided us with sufficient shelter from the weather, we continued to use our six canvas tents to sleep at night even after we entered the forest. I shared a tent with Todd, the sergeant who had been the lone survivor of a Morrok attack on his convoy through Serenity Valley. The first time I had met Todd, he had been disheveled and terrified, having not eaten or slept since escaping the Morroks with only his life and his story. Over the last several weeks, I had found that he didn't have much more confidence when he was around his military superiors, however well-fed and well-rested he might be now. He simpered and second-guessed himself constantly in front of Fallon and the other men, and although this quality made him easy to live with, as he was always willing to give up more space in the tent and carry our shared supplies, I often felt guilty about taking advantage of him.

One morning, after we had been in the forest for about a week, I woke early to find Fallon and Cyrus sitting on the forest floor poring over a map that Todd had sketched. Todd was on his feet hovering near them, pointing out what he thought to be inaccuracies.

"There may or may not have been a river there," he said. "We probably would've seen it by now, though I'm not entirely sure if we've gone as far as we should've before crossing the Gravel Lands to get to the forest. No matter, though, no matter; this scale may be completely off anyway. The first few weeks of my first trip were just such a blur, I can't always remember—"

"Thank you, Todd," Fallon said without looking up.

"Where are we?" I asked, joining Todd behind the other men.

Fallon, seeing that I was the one who had asked, considered for a moment and then pointed to a spot barely an inch south of the beginning of the forest and about halfway between Warrior Peak and the western end of the mountain range. "Here," he said. "We may be close to the first settlement. It's supposed to be about a month and a half west of Warrior Peak and a week south of the entrance of the forest, if you're traveling at our pace."

I laughed. "Who wouldn't travel at our pace? Who wants leisure time?"

"You know, Orestes," Todd said seriously, apparently having missed my sarcasm, "when my group came this way, it took us a full two days more to get to this point, and that was a group of trained men who—"

"Careful, Todd—now you're among untrained women who won't take kindly to such a comparison," I said, beckoning at Levina and Joanne as they emerged from their tent.

Cyrus too gazed at Joanne as she shook out her tangled hair. Glynis always said that Joanne was "aging gracefully" with her slender figure and her still mostly chestnut-colored hair. Fallon teased Cyrus constantly about needing to take the initiative to rescue both himself and Joanne from widowhood.

When Cyrus saw me watching him, he cleared his throat. "Orestes, why don't you and Todd check the time for us?"

I saw a grin spread across Fallon's face; he alone could tolerate Todd for more than a few minutes at a time, and no matter how much Cyrus might have liked Joanne, he couldn't contain his impatience with Todd to appear gentle and kind in front of her.

I seized Todd's upper arm and directed him away from the older men.

"I'll come too," Ritter said as he ducked out of his own tent. Ritter and I had become practiced at using the many branches and vines to climb the colossal trees. With each passing day as we journeyed more deeply into the forest, the canopy became thicker and more tangled so that less and less light made it to the forest floor, and we were forced to climb up the trees a few times a day to check the position of the sun.

"I wonder if I could walk from this tree to that one," Ritter said once we had reached the canopy. The sun was much brighter here, but several feet of thin branches still swayed above our heads. We each stood on the base of a different branch in the canopy and held onto the same tree's trunk. Ritter sidled along his branch, testing his weight with each step. I held my breath as he let go of the tree, but the branches didn't buckle. He moved cautiously along the branches to another tree trunk five yards away as if he were walking on solid ground.

"We should travel like this," he called.

"Just because you didn't break your neck walking fifteen feet doesn't mean we can traipse the whole canopy loaded down with tents and supplies," I said before Todd could give us the particulars of his professional opinion. "Come on, let's do what we came here to do."

We climbed with a little more caution onto the higher, thinner branches until we broke the surface of the trees. It was barely midmorning. We could still make out the mountains in the distant north, but in every other direction lay trees as far as the eye could see.

"Hey, do you think that's a clearing?" Ritter asked, waving at an area southwest of us.

I squinted across the surface of leaves and noticed a gap in the green.

"I bet it's Settlement Six!" Todd said. "There usually aren't big areas without trees unless there are Humans. We must tell the colonel!"

Ritter and I exchanged one amused glance before following Todd back to the forest floor. The others had collapsed most of the tents by the time we dropped to the ground.

"Colonel, Ritter spotted what very well could be Settlement Six," Todd said to Fallon. "And as it's not quite midmorning, I daresay we should be able to reach it before nightfall."

"Very good, Sergeant. You and Orestes pack your tent, and then we'll move out."

Todd and I were ready within minutes; it had taken weeks of practice, but everyone had fallen into a rhythm of setting up and breaking down camp. The first few mornings of the trip, we had run into each other, done the same jobs twice, and rechecked every detail so many times that it had taken more than an hour to get ready to travel. Now we could wake up and start moving within fifteen minutes, which saved us precious time as we searched for the first settlement.

Once I had shouldered my own pack, I found Levina and took her tent as well.

"Is it silly that I love being here?" Levina asked once we had set off.

I laughed. "No. I'd be worried if you missed the Gravel Lands."

"No, no, I love being here as opposed to Warrior Peak. Everyone keeps saying how much they miss it already, but I love Serenity Valley—all the trees, how quiet it is, living off the land, the adventure—everything."

"I like it here too. Just feels right somehow. I know the country's huge, but I'm actually disappointed that we aren't going to see parts of the land. There aren't any settlements in the southwest, and some of the reports from Settlement Eleven say that the trees just stop a few days west of them. That would be interesting to see."

"The trees just stop?" she repeated.

"You can supposedly see where the mountain range ends too."

"Imagine that," she whispered in an awed voice. "All I've ever known is the mountains. I never even thought about them having an end. When I was little, I thought Warrior Peak was all there was to the world, you know?"

She said the last words rhetorically, but I was suddenly very uncomfortable with the conversation. The mountains didn't hold the same mystique for me, because I had grown up not knowing they existed—not knowing anything beyond a desert and a black tower.

It was this thought and others like it that kept me from getting closer to Levina, even after the night we kissed at Warrior Peak. I had seen the consequences of deeper relationships; because of Fallon's close friendship with Cyrus, it had been impossible to conceal my past from him and Ritter, and although they, at least, were careful never to mention it, I couldn't bear to risk Levina looking at me the way she had when she saw me kill the Morrok at the end-of-year tournament.

I knew she had been confused and even angry when I avoided her during the first days of our journey to the forest. Luckily Fallon hadn't allowed anyone to break off from the group the whole time we were in the desert, so she had given up on trying to talk to me in private about that night. So now, as always happened when our conversations took a dangerous turn, I changed the subject to more lighthearted matters, though the knot in my stomach only ached more each time I pushed her away.

*

"Where the hell is Ritter?" Fallon demanded several hours later. Everyone was irritable. Fallon had insisted that we stop every hour to climb the trees and check that we were going the right direction. No one found this to be necessary except him.

"I swear he's obsessed with walking on the canopy now. You should never have sent him up there all those times," I said. I threw off my packs and strode to the nearest tree, which Ritter had disappeared into more than ten minutes before. "I'll get him. He'd better not be hurt."

It was nearly nightfall. Dusk's light hardly reached us on the forest floor, but I could see clearly once I reached the canopy. I circled the tree I had climbed but saw no sign of Ritter.

"Ritter?" I called. "Ritter, come on, we're waiting. Ritter!"

There was some shuffling several feet away, and Ritter emerged from behind a distant tree. He picked his way back to me with surprising speed.

"Sorry, is it time to go?" he asked. His face was flushed.

I scoffed. "What do you think, idiot? How close are we to the village?"

"Oh, very close. Just another half hour's walk. I didn't realize we were in such a hurry."

I shook my head, hoping that he was joking. We had hardly stopped for a meal and had traveled half the day at a jog. Maybe he was just delirious from exhaustion. That would have been better than him believing that Fallon was a patient man.

We traveled the last half hour in silence, but it was hard to keep up any resentful feelings when we finally saw the village's clearing from the forest floor. The village itself was actually an enclosed square-shaped fort. High, thick wooden walls blocked any view of the houses and people we knew filled the space between them. The only signs of life were patches of crops spread haphazardly in the areas between the walls and the man-made tree line.

Although the light was dim, I couldn't miss the rise in emotion in my elder companions' faces as they beheld the village. Almost all of them had worked their whole adult lives to ensure that these settlements were successful and cared for, and before a couple months ago, they probably never thought that they would see the settlements in person. Levina also looked as if she wanted to run the distance to the clearing; her parents lived in one of the eastern settlements, but I guessed she probably wondered how they lived in the forest, although she would never admit this aloud.

"If they're ever attacked, they'll shut themselves in and starve," Jacob commented as we walked through the disorderly farmlands in search of the fort's gate.

"They have storehouses. I don't know how they farm in the first place, though," Fallon replied, waving a dismissive hand over the land. "You'd think they would want some organization. Ah, here we are." We stopped in front of two large doors that almost blended in with the walls. Fallon unsheathed his sword and pounded the door with the butt of it.

"Identify yourselves," a voice called from the other side.

"Colonel Fallon and eleven others, all of Warrior Peak."

A pair of eyes peered from over the top of the wall. "Colonel Fallon? But we haven't had word. . . . It's been more than two years. What's been going on? We've had no letters, no groups making their rounds. . . . We thought you'd abandoned us."

"My friend, I will be happy to tell all once you have let me and my companions into your home and allow us a night's rest."

"Of course, sir. I'll be back in a moment. It takes more than one man to lift the bar."

The guard must have run, for after just a few moments, the door rattled and then opened with a groan.

Even from my view at the threshold under a dark sky, I could see neat rows of uniform two-story houses and well-defined streets running from the place where we stood all the way to the opposite wall. A growing number of people were wandering outside their homes so that they blocked us from coming more than a few steps inside. They were not so different from average

Warrior Peak citizens, but they seemed more rugged somehow—hardened from their exploration and labors in a wild country, perhaps. Most of their clothes were made of rough, frayed cloth and varied in color from tan to brown. The younger ones stared with shameless fascination at our military clothes and equipment, which were all branded with Warrior Peak's symbol.

A man in his early forties cleared his way through the crowd and gazed at each of the older men in our party. There was silence as he considered each. Finally he reached out a hand to Fallon, who shook it heartily.

"How do you remember me, William? You were only a boy when we met," Fallon said, smiling.

"My father spoke highly of you," the man, William, replied. "You were still in school when our colony left, but he insisted you would be our leader one day. He was right."

"I was very sad to hear of his death, but you have taken on his leadership of this village wonderfully, my friend. Now, let me introduce some people you've known only on paper all these years." Fallon rattled off all our names, and William reacted with varying degrees of recognition but with equal delight at all. The crowd around us had stopped growing, and so I assumed the whole village now stood in a semicircle around us and their open gate. There were about three hundred in all. With each introduction Fallon gave, their murmurs increased until I could barely concentrate on what Fallon and William were saying.

"I'm afraid I don't come with good news," Fallon said.

William nodded. "I guessed as much. Let's not discuss it now, though. You must be tired."

"Yes, I was hoping we could set down our gear, and then you and I could speak in private tonight before we introduce ourselves to the entire village."

"Of course," William said. He squinted out among the crowd. "Let's see—Robert, I know you have an extra room. Why don't you invite Colonel Fallon and Glynis?" One by one, William assigned us to an empty room in different houses around the village. Levina left with an old couple who spoke as if boarding one of Fallon's subordinates was the honor of their lives. My host was a young man who barely gave me a word of greeting before setting off. I followed him past several streets to the row of houses farthest away from the gate.

"These are the newest buildings," he said as we turned the corner and the noise of the crowd around the gate died completely. "My wife and I were living with her parents for a while with our first child. The houses have only four tiny rooms upstairs. Luckily young couples were allowed first opportunity to move in these new ones. I don't know what Victoria and I would've done if we'd still been living in one room when the second one came. We're right here."

He stopped at one of the few houses that had candlelight flickering in the first-floor windows.

"I didn't catch your name back there," I said as I followed him inside. The large front room was furnished with only two chairs, a table, and some children's toys.

"Richard. And this," he added as a woman with a child on each hip appeared from the back room, "is my wife, Victoria, my son, Connor, and my daughter, Lila. Darling, this is Orestes. He's from Warrior Peak."

I wasn't sure if Victoria was more shocked or confused by my presence. She set down the boy, Connor, who wobbled on his pudgy legs, and then shook my hand mutely. Now that we were in the light, I noticed that both Richard and Victoria looked to be only a couple years older than Levina and I were.

"Warrior Peak? But I thought—I don't understand why . . ."

"Apparently we haven't been abandoned after all," Richard said with a sardonic grin. "They've brought quite a different group this time as well. Everyone ranging from Colonel Fallon to a teenage girl."

A wave of defensiveness for Levina swept over me, but I decided to let it pass.

"And now we're going to host Orestes for however long they're here," he finished.

Victoria blinked several times in quick succession, as if to clear her confusion. "Welcome to our home, Orestes. I'll show you your room, and then we can sit down for the evening meal. Everyone's been taking their meals in their homes rather than the mess hall. We can't afford to waste anything this year."

She handed the second baby to her husband and motioned for me to follow her. She led me to the back of the house into a kitchen area, where there was a narrow staircase off to the side. It was difficult to fit myself and my packs up the steep, suffocating incline, and the upstairs was hardly more inviting. A similarly narrow hallway had four doors leading off of it, two on each side. My room had only a low bed and several boxes, and the ceiling was slanted so that I couldn't stand up straight except near the wall facing the hallway. I threw down my belongings and hurried back to the lighter, larger rooms downstairs.

"We usually use that room as a storage space, so sorry for the mess," Victoria explained as she ushered me into a chair around a badly carved table in the kitchen. She seemed to be in her element now that she understood why she had a houseguest. "I never imagined we'd host an officer from Warrior Peak. It must've been—I think we were nineteen when they came last, weren't we, Richard?"

Richard entered the room and stuffed his children into chairs that had trays attached on the arms to keep them upright.

"Lila hadn't been born yet, so I would say we were around nineteen, yes," he said.

"I'm not an officer, though," I said as Victoria rummaged among the baskets and cabinets in search of food. "I left school to come on this journey, so technically I'm a civilian unless I'm allowed to complete my training whenever we return."

"You can't be too far away from graduating, though," Victoria said, stopping to scrutinize me. "I thought the military students are finished at nineteen?"

"Generally."

"And how old are you?"

I thought for a moment. I didn't know my real birthday, of course, but Fallon and Glynis had guessed that I was born in the year 308, so I usually changed my age with the new year. "Eighteen."

"Well, hopefully they'll let you finish up when you return," Richard said. "Except for the oldest folks, we're all civilians here, but my father tells me that that's not a favorable role at the Peak."

"Not at all," I replied.

We talked through the meager meal and long afterward, though we were periodically interrupted by the demands of the two small children. It surprised me how little the couple knew about Warrior Peak, and they ate up every scrap of information I mentioned. To them, the Peak was as much of a reality as Serenity Valley had been for me; each of our parents described the other place to us at length, but as much as we were connected to it, we still felt like aliens in a foreign land.

Their lives seemed much slower paced than what mine had always been, but they were still hard workers. They didn't have formal schooling but instead worked alongside their families to keep their village functioning. Everyone was essential to everyone else's survival, and as much as such dependence intrigued me, I concluded that I would have been bored with such a narrow realm of existence. I couldn't have met everyone in Warrior Peak even if I wanted to, but Richard and Victoria knew everyone around them in intimate detail. Victoria laughed as she said that marrying Richard was no great leap of faith because they were two of less than a dozen children who shared the same birth year and so had always known each other very well.

"It's getting late," Victoria said when there was a break in the conversation. The babies had fallen asleep where they sat. "I'm sure we'll all need to be up early tomorrow to hear from Colonel Fallon. Did you get enough to eat, Orestes? I'm sorry we don't have more to offer."

"I'm as full as can be, thank you," I lied. "May I ask why crops are so bad this year? Do you ever get much rain? Farming in the mountains can be awful, but I would imagine you'd have better luck around so many streams and so much good soil."

Victoria and Richard glanced at each other. The former brought the smaller baby to her lap like a child reaching for a comforting toy. It was Richard who answered.

"Last winter, two small children, both of the same household, were lost. They were just outside the walls with their families—nothing unusual—but later, when their parents noticed that they were missing, they were nowhere to be found. It's been speculated that they wandered away and got lost, which, believe me, is more than plausible, given the size of the wilderness, but they were toddlers, so I'm not sure how they could've made it so far in so little time." He cleared his throat and took the other child in his arms. "We combed the area for weeks, but the only trace we found of the children was a few scraps of clothing in the farms right outside. We tore the fields apart looking for more signs of them, for a trail, anything, but it came to nothing, and now we're running low on food because of all the ruined land."

As I lay in my uncomfortable bed that night, my stomach groaning with hunger, I wished being low on food was all we had to worry about. As strange as the forest had been for me, it had never struck me as frightening. It seemed like years since I had spoken to the General before my last school tournament, but through the memories of the long Laconic Warrior narrative, his words suddenly gave the silence of the forest an ominous twist. *No, the Morroks steal their enemies' children. They build up their military by taking away from ours. So essentially, Morroks are you and I without love and compassion. The serum takes care of those.*

Our worst fear had been to find the villages destroyed, but the Morroks were just beginning their attack. Hopefully Settlement Six was only the first.

Chapter Twelve

A Voice in the Forest

EARLY THE NEXT MORNING, the forest Warriors rose at almost the same time, just like at Warrior Peak. I woke to the sound of people chattering in the streets below, and once I had dressed, I followed the crowd toward the back of the village, away from the front gates. Past the rows of houses was an open square with a few large wooden buildings surrounding a water well in the center. Patches of dead grass dotted the open space, looking as if there used to be mostly green space with dirt paths that people had ignored to the point of killing the grass.

William, the settlement leader, was herding everyone into the largest building, which turned out to be the mess hall. As people crammed inside and filled the benches and tables, dust started to kick up, and I remembered Victoria's comment the night before about everyone eating in their own homes rather than here. Fallon, Levina, and the others were sitting on a small raised platform at the back of the hall, all of them looking clean and refreshed. I sat next to Levina just as Fallon left the platform to settle an argument about whether or not the children ought to be allowed to stay for the meeting.

"You shaved," Levina observed.

"I'm a new man," I replied. I took her wrists and brought her hands to my jaw. "Why, don't you like it?"

"Stop that," she said, ripping her hands away. "We're these people's only link to the outside world—a very dangerous outside world. Do you want to make us look like just a couple of silly teenagers the first day we're here?"

"I wouldn't dream of it."

"Besides, I thought you were traditional. You shouldn't have let your beard grow out that far in the first place, not without being married."

I grinned, surprised she would say that. I was one of the few men older than eighteen who adhered to the old custom of unmarried men remaining clean-shaven and short-haired. Most men pretended that the tradition didn't exist because they wanted to look older or didn't want to stand out among their peers; I had just been lazy with only the desert and forest to hold me accountable. I was about to tell Levina this when the argument nearby grew to shouts.

"The children will stay!" William bellowed over the rest. "They will sit in the back where they can ignore us if they like, but they will stay in this room! This concerns us all."

The chattering subsided at his last statement, and everyone settled into place. The building was so packed that I couldn't see the floor beyond our platform, and the room was stiflingly hot despite the early time of day and all the windows being open.

"Very good," William said. "I have little to say except that I agree wholeheartedly with everything Colonel Fallon is about to tell you. I'm relinquishing all my authority to him until he decides we are safe enough for his group to leave. Colonel, they are yours to command."

He left the platform and took a seat among his people.

No one reacted beyond a few frowns when Fallon first said "Morrok," but as he described them, the older people began to whisper among themselves. Fallon dwelled just long enough for the people to understand the gravity of the situation and then changed tactics by describing the training programs and increased defenses we were hoping to establish in their settlement. Most people nodded as he spoke, whether out of fear of the Morroks or awe of Fallon I couldn't tell, but there were a few scattered throughout the crowd who sat with their arms crossed, resistant to any change, however good for them.

"If it's as dangerous as you say," a woman in the front row said when Fallon opened the floor for questions, "if the Morroks could come to the forest and are as powerful as you describe, why not leave? We are vulnerable enough to the elements as it is. We live a hard life, Colonel; I don't know if we could survive outside threats."

"But this is our home," a younger man near her said. "We can't abandon it. I've worked hard here all my life, and my father worked hard here all his life. We can't just give up because of some stupid Morroks."

"Watch your tongue, boy," an older man barked. "Didn't you hear what the colonel said? This is serious. You can't just ignore the Morroks."

"Yes, but the colonel also said we might be valuable for Intelligence by staying in the forest," yet another said.

"All your observations are valid," Fallon said as more people began to speak at once. "And it is your decision to make—whether to stay or leave. I cannot stop you; I know that no command or authority will override the need to protect your families. I believe the time will come when the forest Warriors will have to unite and attack from the south while our brothers attack from the Peak. That time is not now, but while you wait for me and my family to warn all the settlements, you will need the defenses I hope to build up for you. According to the last Intelligence reports before we left, the Morroks have taken control of nearly half the desert. Warrior Peak has done little to prevent this, and because of it, we had to travel a wide berth to bypass their patrols. Their ultimate strategy is unclear, but I believe that we must, at any cost, keep them out of Serenity Valley. The Morroks will not be able to match us on two fronts, and so I plead for the continued presence of Humans south of the Gravel Lands."

I bit my lip against the skepticism that sprang to mind. We had no idea of the Morroks' numbers, but I doubted that the mere few thousand Humans in Serenity Valley would be able to stand for very long, even if we could ever successfully unite them, which, given the size of the land, seemed more and more unlikely by the day. And, I realized with an unpleasant jolt, the Morroks were already in Serenity Valley. Richard's story from the night before had proven that. I wasn't looking forward to telling Fallon.

"I will not ask you to make such a decision now," Fallon continued. "Now I ask only for your cooperation. William and I have discussed this and have agreed that from today until we leave, the entire village, down to the last child, will be divided into three groups that will rotate duties each day. One group will farm and do all that is necessary to keep the village running; the second will help with reinforcing the walls; and the third will train with weapons and receive additional teachings on the Morroks, healing, and strategy. I will not trouble you with any more details at this moment. For now, we will attempt to make these groups. To be accomplished this, I ask that you reassemble outside the walls and stay close to your families, particularly those of you who have small children. Let us proceed."

The once boisterous group was now morose as they filed one by one out the single door of the mess hall. I caught Fallon's arm when he began to follow.

"How important is it for you to be the one to divide these people?" I asked.

"Why?" he asked as he kneeled next to my seat so that only he and Levina could hear me.

"I heard something very disturbing last night." Conscious of wandering ears, I recounted Richard's tale in as little detail as I could manage. "I'm sure it was Morroks," I concluded.

"How can you be sure of that?" Fallon asked. His tone was more skeptical than dismissive. "All I understand from that story is that two toddlers wandered into the forest and never returned. You said they disappeared in the daytime. How could the Morroks hide?"

"It's more than possible," I said. "They snuck into Warrior Peak, didn't they? All it took was for a single Morrok to wait in the shadows for a child to stray into the forest alone. These people know the trees around them; the children couldn't have wandered beyond their reach in so short a time. The Morroks wouldn't begin a war with us if they didn't have the manpower. There have been no missing children from Warrior Peak, so where are their numbers coming from? Ask William if any other babies have disappeared or 'died' in recent memory."

Fallon's stare was inscrutable. Eventually he stood and said we would discuss the matter later. It was only when he left that I turned to Levina. We were the only ones left on the platform.

"What did you mean by 'where are their numbers coming from?'" she asked. "I know that baby disappearances historically come along with the rise of Morroks, but surely you don't mean that—that the children . . ." She seemed unable to finish the thought, and I wasn't willing to do it for her.

"I don't think we're in danger of an attack, not for a long time," I said. "But either way, we need to make sure this village is as ready as it can be. Let's go outside and see how the groups are doing."

*

"Better," I said, drawing my sword away from my opponent's. "But you don't want to give too much slack. Absorb the blow, but don't let the blades come to your chest."

"Whatever happened to throwing off the other person's sword?" the boy across from me asked. He was only a few years younger than I was and had shown more promise than many I had dueled so far. "When you get in a tangle like that—my friends and I make a competition of who can push the other back."

"And that's fine if you're fighting another Human," I replied. "Like we told you at first, these aren't conventional dueling techniques. You have good instincts, but you have to relearn what to do in instances like that. A Morrok's size is balanced by a Human's agility, but there is no match for its strength. You shouldn't even get yourself in a situation where your blades are locked, but if you do, maneuver out as soon as possible."

"I'll keep that in mind," he said. He shook my hand before I walked away.

The training group had been pushed around to several different locations over the past weeks. When we tried to practice inside the settlement, we interrupted the wall construction as old, rotting sections were torn down and reinforced; and when we practiced outside, we distressed the newly reorganized and replanted farmland. Regardless of where we managed to practice, however, I spent my days moving among the pairs of duels, critiquing and demonstrating as necessary. It was almost like being back at the military school training grounds again.

Most of us who had come from Warrior Peak were involved in hand-to-hand combat training, which was exciting for me; since we had left Warrior Peak, I hadn't had a chance to do much more than stare admiringly at my new sword, which I had finished mere hours before we left for the desert. When the people weren't training, Levina gave lessons about Morroks and their history, and Holt's wife, Abby, taught a select few about battlefield healing.

Holt and Joanna oversaw the wall construction. The rest of us tirelessly wove among the foresters, trying to make up for years of informal training in swordplay.

"That will do for today!" Fallon yelled over the clanging metal. "We don't have much daylight left, and we'll want to beat the farmers to dinner, so let's pack up quickly!"

A few scattered laughs accompanied everyone packing up their weapons. Many of them didn't have scabbards, so they simply wrapped their dull blades in cloth. We hadn't bothered having the village blacksmiths sharpen all the blades, because everyone would be using their weapons so much in practice; that project we saved for the last days of our visit, which, judging by the progression in the wall and the people's education, were rapidly approaching.

The mess hall had been transformed into a classroom by day and a dining hall by night. Despite the scarcity of food, Fallon decided that all meals should be cooked for the village in mass quantity because people were so busy during the day now. The building was as full that night as it had been the day we arrived; no family was willing to dare the journey to the Peak, at the very least for fear of a Morrok-controlled desert standing in their way.

Once I had filled my plate, I sat wherever there was room and ate quickly to allow space for the next wave of people. I spoke to those around me only long enough to learn the names of those I hadn't already met. There were few people I hadn't talked to yet, and I never grew tired of seeing how surprised a person was when I remembered his or her name a few days after meeting them.

Just as I was finishing, a hand rested on my shoulder and a voice whispered in my ear, "We already have an audience."

I bade farewell to my dining companions and followed Levina outside into the evening. Most of the children of the village had gathered by the well outside the dining hall. Levina and I had begun a ritual of telling stories in the evening to give the parents a break from their children and to give the children a break from the frightening issues of each day. Levina recited old fables of the Peak and told stories she had created on her own, and I repeated Aldis's tales of

Tyrclopia and, if we had time, the story of James, Caden, and the Laconic Warriors.

"Whose turn is it tonight?" Levina asked the children.

"Orestes!" several of them chanted.

Conscious of their unwavering attention, I stood and paced back and forth, scratching my chin. "Do you remember Acules?" I asked, knowing very well that they did.

"Yes!" came the chorus of high-pitched voices.

"Well, when he was thirteen—about Adam's age"—several heads whipped around to look at Adam, who tried to look indifferent to the attention—"the Morroks captured two of his friends, who were still babies at the time, and Acules decided to go after them, right into the Morrok Facility. . . ."

I proceeded to tell them a long narrative loosely based on my rescue from the Facility, except that I edited myself out and added several embellishments. In the end, Acules had killed a countless number of Morroks singlehandedly, done considerable damage to the Facility tower itself, and rescued dozens of children. Most of the children eagerly absorbed every detail, but Levina was frowning whenever I looked back at her during my tale.

"I thought you'd told me all of Aldis's stories," she said as the children wandered back toward their homes, chattering about the narrative.

"I made that one up," I replied, secure in my honesty.

"Since when are you so creative? All those details about the Facility and the desert were amazing."

No longer confident, I shrugged.

"Either way," she continued, "I don't know if you should plant ideas like that in their heads. Honestly, a thirteen-year-old killing a bunch of Morroks all on his own? What if Adam thinks he can pick up his father's sword and do the same thing?"

"Acules is different," I said. "They understand that. It's just a story. Stories let them escape reality for a little while and give them a little hope, even if their parents don't have it every moment of the day."

By then the dining hall was quiet, and people were dispersing to their respective homes. Levina squinted through the darkness toward the street of her temporary home and sighed. "My hosts go to sleep at about sunset, and I always wake them up when I'm out late. I'll see you tomorrow."

"All right, good night."

She stood there for a moment as if she was expecting me to say something else. Just as I wondered if I should try to kiss her goodnight, she seemed to give up and walked away. A kiss probably wasn't what she wanted anyway. Traveling and now training and building had kept us busy and exhausted the past few months, and by now she was probably tired of waiting. I wasn't sure I could blame her.

After watching Levina disappear down her street, I drifted toward Richard and Victoria's house, but once I arrived, I continued past it. The village gate hadn't been closed for the night. Making sure no one was around to discourage me, I slipped outside the town and into the forest.

I had done this as often as I could since the day we arrived. A small part of me missed the trees, but most of all, I wanted to find some trace of the Morroks that had stolen the two toddlers Richard had spoken of. They were all I could think about. I couldn't fall asleep at night without knowing I had tried to find out what happened, even though months had passed. I knew that the children were lost forever, but I had to know for sure that I had done everything I could.

Although we had passed safely into spring, the air was thin and cold under the cover of the trees. I proceeded slowly, searching the ground for any abnormally large footprints. This became more and more fruitless the further away from the village I strayed. In addition to keeping in the cold, the intertwined branches kept out whatever light the moon might have offered. Just as I decided to turn back, I heard mulch and leaves crunching under another set of footsteps.

It wasn't heavy enough to be a Morrok, but it was unnerving to have the silence of the woods broken. I slowed to make as little sound as possible and followed my ears toward the other footsteps. Whoever it was was speeding up. Had he or she heard me? I quickened my pace as well. I could no longer see my hands in front of my face. All sense of direction gone, I burst into a sprint. My own feet crashing through the foliage mixed with the other's stride until I couldn't distinguish where the noise was coming from.

The crunching abruptly cut in half. I skidded to a halt and strained my ears for the other person. Not another foot fell, but the branches above me swayed and showered leaves onto me. The canopy opened, and I was bathed in moonlight for less than a second. Before my eyes could adjust to the light, the figure had disappeared above the forest floor.

I stumbled backward into the nearest tree and clutched the stitch in my side. How long had I been running? How far away from the village was I? Which way was the village? I didn't dare try to climb a tree to try to see the position of the moon. I could find my way up a tree in the daytime, but doing it blindly was a sure way to end up with a broken arm. Besides, I had no idea who was up there now.

The air seemed much thinner than it had been when I entered the forest. I slid to the ground and tried to catch my breath. There was no sense in moving until the sun had risen so I could find my way back. But it was so cold. Colder than it should have been.

I struggled to my feet again and began to pace and rub my hands together. My breath was unusually warm against my skin, and each intake left a little more chill clinging to my lungs.

"Orestes," said a clear voice from somewhere to my right.

I started and backed into the tree again, wary of leaving my back exposed. "Who's there?" I asked.

"No one you know, not truly," the other replied. It was unmistakably the voice of a man, but it lacked any distinct quality to it, being neither high nor low, neither gruff nor robust. It was almost as if the voice were a whisper carried by the wind.

"Are you the one I was chasing a moment ago?"

"No. That man is a fool and should be of no interest to you."

"If you say so," I said, just to fill the silence. I quieted my breathing as much as I could and strained to hear the slightest shift the other might make. He was only a few feet away, but until I discovered whether he was friend or foe, I wanted him no nearer. "Are you alone?" I asked.

"But for you, yes."

"What do you want with me? Are you from the village?"

"No."

"Then how do you know me? Should I know you?"

"I wished to see you fully grown. I've heard reports, yes, but I wanted to confirm their veracity."

"Fully grown?" I repeated. How could he see me in this darkness? "Then I knew you when I was a child?"

"I told you that you do not know me," the voice said. It was now somewhere to my left, but I hadn't heard a single leaf shift.

"If you knew me but I didn't know you, then I must have been too young to remember you," I reasoned aloud. It was harder than ever to draw a full breath. My heart was pounding, whether from fear or lack of air I did not know. I had to keep the voice talking so I could keep track of where it was. "The only ones who knew me at that age were Morroks."

"Well spoken."

"Then you are a Morrok?" I asked.

"Yes . . . and no."

"I must know."

"Why?"

It was back at my right. It must have been pacing around me.

"Because if the answer's yes, then I must kill you."

The voice laughed. It reminded me eerily of Dirth. Dirth. How long had it been since I thought of him? But Dirth made noises when he walked. I would never forget the sound of him striding down the corridor to my cell, his many weapons clanging against each other as he walked. That sound was the nightmare of my childhood.

"Why must you kill me if I am indeed a Morrok?"

Because Dirth had told me to. "Because the Morroks are my enemy," I said aloud, pushing my first thought aside.

"But you said you lived among them."

"That gives me all the more reason to hate them."

"So much for loyalty."

"Only fear, not loyalty, motivates Morroks, and I no longer fear them," I said.

"Then why does your voice shake?"

"You must not be a Morrok."

"Suddenly confident, are you? Will you kill me now that I am not a Morrok?"

I lost count of how many times he had circled me. I had no idea what I was saying. The sword and dagger hanging at my sides seemed so far out of reached. "I'm beginning to think that I couldn't kill you either way."

"Why is that?"

"I cannot see you."

"That is the lesson I leave with you tonight. The unseen will prevail over the tangible. Remember that. Farewell, Orestes."

The heavy gait of a Morrok marched away, deeper into the forest. The air warmed slightly. The moment I could move my limbs, I pushed away from the tree and bolted.

*

I somehow found my way back to the village, but I didn't go back to Richard and Victoria's. I probably couldn't have slept if I had wanted to, so I contented myself in sitting on the ramparts to watch for whomever I had attempted to follow at first to return to the village. Just as the sky began to lighten, a figure emerged from the trees and sprinted toward one of the construction sites. He slipped easily through the half-built wall and disappeared down one of the streets. If the figure had been a stranger, I never would have been able to recognize it from my angle in such dim light. But I had grown up running alongside that lanky figure. It was Ritter.

Chapter Thirteen

The End of Our World

WE LEFT WILLIAM'S VILLAGE a few days later. The walls were all reinforced, the villagers were educated, and the adults had at least observed the proper techniques for how to fight a Morrok. The entire town saw us to the tree line; everyone was smiling. We were their saviors. As far as they were concerned, they would be ready if the Morroks attacked. I wished I were as confident as they were. I still doubted that the Morroks would attack because we had yet to find evidence of them in the area, but I feared for the village children. It was the kidnappers' job to work without leaving a trace.

"Why so solemn?" Glynis asked a few hours after the village clearing had disappeared from our sight.

"Solemn?" I said. "Do I look solemn?"

"You look solemn anytime you're left to your own thoughts. Are you so old already?"

I grinned. "Not old myself. Just a young man with an old man's thoughts and worries."

"You don't think what we did at the village will make any difference?"

"No, I do think it'll make a difference. Truly," I added when she continued to frown. "If the Morroks attack them, they'll be able to fight like real Warriors. If we hadn't come, they would've woken one day to a living nightmare ransacking their village. I wouldn't have left Warrior Peak if I didn't think what we're doing was going to make a difference."

"Now you sound like Levina."

I laughed. "She's infectious that way. Or maybe just irritating."

Glynis opened her mouth to reply, but Ritter's voice carried over the whole group. "I think I'll just hop up in the canopy and see how we're doing on time."

Something akin to anger seized my insides. I halted and rounded to see Ritter discarding his packs and sizing up the nearest tree as if about to climb it. I had watched him sneak out of the village every night since I first discovered him, and I also had spotted him slipping off during the day when he was supposed to be training. Although I knew it was only because I had seen them both on the same night, I couldn't separate Ritter's ventures into the canopy from whoever or whatever I had met in the forest that night. What if Ritter was communicating with that person? He seemed to know Ritter because he had called him a fool. "Fool" wasn't an accurate description of Ritter, but the voice seemed to have an informed opinion about him.

"Why do you need to check the time?" I asked as calmly as I could. Everyone else had stopped, and Fallon's mouth was halfway open, probably to ask the same question. "We've been walking only a few hours."

"Can't hurt, can it?" Ritter replied without looking at me. He slung off his biggest pack but kept his weapons and a small survival pack of food and water. "In fact, I want to try walking above you for a while. You mind carrying this for me for a little while, Orestes?"

Anger boiled over into resentment. Was no one else suspicious of this? "Sure," I said through gritted teeth.

"Why don't we stop for the midday meal first?" Glynis said. "It'll give me a chance to tell Ritter how worried he'll make me if he tries to walk in the middle of the air like that."

Ritter laughed rather harder than necessary and agreed to stay for the midday meal. As we unpacked and sat down, the women cast worried glances between Ritter and me as we glared at each other. Levina whispered to me to ask what was wrong, but I pretended not to hear her.

"Dad, I was wondering," Ritter said as we were finishing up, "are we planning on traveling to the edge of the forest?"

"What, you mean west of Settlement Eleven?" Cyrus asked. He glanced at Fallon. "I don't think so."

"Do you think maybe I could go while we're at Settlement Eleven? The border's only a few days west, right?"

"Yes, Levina and I want to see it too," I said. Ritter looked around at me in annoyance, but he quickly fixed his face into a smile. I remembered only a moment after I said it that Levina and I had actually discussed the edge of the forest, but that was beside the point; I wanted to keep an eye on Ritter.

"That sounds all right to me," Fallon said. "When we arrive at Settlement Eleven, we'll ask them the best way to go, and after we get a routine started, the three of you can make the trip. Agreed?"

"Agreed," Ritter and I said, staring at each other.

Levina scrutinized us both for a moment. "I guess I don't have a choice. Agreed."

*

A little more than three weeks later, the three of us departed from Settlement Eleven after a long argument over whether or not we needed a guide. Although settlements themselves were nearly identical in shape and size, the people of Settlement Eleven were quite different from those of Settlement Six because while Settlement Six had departed from the Peak when Fallon was a boy, Settlement Eleven had left only a year or two before I came to the Peak. Because of this, almost everyone twenty years old and older had had some training at Warrior Peak, and that made our job much easier. They didn't know any more about the Morroks than Settlement Six did, and their walls needed reinforcement as well; but because they had the same basic training as we did, we needed only to teach them how to fight Morroks rather than having to start by teaching them how to hold a sword.

This fact finally silenced Glynis's excuses to keep Ritter, Levina, and me from traveling to the border of Serenity Valley. She worried about trivial difficulties such as animals stealing our food or one of us falling ill; my concern, however, was with Morroks, but because Fallon didn't believe that they were in Serenity Valley, I didn't advertise my fears. I wanted to find out what Ritter was up to. During the week we had stayed at Settlement Eleven, he had continued to sneak out to the trees once or twice a day.

While we traveled to the border of the forest, his disappearances became more frequent. On the second day, he told Levina and me to travel at our own pace and that he would catch up. After that, we saw him only at mealtimes. He even slept in the trees.

"No Ritter?" Levina asked when she emerged from her tent on the fourth morning since our departure from Settlement Eleven.

"No," I said. I already had my tent packed and ready for travel. Levina always slept later than I did, but I had woken particularly early today because I had a feeling we were close to the border. The trees had thinned some, and we were seeing fewer and fewer animals. Even in the midst of my stress about Ritter, I was excited to see the end of the trees.

Levina smirked as she looked at my packed bags. "I guess we're not having breakfast this morning."

"We can if you want, but I think we're close."

"Fine, no breakfast then."

I helped her pack her tent and secure all her belongings. We were traveling light and were making quick progress with only two people to take care of. I had almost forgotten what it was like to be really alone with Levina, and the last few days that we had passed laughing and talking had already become my favorite of all our time in the forest. At night, though, it was almost impossible to fall asleep knowing that she was only a few feet away in the next tent with no one else around.

Since we were more than accustomed by now to traveling with our heavy packs, we were able to set off at a brisk walk. Not too long after, we were racing each other through the trees, stopping every once in a while if we heard something in the canopy above us. Levina was about to call a truce on the race when suddenly, there were no trees surrounding us. We both froze and shielded our eyes against the abrupt flood of sunlight.

Levina dropped her bags and crouched to the ground. "Is this sand?"

I blinked a few times to acclimate myself to the light and gazed out ahead of us. Not two yards behind us was a full forest, but under our feet was a mixture of sand and dirt, and beyond us was a desolate wasteland, not unlike the Gravel Lands to the north. I turned around and studied the tree line. Not one leaf reached beyond a very distinct point.

"This is . . . wrong," Levina said, following my gaze. "When we entered the forest in the north, it changed so slowly from desert to forest, but this . . ."

I squinted toward the north. No mountains. The end of our world.

"I don't like it here. It reminds me of the Gravel Lands," Levina said. She grabbed her bags and retreated within the tree line. I was tempted to do the same. Every desert I had ever known had contained Morroks. Although this one might not, the association was too strong not to unnerve me. I followed Levina back to the trees.

"Here," she said, tossing me a wooden sword. I caught it and dropped my bags. "I don't want you to hold back this time. I don't care if you hit me."

I grinned. "You will if I do."

We had trained often in the last four days, and she always insisted that I come at her with my all. I always lied and told her I was.

"Stop smirking. I'm serious. If I can't handle you, how will I ever handle a Morrok hitting me?"

She jabbed at me a few times, and I swatted her away.

"At this rate, we'll never fight Morroks," I sighed.

"And that makes you sad?"

"Of course not."

I grabbed her sword by its wooden blade and tugged it out of her hand.

"Your hand would be bleeding if this were real!" she said. "Come on, please do this right."

We traded a few more blows, she with more intensity than before. I decided to treat her at least like one of the young men I worked with at the settlements. Her eyes widened the first time I went on the offensive, but then she smiled.

We continued wordlessly for several minutes. Levina was remarkably improved from the last time I had seen her fight; she parried me with increasing ease and came close to landing a few blows. In her excitement, her swings became wilder and fiercer. Her eyes never left my blade, like I had taught her, and I was glad I had so that she wouldn't see me suppressing a laugh as I watched her face screw up more and more tightly in concentration.

After a time, I misjudged one of her swipes, and my wooden blade collided with her left elbow. She groaned but didn't release her sword. I was halfway through my first apology when she leaped toward me again, slashing furiously, and before I could react, she had given me a few bruises in revenge. No longer trying to hide my smile, I doubled my efforts of warding her off for several minutes. Her blows became smaller and more calculated, again like I had taught her. But before long, she had exhausted herself and retreated a few steps away from me. I followed and engaged her again immediately.

By chance, I hit her again on the same elbow. This time she cried out in pain and backed away from me, nursing her arm.

"You're laughing at me again!" she snapped.

I threw my sword aside, crossed the distance between us, and tugged her weapon out of her hands. She glared at me as I grasped her left forearm and helped her stretch out her surely throbbing elbow.

"You did much better," I said as we sat on the forest floor among our packed bags.

"You were laughing," she repeated.

"Only because it's you," I teased. She continued to glare. "Come on, I wouldn't lie about your progress. I want you to improve as much as you do. You did well. Now why don't you say a bunch of words I don't know so I can be the student for a while?"

The rest of the day passed with the same ease but without any sign of Ritter. Levina and I set up camp and then relaxed, glad to be in one place after four long days of travel. By evening, Levina's elbow was bright purple, and I promised her I would never duel with her again unless we used leaves as our swords.

All throughout the day, I found myself staring out into the desert and caught Levina doing the same. The scene knotted a strange mixture of sadness and fear in my stomach; unlike the Gravel Lands, in which every scrap of landscape seemed never to have lived, this desert seemed dead, as if something beautiful had once existed in it and then drifted into obscurity.

"Did I ever tell you which settlement my parents live in?" Levina asked as the sun began to set. We had given up sneaking looks at the desert and were now leaning against the same tree at the very edge of the forest facing the sand.

"Fallon did. Besides, theirs was the last colony to leave, so I figured they had to be at Settlement Twelve."

"Oh."

I glanced at her, wondering if I should push my luck. Levina usually didn't like to talk about her parents, but she had mentioned them first. "It could be another four months or so before we make it to them," I said.

"I know. I keep thinking that I won't see them somehow, though. They left when I was four, and I never thought . . . I grew up thinking I never would see them again. Always hoping, of course. It just . . . doesn't seem like it will happen."

"Don't you want to see them?"

"I don't know. If they're still living there—still alive, for that matter—I think I would like to see them just once. Promise you'll make me if the time comes. I'll probably get nervous and want to stay camped out outside their village."

"I promise," I said, trying to smile for her.

She grinned weakly in return. After a few moments, she asked, "What about you? You've never told me about your parents."

I stiffened and stared even more determinedly into the desert. "Fallon and Glynis are my parents."

"No, they're not, not really. They're almost too old to have a son so young, you don't look a bit like either of them, you call them by their first names, and you didn't come to Warrior Peak until you were seven when they've lived there all their lives."

"I've lived at Warrior Peak since I was five."

"Then why didn't you start school until you were seven?"

"Fallon and Glynis had to teach me about Warrior Peak. I would've been behind everyone else in school as far as writing and history and the like." That was true enough. Maybe I could make it through the conversation without lying.

"Okay, but what about those first five years?" she persisted. "You must remember some things. It's not very often that a foreigner comes to the Peak. I think you, Acules, and Aldis are the only ones in living memory."

I took a deep breath as feelings of resentment began to swell inside me. "I don't want to talk about it."

"Oh, come on. Please?"

"No."

"Why, is it something bad?" she asked, concern coming over her features.

My face flushed. Of course it was something bad, stupid girl.

"Orestes, you can tell me anything," she said.

"I said no," I growled. Why wouldn't she drop it?

"Come on, I talked about my parents. There's nothing you can tell me that'll make me think differently of you. Please tell me."

"Damn it, Levina, I said no!"

I pushed myself to my feet and began to pace. Levina turned to watch me with hurt in her eyes. I ignored her. I didn't understand how a woman whose entire strength wouldn't have been able to shift my smallest finger could get under my skin as much as the Morroks. I didn't like it at all.

I stopped pacing and perked my ears. Someone was running our way from deeper within the woods, and whoever it was made no effort to conceal his sound. I unsheathed my real sword and told Levina to do the same. She dove at her bag and found it within seconds. She was shaking as she scrambled to her feet.

"Orestes!" the runner called.

Levina and I lowered our swords. It was Ritter.

"Orestes," he said again as he came into view. Pale and breathless, he leaned against a tree and clutched his side as if he were about to collapse. "We have to—we have to leave—get out of here now."

"What are you talking about?" I demanded. This was it. Whatever he had been doing in the forest was backfiring on him.

"No time—leave the bags—come on, we have to—"

We all froze. More footfalls marched our way. They were still distant, but they sounded heavy.

"Morroks," Ritter said, "but that's not the problem."

"Of course that's the problem!" I snapped.

"They'll be taken care of, but only if we leave now," Ritter said. He pushed himself off his tree and stepped up to me so that his face was only inches from mine. For the first time in our lives, I was taller. "Listen to me, we have to go. Into the desert, into the canopy, somewhere—anywhere but here."

I pushed Ritter away. "Levina, get ready to fight."

"Damn it, there are eight of them, you idiot!" Ritter shouted, shoving me back. "Do you want to get killed? Do you want Levina to die?"

I was on the verge of really hitting him when the canopy above us began to shift violently. Ritter swore again and was about to say something else, but a great crash from above drowned out all other sound. Instinctively, I covered my head as foliage rained down on us. Sounds of giant bird wings filled the air. I tried to see just how many birds there were, but feathers had joined the mixture of dirt and leaves stirred up in the air, and I was forced to cover my face again.

"Prepare your swords, Humans," a high-pitched voice commanded once the noise had died away. The Morroks' footsteps were getting closer.

I raised my eyes and saw no less than twenty figures standing in a semicircle in front of us, facing the sound of the Morroks' approach. Darkness had fallen by then, but I could still discern that the figures were Humanlike, except that they each had two huge wings protruding from their backs, springing from right under their shoulder blades and nearly dragging the ground in length. Apart from the wings, the figures were much shorter than I was and thinner than a Human child.

I glanced at Levina; she was gaping and holding her sword stupidly at her side, much like I probably was. Ritter seemed unaffected by their appearance other than the anxiety that he wore every time his eyes flickered to the bird people, as if he were a child caught misbehaving.

The Morroks brought us all back to our senses. They crashed into view and stormed through the bird people's circle as if they were made up solely of feathers. True to Ritter's word, there were eight of them, all tall and fierce as ever.

One of the bird people shouted something in another language, and the twenty of them immediately half ran, half flew out from under the trees and into the desert. Ritter was right on their heels, and, pushing Levina in front of me, I followed.

The Morroks lumbered after us, and before I could turn around, two of them were on me, slashing with speed that shouldn't have been possible for weapons of their size. No less than three bird people immediately surrounded each of them, stabbing them with their short, curved swords and lean spears and then flying away just above the Morroks' reach. Enraged, the two Morroks turned their attention to the bird people, but the moment they were out of my range, another Morrok came at me.

I was prepared this time. I met the Morrok's first strike with its huge mace and my sword penetrated the wood so deeply that I couldn't draw it away again. The Morrok ripped its weapon away, and I could barely keep my sword in my hands. I ducked under a few swings that would have broken my neck in an instant and danced away to get a quick view of what was happening with the others.

Levina and Ritter both were protected by the bird people, who were giving the Morroks the same treatment I had seen with the first two. Hoping I could trust them, I charged at my Morrok, dodging its mace again and lunging forward to stab at its chest. It twisted away with only a graze.

"Fools! Leave the Serenial! Get him!" one of the Morroks croaked.

Within seconds, three additional Morroks surrounded me. Heedless of minor injuries, I parried and shoved my way through them, not wanting to leave my back exposed at all costs. Before long, nearly all the bird people swooped down on the group and scattered the Morroks. Two of the bird people fell to a Morrok's irritated swat, but as I twisted free of the tangle, I saw that two Morroks had fallen as well.

I rushed to Levina, who was dueling another Morrok with the aid of only one bird person. Within moments of my arrival, the Morrok hit the sand, fatally wounded.

The Morroks were now hopelessly outnumbered, but they didn't retreat. They wouldn't have retreated if there had been fifty bird people and fifty Humans. The remaining five died fighting and hating to the end.

A couple of the remaining bird people tended to three who had fallen, but the rest herded Levina, Ritter, and me together so that we were in the middle of a tight circle of feathers. All of them had their swords raised.

"Drop your weapons to the ground, Humans," the one in front of us ordered.

"Don't you dare," I said to Ritter and Levina. I stepped in front of them and pointed my sword at the speaker. "Who are you? What do you want with us?"

"I advise you to cooperate. I know that you are alone, and I have no problem with taking you by force. No help will come, I assure you." He spoke slowly and pronounced each syllable with painstaking accuracy as if the language was unnatural to him.

None of the bird people were taller than five feet, and their arms were barely half as thick as mine; however, I couldn't deny what they had done to the Morroks. I sheathed my sword and glanced back at Ritter and Levina to make sure they had done the same.

"What do you want with us?" I repeated.

"You are to come with us," the bird person said. "We shall hold your swords and tie cloth around your eyes so that you cannot see, and we shall lead you to our nearest village. Our chieftain must speak with you."

"Just me? Then let my friends go."

"No. We shall hold them until we decide what is to be done about you."

I surveyed the group again. Seventeen of them had no more than a few cuts and bruises, and the three on the ground seemed to be alive still, though unable to fight. We would lose if we chose to fight, and I doubted we could escape them with us on foot and them in the air. I had no choice.

"We will go peacefully, but only if we can keep our eyes uncovered. I refuse to be pushed blindly through the forest, unarmed, for you to kill us on a whim. If you do not agree, I promise I will fight you to the death, and then no chieftain will be able to speak with me."

The speaker conferred briefly with the bird people nearest him in their own language. "Very well," he said. "Hand your swords to me, and we shall leave your eyes free. But do not attempt to run from us. We see all in the forest."

Chapter Fourteen
The Interpreter

WE WERE FORCED TO ABANDON any other belongings we had taken on the trip, except that Levina demanded that she be allowed to retrieve her diary. I wasn't sure if Ritter and I or the bird people were more amazed at how bold she was. I took note of the ones who scoffed at her because they were probably the only ones who understood our language.

We traveled through most of the night. They led us in circles so as to confuse us about where we were, but they needn't have bothered; I couldn't have told one tree from another if they had held a sword to my neck.

Levina cradled her left arm close to her body, and I cursed myself repeatedly for ever having dueled with her when we weren't in the safety of a Human settlement. After a while, I picked her up and carried her. She was too exhausted to protest. The bird people kept glancing at us as if they had never considered the possibility of carrying one of their own kind.

Every time I glanced at Ritter, he looked more nervous than I had ever seen him. I tried to ask him what the matter was, but the bird people who understood our language stared at us whenever we spoke. Ritter's face was drawn and his jaw clenched as if he might have thrown up if he opened his mouth anyway.

"We shall climb here," the leader said after hours of walking. "Is your female injured?"

"She'll be fine," I said. I set Levina on her feet and told her that we had to go into the canopy. Her eyes widened, but she nodded.

One of the bird people led the way, and Ritter was close behind him, climbing with equal skill. Levina and I had much more difficulty, particularly because of the darkness. The other bird people stayed below, rustling their wings impatiently, until we had broken through the canopy, and then they joined us.

At first, I thought they had brought us to a random spot in the canopy. Although I wasn't sure what it would look like or how it was possible, I had assumed that they had a settlement of some kind, but where we were now was no different from the other parts of the canopy I had seen when checking the time of day for Fallon.

"Follow me," ordered the same bird person who had been speaking to us.

Levina and I didn't move but continued to cling to the tree trunk.

He sighed. "We have made these branches strong. You will not fall."

I laughed weakly. "I think I weigh twice as much as you."

"Do you think that two Serenial never stand close to one another? You will not fall," he repeated. Ritter had already walked a few paces with him.

Levina stared out to the open canopy as if she were on the edge of a cliff. I nodded to her and led her away from the tree trunk and into the open. Our party moved only as fast as the two of us were willing to walk. It was nearing dawn. With every tree trunk we passed, more and more Serenial—as the bird people seemed to be called—appeared to stare at us. As more light revealed the scene, I realized they were coming out of their houses, which were no more than leaves and branches and other debris piled together into four walls and a roof. The little huts reminded me of nests.

The Serenial themselves looked to me like smaller versions of Humans, but their skin was oddly pink and hardened, like scales. Their hair color was almost uniformly white-blond, and all of them wore it long and slicked back, revealing narrow, pointed faces with dark, almost pupilless eyes. The real distinction among them was their wings; the eldest and youngest among them had thin plumes while the middle-aged had full, thick wings. Their wings were a vast array of colors, ranging from red to gray to gold. I couldn't help but stare as several of them smoothed their feathers or ruffled their wings in mannerisms foreign to us Humans.

We stopped in front of one of the sturdier huts.

"Wait here," the speaker said. "An interpreter will retrieve you whenever our chieftain wishes to speak to you. The door will be guarded."

Ritter and Levina ducked through the curtain that served as a door. I was about to follow them when the Serenial caught my arm. "Never mind. The interpreter is here."

I turned to see another Serenial—this one unusually tall but unmistakably a woman—jogging toward us, her rich auburn wings tucked tightly against her back. When she reached us, she exchanged a few hurried words with the guard in their language while I stared longingly at the curtain that separated me from my friends. What if they were killed while I was being interrogated by this chieftain? If they were going to try to execute me, I was ready to die fighting, but I couldn't stand the thought of leaving Levina and Ritter vulnerable.

"Come," the female Serenial beckoned me.

She set off at a brisk pace, but I stood undecided for a moment, feeling like I had failed but unable to accept that I had. The Serenial who had been speaking to us all this time drew his sword and waved it in the female's wake. I wanted nothing more than to rip his stupid little weapon out of his tiny hands and run him through, but my more diplomatic side held me back. The Serenial might not want to harm us at all, and I had to find out for sure.

Telling myself I was on solid ground, I jogged the distance between myself and the Serenial woman. The sun was beginning to rise, and it seemed as if all the Serenial had risen with it to gawk at me as we passed. I felt like a giant among them. None of them came close enough for me to measure, but I doubted even the tallest male reached my shoulder. Even in whispers, their voices all sounded high-pitched, though not in a grating way. Whenever we drew level with a few of them so I could hear better, they ceased speaking and averted their eyes. Maybe they weren't so different from Humans after all.

Among all the gossiping around us, I almost didn't notice when my interpreter spoke, so low and hurried was her voice. I turned to give her my full attention, but she snapped out of the corner of her mouth, "Don't look at me. No one can know that we've communicated."

Obediently, I looked away.

"There's no time to give you proof that I can be trusted, but I assure you, Orestes, I'm on your side. The chieftain has every intention of executing you publicly tomorrow, along with Ritter and Levina, if we're all not very, very careful."

"Why—" I began, but the Serenial jerked her head once to silence me. I searched my mind for any way I could have unknowingly offended the Serenial, but the only thought that prevailed was an admiration for how much more comfortably this woman spoke in my language compared to the other Serenial.

"No time to explain," she said. "The chieftain doesn't know a word of your language, but I don't think I can say the same for the guards who will be in attendance at this meeting. Therefore, I won't be able to communicate with you verbally, but watch my body language closely—though you should never break eye contact with the chieftain. Depending on your answers to her questions, you may get out of this alive. If you heed to nothing else I say, let me warn you this: Pretend you've never seen a Morrok before today. Pretend all you know is what you've heard in Warrior Peak lore. You've never fought one before today, and you had no idea they were in Tyrclopia or in this forest. Is that clear?"

"Yes," I said, though I was completely bewildered by her instructions and by her knowledge of my life. First, she knew all three of our names, though we had not given the Serenial any of them. Then she seemed to know that I knew all about the Morroks, even that I had fought them before. She also knew about Tyrclopia and Warrior Peak, although neither of those nations knew about the Serenial. And finally, most pressing at the moment, how was I supposed to study this woman's body language if I was not to break eye contact with the chieftain, to whom I was supposed to lie to save my friends' lives?

We arrived in front of a large hut that was reinforced with wooden planks and a real door. It was the most stable structure I had seen in the canopy thus far, but it was also the heaviest. In spite of every other worry I had, I couldn't help but look for some visible means of support for this building as the interpreter spoke to the two Serenial guarding the door. Moments later, the guards threw open the door, and the interpreter and I entered.

The building consisted of only one large room that reminded me of the forest Warriors' mess halls. The only furniture included a long table and low-backed chairs that lined both sides. At the head of the table sat who I assumed to be the chieftain; she was indeed a woman, but she was older than any Serenial I had seen. Her hair was gray as opposed to blonde, and her clothes were much bulkier than the loose, thin clothing most of her younger counterparts wore.

There were only three others in the room: two more guards who stood in the corners of the far wall behind the chieftain and a young man who sat to the left of the chieftain with a quill and parchment at the ready. The interpreter waved me into the chair at the end of the table opposite the chieftain (and notably close to the door, which seemed to be the only exit), and then she crossed the room to stand at the right hand of the chieftain herself.

The chieftain studied me without speaking for what felt like minutes. I knew it would be prudent to fear her to some extent, but I had a hard time finding a leader like her intimidating after growing up with cursing, foul-tempered Warriors such as the General and Fallon. But then I remembered the way the Serenial had fought the Morroks in the desert and that my life was now in their hands.

Finally the chieftain spoke. The Serenial language was bizarre at best. For the most part, it sounded like jumbled Human tongue, but it was punctuated occasionally by clicks and screeches. I tried my best not to flinch every time the chieftain's voice shrilled among a flow of normal language.

Barely a moment of silence elapsed as the chieftain's voice died and the interpreter's began. "I don't know if you're aware, Human, that the Morroks never entered our forest before your people arrived," the younger woman said tonelessly. It took me a moment to realize that the interpreter was repeating the chieftain verbatim, not even changing the "I's" to "shes." "My people used to dwell on the ground as well as in the trees, and when Humans began to invade Serenity Valley more than fifty years ago, we allowed you to have some land. The forest is large, and we are not a violent people."

The chieftain picked up again, and the interpreter spoke over her voice as she continued. "However, as more Humans settled, the Morroks entered the forest as well. We had heard of them only in legend, and quite a few of our children had disappeared before we realized what threat was facing us. Unable to resist the invisible menace, we fled to the trees, where we have lived for the last thirty years. If any Humans knew of us, they have forgotten, but the Morroks have not, though the delicate canopy continues to protect us from their great size—at least for now."

The chieftain paused, and the furious scratching of the recorder's quill buzzed in the silence. In any other circumstance, this story would have fascinated me. As it was, all I wanted to hear was what the story had to do with me.

"In the past few months, the number of Morroks in the forest has increased tenfold. They are destroying the plants and animals that we depend on for food. They are finding ways to chase us out of the trees. They have even constructed a fortress by the great lake in the center of the forest, where most of your people dwell."

I contained my shock over this information to an involuntary twitch in my right arm, my fingers flexing around a phantom sword. The Morroks were already beating us to our own strategy; they were attacking us on both fronts before we could attack them from both fronts, and they had been doing so long enough to build an entire fortress in Serenity Valley.

"It has taken our scouts a while," the chieftain continued, "but we have traced the recent fluctuation in Morrok activity directly to the time when your small group entered our forest. We have been following the twelve of you for a while, as has a small contingent of Morroks, though we didn't understand why until tonight. Not a single Morrok camped out around the Human town where the rest of your group remains, and even when the other . . ."

The interpreter faltered for a moment even though the chieftain never seemed to have broken her speech. I glanced at the younger woman, wondering if this was some signal from her, but she merely took a deep breath and continued. "Even when the other young man with you went into the canopy at night, the Morroks paid no heed to him. In fact, they came out into the open to attack only when it was just you and the woman with you, though my warriors tell me it is obvious they were interested only in you. So it is finally apparent to us that you are the cause of the Morroks' increase, and I, along with all my fellow chieftains, would like to know why."

I didn't realize I was supposed to speak until the recorder had finished scrawling the rest of the chieftain's dialogue.

"I don't know," I said. "I had no idea there was a group following us—either Serenial or Morrok. In fact, I'd never even seen either of your kind before tonight."

"Then how," the chieftain said, her voice rising slightly, though the interpreter's remained monotone, "did you ward off three Morroks at once when it takes four of my warriors to contain just a single Morrok?"

I tried my best to look confused. "I just survived, but so did most of your warriors. Before we left Warrior Peak, my people did extensive training on how we assumed we ought to fight Morroks based on what we knew about their size and build."

The chieftain seemed to expect an answer like this because she fired back another accusation before the last words were out of my mouth. "I know for a fact that one of your number frequently leaves your group—often at night—and that there is sometimes a Human among the group of Morroks following you. Now tell me that you know nothing of Morrok activity in Serenity Valley!"

The interpreter's eyes had filled with tears, though no one but I seemed to notice. For a second time, I wasn't sure if that was some signal, but I was too busy fighting back tears of my own—tears of rage, bewilderment, and betrayal. Finally I knew why Ritter climbed into the canopy every time he left our company. He couldn't leave a trail when he went to visit the Morroks.

"I don't . . . I don't know anything about Morroks following me, and I certainly have not been in contact with them," I said, trying to keep my voice steady. However, on top of the revelation about Ritter, I couldn't shake the memory of whatever figure I had met the night I had followed Ritter out of Settlement Six. It couldn't have been a Morrok, could it?

"You're lying."

"I am not," I said. "Look, maybe my people have caused the Morroks to enter the forest, but just because we're causing the havoc doesn't mean we're the havoc itself. I—and all Humans—have no quarrel with the Serenial, even if you won't stoop to mingle with us, and I assure you that we hate the Morroks just as much as you do. We, like you, have lost people to them, but we, unlike you, are trying to fight back."

The chieftain bristled as the interpreter finished translating my reply. "First, I still do not believe that you do not consort with Morroks. Second, I would like to remind you that the forest is our home, so you—"

"If you didn't want us here, you should have shown yourself and defended your home against Humans long ago. The forest Warriors have worked their whole lives settling a land they didn't think previously inhabited, so they can't be—"

"Our people aren't as quick as yours to start wars and—"

"Start wars?" I repeated. "This war with the Morroks is the first Warrior Peak's had in more than three generations. We didn't ask for this fight either, and there's no basis for you to say that we would've fought your people if we'd known about you from the beginning."

"That's not the issue at hand!" the interpreter shouted over the chieftain's continued retort. "The point is that the Morroks seem to be particularly interested in you, regardless of whether or not you're in league with them. On behalf of all Serenial, I command you to leave our forest and to take the rest of your people with you."

"That won't make the Morroks leave, especially if they're finding ways to attack your people again."

"Then you must root them out of Serenial Valley."

"We can't do it alone!" I said, jumping to my feet. The two guards sprang forward and drew their swords, coming close enough for the tips to brush my cheek. "It's your responsibility as much as ours. If you would just work with us, we could—"

"Leave the forest, or I will kill you where you stand!" the chieftain screamed, rising as well.

"I will do no such thing."

The chieftain and I glared at one another, at an impasse even though it was she who had guards ready to behead me at the flick of the wrist.

"Would your two friends be more of a persuasion?" the chieftain asked slowly. "Guards, bring me the head of—"

Whatever else the chieftain said was never translated. The guards' attention shifted from me to the interpreter as the young woman's arm locked around her superior's throat. Shocked but pleased that I wasn't the only one who wanted to do the same, I took advantage of the guards' surprise and relieved one of them of his sword. I quickly bashed him over the head with the flat of the blade and turned to meet the remaining guard just as he struck at me with his own sword.

The guard's wings extended, making the room seem much smaller as they knocked over a few chairs and blocked the interpreter from my view. The chieftain was lying on the floor, and the interpreter was struggling with the recorder, but both were weaponless, so I felt justified in concentrating solely on the guard before me. Repeating the fighting strategy I had witnessed earlier that night, the guard attempted to fly, but the ceiling was too low for him to lift more than a few inches off the floor. I swung at him with all my might, and even though he had both hands on his sword, he couldn't block my blow. As the guard crashed to the floor again (dead or injured, I did not know), I realized the Serenial were as strong compared to Humans as Humans were to Morroks; unless the individual of the weaker race had considerable strength, he or she could not hope to match the stronger.

"Orestes!" the interpreter called. She and the recorder were on the floor now, the former doing everything she could to cover the latter's mouth lest he cry out for help. Jumping over a few scattered chairs, I raised my sword over the two. The interpreter pushed herself away, and I smacked the recorder's head with the butt of the sword, knocking him out.

Suddenly alone in a room of prone bodies, the interpreter and I simply stared at each other for a moment.

"I suppose you just proved I can trust you," I said.

"Yes," she panted, frowning. "I didn't kill the chieftain, but attacking her is treason enough for execution or exile, so I need to get to the ground as much as you do."

"Why are you doing this?"

She waved off the question as she crossed the room to pick up the other guard's sword. "No one knows what has happened, so we should have time to get your swords before we go to Ritter and Levina. Let's move quickly. Hide your sword, and let me do any talking."

We emerged from the building and closed the door behind us before the outer guards could look inside. The interpreter murmured to one of the guards and then set off without waiting for a reply. She led us out of their sight and then broke into a jog, and within moments, we were outside a small, shabby hut set off from the rest of the Serenial village.

After handing me her stolen sword, the interpreter ducked inside the hut and reappeared an instant later bearing our swords. I cringed at the sight of Ritter's blade, and luckily she handed me only my sword and Levina's. She strapped Ritter's to her back and took the Serenial swords from me, presumably for her own use.

Just as we finished arranging our weapons, cries of alarm sounded in the distance.

"They must have found them," the interpreter said.

"Let's hurry before they do anything to Levina and Ritter."

After only moments of running, we were back among dozens of Serenial—young and old, armed and not—spread out searching for us with hatred in their eyes that only a mob mentality could bring on. They spotted us immediately, but we paid no attention to them as we barreled our way through the mass of feathers toward the little hut where I had left Ritter and Levina not an hour ago.

We reached our destination after several minutes of dodging and batting away both weapons and grasping hands. I thought I saw the interpreter receive a deep blow to her leg; she didn't cry out, however, but merely hobbled the rest of the way to the hut.

The interpreter made it inside first. She pushed away the heavy curtain; I cut it down. I glanced inside long enough to see the floor mats in disarray—bloodied and covered with leaves and soil.

With the interpreter still inside, I blocked the entrance with my body and swung my sword wildly at the oncoming mob, hoping to frighten them with my size and strength. It worked for a moment as they all stopped a few feet short of my reach. Then I glanced up.

About a dozen Serenial beating their wings steadily above me each had an arrow trained on my chest. I stopped moving my weapon and tried to decide if I could throw myself inside quickly enough. At least then I could die fighting, with some control over my life. Being shot would have been the worst way to go.

"Orestes, they escaped! They dug through the canopy! Come here! Look!" the interpreter hissed from inside the hut.

None of the Serenial reacted. Either no one heard or no one understood. I took a deep breath and dove into the hut.

The mob collapsed on the doorway immediately but not before I saw the interpreter tuck her wings close to her and slip through a hole dug through the intertwined tree branches that had once served for a floor. Heedless of the height from which I was about to fall, I launched myself headfirst through the hole, for once turning my back on dozens of pursuing blades.

Chapter Fifteen
Ritter's Love

A PAIR OF THIN ARMS locked around my waist the moment my body broke through the canopy. The interpreter beat her wings furiously in an attempt to stay airborne, but to no avail. The patched light from the canopy swirled around us, but I couldn't close my eyes against the looming impact. I tried to lift my head, hoping to protect my neck, but at the last moment, the interpreter jerked on my torso upward, and we landed sideways on the forest floor. We bounced and rolled, and I landed on top of her so hard that I was sure I had crushed her wings.

I sprang to my feet and whirled around to help the interpreter, but she was already up and stretching out her great wings. We heard shouts from above, and angry faces smashed into the hole from which we had escaped. The interpreter and I darted in a random direction, she with surprising speed for one so small.

"They'll pursue us for a while, and they'll be hard to lose because they can see us from above, especially since it's broad daylight," she said.

"Will they shoot at us?" I asked.

For several seconds I heard only her panting.

"Yes," she said finally.

"We might as well yell for Levina and Ritter if the Serenial know where we are anyway. Then we have to run and dodge, even if they're not shooting. We'll give them two moving targets. We might have a chance."

She didn't acknowledge me further but started screaming our companions' names.

We ran for hours, occasionally throwing ourselves behind trees or circling around them to confuse potential pursuers. If there were any, they never showed themselves. Not one arrow rained down on us, not one tree branch shifted above us, and not one feather fell in our path. The interpreter tried to tell me once that Serenial weren't violent people, but I found it hard to believe anything positive about them at the moment.

After nearly three hours of searching, the interpreter held up a hand for silence. I stilled my croaking voice and strained to listen. "Sylvia! Orestes!" Two faint voices from somewhere to our left. The interpreter and I hesitated for only a moment and then darted toward the sound.

Ritter and Levina came into view, both of them looking much like we probably did—red-faced, wide-eyed, and hair disheveled—but they had the added detail of scraped and bloodied hands.

At the sight of Ritter, I was sure that if I didn't kill him, the anger that was springing up inside would kill me. But I forgot about him completely as Levina stumbled into me and I caught her up in my arms. I didn't realize until then that all my anxiety from the last few hours had not been for myself but for her—if the Serenial would spot *her*, if one of their arrows would hit *her*. I wasn't sure if I kissed her or she kissed me first. It didn't really matter, as long as she was safe and mostly whole.

"We should keep moving," Ritter said.

Embarrassed, Levina stepped away from me, but I marched toward Ritter with my hand flexing over my sword hilt. I opened my mouth to unload all my accusations on him, but the interpreter stepped in front of him, though the top of her head barely reached either of our shoulders.

"Wait, Orestes," she said. "I know what you're thinking, but the chieftain was wrong. Please listen to me—but while we move. We really need to get back to Settlement Eleven before we can be safe from anyone—Serenial or Morrok."

I glared over her head while Ritter stared back impassively.

"Fine," I growled.

After determining which direction was east, we set off, hoping that that would lead us close to Settlement Eleven. The Serenial, with her short, thin legs, had trouble keeping up with us, but she was determined to speak even through short puffs of breath.

"I'll start with my history," she said. "My name is Sylvia, and I am twenty in your years. Serenial become adults when they are eighteen, and to mark that, we travel the forest for as long as we want with no real obligation to return home if we wish to start our adult lives elsewhere. I have been on that journey for more than two years now, so I was just a visitor in the village we just left. All they knew about me is that I know the Human language very well."

"Where is your real home?" Levina asked gently. That seemed like a silly question to me when Sylvia was in the middle of trying to clear Ritter's name, but then I noticed what Levina had—that the other girl was close to tears.

"Far northwest of here, nowhere near any Human settlements," Sylvia replied. "As I child, I had heard of Humans, of course, but I always wanted to see them for myself—how they traveled or even stood upright without wings to balance them." She paused and laughed a little. The rest of us smiled as well, a relief after the previous night's events. "The Serenial have always observed Humans without their knowledge, and so some of us know your language and culture very well. Humans fascinated me as I traveled throughout Serenity Valley, but I was never allowed to see one up close in the interest of preserving Serenial secrecy."

Sylvia paused again. I thought she was just catching her breath, but Levina again seemed to know something I didn't as she stared at Ritter, who was grinning broadly.

"I got clumsy one day, though," Sylvia continued. "I came across your group not too long after you entered the forest, and I followed you for a few days, confident that you would lead me to a Human settlement. I never imagined that any of you would climb into the canopy, and so when Ritter did one day, I was completely unprepared and couldn't hide before he spotted me."

Ritter chuckled. "She almost killed me to keep me quiet."

"But he was just as curious about me as I was about him, and we ended up talking for hours. After that, I followed your group for months. Ritter and I taught each other about our languages, I showed him how to move in the canopy, and he told me all about Humans and Warrior Peak. He took every opportunity to join me in the trees, and as time went on, he snuck out at night to see me as well. I thought we were being careful, but I guess the Serenial who were officially tracking you saw Ritter leaving your group and thought it was Orestes going to see the Morroks."

"That still doesn't explain the Human whom the Serenial saw traveling with that group of Morroks," I said.

"No, it doesn't," Sylvia agreed. "And that's troubling, but we can't do anything about it, especially considering that the Morroks you killed last night may have been all there was to the group that was following you."

Levina stopped running. "There's been a group of Morroks following us?" she asked, aghast.

"Yes," Ritter replied.

I halted as well. "Wait, you knew?"

"Sylvia overheard the chieftain saying so yesterday evening," Ritter said. "The Serenial saw the Morroks moving in on you and Levina, and they were planning to intervene and bring you up to the canopy for questioning. Sylvia told me, and I was rushing to tell you in case the Morroks got there first or the Serenial decided to kill you on the spot."

"Sorry I didn't listen to you," I said grudgingly.

"That's all right. You had every right to doubt me, but I swear I don't have any more secrets. We just couldn't risk the Serenial finding out about me or the forest Warriors finding out about the Serenial. I think the Morroks are enough to scare everyone right now."

"Ritter's right," Levina said. "But what will you do, Sylvia? I'm sure you can't go back to the canopy."

"No," Sylvia said. "I don't mind exposing myself to the rest of your group. I know Ritter has hated keeping it from all of you. I can stay on the forest floor while we're traveling, and whenever we arrive at settlements, I'll stay in the canopy close by. Serenial villages are usually as far as possible from Humans, so I should be safe."

We all agreed to this and started to jog again in silence. I tried to organize all the events and revelations in my mind to report to Fallon later, but it took all my concentration to keep one foot moving in front of the other.

About midday, we all collapsed on the forest floor, too tired to go on or to care what might attack us in our sleep. Ritter and Sylvia curled up together and were asleep within moments.

Levina caught my eye, and we both laughed. "They were just curious about each other's cultures, right?" she asked.

"Purely intellectual."

"Well, I hope he's better with her than he was with all his sweethearts at Warrior Peak. Did you know that he didn't even say good-bye to the last one when we left?"

"He ought to be shot."

Levina rolled her eyes. "Good night, Orestes."

"Good night, Levina."

Despite not having slept for so long, I couldn't rest peacefully. My sleeping mind conjured images of Morroks and feathered Humans, both frightening and unsettling in their own way. Every time I woke, I wondered if I had imagined the last two days, but one glance at Sylvia destroyed every doubt.

One thought in particular continued to echo in my mind: that a small band of Morroks had been following me since I entered the forest. That meant that the Morroks knew who I was and knew my face—perhaps even my name. My name! Of course they knew my name. Dirth had given me my name. But how could he contact the Morroks on this side of the mountain? What did he want with me after all these years? Perhaps I knew too much. But it wasn't as if my insight into the Morrok psyche would help the forest Warriors stop the army of them that had apparently descended on Serenity Valley. *The unseen will prevail over the tangible. Remember that.* Or so the strange Morrok voice had told me. I highly doubted that this would hold true when the Morroks so outmatched us in strength and perhaps in number.

When I woke from my uneasy sleep for the umpteenth time, night had fallen. Ritter and Levina were fast asleep, but Sylvia sat up, clutching her knees to herself and weeping softly.

Careful not to wake Levina, I scooted closer to her. "Are you okay?"

She flashed me a small smile. "Oh, I'm not hurt. Don't worry about me."

"I bet you're glad you got involved with Humans now, aren't you?"

She laughed weakly. "Ritter and I discussed all the risks that came along with our relationship, but I suppose we never expected the worst to happen. This was definitely the worst."

"Sylvia, I'm sorry. I feel like this is all my fault. We didn't have to attack the chieftain and the guards."

Sylvia sighed. "Yes, we did. Ritter and I—we couldn't—we didn't want to—hide forever. I guess I used to imagine us bringing our people together somehow." She laughed again. "So childish. So foolish. The Serenial have watched your people from the day they arrived, but we never interfered. Serenial—well, we're so different from you, especially in my part of the country. We're very reserved—very concerned with survival, but not with truly living. We don't laugh as loudly or cry as often or touch as much."

"Which is the opposite of Ritter."

"Exactly."

"But with all that Human watching," I said, "your people must have seen that we aren't evil—not at all like Morroks."

"No, but I'm sure that, had *your* people scrutinized *mine* for so long without our knowledge, you would no sooner give your daughters to our sons in marriage than we do now. Time has a way of exposing flaws no matter how good the people, especially when the observer is so predisposed to dislike the ones being observed. Humans have always just been a nuisance that we hoped would get bored with the forest and leave."

"Do you think we'll ever be able to contact the Serenial again?"

Sylvia shook her head and lay down next to Ritter again, her shoulders still quivering. I had asked solely for political and military reasons because I knew Fallon would have asked the same had he been here, but as with everything Serenial thus far, I seemed to cause nothing but strife. *Leave here, or they will die.* That was what the Morrok that invaded my last end-of-year tournament had warned me. But I had left Warrior Peak, and people were still going to die. I was truly nothing more than a dangerous fool; dangerous because I had once been a Morrok and a fool because I still listened to them.

Long after Sylvia's breathing quieted, I sat fully awake, perhaps out of continued paranoia over the Serenial or Morroks or whatever else dwelled on this side of the mountains. But mostly I watched Levina's slender form rise and fall in a steady, soothing rhythm and wondered what I would have done if she weren't beside me.

*

By some miracle, we found Settlement Eleven after only ten days of blind searching. Ritter and Sylvia ascended into a tree close to the edge of the village's clearing while Levina and I proceeded to the gate, which was closed despite it being the middle of the day. I noted that most of the outer wall seemed finished—quite a feat, considering that construction had started only three weeks before. The whole village must have been working on it.

Several minutes passed before someone answered my pounding on the gate. Fallon poked his head over the parapets and cursed. "Where's Ritter? What took you so long? It's been more than two weeks! You were supposed to be gone ten days! Where are all your supplies?"

"Fallon, please, just let us in. There's too much to explain."

The atmosphere inside the village was different from how we had left it. Although smaller in population, Settlement Eleven was strikingly similar to Settlement Six in everything from the structure of the village to the positive attitude of the people. Now, however, hardly anyone was on the streets; no one was working, no one was in the mess hall, and no one paid us much attention as we passed, though Fallon was still berating me and asking questions without waiting for answers.

When he paused for a breath, Levina asked, "What's wrong with everyone?"

Fallon grimaced, murmured, "Wait until we're inside," and was silent until we reached the mess hall. I had never been so grateful to Levina.

Jacob, Cara, Holt, Abby, Glynis, Cyrus, Joanne, and Todd—everyone with whom we had set out from Warrior Peak—sat in the mostly empty building with the leader of Settlement Eleven, Frederick. They all looked strangely small sitting in such a large room hunched over in chairs, silent and staring at the floor as if in mourning. They brightened considerably on seeing Levina and me, but that didn't last long as they repeated Fallon's long list of inquiries, ending with a last, more desperate, "Where is Ritter?"

"Ritter is as safe and alive as the two of us," I assured them. "However, I think it's best if the rest of our story doesn't leave this room." Then, sparing no detail, I related the events of the past few days, ignoring any interruptions from anyone else in the room until I had finished. I could see in Fallon's eyes that he was calculating and recalculating with each new revelation, and a strange feeling of possessiveness pervaded my inner thoughts. Fallon was the one who was going to decide how we would act, but what did he know? He hadn't been there. He hadn't made my mistakes, but neither had he made sure that the four of us had survived the past few days. Why was it now so hard to trust Fallon of all people?

"Well," Fallon said once I had answered everyone's questions twice over, "alienating the Serenial like that complicates our entire mission, to say the least, and our call to the great lake in the central Valley is now more urgent than ever. However, before we discuss that, I should tell you what's happened here." He cleared his throat as everyone shifted their attention from my terrible topic to his. "Last night, eight children were kidnapped from under their parents' roofs. Five boys, three girls, all under the age of two. In each child's bed was left a note."

Frederick, a rotund and bearded man bordering on old age, produced a handful of paper scraps. One by one, I unfolded them, and each one had the same message in the same large, scratchy writing: "There are only Eight whom the Morroks fear."

"Eight?" I said aloud as I handed the notes to Levina. "Do they mean those eight children they stole?"

"That's unlikely, don't you think?" Levina said. "What are the chances that all eight whom the Morroks supposedly fear are in one village? Out of all Humans—Warrior or Tyrclopian—and all Serenial, they fear only eight."

"Besides, why would they fear children?" Cyrus asked.

"And why would they want to keep the ones they fear close to them?" Jo-anne added. Cyrus took her hand.

"A more poignant question would be why *wouldn't* they keep the ones they fear close?" Fallon said. "I agree with Levina; I don't think they fear the babies they kidnapped. I believe the crime was symbolic—just some sick ploy of the Morroks. I don't know what they meant by it or why they think we need to know whom they fear, but the more immediate problem is that the Morroks are moving among us and making their presence blatant now. But what shall we do about it?"

"We could track them—at least the ones that stole the children," Frederick suggested. "They can't be too far away, and even if we fail, it would be a comfort to the parents that we tried. But if we succeed, perhaps we'll find out where exactly the Morrok stronghold is."

"The Morroks cannot be tracked," I said. "You can try all you like, but you will never find evidence of them. I'd stake my life on it."

Frederick tugged at his beard. "Well, I can't just do nothing! You say they're monsters—seven or eight feet tall—but they came into my village—into our very houses!—without so much as being seen. I can't let this happen again."

"How does one fight an enemy that won't show itself?" Holt mused.

I was strongly reminded of my last conversation with the General. He, like most, had believed that the Morroks would fight us face to face, and now, finally, my family was learning that that was not how they operated.

"We can't, that's all," I said after a few moments' silence. "We have to wait to be attacked. If the Morroks have built a stronghold in the forest, I bet it's as dangerous as a Facility, and no one leaves a Morrok Facility alive." Except Acules and me.

"If that's the case," Frederick said wearily, "then I feel we need to be better prepared than this. I agree with Colonel Fallon's earlier sentiments, now more than ever. If the Serenial will do nothing about the Morroks, then Humans must bear the burden of rooting them out of the forest. Our best chance at doing that would be to unite among ourselves."

"We are of one mind, my friend," Fallon said.

"Then I propose we waste no time," Frederick continued. "I will take my village north to join William at Settlement Six. Then we will proceed together to the lake in the heart of the forest, where your group will be by then."

"What about the dangers that the forest now holds?" Glynis asked. "Your village has children and elderly. What about the Serenial? The Morroks? If they were able to penetrate the village walls to kidnap a few children, what will happen to you when you're exposed in the forest?"

"The twelve of us have survived," Jacob said. "Frederick's village numbers more than a hundred."

"What do you think, Colonel?" Frederick asked.

Everyone looked at Fallon like fearful children to a parent.

He sighed. "If you think you can head such a large undertaking, Frederick, then by all means, I support you. My conscience would be relieved if I were to escort you to Settlement Six myself, but I feel the twelve of us must press on toward the central Valley with all speed, as you said."

"It's decided then," Frederick said, his voice shaking. "There's no need for us to finish construction on our walls, so tomorrow we will begin preparations for departure. Today, however, we ought to rest and remember the eight children who spurred our mobilization against the Morroks."

Chapter Sixteen
The Cost of a Prisoner

COMPARED TO WHAT SYLVIA told us about the Serenial, Warrior marriage ceremonies were very dull. As the highest-ranking officer available in the absence of an Inventory division officer, Fallon had the authority to write the notification that we would turn in to the Inventory division whenever we made it home: "On the two hundred and eighty-first day of the year 326, Cyrus, son of Jesse and major of Intelligence, and Joanne, daughter of Helena and captain of Intelligence, were married in the eyes of Warrior Peak. I, Fallon, son of Harold and colonel of Intelligence, administered this marriage, and the undersigned were witnesses to it."

We had been gone from Settlement Eleven for two months now, and the thought of having a wedding in the middle of the forest seemed almost too absurd to go through with. Still, we all dressed in our finest (which meant the least torn and dirty tunics we had) to witness Fallon write the marriage certificate, and then, one by one, we signed, beginning with the highest ranking among us and ending with Sylvia, who was not a citizen of the Peak. I had always despised weddings because at Warrior Peak, it was a law that everyone present who would remember the event had to sign as witnesses. Fallon, being a prominent officer and a friend to many, was invited to nearly every wedding imaginable, and so a large portion of my childhood had been dedicated to watching hundreds of people promenade forward to scrawl their names across foot-long scrolls of paper.

After the mercifully small number of witnesses at this wedding had performed their duty, we watched Cyrus and Joanne—widower and widow—exchange the marriage gifts as giddily as if they were twenty years old again. Cyrus gave Joanne a bracelet because, traditionally, women did not wear jewelry of any kind until they were married and their husbands provided it for them. Impatient young girls and greedy jewelers often marred this practice, but it remained part of the marriage ceremony all the same.

Joanne's gift was more symbolic. First, she took Cyrus's shaving knife from him and pinned it firmly into the earth between them. Then she handed him a long, thin piece of hair-tying cloth that, traditionally, she would have sewn herself. Until marriage, men were supposed to remain clean-shaven and keep their hair cut short. This tradition was breached even more than the women's because men often associated lack of facial hair with boyhood, and no man wanted to appear to be a boy just because he didn't have a wife. Ritter and I had been among the few who adhered to this practice, but since Sylvia had begun traveling with us nearly two months ago, Ritter's beard was nearly full and his hair hung around his ears.

With the ceremony completed (to my delight in under twenty minutes), we settled on the forest floor for a poor substitution for a marriage feast, which consisted of a small rabbit for the newlyweds and berries and roots for the rest of us. We had become unwilling hunters in the past month and a half, ever since half our food supply "disappeared." We had traveled two weeks away from Frederick's village—just far enough not to be able to call for help—when we woke one morning to find the camp robbed of everything that wasn't in the tents with us: tunics, utensils, secondary weapons, firewood, and most of our food.

Living off the land wasn't terrible, but it had been a tough, sometimes frustrating adjustment for all of us who had grown up having our meat skinned and cut for us by the Warrior Peak butchers. We did, however, learn to become better archers and trappers, and the forest was overflowing with edible plants, though they too had given us trouble at first. In the first week, half the group had eaten a root that kept them in a state of weakness and vomiting for nearly a week. From then on, all food passed before Sylvia's eye for approval before anyone touched it since she had grown up eating forest plants, but there was no making up the week we lost to sickness while the Morroks were working on their stronghold by the lake.

After the food robbing, Fallon decided that we would have one person awake at all times to keep watch over the camp and alert the rest of us in case of an ambush. At first, lack of sleep and food made a disaster of watch duty. Every other night, whoever was on watch would wake the entire camp, insisting that he or she had seen or heard a Morrok. Although I tended to believe that the Morroks really were lurking nearby, Fallon often dismissed these alerts as the paranoia that came with being the only one awake under the blackness of the canopy. From then on, he had two people on watch at all times, and the middle-of-the-night alarms subsided for the most part.

As I was finishing my portion of the wedding meal, Fallon tapped me on the shoulder. "I want to travel straight through for a couple days, but we need supplies. Get Todd or Ritter or Levina to help you hunt and gather a bit before you lose the light."

I nodded and looked at my potential candidates. Ritter didn't seem like a likely choice since it was his father who had just been married. Also, he had barely left Sylvia's side ever since she had announced that she was pregnant and had been for a couple months already. Sylvia said Serenial pregnancies and births were no different from Human ones, but we were all waiting in quiet speculation to see how the mixed child would turn out.

Levina and Todd both had dark circles under their eyes, and their smiles were strained as they listened to the others talk. Neither had slept much in the past weeks. After Sylvia joined our group and Cyrus and Joanne's relationship had developed, there had been some tent shuffling, and Levina was left alone in her tent—a prospect, she informed me, that was as unsettling as doing watch alone. And as his tent mate, I knew that Todd hadn't been sleeping well either, though I wasn't sure of his reasons. He did, however, seem pleased to leave the party to hunt with me.

After stringing two small bows and grabbing quivers, we headed eastward away from camp. No one noticed. We worked in silence for a while, finding suitable plants but no animals, which was strange. The trees had been thinning out over the past week, but the presence of wildlife hadn't changed until recently.

"Do you think we're lost?" Todd asked abruptly once we had given up trying to sneak around so as not to scare off any animals.

"Lost?" I repeated. "Camp's only a few minutes back—"

"No, not now. I mean our route to the lake. The colonel hasn't found any of the landmarks Frederick marked on our maps, and none of us have gone in the trees to check our direction because of the Serenial. Now the trees are thinning. What if we're getting close to the Gravel Lands instead of the lake?"

I stopped foraging and stared at him. Surely Fallon wouldn't let us travel blindly like that. "I doubt we're straying that far north."

"The thing is," he persisted, "this is what happened to us last time—two years ago. The Morroks stole our supplies. Then we kept seeing them or hearing them at night. Then they attacked. I mean, just the other night, Sylvia and Levina swore they saw two figures hovering around the edge of camp. What else could it have been?"

"The imagination of two women who talked themselves into seeing something that wasn't there," I replied, reminding myself of Fallon. "Is this why you've been having—" I stopped myself. There was no good way to ask a man about nightmares he denied to everyone else, especially when the nightmares had real fear behind them. Todd had been the only survivor of his group that traveled through Serenity Valley two years ago, and I understood better than most the lasting horror of Morrok encounters. "Well, we're prepared for whatever happens," I finished.

I leaned over to continue rooting a few more berries out of the nearest shrub, but Todd spoke again. "All the same, do you think we could climb in the canopy, just to make sure we're not near the Gravel Lands?"

I laughed. "And defy the colonel's orders? I never would have expected it of you."

"Orestes, please, what can it hurt?"

I glanced at Todd again, noting his pale skin and bloodshot eyes. Our chances of climbing directly into a Serenial village were probably slim even though Sylvia insisted that the Serenial outnumbered Humans—both forest Warriors and those at the Peak—at least twice over. I also still doubted that we were really lost, but if proving it would help Todd sleep at night, then the small risk was worth it.

"All right, let's go."

Todd was even clumsier than I was trying to climb the nearest tree. Unlike the trees in the west, these had few decent handholds, and no branch seemed willing to hold our full weight. We ended up having to use our daggers to claw our way up. To maintain some of our dignity, we heartily abused the bad luck that brought us a branchless tree and the ludicrousness of grown men needing to climb trees at all.

Although the trees were thinner, the canopy was still solid, and as we hoisted ourselves onto the thicker branches, I couldn't quell the fear in the pit of my stomach as I thought of the Serenial. Todd remained pinned against the tree trunk as I took a few cautious steps away from it. As far as I could see, there were no huts or nests that made up a Serenial village, but that was the least of my concerns as the branches I stood on swayed dangerously under my weight. I retreated to the tree trunk with Todd.

"I thought Sylvia said the Serenial walk up here all over the country," Todd said.

"If that's true, then they are far braver and more talented than I," I replied. "Let's just do what we came to do."

Just as we moved to pull ourselves farther up the tree, a shriek cut through the forest's silence. Bewildered, I looked at Todd, who cocked his eyebrows. He opened his mouth to speak, but another strangled cry interrupted him.

"It sounds like a woman," I murmured. I thought of Levina, Glynis, and the others, and my pulse quickened.

"It's coming from the opposite direction of camp though," Todd said. "I thought there weren't any villages between Settlement Eleven and the lake."

"It doesn't matter. We have to see what's happening." I scrambled to find an opening in the branches so we could descend to the floor again.

"Wait, it sounded like it was coming from the ground," Todd said. "Why don't we stay up here and find out what's going on? We'd have the element of surprise in case it's something dangerous."

I gazed doubtfully across the expanse of canopy between us and our goal. Todd had no idea how hard it was to tread branches that the Serenial had expertly intertwined, much less branches in thin, uninhabited areas. But before I could say as much, Todd pushed himself away from his tree trunk and started toward the source of the screams. The branches immediately began to buckle under him, but before they folded, Todd leaped to the next set, holding higher branches and vines for additional support. For a moment, I did nothing but marvel at how the usually awkward, sometimes sniveling Todd had transformed into a man of such action and purpose. Impressed, I followed.

Jumping from one unsupportive branch to another was much slower than running on solid ground, but the woman's voice continued to lead us as she moaned and cried in pain. I hoped our clumsy crashing through the leaves would not be noticed as we neared her.

The woman's voice muffled abruptly as we drew parallel over the noise. Todd and I froze where we stood, though the branches under us continued to sway. Halted grunts, so low that we could barely hear, replaced the feminine wail.

"Tie her and put her back in the bag. We're close to the lake, and we can't have the Humans finding us before we get to the fortress."

"Two of them are out hunting. Shall we kill them?" another equally scratchy voice asked.

"No," the first growled. "One of them could be Orestes. Now shut your mouths and keep that damn girl bound."

I glanced at Todd, and he nodded in silent agreement. These were unmistakably Morroks. We didn't need to risk sticking our heads through the canopy to check. The Serenial had made it clear that a group of Morroks was always following our group, but it was unsettling to hear that they knew exactly where we all were at any given time. And they knew my name. To hear my name on Morrok lips after all these years was enough to make me want to drop from the trees and fight them all.

"We need to alert the colonel," Todd whispered. "Maybe if we can rally everyone in time, we can catch them off guard."

I ignored Todd as I sifted through the layers of leaves and branches below me. After a few moments of silent work, I made a hole in the canopy large enough for me to view the scene below. Sure enough, a cluster of eight Morroks stood or sat in a loose circle below us. They had no equipment other than their weapons and the ragged clothes on their backs. I shifted to make sure I had observed every possible angle. Eight again. Eight Morroks had attacked us the night we met the Serenial. Eight children had been kidnapped from Settlement Eleven while we were gone. There were only Eight whom the Morroks fear.

"You go ahead. I want to watch," I said to Todd.

"I don't think that's a good idea."

"I'm not leaving. They have a prisoner down there, and I have to make sure nothing happens to her."

Todd didn't move for a few moments, but he seemed to realize that even though he outranked me, he wouldn't be able to force me to listen to him. As Todd's uneven footsteps receded into the distance, I strained to hear more conversation, but I was disappointed. Morroks had little to say to one another besides passing on orders, and Morroks never questioned orders.

At least we now knew that we were close to the lake. But we were also near the Morrok fortress that the Serenial chieftain had told me about. I assumed that the Humans the Morroks had spoken of meant me and my group, and they apparently believed that they needed more than the eight of them before they revealed themselves. But surely if Morroks could overpower normal men two or three to one, then eight on thirteen would be no problem for them. What were they waiting for?

One of the Morroks interrupted any further musings. It rose and padded across their circle to a large, lumpy sack I had missed in my earlier sweep of the area. It bent over the mound and, after a moment's pause, straightened up again. "Still breathing," it said to no one in particular.

The crying woman. They had literally put her in a bag. Instinctively drawing my sword, I crawled closer to where the woman lay. Once again, it took all my willpower not to climb down and face them myself.

My struggle to mollify such thoughts was cut short by a sudden chill in the air. There was no breeze, but I could neither stop the shiver that ran the length of my body nor ignore the icy pain of drawing in a single, unsteady breath. Below, the Morroks seemed to feel it too because they all stiffened where they stood. One of them, reluctant but frightened, suddenly left the circle and disappeared out of my range of sight. Equally quickly, it was back, shaking so hard that I could see it doing so even from my perch. "The Humans are coming. We fight."

Without a word, the remaining Morroks unsheathed their weapons and followed the speaker in the direction of my camp. Only one stayed, assuming a guard position next to the sack. Elated by my luck, I crawled several feet away so that I could ease down a tree out of the Morrok's hearing.

Once on the forest floor, I was aware of how vulnerable I was to any Morroks that might be lurking nearby. Looking over my shoulder every few seconds, I quieted my footsteps and approached the lone guard. I suppressed shudders as the cold, still air pressed in on my lungs. As I came up behind the Morrok, I could tell it was having similar symptoms. Barring myself from any empathy, I raised my sword and plunged it into its back.

The Morrok reacted so quickly that the blade hardly sank in an inch. It twisted away, hissing and drawing its war ax. Conscious of the Morrok's huge and uncaring feet, I wedged myself between it and the sack.

The Morrok swung at my side. I threw myself out of the way and landed on the ground with only a graze across my ribs. I was barely on my feet again before the Morrok was delivering another blow. Determined to lead it farther away from the woman in the sack, I danced backward, swinging my left arm behind me to warn me of any trees and keeping my sword arm steadily in front of me.

One arm wasn't enough to contend with a Morrok's strike, and so my plan came to an end as I met a heavy blow from its ax. We struggled for a moment, weapons locked, but it was obvious the Morrok would win. I slackened my grip and dove away again.

No longer satisfied with defensive strategy, I pushed off a nearby tree and drew my dagger. The Morrok easily batted away my outstretched sword, but I kept the rest of my body moving forward so I got close enough to pierce its side with the dagger.

The Morrok didn't react to the dagger at all except that there was new anger behind its strikes. I parried and dodged blow after blow, waiting for a new opportunity to attack. Finally, after several minutes, the Morrok stumbled, dropping one hand from its weapon to clutch at the dagger still buried in its side. Seizing perhaps my only opportunity, I threw all my weight into a thrust at the Morrok's chest. I drew the sword out quickly to cut its throat, but there was no need; the Morrok slumped over, either dead or fainted from blood loss.

Leaving the Morrok to suffer its death throes alone, I plucked my dagger from the Morrok's weak grip and wiped its blood from the blade in the soil by its side. Dagger still in hand, I scrambled over to the sack and sliced it open until it was in shreds.

Inside was a woman so bruised, bloody, and diminished that I couldn't begin to guess her age or what she might have looked like before becoming a prisoner of the Morroks. She had layers of thick, black hair that might have been smooth and beautiful if it hadn't been tangled, matted, and caked with blood. Like any Human who had spent years under Serenity Valley's canopy, her skin was pale, and what was left of her dress indeed looked like the dull-colored but well-made clothes of the forest Warriors. She was unnaturally thin, but my heart leaped when I saw her stomach rise and fall slowly. At least she was alive.

After gathering the wisp of a woman in my arms, I hurried in the direction of my camp. Images of my family fighting seven Morroks flashed through my mind. Each of my pounding footsteps sent a jolt of fear for their safety blazing from the soles of my boots to the forefront of my mind. I expected to hear the sounds of battle as I approached, but my ears were filled only with my own panting.

My anxiety was at its peak when I came upon our cluster of tents only to find a pile of dead Morroks and most of my family standing. Bloody, shocked, and horrified—but standing. Only a few cries of relief escaped the women before they all froze, gawking at me. I was so glad to see them myself that I forgot about my charge until Glynis gasped, "Orestes, who *is* that?"

I glanced down at the half-naked, bleeding woman in my arms. She seemed to be breathing still, but her head and limbs lolled lifelessly from her body.

"I don't know," I said, "but the Morroks had her. She needs help."

The camp sprang to life again. The woman was whisked out of my hands and taken to Levina's tent. Holt's wife, Abby, a skilled healer, appeared out of my tent and rushed to Levina's, calling for water and clean cloth. I caught Sylvia's arm as she passed and asked, "Who's in my tent?"

"Todd," she said. "He was the only one seriously hurt. Abby won't say . . . if he'll . . . he fought bravely."

With that, she dashed off on whatever errand she had been on. The rest of the men had busied themselves with hauling the Morroks' bodies farther away, whether for burying or burning or merely relieving us of their presence, I did not know. I promised to join them shortly, but not until I had seen Levina.

Just as I was about to call for her, she appeared in the camp, bearing damp cloths she had moistened in a stream nearby. She let out a dry sob when she saw me but held up her load as her excuse for not doing more. Satisfied that her jog betrayed no wound, I caught up with Fallon, Cyrus, Jacob, Holt, and Ritter, all of whom bore some bruises and abrasions but ignored them as if they were paper cuts. We dragged the huge corpses farther and farther from the camp, pretending the women's frantic instructions to one another didn't alarm us.

The night passed in the same way. The men took turns digging a hole for the Morroks and guarding the camp. The women flew from one tent to the other without giving us updates. No one really understood what was happening with the patients except Abby and Sylvia, but it was clear from the amount of time that they spent with Todd that he was the more serious case.

When we finished burying the Morroks, I expected to see the dawn sun peeking through the canopy, but the moon and stars showed no sign of giving up their places in the sky. Weary and resigned to acknowledging our own wounds, we washed and clumsily wrapped bandages around ourselves. We found the camp considerably quieter now that Abby had ordered the other women to bed. The men were similarly banished, but I heard everyone talking even after they retired to their tents. Since Abby, Sylvia, and Todd occupied mine, I sat outside in the middle of the gathering of tents listening to the hushed murmurs of their occupants. After a while, Levina came outside rubbing her eyes and wiping sweat from her brow.

Wordlessly, she dropped to the ground and hugged me. Too exhausted—both physically and emotionally—to speak, we sat there for a long time, alternating between embracing and kissing and listening to each other breathe. After a while, we broke apart. I expected to see Levina's eyes filled with tears, but there were none. Her face was rigid and determined, like it had been that night in her room at Warrior Peak when she had told me she was going to Serenity Valley no matter the obstacle.

I nodded to Levina's tent. "How is she?"

Levina gazed in the same direction and sighed. "She's sleeping. She opened her eyes for a few moments earlier but didn't say anything. Abby says there's nothing seriously wrong with her—no broken bones, just bruises that'll heal in time."

"Good."

"Orestes, what happened exactly? Todd came back from hunting without you and just told us to get ready to fight. He said we had to draw the Morroks away from you. I thought—we thought—that you were being attacked . . . that you wouldn't survive. . . ."

As briefly as I could, I told her what had happened. Sylvia's occasional coming and going from my tent always stopped me midsentence, but rather than giving us any information, she shook her head and continued with her task.

When I was finished, Levina told me what had occurred once Todd arrived at camp. "All he said was that you two found eight Morroks and that you were still with them. He gave Sylvia and Ritter your hunting bows and told them to follow us from above. He led us toward the Morroks, shouting and making as much noise as he could. Seven of them met us, but Sylvia and Ritter shot down two of them before they got close enough to fight. One Morrok had a bow, and he shot—"

"It."

"—it shot at Ritter and Sylvia while the other five attacked. We outnumbered them two to one, so we held them fairly well. Sylvia cried out, and we thought the Morrok archer had hit her, even through the canopy."

"She doesn't seem hurt."

"She's not," Levina said. "She said the arrow just came alarmingly close to her stomach, and she got scared because of the baby. She and Ritter couldn't see the forest floor, but the Morrok could tell where they were by the swaying branches. They were trying to find a way down when the arrow nearly hit Sylvia. That's when Todd went for the archer, all on his own, to give Ritter and Sylvia a chance to get away.

"I saw the Morrok slash him," she continued, shuddering. "It was diagonal, from his left shoulder to his right hip. Todd fell, and by then, Sylvia and Ritter made it down. Everyone saw Todd on the ground and went crazy. We killed them all—not quickly and not easily—but we did it."

Levina's voice fell, and I didn't know what to say. I couldn't help but feel that Todd's injury was my fault. He had rushed everyone into battle because I was too stubborn to return with him and plan a real strategy. I understood better than most Todd's unease with Morroks; he must have been panicked by the mere sight of them, but I had been too caught up in my own anger to assure him I wasn't going to attack all eight by myself.

Just as dawn finally muscled its way into the sky, Abby ducked out of my tent. Levina leaped to her feet, throwing me off-balance and waking me from my doze. I rose as well when Sylvia exited after Abby.

"He's gone," Abby choked, covering her face with her hands. Sylvia wrapped an arm around the woman and led her to her tent. Then, not glancing at either of us, Sylvia disappeared into her own tent, leaving Levina and me standing dumbfounded and unable to believe that less than twelve hours ago, we had been attending a wedding.

I tried to mourn for Todd, but all I felt was a burning in the pit of my stomach, in the back of my throat, in the tips of my fingers that rested on my sword. Not for the first time that night did several minutes pass without

Levina and me moving or speaking. And not for the first time did Levina voice what I felt inside when, dry-eyed, she whispered, "I hate them."

I gathered her into my arms again and let her cry until everyone else awoke and cried with her. I could never make my mouth say it, but all day long, the thought resounded as surely as I drew breath: "I hate them too."

Chapter Seventeen
The Empty Settlement

WE BURIED TODD THE SAME MORNING and left the place behind. Fallon and I each spoke a few words about him, and our testimonies agreed that he could have been a great leader one day. Although they would never admit it, no one else thought the same of Todd because they knew him only as a young soldier eager to please his superiors. Fallon had always seen through that, and I could tell he regretted not helping Todd grow to his potential. I too realized I had taken Todd for granted; I thought I didn't need a friend beyond Ritter and Levina, but as we traveled, Todd's absence drowned out all other company.

The only diversion from everyone's grief and anger was the new addition to our group. As the days passed and the bruises faded, it became clear that the woman I rescued was really a girl, no older than Levina and I. She slept the better part of her first few days with us, so the men took turns carrying her. On the fourth day, she walked on her own, though with a slight limp. Abby was the only person she spoke to, and even then it was only "yes" or "no" to her medical questions. Fallon was bursting to ask her a list of questions he recited to me at least twice a day, but Glynis refused to let him interrogate the girl while she was still in such a fragile state.

Yet even in her silence, the girl changed the dynamics of our group. Feeling it would be rude to leave her out, the women tried everything to include her in their conversations. Sylvia in particular carried on one-sided discourses with the girl for minutes on end, pausing every once in a while in hopes of receiving a response. At his wife's prompting, Ritter turned on his old charm to try to cajole the girl into speaking, but he gave up quickly when she only stared at him, expressionless. The rest of us men left her to her silence, though I dearly wanted to know her name. After a few days, her true white skin overcame most of the cuts and bruises on her face, and she began to remind me of a girl I had met one time or another at Warrior Peak, but I didn't have a name to put with the face.

A week after Todd's death, she finally spoke. The trees had thinned out to the point that there was no canopy, and the grass under our feet told us we were nearing the lake. Everyone was heartened, and Fallon hardly wanted to stop to sleep. Every day we traveled later and later, and the week after Todd died, it was completely dark by the time we stopped, had a brief dinner, and then crawled into our tents, exhausted.

On that night, the girl and I were the last two left outside. She was still eating her second helping, which delighted Abby, who said she had lost too much weight in too short a time to be healthy. I had first watch alone and was idly sharpening my sword in anticipation of a few hours of solitude. Assuming a girl who stayed silent for so long would have a similarly muted voice, I was surprised when she asked, her tone strong and clear, "Are you Orestes?"

Immediately losing interest in my sword, I put it aside and did my best not to look shocked that she had spoken. "Yes."

"I thought so."

I waited for her to say more, but, apparently satisfied, she went back to her food. Her silky hair fell forward and shielded her face from my view.

"Why do you say that?" I asked cautiously.

She returned my gaze and held it unblinkingly. "The Morroks often spoke about you. They never seemed to know which Human you were, only that you were one of the men in this group. At first, I didn't know why they were so concerned about you, but now that I see you, I think I do."

Although unnerved on many levels, I hid my curiosity enough simply to reply, "Why's that?"

"Your demeanor. It's like a Morrok, in a way. Intense. The way you walk—with purpose, determination, like no one could stop you even if he wanted to. And if you're not talking or engaged with other people, the look in your eyes—so distant, so sad, almost angry. Well, the Morroks are angry. Perhaps with you, it's passion."

"What's the difference?" I asked, trying to keep my voice steady. I wished she had never spoken. For the past thirteen years, I had worked hard to separate myself from the Morroks, but now a complete stranger was telling me I reminded her of them.

"Unbidden anger like theirs comes from long-standing bitterness or fear, I think," the girl replied. Her fork was halfway to her mouth, but she seemed to have forgotten it in her pondering. I couldn't believe she could speak of her tormenters so lightly. "Only a person whole enough to be dedicated to something has passion, whether it's for a person or place or cause of some sort."

"Can't you hate something or someone enough to call it a passion? That sort of passion would be along the same lines as anger."

"Perhaps," she replied thoughtfully. "I always thought of passion as something positive, though, like as in the passion of a master for his craft. The passion of a crusader to his cause. The passion of a lover."

Unsure of how to respond to that, I went back to my sword sharpening. I mentally ran through Fallon's list of questions for her but couldn't pick one that wouldn't scare her off from talking to me again. Instead, I decided to return to her earlier observations, however much I hated them. "You say that I remind you of a Morrok and that that's why the Morroks are so 'concerned' about me. But why would Morroks be concerned about someone like themselves?"

"It's obvious, isn't it?" the girl asked, her eyebrows rising. "The only real threat to Morroks is their own kind. Humans can't stand up to them. I mean, look at what happened to that man in your group who died when he tried to fight a Morrok all on his own. . . ."

My face must have betrayed my horror at her statement because she immediately clapped her hands over her mouth.

"Oh, I'm so sorry," she whispered. "It's been so long. . . . I mean, you forget decorum—not even decorum . . . sensitivity, any sort of humanity—after being around Morroks for so long. I'm so sorry. I'm sure your friend was a brave man, and I would never—"

"Don't worry about it," I mumbled, knowing her words to be all too true. "So how long were you with the Morroks?"

The girl pursed her lips and looked away. Cursing myself for attempting one of Fallon's questions, I opened my mouth to tell her to forget it, but the girl spoke first, though she stared at her empty plate rather than at me.

"I lost count of the days," she answered, her voice barely audible. "It felt like longer than it actually was, I'm sure. It was more than a year but probably less than three. I don't know . . . just one long nightmare. . . ."

I was burning to ask her where she had come from or how she came into the Morroks' possession or especially why they had kept her alive, but I knew I had already gone too far. We sat in silence for a few moments before she rose, piled her dishes with the others, and strode toward Levina's tent. Levina's dress hung oddly on her figure; it was too short in length, too broad in the shoulders, too big in the waist, and not big enough in other areas. Just before she entered the tent, I blurted, "What's your name?"

She froze as if I had shouted an insult at her. Turning back to me, she scrutinized me for a moment as if suspicious about why I asked. "Cassandra," she replied finally.

"Cassandra," I repeated, closing my eyes and listening to the tent flap close behind her. "I've never heard that name before."

*

The next morning brought what we had been working toward for more than two months: the lake. I was the first to see it as the sun rose. I hadn't slept all night. Cassandra's words had echoed in my head as I paced the dark camp hundreds of times, trying to brace myself against a suffocating cold that lifted only when the early risers crawled out of their tents. We had settled comically close to the lake not to have noticed it the night before. For the lake was colossal; from half a mile away, we could see that its shoreline extended beyond our vision. With excitement unbecoming of people our age, we packed our tents in record time and sped toward the hazy horizon that only a great body of water could create.

For everyone—except Sylvia and maybe Cassandra, who hadn't grown up among mountains—the lake was fascinating. Out from under the cover of any tree, it sat unguarded by anything but millions of tiny blades of grass and unabashed in the middle of a country in which the trees meant everything to its inhabitants. The lake truly seemed to have no end; not only did the shore under our feet stretch beyond our imagination just like the mountains in the north, but we also saw no evidence that the water ever stopped, like the oceans we had read about as children.

Much to Fallon's distress, everyone dropped their packs and waded waist-deep into the water, exclaiming at the cold and at the strange sensation of being enveloped in liquid. Most of us laughed aloud when Cassandra marched straight through our ranks and dove headfirst under the water. After a few moments of complete submergence, her head popped up several feet away, too far for any of us to walk to her. Feeling suddenly inadequate, I realized I would have to learn how to swim if I was going to spend any amount of time around the lake.

Sylvia surprised us all more than Cassandra when we heard a beating of wings from the edge of the water. Mumbling about damp feathers and a pregnant belly, she had refused to come farther than ankle deep, and now, without a word, she was rising above us and squinting southward.

Ritter shielded his eyes against the early-morning sun to follow her movement. "What do you see?"

"I don't know," she called back. "A tower maybe? I don't think it's a tree. Too big and too isolated."

I froze and reached reflexively for my sword even though it was piled with our bags on the shore. "Can you see the color?"

"No," Sylvia answered, "it's too far away. If I had to guess, I'd say black, but again, that could be due to the distance. Why?"

"Fallon, we need to leave!" I shouted over my own splashing toward the shore. The Morrok's words from a week ago, their meaning now painfully obvious, rang in my ears: "We're close to the lake, and we can't have the Humans finding us before we get to the fortress." The Serenial had warned us about this months ago—the fortress by the lake. But what were the chances that we would exit the trees this close to it? And why was it a tower, a Facility tower just like in Tyrclopia?

Fallon, who had just given in to the lake's distraction, took my distress to heart and ordered everyone out of the water. Sylvia landed just as we reached shore, shaking water from ourselves like animals and scrambling for our bags. Between slinging packs on their backs and strapping weapons to their waists, everyone, including Fallon, threw me bewildered glances, but I ignored them all. Only Levina mimicked me in staring in the direction of the tower, but I couldn't see even the shape of a building.

"Hawk eyes," Sylvia whispered in my ear.

I roused from my stupor and stared at her. She tapped the corner of her own eye and winked.

In no mood for Sylvia's comparison of Human sight to Serenial, I made my way to Fallon. "We were going to go along the northern edge of the lake anyway, right?"

He nodded. "Yes, that's what I had planned. We should come across Settlement One today or maybe tomorrow depending on our pace."

"Let's make it today. The Morrok fortress we've heard rumors of—I think that tower is it."

"Then we'd best put some distance between us and it."

"As if distance will stop them," I muttered.

"Delay is what I'm aiming for," Fallon said with a grim smile. "I think we all know the inevitability of our circumstances by now, don't you?"

At Fallon's command, we set off at a brisk march. I dropped to the rear of the group as Fallon explained my suspicions to the rest. The tree line was probably our biggest threat. We would be able to see any Morroks coming from ahead or behind, and I didn't think Morroks could swim. Then again, all the Morroks I had known lived in a desert.

"Did the colonel say Settlement One?" a voice to my right asked.

Again startled out of my musings, I glanced down to see Cassandra walking next to me with the tent she and Levina shared packed on her back. It was heartening to see that she was healthy enough to start pitching in; now a weapon was all she needed to look like one of the group.

"Yes, do you know it?" I asked.

"Yes."

I almost laughed at how difficult it was to talk to this girl. "Um, *how* do you know it?"

"That's where I . . . it's my home."

"Really? That's great. I'm sure your family will be thrilled to know you're ali—that you're safe."

"If they're still alive," Cassandra murmured.

"What do you mean?"

She started to answer but faltered, and I knew I had asked the wrong question again.

"Well, we'll be there soon enough, and you'll have a great reunion," I said bracingly. "So you never lived at Warrior Peak then? Never even visited?"

"No."

"I could've sworn I'd met you before, or maybe you just look like a girl who was in school the same time as I was. I think she was younger though—how old are you?"

"What's the date?"

I shrugged as well as I could with all my packs. "Latter part of the year 326. Maybe the three hundredth day or so."

"Then I'm eighteen, I guess, or at least close to it."

"Oh. That's how old Levina and I are."

Cassandra didn't say anything to that. We walked in silence for a few moments before she drifted ahead, apparently having gotten all she wanted from me. Upon reflection, I realized Levina probably would have asked Cassandra about her family and her home to try to make her feel better. Maybe Cassandra would know better than to talk to me from now on.

The day passed in a blur of nervous energy. Always glancing behind in fear of a group of pursuing Morroks, we alternated between walking and jogging and never stopped for a meal or rest. I couldn't stop thinking about the tower even though I hadn't seen it. Instead, images from my childhood flickered in and out of my mind—the black tower, set at the bottom of a deep and perpetually unfilled dune. From the base of it, the tower seemed taller than possible to build. From the top of the dune, the tower seemed both to plunge into the earth and to pierce the clouds, as if it connected the sky and whatever was below the sand, as if the land would break apart without it.

"Is that a building?" Glynis asked wearily late into the afternoon.

We raised our heads with equal enthusiasm and mumbled a cheer of assent. Fallon quickened his pace, and the rest of us were forced to keep up.

"Shall I fly ahead, Colonel?" Sylvia offered.

"No, the sight of a Serenial would alarm them. Thank you though."

As we drew near, Settlement One looked much the same as the other settlements except for its size. As the oldest settlement in the forest, the village had grown to twice the size of the ones we had seen. The outer walls had been reinforced at least once so that they were as strong as Settlements Six and Eleven now were. In addition to the original structure, new wings had been built on so that the village formed an odd *t* shape. The farmland outside the settlement walls was nearly as large as the settlement itself, and it also had tall fences surrounding it to protect the crops from animals. Fallon, Cyrus, Jacob, and Holt murmured their approval to one another as we approached the outer doors of the village.

"I wonder why no one's tending the fields," Levina said.

"Maybe harvest is over," I said, though I was unnerved too.

Fallon pounded on one of the doors and stepped back. We all glanced up at the parapets, expecting a sentry or gatekeeper to ask us for identification. No one appeared. Fallon knocked again, this time more insistently.

"Sylvia, fly over and see if anyone's inside," Fallon said after several minutes of agonizing silence.

Ritter looked unhappy at his pregnant wife going over alone, but Sylvia unfurled her great auburn wings and soon disappeared to the other side of the wall. A few tense moments passed in which I half expected to hear a scream of pain. Ritter seemed to fear the same because he drew two daggers and marched toward the wall, ready to scale it. Luckily Sylvia flew into sight again and perched on the parapet above us.

"There's no one in here, Colonel," she reported. "No one on the streets at least. I tried to peek into a few windows, but the curtains were drawn. Shall I try to break into a house?"

"No," Fallon and Ritter barked simultaneously. Ritter grinned sheepishly and held out his hands to Fallon in supplication. Fallon continued, "Ritter and Orestes will climb over and help you open the gate."

Ritter and I shrugged off our packs, and I drew my dagger as well. Jacob produced a rope that hardly looked thick enough to support our weight, but we took it without protest. Sylvia descended, took one end of the rope, and resumed her place on the rampart.

"It's tied tight," she said a moment later and threw out the slack. Holt and I lifted Ritter as high as we could, and he clambered up the rest of the way, using the rope and knives for support. I did the same with the added help of Ritter and Sylvia hauling the rope up toward them.

A few minutes later, we had the doors opened enough for the rest of our group to file inside. Before Fallon could give us orders, Cassandra drifted away from the cluster and down one of the streets of houses. Her eyes were clouded over, and her mouth hung open in apparent shock. Her limp was suddenly gone, and she seemed to float away from us, her dark hair billowing with each step as the only proof that her feet still touched the ground.

"I'll go with her," I said. No one objected, so I followed her at a jog. She didn't turn around as I approached, and I heard her counting as we passed each house. Finally, when we were almost to the end of the street, she turned and walked up to one of the houses. Her hand rested on the latch of the door as she leaned on the wood and simply breathed, her eyes closed. I thought she was about to faint, but before I could get close enough to check, she pushed open the door and glided inside. Concerned, I followed.

The house we entered seemed frozen in time. The front room was furnished with cushioned chairs, couches, and rugs. A half-sewn cloak with a needle and pins sticking out of it lay across a small table. Hand-carved dolls wearing homespun dresses sat in a semicircle on the floor with a gap wide enough for a little girl lying on her stomach to play with them. Another doll, shaped but not painted, topped a pile of woodchips and a whittling knife in the corner. I absorbed all of this and tried to quell the horror rising inside me. There was no blood, and not a piece of furniture was overturned. But Morroks hardly ever left a trace if they didn't want to.

Cassandra proceeded through the room, skirting furniture with a familiarity that told me that this was her home. She disappeared into the back room, and I heard the narrow staircase creak as she ascended.

Hand on the pummel of my sword, I poked my head out to the street again. My family ran in and out of houses without Cassandra's reverence.

"Is there no one here?" I asked in hushed tones as Glynis passed.

"Not that we can find. But there are no signs of struggle, except that I've noticed empty weapon hooks in every house. Perhaps the battle took place outside the village."

"And the children taken when their parents lost."

Glynis nodded, her eyes filled with tears.

A moment later, Fallon jogged down the street. He paused when he saw Glynis and me. "Anything to report?"

We both shook our heads.

"As soon as we make sure there's no one here, we will proceed to Settlement Eight with all haste. Maybe they will know what happened."

"I think it's obvious what happened," I said.

"They could have abandoned their village to join the others," Fallon replied.

"Without taking anything but weapons?" I said. "Besides, this has to be the best village around the lake—large, well-fortified . . ."

"Fallon," Glynis said before an argument could break out, "what if . . . what if they're all deserted—every village? What would we do? We would have no hope standing up to the Morroks—"

"We can't think that far ahead, my dear," Fallon said gently. He put a hand on each of our shoulders, and for a moment, we were father, mother, and son again, not Colonel Fallon and two of his subordinates. "Finish checking this street for any clues, and we'll meet back at the doors."

With that, our link was broken; Fallon jogged off again to check on the others, and Glynis trudged to the next house. I reentered Cassandra's.

This time I strode past the front room and went to the stairway in the back. On the second level, I found the four small, dim rooms characteristic of forest Warrior houses. One of the doors was open, and inside I found Cassandra on her knees in the middle of the room, her head bowed. I would not have known she was crying except that the hands in her lap were soaked with tears.

"Cassandra?" I said.

She lifted her head and stared at me, her lifeless amber eyes still leaking their silent tears.

"We have to . . . we have to leave. We have to get to Settlement Eight. Fallon thinks that this village might have been deserted by choice. There's still hope. . . . We have to make sure."

She continued to stare. I wanted to say or do something to comfort her, but I couldn't think of how to do either. My more pragmatic side was concerned just with figuring out how to get her to move.

Luckily I didn't have to act at all as Cassandra rose to her feet. With an air of dignity beyond her years, she picked up a bag and circled the room, gathering what I realized must have been her belongings—clothes, personal care items, and the like. Last of all she thrust an arm under her bed and produced a short, curved sword encased in a scabbard without a speck of dust on it. She arranged these possessions on her body and marched to where I stood in the doorway. After gently ushering her into the hallway, I shut the door behind us and sighed. I wanted to tell Cassandra that I understood what it felt like for the Morroks to terrorize her and take everything from her. But my shame crippled me yet again, and I contented myself in following her down the stairs and respecting her silence as I wished no one ever would have respected mine.

Chapter Eighteen
The Outpost

NIGHT HAD FALLEN BY THE TIME we reached Settlement Eight. Even from the outside, we could see that it was different from Settlement One because the farmlands were overgrown with weeds as if they hadn't been plowed in years. When Fallon knocked at the outer doors, no one answered. Ritter, Sylvia, and I repeated our procedure for opening the village, and we made a quick sweep of all the houses. We found no Humans again, but unlike Settlement One, everything of value was gone. After several minutes of searching for clues, we gathered again at the town's entrance. We were exchanging exclamations of bewilderment and suggestions for future action when Ritter and Sylvia reentered the settlement from the outside. In our confusion, no one had noticed they had left.

"Fallon, isn't Settlement Twelve supposed to be a few hours south of here?" Ritter asked.

"Yes. Why?"

"Well, there's a great structure within eyesight—even our eyesight," Ritter replied, gesturing to us Humans instead of Sylvia. "It's bigger than Settlement One—almost like a city."

"But is it a Human structure?" Fallon asked.

"It is, sir," Sylvia said. "I flew ahead a bit and saw sentries marching around the ramparts. It really is a magnificent place. Hundreds of buildings inside a great stone wall. Room enough for thousands of people."

Fallon sighed in relief. "Finally something to rejoice about. Let's go, everyone."

Stumbling with exhaustion but too close to quit, we abandoned Settlement Eight and headed south. It was hard to believe we had missed Sylvia and Ritter's discovery before we entered Settlement Eight. Even in the dark and at a distance, the walls of this new settlement were taller than we thought possible to build in the forest. Neat stone blocks stood at least three stories above us, and thin, sturdy watchtowers rose out of each of the four corners. Spiked parapets lined the entirety of the thick ramparts with gaps between just wide enough to shoot arrows through. As we neared, we saw that the front gates faced the lake and that the entire structure was bordered by rivers on either side and by the forest in the back.

When we reached the thick wooden gates, we did not have to knock, because the sentries had already seen us. Two faces peered down at us from over the top of the parapets.

"Declare yourselves," one of them called.

"I am Colonel Fallon, and I have with me twelve others."

"Colonel Fallon of the Intelligence division at Warrior Peak?"

"Yes."

"Just a moment, sir."

We were left standing outside the gate for so long that we thought they had forgotten about us. One by one, we slumped to the ground and leaned on our packs, almost too tired to stay awake. Fallon was the only one left standing when the double doors began to creak open. We nudged each other and hauled ourselves to our feet, picking up our packs for what we hoped would be the last time.

The reason for the delay became apparent once we had squeezed through the partially opened doors. Ten older men dressed in their pajamas with military coats thrown hastily over them stood before us in greeting. They each held a candle and torch, which lit up our gathering as if it were daylight.

"Welcome, Colonel. We've been waiting to hear from you," one of the men said. He stood half a step ahead of the rest, and his coat was the most decorated with the small, intricate stitching of Serenity Valley's crest on it. "How many are in your group? Thirteen? That's enough that you can have your own house. Corporal!" A fully dressed sentry appeared, bearing yet another torch. "Take these people to one of the empty houses closest to the fort. Will eight rooms be enough, Colonel?"

"Yes," Fallon replied.

The whole party moved farther into settlement, and a few sentries shoved the doors shut behind us. The corporal whom the leader had called continued straight ahead along a line of houses, but the other men veered right across an open field. Fallon waved the rest of the family on with the corporal, but he caught me by the arm.

"Come with us," he said.

I followed the old men past a few buildings larger than any of the mess halls of the other settlements, past a huge, open pin of livestock, and finally to a great stone building toward the rear of the entire settlement. It was the stone building that we entered, and I barely lifted my head to gaze around the interior before we swept into a small room in the corner of the building.

After I closed the door behind us, the men spread their torches and candles around the room to reveal the space as square, undecorated, and filled only with a long table and a dozen or so chairs. Fallon and I waited for the other men to sit before we took the remaining chairs at end of the table opposite of the man who appeared to be their leader. He was a stocky man with a square face and dark hair shaved so short that he appeared almost bald. A raised scar ran along his left jaw line.

"Colonel Fallon," the leader exhaled, "my name is Mark, and I am the general of this place, which we call the Outpost. The people who live here are from Settlements Two, Eight, Twelve, and the survivors of Settlements One, Five, and Nine—though I must admit that there are not many to speak of from One and Nine."

Fallon absorbed all of this without visible reaction. I couldn't fathom how, though, because I was still trying to remember where exactly all those settlements were located.

After a pause, Fallon said, "Well, General, I'm afraid I don't recognize your name, and I was unaware that there was a general in the forest."

"No, sir, I don't expect you to know my name or acknowledge my title. In Warrior Peak's eyes, I am a civilian, but the hardships we've seen in the forest have forced us to organize ourselves as an army."

"I understand, and I trust that you are acting in the spirit of the Peak in doing these things," Fallon replied. "However, I am at a loss as to how all of this has occurred without my knowing. Up until two years ago, I have had regular contact with all twelve settlements, and I have heard nothing about the Outpost, your new hierarchy, or the apparent destruction of some of the settlements. I assume that this is all due to the Morroks, but there was never a report of Morrok activity in the forest; in fact, we did not know about them at the Peak until two years ago. I doubt you could have built this settlement and formed your government in only two years."

Mark shook his head. "No, sir, this is the result of decades of work, almost since the founding of Settlement One. The Morroks have been attacking our people for generations. From the first, our fathers sent messengers to the Peak to warn you as much as to cry for relief. It took a few years before they realized that anyone who had knowledge of the Morrok presence in Serenity Valley was killed. The Morroks hid themselves whenever your groups came through the forest, and we knew better than to tell them of our plight for fear of their lives being lost."

"But surely my messengers would have seen this building?" Fallon said.

Mark smiled humorlessly. "We put on quite a charade whenever your people came through the forest. We kept Settlement One filled at all times because that's the only one your groups visited. If they were coming from the west, they always went to Six, Eleven, then One, or if they were coming from the east, they went to Ten, Seven, Three, Four, then One because they could just as easily pick up the other lake settlements' reports from One as visit them individually."

"How could the Morroks know whether or not the messengers knew about them?" I asked.

"That we don't know," Mark said. He turned and looked me in the eye as he answered, and I knew then that I liked him. "My guess is that they allowed Fallon's groups through the forest so that no one at the Peak would be suspicious. We knew that most groups made it through because we would always ask about the previous messengers under the guise that we had grown close to them during their stay."

"So am I to understand that for years all the status reports my messengers gave me from the settlements were made up?" Fallon asked.

"Yes, sir," Mark replied, unapologetic. "It was necessary, Colonel. Did the other settlements ever mention anything of significance?"

"What, the ones to the east and west?" Fallon said. "No, nothing about their reports ever raised an alarm at the Peak. Are you not in contact with Six and Eleven to the west and with Three, Four, Seven, and Ten to the east?"

"No, sir. All our attempts to reach them have failed, and if they ever tried to contact us, we did not know. Have you visited any of them, Colonel? Actually, we'd like to hear how you yourself came to the forest in the first place, sir, if you don't mind."

For the next hour or so, Fallon and I related what had happened at Warrior Peak ever since Todd brought news of the Morroks being in the desert. A bear of a man named Frank, who had been the leader of Settlement One, remembered Todd from his visit to the village more than two years before. We couldn't determine if Todd's group had learned a piece of information the Morroks didn't want to reach the Peak, but then I remembered that the Morroks that had attacked Todd's group had let him go on purpose to tell the Peak that they existed. Frank also reported that it was shortly after the departure of Todd's group that Settlement One was attacked.

"Everyone was killed," Frank sighed, shaking his head. His long, gray ponytail flopped from shoulder to shoulder. "I left one evening to tell Mark that your people were on their way back to the Peak. The next morning, I came back to find the settlement ravaged. All the adults were dead and all the children disappeared. We gave the adults a proper burial and cleaned the settlement in case we needed to fill it again for the benefit of more messengers. No one would live there again though; it was too dangerous for so small a purpose."

"Do you remember a girl named Cassandra?" I asked him.

Frank thought for a moment. "Oh yes, of course I do. She often acted as recorder for our meetings. Stunningly beautiful girl—always distracted our younger council members. Hers was actually the one body we did not find."

"That's because she lived," I said. "We found her not a week ago being held captive by a group of Morroks."

"What wonderful news that she is alive! I'll have to speak to her later."

Fallon and I continued our tale. The men listened in silence, merely nodding their heads as if they expected us to report as such. They were, however, shocked to learn about the existence of Serenial. They couldn't believe they had overlooked Sylvia's odd appearance when we had arrived earlier and insisted that they meet her the next day. Like any good military council, they wanted to know if there was any hope of gaining the Serenial as allies, but I assured them that we weren't likely ever to see a Serenial other than the one already within our walls.

The men were also surprised that Settlements Six and Eleven had never heard of Morroks, but they attributed this to the Morroks amassing in the central Valley and spreading across the Gravel Lands before they looked to the rest of the forest. Guessing at the Morroks' strategy inevitably led to strategy talk of our own. The one unanimous opinion was that we needed to gather all the forest Warriors together in one place so we could either root the Morroks out of the desert or fight our way back to Warrior Peak or both.

"Settlements Six and Eleven should be traveling this way by now," Fallon said. "That leaves Three, Four, Seven, and Ten. The latter two are quite a problem because they are months away; however, Settlement Four is only about ten days from here, correct?"

"Yes, sir," answered one of the men who hadn't introduced himself.

"I propose we send a platoon—perhaps three dozen soldiers—to escort them here. Your men are trained, aren't they?"

"Yes, sir," Mark said. "The large opening right inside the gate is our training grounds. All the children are schooled daily, and all adults are required to prove their continued skills with a blade at least once a month. The more talented the fighter, the higher the rank in our society."

"Excellent," Fallon said. "I would like Lieutenant Orestes here to lead that platoon to Settlement Four. Although I have great confidence in your officers, Orestes is well-versed in traveling through the forest, and he is unmatched in his fighting skills, particularly against Morroks."

The other men glanced at me with new interest as I tried to keep my face impassive in spite of hearing Fallon both praise me and randomly assign me a military title in the space of a few seconds.

"Very well," Mark said. "When would you like to leave, Lieutenant?"

I opened my mouth, but nothing came out for a moment. Not only had I never been in charge of others, but this mission was as new to me as it was to them. "I'd like to spend a few days here to get my bearings," I said finally. "Perhaps we could leave three days from now? Does that give you enough time to gather the platoon, General?"

"I could have them tomorrow if you'd like, but I understand the need for rest and orientation. I expect this will be your home for some time. And on that note, Colonel," Mark continued, shifting his attention to Fallon, "you have brought yourself and twelve others, some with titles, into a world where those titles have different meanings. As I said, I am a civilian at Warrior Peak, but I have been elected a general in the forest. How do you propose we resolve these differences?"

Fallon smiled the smile of a proud teacher. Mark was impressing him with every word that came from his mouth. "General, it sounds like you have done an amazing job of keeping our people alive and united against our enemy, and I would never take that away from you. I would like Orestes and myself to be on this council, but you will maintain your leadership. As for the rest of my group—they will work for the good of the settlement wherever you place them. They are all very talented, and I trust you to use them to their best advantage."

"Thank you, sir. I cannot tell you how glad I am to hear you say that," Mark replied. "You and Lieutenant Orestes are more than welcome on this council; in fact, I would object if you didn't participate. But for now, let us dismiss; you've had a long journey."

We all stood and shook hands before we left the room. Outside, Mark found a note from the corporal from the night before, which told him in which house our family now resided. Mark walked us out of the stone building and pointed us to a row of houses nearby. Although the sky was turning gray with the first signs of daylight, Mark bade us good night and left for his own home.

"Lieutenant, huh?" I laughed as soon as Mark was out of earshot.

"At Warrior Peak, that is the highest ranking I can give you by my own authority," Fallon replied. He began to march in the direction of our house without looking at me.

"Since when do I get to come to meetings and lead a troop of soldiers?" I pressed.

"You're old enough now."

"Since when does age give you magical leadership abilities?"

Fallon stopped walking abruptly and grabbed me by both shoulders. "Orestes, I need you to be in the thick of things now. There's no denying your influence on the Morroks and vice versa. Your name has spread throughout this forest among Morroks and Serenial alike. They have made you an entity in this war, and I think you're up for the challenge of it. You are not a child anymore, and it's probably best that no one knows I've been your father these past thirteen years. You are a lieutenant at Warrior Peak and will be more here, and these people must know that you have achieved these things by your own merit. You need the freedom and respect to act as you feel is necessary, and I am helping you to receive that freedom. Do you understand?"

Bewildered, I blinked at him several times. When had he decided all this? "Yes, Colonel," I replied faintly.

"Very good, Lieutenant."

I trudged after Fallon in a daze, and within moments, we had arrived at our house. The homes were two stories like typical settlement dwellings, but the roofs were flat. Inside both floors were exactly the same: a narrow hallway with four rooms branching off. We poked our heads in the first-floor rooms and found that the older adults had claimed them. Fallon joined Glynis, and I proceeded up the stairs. Ritter and Sylvia had taken one room, and Cassandra and Levina each had their own; the last door I tried was empty except for a bed, a small table, and a chair. Too exhausted to undress, I flopped down on the bed and remembered no more.

*

By the time I woke the next morning, everyone else had risen and left the house. It took me a few moments to remember where I was, and when I did, I dressed as quickly as I could and ran outside.

It was nearly midday, and the Outpost was alive with activity. Although the housing area was deserted, I heard voices from every other direction; I picked one and followed.

Next to the fort (as the stone building we had met in last night seemed to be called) was the back of a long building that seemed to run half the length of the settlement. I walked along the back of the building, putting my ear up to the wall every few steps to try to guess what was inside. As I neared the end of the building, I knew that at least part of it was used as a blacksmith.

When I rounded the corner, I wasn't disappointed. A similar long building ran parallel to the first, creating a narrow street that was filled with people carrying all sorts of wares and goods. Curious, I squeezed my way through and earned several curious stares along the way. Even in a settlement of more than a thousand people, a new face stood out quickly.

The street between the two buildings seemed to be the place to buy anything one would ever need. There was a blacksmith, a carpenter, a tailor, and many goods to be sold or distributed; I couldn't tell if the Outpost had some sort of currency or not. I saw some people exchanging paper notes for products, but the jeweler accepted my old Warrior Peak coins for a necklace that caught my eye.

After running the gauntlet of the market street, I wandered farther away from the fort and found myself on the training grounds Mark had mentioned the night before. True to his word, there were hundreds of children in groups all around the field. For a moment, I felt I was back at Warrior Peak. The smallest children sat on the ground touching weapons for the first time while their teachers rattled off safety procedures. Slightly older children were studying the most elementary battle strategies and looking longingly at the teenagers, who were dueling one another or shooting targets lined along the settlement wall.

Not surprisingly, most of my family walked among the children, observing their training with approving nods. Levina spotted me from several feet away and wove through several sparring matches to greet me with a hug and a kiss. Her face was shining.

I laughed. "You're in a good mood."

"It's wonderful here, Orestes. It's more than we could have ever hoped for. You missed the tour this morning, but oh, it's exactly what we need! The walls are high and strong, and there's enough food stored in here to keep more than two thousand people fed for months. Even if the walls are breached, the fort in the back is made completely of stone, and the armory and infirmary are already in the fort, so it's the perfect place for a last stand if the worst should—"

"So this place can handle a siege," I said, grinning at her enthusiasm. "Go on."

"Well, let me give you the tour myself, and I'll tell you all about it."

Levina escorted me to every corner of the Outpost. In the few hours I had wasted on sleep, she had become an expert on the storage barns, livestock pins, kitchens, mess halls, armories, infirmary, and every other feature I didn't convince her I had already seen.

By day, the interior of the fort seemed to be the most hectic place in the settlement. Although the Outpost used currency, many of a person's needs could be taken care of by applying at the fort's offices for his or her desired object, including a new sword, military uniform clothing, and even a place to live. Most of the offices in the fort would have fit in the Inventory division at Warrior Peak, and indeed, the extent of the Outpost's organization would have made the most meticulous Inventory officer proud.

I expected the midday meal to be pandemonium, but Levina explained that everyone ate in shifts and took turns helping in the kitchen. The mess halls were nothing more than three open-air buildings that had long rows of benches and roofs overhead in case of rain. Levina and I met several new people just by sitting on the same bench for an hour. They were as delighted to hear about the Peak as we were to hear about day-to-day life at the Outpost. Everyone, including Levina, was surprised to hear me introduce myself as Lieutenant Orestes, but I told Levina I would explain later and hoped that the rest thought me older than I was.

After eating, we strolled along the ramparts, and I signed up for regular shifts of guard duty. Levina didn't have quite as much to say about the exterior, so I had a chance to fill her in on the previous night's events. I must not have explained something correctly, though, because Levina was thrilled when I told her about my promotion and upcoming mission to Settlement Four. It was only after I mentioned Fallon's flouting of his role as my father that she seemed to realize I didn't really know what to do with my new position.

"Will you come with me?" I asked finally. We had wandered out of the Outpost, over the bridge of one of the rivers, and to the fields beyond, where yet more people worked in the hot afternoon sun.

"To Settlement Four?"

"Yes. I'm going to have more than thirty people that I've never met under me. I doubt Ritter will go since Sylvia's getting bigger and should be resting, and Cyrus and Jacob and the rest probably have jobs by now. . . . Hell, I just want you to come."

I watched Levina struggle with herself, torn between looking stern at my cursing and being flattered by what I was asking.

"Fine, I'll go," she said, "but I have something to ask you too."

"Go ahead."

"I—I found my parents," she said, her voice suddenly small. "This morning I asked around in the fort offices, and someone told me that they moved here years ago with the rest of Settlement Twelve. I have their house number. . . ."

"Then let's meet them. Tomorrow evening before we leave. I'll track them down earlier in the day so they aren't shocked when we show up at their door. It'll be great, I promise."

"Thank you," she whispered.

"Now let's find Cassandra. I want to learn how to swim, don't you?"

"You're going to be leading a troop of soldiers into a Morrok-infested forest in less than two days, and all you want to do is swim?"

"Of course. Besides, Cassandra needs a friend."

Levina hesitated a moment before answering. "All right, let's go."

Chapter Nineteen

Reunions

My second day at the Outpost was not quite as leisurely as the first. Fallon roused me at sunrise for a council meeting that resulted in obsessive, fruitless speculation about what we would do once we gathered the settlements: either attack the lake fortress or attack the Gravel Lands Facility. After two hours of trying to remind them of the insanity of attacking the Morroks at all, I gave in to the possibility and cast my vote for attacking the Gravel Lands because it was the largest, most central gathering. But the condition to that plan was that we needed Warrior Peak to attack from the north simultaneously as we attacked from the south. That would mean we needed to communicate with the Peak, and while the Morroks had an ever-firming grip on the desert, this did not seem likely.

"What if we sent the Serenial? Couldn't she just fly over them?" Frank, the former leader of Settlement One, suggested.

"She can't fly indefinitely, Colonel," I said. "It took us half a week to walk the desert. She couldn't make it without landing, and they'd kill her when she did. Besides, she's pregnant."

"Point taken, Lieutenant."

"Even if we do find a way to contact the Peak," Mark said, "what's to say that the forest Morroks won't attack us from behind when we march on the Gravel Lands?"

"It depends on how many Morroks are in the forest," Fallon said. "There may not be as many as we fear, and we don't know how spread out they are. The size of the forest is not a problem particular to us Humans."

"There might be a way to find out," I murmured, more to myself than the others, but all eyes turned to me. Aldis's voice filled my ears—stories of how Zachaes and Xander had sauntered into the Facility without harm coming to them. Also I remembered my rescue—how Acules was allowed to leave the

Facility unharmed and managed to kidnap three children along the way. Perhaps I would receive similar immunity. . . .

"Lieutenant?"

Suddenly jerked back to the present, I shook my head. "If we don't think of a solution before I come back from Settlement Four, then I will tell you my thinking. It would be quite risky."

They seemed to want me to elaborate, but I said no more. Fallon nodded his approval. Perhaps this was the freedom to act that he wanted to give me. I looked away from him.

"On that note," Mark said, "let us go to our own tasks. It must be mid-morning by now."

"We really need a window in here," one man grumbled as we filed out. I had a feeling someone said this at least once a meeting, and I made a mental note to uphold the tradition next council.

Before leaving the fort, I went to the office that assigned everyone's weekly duties to find Levina's parents. The council room was actually a very small portion of the fort. Most of the building was dedicated to emergency food and weapon storage, and the rest was filled with offices that took care of civil matters. The lines of people who needed to visit these offices stretched all the way outside the fort, but I decided to abuse my council position to cut in front. I scanned the list of everyone's jobs and found that Levina's mother was a regular cook and her father was a low-ranking officer who oversaw adult fighting skill checkups. I also found my name on the list for sentry duty that night.

Since the kitchen was directly across from the fort, I decided to visit Levina's mother. Even though breakfast had ended and the midday meal was still a few hours away, the shouts and bustle of the kitchen reached me even before I opened the door. When I crossed the threshold, the heat immediately slapped a layer of sweat onto my forehead, and the smell of smoke made me sneeze a few times in spite of the many chimneys. Dozens of ovens lined the walls, several long tables loaded with food sat in the middle, and hundreds of pots and trays were scattered on counters, hearths, stoves, and the floor.

It was obvious who the regular cooks were because they were the only ones who stood in one place. In contrast, the weekly helpers dashed to and fro, bringing the cooks wood for the stoves, ingredients for stew, flavor for drinks, and spices for meat. Most of the helpers were old enough not to spill anything but young enough not to know they were being taken advantage of.

I caught one such helper by the arm as he hurried toward the door, doubtlessly to fetch something from the separate storage building behind the kitchen.

"Could you point out Margaret daughter of Daniella?" I asked.

"Along the back wall, one of the cooks. Light brown hair, yellow apron, kind of skinny."

"Thank you."

Dodging more helpers and resisting the urge to taste everything I passed, I made my way back to Margaret. Where the other cooks barked out commands and screamed if their orders weren't accomplished correctly or quickly enough, Levina's mother was soft-spoken and hailed a helper only if he or she seemed to have nothing else to do. When I reached her, she was bent over a low-burning stove, poking at a piece of meat.

"Excuse me, ma'am, may I speak with you for a moment?" I asked.

She straightened and wiped sweat off her brow. If she responded to my question, I didn't hear, because I was momentarily taken aback by her appearance. She looked just like Levina. She was the same height and build, and their faces were the same, except for the eyes. Although Margaret's eyes were brown like her daughter's, they had no life and no beauty in them.

"I'm here on behalf of your daughter Levina," I said after a stretch of silence that drowned out the sounds of the kitchen.

"Levina?" Margaret repeated. "But she's at Warrior Peak with her grandparents. How could you . . . ?"

"She's here. She arrived with Colonel Fallon's group two nights ago." I watched her face for a reaction before I continued, but she gave no indication of her feelings besides her eyes misting. "She wants to see you and your husband tonight, an hour or so before dark. Will both of you be at home?"

"I, um . . . I'll have to check . . . well, all right, we'll be there."

"Good. See you tonight."

I left the kitchen with every intention of finding Levina to tell her that her parents were delighted to see her, but I had hardly taken two steps before Frank, the former leader of Settlement One, spotted me and swept me to the mess hall to discuss the next day. He told me that my three dozen soldiers had turned into an even two score and that they had all been informed of their upcoming task. I also had two sergeants under me with whom I could consult or leave in charge in the event of my absence. Frank had arranged for me to eat my midday meal with them in the fort to give us some privacy as we discussed our plans. All our supplies were already taken care of, and luckily he wasn't too upset when I told him I had invited an extra person.

"It shouldn't be a problem to pack up food for one more," he said. "Who is it, your wife?"

"No, sir," I said, "but she won't be a soldier either, because she won't follow my orders. So I guess for the most part she'll take on the typical wife of the officer role except that she's one hell of a fighter."

Frank chuckled. "Excellent."

Although we were in the shade, sweat peppered his forehead and was beginning to show under his arms. He wasn't a particularly heavy man, but I wondered if his thick hair was keeping his neck and shoulders from staying cool.

"Did you get a chance to talk to Cassandra?" I asked.

He sighed. "Yes. She's much changed. She used to be all charm, very popular with the young men, but yesterday she hardly wanted to speak to anyone at all, much less to me. I didn't mention her captivity. Mostly we just reminisced about her adoptive parents and other friends."

"She was adopted?"

"Yes. She came to Settlement One as a young teenager, after Settlement Nine, where she was born, was nearly wiped out. We just found her on the lake's shore one day; we think she swam most of the way to escape the Moroks."

I absorbed the news without comment, but my admiration for Cassandra deepened even more. She had survived two Morrok attacks with remarkable resilience, and although her silence these days proved that she had deep mental scars, she kept moving forward in spite of the Morroks' continued looming threat in the forest.

"Thank you for seeing her, Colonel," I said. "She was with our group for a week before she uttered a word, and I'm sure it was encouraging for her to see a familiar face."

"It was my pleasure, Lieutenant." He wiped his brow and tried to smile, but his face had become drawn and sallow.

"Are you not feeling well, Colonel?"

"Not especially, now that you mention it, Lieutenant. I think I might lie down for a while."

Once I saw Frank home, my day filled up for me. I had enough time before the midday meal to tell Levina what time we were meeting with her parents. She hardly pieced together a coherent sentence before retreating to our house. There I knew she would confide in Sylvia, who had secluded herself inside, partly due to her pregnancy and partly to avoid the stares and repetitious questions of curious Humans.

My meeting with Scott and Caleb, the two sergeants assigned to me, was a pleasant one. Both of them were bachelors who had a good sense of humor, and they seemed to be good friends already. They were in their midtwenties and talked to me like I was the same—not an eighteen-year-old who had just stumbled into a title higher than theirs.

Fallon, however, who knew how I got my title, grabbed me the moment I left Scott and Caleb to give me his expert advice on how to be a real officer. He spoke for an hour straight and left me wondering why he had trusted me with this mission in the first place. None of his tips stood out in my mind except that the only way to learn was to experience it. That didn't comfort me much.

Once I had escaped Fallon, I was anxious to leave the settlement before anyone else could keep me sitting in one place for more than five minutes at a time. I crossed most of the fort without delay but had to stop when I came across the children training. I couldn't resist meeting a group of ten-year-olds who were drilling their thrusts and swipes with blunt blades. They asked me if I had ever been in a "real" battle and if it was as scary as all the adults warned them. Levina would have thoroughly disapproved of my answers, which included several degrading remarks about the Morroks and glorifications of the Human potential.

When I made it to the lake, I found that its shore was the place for children too young to be in school. Some mothers cradled newborns while others screamed at toddlers to get away from the water. The only person within eyesight not engaged in a game or conversation was Cassandra, who sat by the mouth of the river that divided the Outpost from its fields. Disheartened that she hadn't found any friends or even a job to occupy her, I stepped over and around the children to join her.

"Hello," I said, flopping down next to her.

She was hugging her legs to herself and didn't let go as she turned to me. "Hi."

"Do you want to swim?"

"Is that your therapy for me?"

I laughed. "Maybe. I also don't know any other way to entertain anyone except dueling, and I doubt you'd want to do that."

"Why not?"

It seemed that anything less than bluntness would never work with this girl. "After surviving two Morrok attacks, I thought you would want to stay away from anything violent."

She released her legs and turned her whole torso toward me. "Two attacks?"

"Frank told me about Settlement Nine. I had no idea you had been through so much. Settlement One is enough of a trauma for anyone. I wouldn't blame you if you never wanted to pick up a sword again."

She scoffed. "You think I would react to violence with pacifism? Is that what you do?"

"No, I wouldn't, but I didn't know if normal people—" I stopped myself, realizing that I was about to align myself with the Morroks again, as Cassandra had done in our last conversation. She made it far too easy for me to talk about my past. "I didn't know if women felt like that."

"Women are the only people who are normal?" Cassandra teased.

"No, that's not what I meant. I misspoke."

"Orestes, I know better than most that the Morroks are after you for some reason, so you can stop pretending like you're not curious about what I learned among them. Just ask."

Impressed with her grit in the face of such a past, I decided to take her at her word. "All right, here's what I'm most curious about: Why did the Morroks keep you alive? The Serenial told me months ago that a Human was 'traveling' with the group of Morroks following me. The fact that the Morroks escorted you, however violently, from Settlement One to the far west side of the country is quite unique, considering that most of the Morroks' victims hardly take two steps before the Morroks kill them."

"That's a good question," Cassandra replied. She brought her knees back to her chest and rested her chin on them. For a moment, I thought she was staring at me, but when I followed her gaze, I realized she was looking past me, in the direction of Settlement One. "You know, that man, Frank, seemed to think I had no idea that our home was destroyed, but I did. The Morroks attacked—not many of them, but enough to win—and I was the last left alive. There was a town meeting that night, but I stayed home to sleep instead. They broke in and slaughtered everyone almost within the same building, and then they combed all the houses to take the children. I had heard the screams, but I was too terrified to investigate. Then they came to my room.

"I was sure I was going to die, but they just put a bag over my head and pushed me in the direction they wanted. I think I must've fallen down the steps because I blacked out and got a lot of bruises. When I woke up, we were in the forest."

"So they knew in advance that they were supposed to kidnap you."

"Probably. Morroks don't have ideas of their own. They always got orders from something that followed us around the forest. I don't know what it was. It would just get cold all of a sudden, and one of the Morroks would go out of sight and come back with instructions for what to do."

I nodded, not trusting myself to speak. So it had been a Morrok I had met all those months ago by Settlement Six.

"I think," Cassandra began again, hesitantly, "they captured me because of you."

"Talk of guilting a man!"

"No, not that it's your fault," she amended. "I just think you played into their hands by rescuing me. Just think for a moment," she went on quickly when she saw me about to protest. "Why else would they not take me to that fortress across the lake or to the Facility in the desert? That group of Morroks your group killed was concerned solely with following you, so why else would I be captured and sent with them if not for some plan they had for you?"

"But I did rescue you, and nothing happened."

"Well, they probably didn't anticipate your friend drawing seven of them away while you had to contend with only one."

"Probably not."

Glancing up at the sun, I was surprised to find it was nearing evening. As much as I was glad to have Cassandra open up to me, I wasn't sure how much stock I wanted to put in her theory about me being the cause of her trauma.

"I need to be going," I said. "Take care of yourself, Cassandra."

"Bye."

Already comically tired from spending a day just talking to people, I hurried inside the walls and made my way to my house, where Levina still sat. She looked ill when I told her it was time to go and walked in silence as we searched for her parents' house.

A girl in her early teen years answered the door. She had light brown hair and was rather tall, but she was definitely Levina's sister. Levina and I were both speechless; I hadn't considered the possibility of Levina having siblings, and the shock on Levina's face told me that she hadn't either.

Levina's family owned an entire floor of a house and so had a separate room in which to host guests. Her sister led us up the stairs and opened the door to that room, where six people already sat: Levina's parents and four more siblings, two boys and two more girls.

Levina's parents both rose when we entered. Levina had inherited her father's dark brown hair while her sister had taken his height. Although my prior knowledge of him might have colored my opinion, I instantly disliked the look of the man. He was tall but did not stand up straight. He greeted me but did not look me in the eye. He shook my hand but did not grip it with strength.

"Please, sit," Margaret said after she and Thomas (as Levina's father introduced himself) had exchanged awkward embraces with their oldest daughter.

Levina and I looked about the cramped room doubtfully before Margaret ordered two of her children off the chairs that she and her husband weren't occupying. Levina started to protest, but I shushed her and accepted the kindness for us.

"So these are your children?" I asked after a few moments of uncomfortable silence.

"Oh, yes," Margaret said in a rush, as if grateful to have something to fill the air. "Little Thomas and Aiken are the youngest two." The boys looked up at their names but then went back to their toys. Neither of them looked older than five. "Then there are Edlyn, Wren, and Holly, in order of age." The girls, none of them older than thirteen, had been staring at Levina from the moment she entered the room and hardly blinked at the mention of their names.

Levina turned her strained smile to the girls. "I'm very glad to meet all of you."

When the children said nothing in return, Margaret asked, "How are my parents?"

"They were very well when I left them. Grandfather is making a lot of money with his carvings and Grandmother with her paintings."

"They didn't draw you into their life of being civilians, did they?" Thomas asked.

"No," Levina snapped.

Everyone seemed surprised at her tone, but I knew it was for love of her grandparents and not for pride of herself that she answered that way.

"No," she repeated, softening her tone, "I went through school until we left for Serenity Valley."

"How did you do in the tournaments? Win any?" Thomas asked.

"Fighting wasn't my forte in school, though I have gotten better since we've been traveling."

"She means since she's been training with me," I teased, trying desperately to add some lightness to the conversation. No one smiled.

"So how long were your travels?" Margaret asked after a pause. Her jaw was locked into a smile, and her voice was as light as if we had just returned from a leisure trip around the lake region.

Levina and I glanced at each other, confused. Time had passed so strangely for us since we had been in the forest. A single day of hard travel could feel like a week, but a month at a struggling settlement seemed to pass in a day.

"A year, maybe a little less," Levina said. Her smile was the same as her mother's.

"A year?" Thomas repeated. "It should take only a couple weeks between here and the Peak. That's all it took us when we first came here thirteen years ago, and we were leading upward of a hundred—"

"Fourteen years ago," Levina whispered.

"Excuse me?" Thomas said, leaning forward to hear.

"You left when I was four. It was fourteen years ago when you left. I'm eighteen now."

The silence went from awkward to volatile in as long as it took for her to speak those words. I found myself clenching my fists in anticipation of what Levina would say next. I knew she had questions—painful questions—that had kept her up at night all those fourteen years, and I knew this was her time to ask them. She wanted them to tell her—the adult Levina, whom circular logic could not divert—why they had left her, if it was really worth it to break apart their family for a settlement that now lay abandoned, if they regretted what they had done.

But she asked none of these things. The silence lost its threat as one of the children, oblivious to the tension, interrupted, saying, "Can we go outside,

Mommy?"

Margaret turned to the girl with garish enthusiasm. "Of course, my dear. Come back soon, though; it's already getting dark."

One by one, the little Levinas trooped out the door, their arms laden with toys. Only the oldest girl hesitated at the door as if deciding whether the tension was worth participating in adult conversation. She left, of course, and the silence returned.

"So," Margaret began again, her smile bigger than ever, "what do you think of the Outpost? Have you signed up for any jobs yet?"

I waited for Levina to answer, but she had fixated on a spot on the wall between her parents and seemed unwilling to speak. When I nudged her leg, she shook her head ever so slightly, and I knew I was on my own for a while.

"I'm trying guard duty tonight," I said, "but we haven't had much of a chance to breathe yet, much less take up new jobs."

"Idle hands," Thomas said, clicking his tongue, "don't do anyone a favor, least of all yourself."

Without meaning to, I felt my face freeze into the women's smile. "I don't know if you're aware, sir, of why it took your daughter a year to make it to the Outpost, but I assure you that her hands were not idle."

Levina seemed to sense the strain in my voice and took over. "Orestes and I have been working under Colonel Fallon for some time now to warn all the settlements about the growing Morrok threat. We hadn't received messages from the forest for more than a year before we left the Peak, and so we had no idea—"

"Colonel Fallon, huh?" Thomas interrupted. He was clearly impressed. "So you were able to make some good connections in spite of—well, your grandparents weren't going to get them for you. But you went right to the top. Quite impressive. You take after me that way."

"Damn, I hope you're a joking man," I growled.

Thomas cupped a hand to his ear as if he hadn't heard me. "What's that?"

"Maybe you like to weasel your way up to great men to make yourself look important, but Levina is not—"

"Exactly who are you again?" Thomas snapped.

A few profanities escaped me before Levina jumped from her seat. Gripping my shoulder with strength I didn't know she had, she said, "Thank you for having us. We have to leave now."

"We should do this again sometime!" Margaret said shrilly as she and Thomas rose awkwardly from their chairs.

I bit back my sarcastic retort as Levina pushed me toward the door. We let ourselves out of the room, down the stairs, and out the front door into the twilight, and then I burst. "How could you let them treat you like that? You've cut me to pieces for not remembering to say good morning to you, but you let them act like they owe you nothing—no explanation, not even a shred of decency! Did you hear that man? Levina, those people have no right, no claim to you and what you've—"

"Orestes, please stop," Levina choked. She was biting her lip, massaging her temples, and doing everything not to burst into tears.

"Oh, I'm sorry, I didn't mean to upset you. Maybe I shouldn't have come. Maybe they would've acted differently if I hadn't—I just can't believe—"

"Damn it, Orestes, just shut your mouth!" she shrieked. A few people down the street looked around in concern.

Realizing we needed privacy, I put my arm around Levina and ushered her away from her parents' house. Somehow we ended up in the mess hall furthest from the kitchen, and I vaguely recalled that I had not had dinner. After taking a seat on one of the long benches, I pulled Levina onto my lap, and she gave up trying not to cry and sobbed into my neck until the sun had set. I waited until her breath had steadied before I asked my question again, though this time in a gentler tone.

"Levina, what happened?"

"They have five kids," she sniffed.

"And . . . ?"

"And my grandparents always told me that the reason they left me at Warrior Peak was because they thought the forest wasn't a place to raise children."

"Maybe once they got here, they realized that it wasn't too dangerous—that other children grew up safely and normally."

"Then why didn't they say that?" she said, pushing herself back to face me. "They've moved on! They never expected me to show up here. They never sent for me and never once wrote to me even while Fallon had messengers coming regularly through the forest. I was so stupid to think they'd want to see me now! All they had to say to me was what they'd ask of any girl they've never met—not a daughter. It's like they didn't care to know me better than that, even now that they have a second chance."

"I'm sure if we give them a little more time, they'll—"

"You don't have to pretend to defend them for me. I'm too old to be chasing after my parents' affection or approval. This whole thing is silly. We have separate lives, and I accept that. It's idiotic for me to be upset about it."

I smiled at her. "You don't have to pretend for me either."

She laughed weakly. "I don't know how you do it. It never seems to bother you that you don't know who your parents are, or if you do know, you don't care that you never see them."

"Fallon and Glynis are my parents, and that's good enough for me."

Thwarted again in her attempts to have me reveal my origins, Levina frowned and looked away.

Feeling guilty, I continued, "They're your parents too, you know. And since you don't have a title, Fallon won't mind you being associated with him."

She laughed again and kissed me. We talked for a while longer until it was time for my guard duty. After a few moments of bickering over whether or not I should go, I walked Levina home and then hastened to the front gates. I checked in at the gatehouse, and the officer on duty there assigned me to a partner: a man at least fifteen years my senior who stood a head shorter than me and who had an endless need to talk.

What I thought would be a peaceful few hours strolling around the ramparts turned into a challenge to fit in a word with my partner. He stopped chattering only when we reached the southwest corner of the wall and I held up a hand for silence. Tipping my torch over the wall, I pointed at a figure who sat by the lake, exactly where I had left Cassandra earlier in the afternoon.

"Do you know who that is?" I asked.

"Yes, my wife told me about her," my partner answered. "She's been there almost all day. My wife saw her when she was outside with the other mothers, and before you came, the officers sent me out to tell her we were about to close the gate for the night. She said she'd be all right staying outside. We've been keeping an eye on her."

"A really close eye, I hope."

I continued reluctantly but couldn't keep my mind off Cassandra. She of all people should have known how dangerous it was to stay outside the walls. If she were attacked, someone could be there in maybe two minutes, but it took less than two minutes to kill or capture a girl.

"It's too bad what happened to Colonel Frank, isn't it?"

"What?" I asked, coming out of my reverie.

"Didn't you hear? It happened just a few hours ago, but I guess the general's trying to keep it quiet. Colonel Frank was found dead in his room just after sunset. No one's sure what happened."

"But I saw him just this morning," I said, aghast. I remembered his sweating and his strained smile, but I hadn't thought it serious enough to find a healer for him. "He didn't look all that ill."

"Just one of those sicknesses, I guess. It comes on you, and the next thing you know, it's taken you. It's a shame though. They buried him really quick out in the forest in case it was something that'll spread."

"So . . . so no one was with him? No one . . . the body—he, Frank—wasn't injured, like he had been attacked in any way?"

My partner shrugged. "I don't know." This was no more than gossip to him, but it bothered me beyond explanation. Suddenly I was fifteen again and had come upon Aldis's broken and lifeless body. Both Frank and Aldis had been going about their business in the morning and then were found dead a few hours later. I knew it was impossible for a Morrok to enter the Outpost if for no other reason than the number of people inside who would have seen it. The physical parallels were haunting, but the motives couldn't have been the same. Aldis had been killed to hurt and warn me; I had known Frank for only two days. Surely yet another death couldn't have anything to do with me.

Yet all night as we circled the ramparts—passing Cassandra as she lay by the lake and passing the forest, which was emitting an icy breeze—I thought of Frank and how he had survived the slaughter of Settlement One only to give way to sickness. Most of all, though, I wondered what the forty of us who were venturing out to the forest the next morning would discover about the fate of another settlement and, more importantly, of hundreds more Human lives.

Chapter Twenty

The Weight of a Title

TRAVELING WITH FORTY PEOPLE made trudging through the forest a new adventure. When we first assembled early on my third morning at the Outpost among fog from the lake and dubious glances at me from the soldiers' parents and wives, I thought us a motley contingent at best. I hadn't met many of the soldiers before that morning, but I knew the group was composed mostly of men from my age up to their forties and also a handful of women, few of whom were married and none of whom were mothers. Most of them had never been more than a mile away from the Outpost and so were excited and enthusiastic about our journey, even if we did sleep without cover, carry our own food supply, and keep a pace even Fallon would have thought extreme.

Within two days, I had learned everyone's names, and within five, I knew their weapons of choice and a little about each of their families. My sergeants, Scott and Caleb, quickly became my friends and Levina's as well, though I had to work not to become jealous of them as they teased and flirted with her.

To her credit, Levina defied my earlier assertions and aligned herself with the other soldiers, even to the point of being insulted when I didn't assign her equal duties in watch, cooking, fetching water, and the like. The two of us learned more about forest Warrior life after a week of sitting fireside with our new companions than we had after months of searching for settlements. We learned songs, dances, stories, and all sorts of other traditions the southern Warriors had formed over the years, and the foresters were just as curious about life in the mountains.

One night, eleven days into our travels, we were comparing funeral practices. Most of the platoon had finished eating and were rolling out sleep mats and setting up for the night. A handful of us sat on a fallen tree in front of a dying fire, our empty dinner plates in our laps. The forest Warriors were horrified that we typically cremated people simply because there wasn't enough room to bury everyone on the mountain. Levina and I were equally disturbed that the foresters threw a party after burying someone in order, as they put it, to celebrate a life well spent.

"We're too young to be talking about death," Scott, one of my sergeants, yawned as he scratched at the dirt beneath him with a dagger.

"*Some* of you are," a bearded man said. "Others of us have to consider these things."

"What things?" Scott snorted. "You're only thirty-six, and there's no reason you ought to fear death any more than the rest of us."

"Oh, I don't know about that," I said. "The older you get, the harder it is to swing your sword the same way."

"Not you too," Scott said. "How old are you, then, Lieutenant, if your arm's already tired?"

"Twenty-five," I replied without hesitation. Levina's eyes darted to me in disbelief. "And my sword arm's fine; this is just what I hear from my more experienced companions."

"And you, Levina? Are you the same age as Orestes?" asked Caleb, my other sergeant.

Levina released me from her stare long enough to smile at him and answer, "Yes."

"You filthy liar," I whispered as the conversation turned to a livelier topic.

"I said only that I was the same age as you. *You* are the one who lied about that age," she said, tapping my nose.

As the last few people finished eating, the ring around the fire widened to accommodate the one pastime that transferred flawlessly from Warrior Peak to the forest: sparring. Every night without fail, someone produced a couple dull or wooden swords, and a miniature tournament commenced. I had avoided participating and enjoyed watching instead, and I was excited to see that tonight my most-anticipated match was about to take place: Scott and Caleb. Caleb was the more skilled and pragmatic of the two, but Scott was the more daring; he took risks that sometimes earned him several bruises but other times won him the match.

"I think Scott will win," Levina said as we crowded among the audience.

"Really?" I asked. I positioned her in front of me to give her a better view, and a thrill rushed through me as she let her body lean against mine. "I was going to bet on Caleb."

"Scott's more like you, except you're luckier."

"Luck?" I replied with mock indignation. "You think that's why I do well?"

Smiling coyly, she shushed me and pointed to the match. To my satisfaction, Caleb did seem to have the upper hand, though it was difficult to tell with the limited light that the small fire provided. The two of them danced dangerously close to the flames, Caleb beating Scott backward, Scott dodging wildly, and both of them guffawing with every movement. Finally Caleb smacked Scott's sword hand, causing him to drop the weapon.

Scott cursed and dove at the wooden sword, catching the pummel of it just before it hit the ground. A few people in the crowd gasped, but Caleb seemed to have expected Scott's quick reactions because he met his next strike without blinking. They exchanged a few blows before Scott clutched at his sword hand in obvious pain. Whether he noticed that or not, Caleb backed away to the other side of the fire while Scott weighed his sword experimentally in his left hand.

Then, without warning, Scott broke into a sprint and leaped over the fire. Gratified by the shrieks of several women, he landed, unscathed, more on Caleb than on the ground, and as they both overbalanced, Scott tugged his opponent's sword from his hands. The crowd scattered when they crashed to the ground, and before anyone else had regained their senses, Scott had brought one of the swords to Caleb's neck, thereby winning the match.

As the crowd applauded and Caleb grumbled halfheartedly about cheating, Levina turned around and said, "Ha!"

"He got lucky," I muttered.

"Which proves my point."

Before I could come up with another intelligent retort, I heard a panicked voice among the several still discussing the match. After a moment, the latter became subdued enough that I could hear the repeated command: "Douse the fire, douse the fire." A few people bearing buckets of water complied just as the owner of the panicked voice made his way through to me. It turned out to be Nicolas, a small, lanky man no older than I was who had been acting as my scout. I drew him away from the crowd and into a patch of moonlight so I could see his face. He was pale and on the verge of tears.

"What happened, Private?" I asked when he did not speak. Levina, Scott, and Caleb found me, and together we surrounded our rattled messenger.

"Lieutenant, I found Settlement Four, but I wasn't alone," Nicolas panted. "A host of Morroks is camped not twenty yards to the north of the settlement."

"A host?" I repeated. "I need more definite numbers than that. Is Settlement Four aware of them? Are they preparing to attack? How close to Settlement Four are we? Did you communicate with any Human, or did the Morroks see you?"

"I, uh," Nicolas began and then faltered.

It was all I could do not to shake the answers out of him. Unnoticed by anyone in the circle, Levina put a cool hand on my arm, and I remembered to breathe.

"I think . . ." He shook his head. "I *know* there are at least two hundred Morroks. I did not contact Settlement Four, like you told me. I saw the clearing with the village and turned to come back to our camp. The gates were closed, so they may know about the Morroks. I saw the Morroks when I circled the settlement to check its walls, like you told me—the walls look like they're stone, by the way, so they ought to be safe. I don't think the Morroks saw me, but I ran all the way back here all the same. We're not half an hour from Settlement Four if we hurry."

"Is Settlement Four directly east of us like we thought?" I asked.

"Yes, sir."

"What direction is their main gate facing?"

"West."

"Good. Caleb, tell everyone to ready their weapons. Leave everything else behind for now. And quietly—no torches either. Scott, I heard you telling

Grace and Sandra that you can travel through the canopy. Can you really, or were you just trying to impress your audience?"

"Yes, sir, I can really do it," Scott replied. He seemed unperturbed by my asking.

"Nicolas, can you climb a tree?"

"Yes, sir."

"All right. Nicolas, lead Sergeant Scott to Settlement Four. If there's any sign of the Morroks, flee to the trees, and Scott, you travel the rest of the way in the canopy, even if you have to leave Nicolas behind. You'll both be safe in the trees. Once you get to Settlement Four, get in as quietly as you can without alerting the Morroks. Tell the men there to be ready to open the gates at a moment's notice and to shut it just as quickly once we're in. If all goes well, stand atop the gate so I can see you from the forest. We need to get our people inside the Morroks noticing. Our combined forces and the security of the walls is our only hope of surviving. Go."

Scott and Nicolas scrambled to gather their weapons and then took off eastward. By the time Levina and I found our own swords, the rest of the soldiers were armed and ready to go. As briefly as I could, I relayed Nicolas's report to the platoon and told them my plan. When I was finished, I paused, expecting suggestions or critiques like my family always gave to Fallon. My platoon gave me neither. Pleasantly surprised, I organized everyone into loose ranks and led the way toward Settlement Four.

Even in the company of forty other people, the forest had never been a more frightening place. We were deep enough into the forest that the canopy permitted only the occasional beam of moonlight to struggle through its thick branches. People touched one another on the shoulder every few minutes for reassurance that we were still together and stumbling in the right direction. The only sound that accompanied us was the crunching of our own feet; every time someone brushed against a bush or tripped over a tree branch, half of us would draw our swords, ready to face the Morrok that our imaginations told us was barreling toward us.

After what felt like far more than half an hour, I saw a large clearing ahead.

Once I had signaled for everyone behind me to stop, I asked Caleb to make sure everyone was still with us and told him that I was going on ahead to see if Scott and Nicolas had made it.

The last few yards to the settlement clearing were perhaps the most nerve-racking because I had spent the last thirty minutes imagining the Morroks spreading out and surrounding the village. However, I came across no such arrangement and made it to the very edge of the trees without interruption. Scanning the wall, I was relieved to see Scott's legs draped over one of the thick outer doors of the village. The walls did have at least a layer of bricks around them and were also thick enough to have ramparts and parapets, which was more than I had hoped for after spending months at Settlements Six and Eleven. Satisfied with my findings, I retreated back to the platoon.

"All's well, at least for now," I whispered to Caleb and Levina when I reached them. "I'm going to tell them to open the gates. We need to move quickly in case the Morroks have patrols nearby. Bring everyone to the forest's edge, and then wait for my signal."

"Yes, sir," Caleb said.

I jogged back to the clearing and slowed as I left the cover of the trees. The moment I did so, Scott sprang to life and hissed at someone at the base of the other side of the wall. Picking up my pace again, I reached the outer edge of the settlement and said in a raised whisper, "Open the doors wide enough for just a few people at a time to come in. I'm going to send them across in small groups, and I'll be the last—"

The familiar sound of metal striking metal stopped me midsentence. Cries of alarm and pain followed soon after. Before I could tell Scott to keep the doors closed, one of them creaked open to my specifications.

"Scott, get some archers ready to shoot at anything that comes through here that's not Human!" I yelled, panicked out of my attempt at secrecy. "Make sure there are people inside ready to fight, but don't, under any circumstances, let them leave the village unless I order it!"

I didn't wait for Scott's response before I bolted back to the forest. There I found a battle already broken out. We outnumbered the Morroks nearly four to one, but the Morroks were holding their ground. My soldiers were trying to surround and isolate each one, but the Morroks proved to be as unnaturally agile as ever as they used their great weapons to keep the Humans herded in front of them.

"Retreat to the village!" I bellowed over the fray. "Stop fighting—cover each other and go! Go!"

Again I expected someone to protest, but as they were able, everyone turned and fled their respective duels to sprint toward the village. The Morroks were quick to pursue, but one of them peeled off northward, doubtlessly to call for reinforcements. I considered following it to silence it before it could raise the alarm, but there were too few of us holding off the nine remaining Morroks while the rest of my platoon dashed to the settlement.

The fighting quickly resumed in the clearing. I killed one Morrok and glanced at the gate, where everyone was squeezing in one by one. About a third of my soldiers had made it inside, but now two Morroks, though pierced by several arrows, were trying to push their way inside as well.

Levina made her way to me, and together we took down another Morrok. She screamed as, in its last moments of life, the beast dug its claws into her ankles. Before I could do it for her, she struck and nearly severed its hand. Surprised by her newfound pluck, I saluted her as we moved on to our new target.

More than half my soldiers were inside now, some of them limping and bleeding and some being dragged by others. A third Morrok was hacking its way toward the door. Five of my soldiers took it down before it made it inside. There were only three Morroks left fighting outside.

"Widen the opening! Open the gate!" I shouted. But just as I said it, another, much larger, group of Morroks began to materialize from the northern edge of the clearing. The gate opened further, and almost everyone part of the original battle flooded inside, Human and Morrok alike.

"Shut the gates!" I screamed, unable to tear my eyes away from the new Morroks only a few yards away from us. I shoved Levina ahead of me and picked up a corporal named Daniel, who lay on the ground, unmoving. I was the last inside before the gate was pulled shut.

Four Morroks still stood inside the settlement. As I set Daniel against the wall, the Morroks on the outside began to batter at the doors. The four inside immediately abandoned whomever they had been sparring and tried to shove the doors open again from the inside. Our archers bellowed for people to clear the way. Soon the Morroks' exposed backs were spotted with arrows, but still they pushed, and to some success. I barked at the archers to stop and rallied my soldiers again.

Three of the Morroks turned and formed a barrier around the fourth as it continued to push. Now impossibly outnumbered, the three guards were cut down within seconds. The fourth met a similar fate, but it took the strength of every man who could grip the door to drag it shut against the oncoming flood of Morroks. A group of men from Settlement Four shoved the appropriate bars and locks in place until the door was secure.

Although the Morroks outside continued to pound, all the Humans around me began to relax. Some flopped to the ground where they stood, others checked themselves for injuries, and still others tended to the wounded.

"It's not over yet," I said. "The Morroks are still out there, and they could lay siege for days. Who's the commanding officer here?"

"I am," a middle-aged man replied as he stepped out of the crowd. Unlike the out-of-shape settlement leaders I had met in the west, this man was robust and had scars up and down his arms to tell of his many battles. He was as tall as I was and had his dark red hair tied tightly behind him.

"Good," I said. "I'm Lieutenant Orestes, and I've been sent from the Outpost to escort your village to the lake region, where most of the forest Warriors have gathered to fight the Morroks. Is this the first time you've been attacked?"

"No."

"Good, then your people know how to fight them. Now I'm taking command of the fighters here, but I'm going to need your help with—"

"Why are you taking command?" the man interrupted, crossing his arms over his broad chest. "I've defended this village for years, and you've barely a beard to show for your experience."

"I'm older than I look, and age is hardly a measure of experience," I said, my frustration mounting. "Colonel Fallon himself sent me here to—"

"The colonel is in the forest?" the leader said. His entire countenance changed to that of a boy who had just heard that his hero was passing by his house.

"Yes," I said, seizing my advantage. "He is at the lake at this very moment awaiting our return. Now, as I said, I'll need your help to wage this battle. Have all your men been called out to fight?"

"No, Lieutenant, but I can—"

"Send someone to do it," I said. One of the Settlement Four men flanking him jogged off in the direction of the houses. "Now we need to reinforce these doors as much as we can, and we need to have a constant guard on the ramparts in case the Morroks have ladders. Scott, Caleb, you take care of that—the ramparts."

"Yes, sir," they said. Another Settlement Four citizen led them and most of the rest of my soldiers to the ladders that led up the wall.

"I'll leave you—what's your name?" I asked the leader of the village.

"Christopher."

"Christopher, I'll leave you in charge of reinforcing this and any other entrance to the village. Now I need to know where we should take the wounded, and I'll also need someone to give me a quick tour of the village so I can learn its resources and weak points."

"Yes, sir, Lieutenant," Christopher said. He conferred with the last few men standing behind him. One of them led the way to the infirmary. The rest of my healthy soldiers, including Levina, helped carry the six who were either dead or too injured to stand. Christopher delegated the gate reinforcement to yet another man and volunteered to give me the tour of the village himself.

"Thankfully we have only one entrance," Christopher began, speaking at top speed as we nearly ran through the village. It was laid out like any settlement, but the people who darted through the streets had a sobriety in their movements that only experience with Morroks could instill. "Unfortunately, the doors are hinged so that they can be pushed or pulled open, which makes the possibility of battering them open very likely. However, our walls are strong—foundation of stone, thick of wood, recently enforced with brick."

"How so?"

"It was a difficult task. The Morrok attacks have been increasing these past few months, and we began to fear for the strength of our walls. We decided merely to add an outer layer of brick to the wood already standing. The bricks themselves are rather hastily made, and not all of them are attached very securely to the wood because we were forever dodging ambushes while we worked."

I swallowed hard and tried not to panic about the walls not being as secure as I had first hoped.

Christopher continued, "The parapets are tall to protect our guards from arrows as they walk the ramparts. Roughly five hundred people live here, more than three hundred of whom are able-bodied fighters. We have enough food stored to last us for weeks, even with your additional men. We also have extra clothes and weapons that are yours upon request. What numbers are we facing exactly?"

Christopher and I spent a few hours discussing everything from battle strategy to mundane matters such as how to rotate watch duties and how many people we needed on guard at all times. Every few minutes, a man or woman from either my platoon or Settlement Four interrupted us with a report or complaint. Those patrolling the ramparts spotted figures moving constantly just outside the clearing, though they could neither shoot the Morroks nor discern what they were doing. I didn't know what to tell them except to keep watch and alert me the moment one of them strayed out of the cover of the trees.

The Morroks had stopped hammering the door fairly soon after we shut them out, but less than an hour later, we heard an odd *thunk* on the outside of the western wall. Concerned, Christopher and I ascended the nearest ladder to the ramparts, where Caleb was already sticking half his upper body through an opening in the parapets to search for the noise's source.

I poked my head out as well. I scanned the forest and, just as the all the soldiers had reported, saw several silhouettes at the edge of the trees. But I didn't see anything that could have made that noise.

"Look down," Caleb said.

Sure enough, at the base of the wall was a large stone—bigger than a Human head—that apparently had been thrown from the forest and then bounced off the settlement's outer wall.

"Why would they do that?" I asked.

"I can't figure it out," Caleb replied. He squinted at the stone as if the mere look of it would help him glean an answer. "Well, if they keep doing it, the only purpose it's going to serve is to annoy the hell out of us all. Judging by how far away the trees are from the walls, they must have some sort of gigantic slingshots to fling the rocks so hard."

"Very strange," Christopher murmured. Another *thunk* resounded across the village, though this time it seemed to have come from the eastern wall.

"I suppose there's nothing we can do about it," I said. "Just let me know if it accomplishes anything."

Dawn arrived, and the rocks had done nothing except, as Caleb said, annoy us. Everyone had been awake for hours anyway. The nonfighting women, children, and elderly knew to barricade themselves in the mess hall once the fighting began, but before that time, the mess hall served meals nearly twenty-four hours a day as people came on and off long, crowded watch shifts. The citizens of Settlement Four cleared out rooms—and in some cases, entire houses—to make space for my soldiers to sleep and relax as much as they could.

Christopher saw to it that I had my own room that no one else was allowed to use or disturb, but I didn't enter it all our first day there or the next. I had been positive that the Morroks would attack as soon as the sun rose on our first morning at Settlement Four, but dawn came and went without a sound other than more rock on brick.

Everyone else must have lost themselves in their duties to avoid worrying about the impending attack, but no matter how hard I worked at one task or another, I couldn't keep my mind off it. I invaded the ramparts even when I wasn't on watch duty; I drew my sword every time I passed the village gates, which were now thick with additional boards nailing it shut and sacks of flour wedging it in place; I flinched with every stone that pounded the wall; I took my meals outside so as not to delay my hearing about an attack. By evening on the second day, my outward appearance must have been horrifying because Scott and Caleb personally escorted me to the house where my room was and promised that someone would be guarding the door until there was significant Morrok activity to report.

In the first two hours of my confinement, I gained maybe twenty minutes of sleep strung together. I wasn't sure if I could actually hear the rocks from my room, but still their reverberation echoed at the edge of my every thought. Finally I gave up trying to rest and lit a candle because I knew I couldn't handle opening the curtains and seeing the activity going on outside. Instead, I contented myself in pacing restlessly around the room. Like all settlement bedrooms, it was large enough for a bed, a small table, and enough space to take a few steps, turn, retrace the steps, and do it all over again until I thought my body would rid itself of my racing mind.

A knock on the bedroom door broke through my inward struggle. Sure that it was someone bringing news of the Morroks, I yanked the door open. On the other side stood Levina, her arms laden with fresh clothes and a plate of food. Her calm expression told me that nothing of interest had happened, but I was still elated to have such a pleasant interruption to my fevered musings. "Come in," I nearly pleaded. She strode past me and plopped herself and her load onto my bed. I shut the door and joined her.

"I thought you were supposed to be sleeping," she said, searching my face for any sign of rest.

"And yet you brought me food."

She grinned. "I know you."

She handed me the plate and watched me eat, occasionally taking a bite for herself.

"What are you thinking right now?" she asked after several minutes of silence.

I discarded the plate on the floor and took one of her hands in both of mine. "I'm afraid I'm going to fail. And it's not about pride of my new title or the fact that the Morroks need to die. It's that all these people are going to be following my orders—fighting on my orders, fleeing on my orders, dying on my orders. Two have already died—two people I knew and two people who trusted me. It was fine playing lieutenant these past few days—organizing the platoon, setting the travel pace, and all that—but I never dreamed I would have to mobilize the village like this. We came out here to escort these people to the Outpost, but now . . . now I'm commanding three hundred and forty people in a battle against two hundred Morroks. How could this happen? We're impossibly outmatched, and that won't change regardless of what kind of commander I turn out to be."

"Orestes, you've acted so bravely these past few days," Levina said, her voice full of warmth and sincerity. As she spoke, she stroked my face with her free hand. "I've known you for two years, and I've seen you grow from a cheeky teenager who trails after great men like Acules and Fallon to a man to whom others entrust their lives. You haven't made one wrong move from the time Nicolas ran into camp to this very moment. I know you feel responsible for the two who were murdered, but their trust in you was not misplaced, because they did not die in vain. You haven't failed us yet, and you won't fail us now. These people will follow you into battle, and no matter what happens, you won't fail them. If we win, you will have been the one who took the most risks and gained the most kills. We may end up having to run for our lives, but you will be the last to leave because you'll stay behind to give us cover, just like you did not two days ago when we were fighting our way into the settlement. Most of the members of this village don't know how well-placed their trust is, but the platoon does . . . and I do. I know you," she said again, her voice now shaking with emotion. "I know you, and I trust you, and I love . . . I love you. If these people don't feel the same, then their blood is on their own heads because you are our one hope."

I couldn't speak for several moments and had to look away from Levina, whose eyes were shining with tears. She was too beautiful for words. It didn't matter that her dress was torn and stained after an endless day of fighting and working or that her hair was tangled and matted or that her skin was smeared with sweat and grit. When I had mastered myself enough to look back, I realized we were gripping each other's hands so hard that our knuckles were white. I relaxed my hold, and we laughed.

"Have we really known each other only two years?" I asked huskily.

"Hard to believe, huh?" she sniffed.

I struggled with myself for a moment, thought after thought racing through my head, but I couldn't focus on anything long enough to form the words. Finally I made myself whisper, "Thank you, Levina."

"You're welcome," she said, bringing all four of our hands to her face to wipe away her tears. "Now I brought you fresh clothes, some soap, and a shaving knife in case you want to get cleaned up. If you can't sleep, at least lie down and rest a bit because it would really—"

"Levina, I don't want to shave anymore."

"Excuse me?"

"I don't want to shave my beard, and I don't want to cut my hair," I said, my heart pounding.

"Well, that's your choice, but I always thought you secretly preferred being clean-shaven anyway, no matter what tradition—"

"No, Levina." I dropped her hands and rummaged in my vest pocket for the necklace I had bought two weeks ago at the Outpost. When I produced it, Levina's eyes widened. "I don't want to shave my beard, and I don't want to cut my hair, and I want you to wear any and every piece of jewelry you can lay your hands on." I wanted to say more, but my throat had tightened beyond relaxation. Instead, I put the necklace around her neck and laid the shaving knife across her open palms.

Levina weighed the knife in her hands, learning the grooves of its handle and brushing a thumb along the edge of the blade. I could almost hear her mind weighing the question the knife presented. She was telling herself that we were too young, that we were in the middle of more important matters, that I was just being foolish and impetuous.

Then she touched the necklace tugging on the back of her neck and weighing on her chest, and she knew this wasn't the first time this question had crossed my mind. Finally she straightened where she sat and hefted the knife in one hand. With an expert touch, she flung it to the ground, where it buried itself between the floorboards. For the moment, that was answer enough for us both, and for that moment, we escaped all the pressures and fears of our world, which, from then on, we would face together.

Chapter Twenty-One
The Battle of Settlement Four

I KNEW IT WAS TIME before the others sent a messenger to fetch me. Panicked voices in the street below roused me from my sleep, and one peek through the window confirmed my fears; although it was the dead of night, women were carrying children in the direction of the mess hall, and soldiers wove through the flood, brandishing weapons and raising the alarm. I was dressed and searching for my weapons by the time I heard someone crash through the front door below.

The seconds it took the messenger to thunder up the stairs seemed to stretch into minutes as my gaze rested on Levina. Her arms lay perpendicular to the rest of her body as if I had never left her embrace. I would have given anything—even the night we had just spent together—to have her be somewhere else at that moment—the Outpost, Warrior Peak, Tyrclopia, anywhere where she would have been safe.

Before I could begin to swallow my anxiety, Levina woke and observed me, fully dressed and armed, with a scoff. "Were you going to let me sleep?"

"I was thinking about it," I mumbled sheepishly.

She too dressed within seconds and had her hand on her own sword when there was a knock on the bedroom door. When I opened it, the messenger, who was no more than fifteen years old but still armed to fight, seemed surprised to find me awake but didn't hesitate to say his piece. "Christopher and your sergeants are on the ramparts by the gate. They'd like you to come as quickly as possible."

"What's going on?" I demanded.

"The Morroks are gathering on the west side, near the gate. They haven't attacked yet, but Christopher told everyone to get in position."

"Thank you."

In the same minute, Levina and I were jogging through the cool, windy night air, dodging women, children, and soldiers alike. The hundreds of lit torches gave the illusion of daylight, particularly on the ramparts, where I knew dozens of soldiers were squinting into the black forest for any sign of Morrok activity. When Levina and I reached the front gates, I stopped short of the ladder leading up to the ramparts.

"When the fighting starts," I said, "I'm handing the lead off to Christopher, Scott, and Caleb. I need to fight, not run around and try to judge what move to make next. I want you to stay as close to me as possible, all right? I need to know you're safe."

Levina's jaw clenched, and I knew I had said something wrong.

"You can't do this," she said.

"Do what?"

"You can't let the fact that we're going to be married cause you to neglect your role in battles. You just said you have to be free to fight, and up until now, you have always trusted me to myself in battle. I am a daughter of Warrior Peak as much as you are a son, and you've trained me yourself for nearly a year."

I ran a hand through my hair, nearly ripping some out along the way. A dozen arguments sprang to mind, but this wasn't the time for this talk.

"Fine," I said. "What were you planning to do?"

Levina waved a hand to the activity behind us. "I was going to help guard the gates." Several soldiers were already forming a ring around the doors, ready to repair the newly added reinforcements if the door began to give or to guard it from the inside should any Morrok infiltrate the village.

I took a calming breath before responding. "That sounds fine, but you have to promise me that if we lose control of the gates, you'll find me. At that point, we'll either have to fight the whole army at once or be forced to flee, and we need to be together should either of those events occur or we may never see each other again. Agreed?"

"Agreed."

We kissed and embraced each other for a long moment until we heard a loud, familiar *thunk*. Knocked back to the present, Levina dashed off to the doors, and I flew up the nearest ladder.

The ramparts were crowded with at least half our forces. The walls were only thick enough for three people to stand beside one another. Archers of all ages and sizes lined the outermost section; most of them already had arrows nocked loosely in their bows and propped between the narrow gaps of the parapets. An equal number of soldiers clutching melee weapons stood against the inner edge of the wall, looking terrified and hopeful that there would be no need for them. Between the two lines of soldiers ran officers who acted more like heralds as they delivered orders up and down the length of all four walls.

"Lieutenant! Excellent," Christopher said once I had wedged my way atop the wall. Scott and Caleb were there as well, though neither of them had their usual alacrity. Both of them were so grim I could hardly remember the look of their easy smiles. "The majority of their troops seem to be here on the western edge of the trees, but they're flinging more stones at the eastern wall."

"So they've got something planned," I said, "but the two activities don't seem to serve a common purpose. Are they trying to distract us with the noise on the east so they can attack on the west or vice versa?"

Before anyone could take a guess, a voice from somewhere down the wall interrupted our discussion. "Christopher! Lieutenant!" the female voice called. "Clear the way! Christopher!" The owner of the voice squeezed and elbowed her way through until she stood before us, looking comical in armor far too large for a woman who could not have been past her early twenties. "You ought to take a look at the eastern wall. It's, um, breaking apart."

"What do you mean?" I demanded.

"Let's just see for ourselves," Christopher said. Rather than trying to cram his way through the narrow ramparts, he swung onto the nearest ladder and took off at a run through the village. I followed suit.

Unlike the western wall with its air of subdued apprehension, the eastern wall was blatantly consumed by fear. The archers had abandoned their bows and their positions against the parapets in favor of huddling in the middle of the walkway with their fingers stuffed in their ears. The close-range fighters were not much better as they had their weapons sheathed and were crouching rather than standing in their positions. Some of the soldiers leaped to their feet at the sight of Christopher and me, but none of them stopped guarding their ears. I didn't blame them. While a rock hit the western wall every few minutes, the eastern wall had a constant barrage. None of the stones came over the wall, but several people cried out when I started to peek through an opening in the parapets.

"They're shooting if they see someone," a woman from Settlement Four warned.

"Well, do we know what's happening?" I asked as I knelt among the frightened soldiers.

"The bricks are breaking apart," a man said.

"Is that what they're trying to do, or is it just a side effect?" I asked no one in particular.

Christopher swore loudly, causing several people around him to jump. "Under the bricks—of course they're breaking the bricks—wood, that's all there is."

I leaped to my feet and forced Christopher to look me in the eye. "You don't think . . ."

"Fire."

Just as he said it, there was an almighty crash that shook the wall under our feet. Curiosity overrode fear, and everyone on the rampart threw themselves on the parapets to see what had happened. I, however, stayed where I was and exchanged an alarmed glance with Christopher.

"Tell me again exactly how these walls were made," I said.

Christopher stood, mouth agape, as if he couldn't accept what was happening. Just as I was about to repeat my question, this time more forcefully, he mastered himself enough to speak. "They're made of wood—boards carved from trees—smoothed over on top so we can walk on them. The parapets are made of wood too. A few months ago, when the Morroks started attacking, we came up with the idea of adding the layer of bricks. . . . We made the bricks from whatever we could find and then layered them against the wall, but they were never very secure. Weather and water wore them down more . . . eroded the cement, cracked the brick—why didn't we fix it?"

"Too late for that. It sounds like they just broke half the eastern wall, and I think you're right—they're going to set fire to it the moment the bricks crumble, but not if we can wet the wood first. How big is your water supply?"

"Quite large, but it's distributed among the houses and—"

Another sickening crash drowned out whatever else Christopher said. This time, he and I shoved our way to the parapets to assess the damage. Most of the eastern wall was laid bare, its wooden backbone dripping cracked cement like an animal shaking out its fur after a swim. The thin bricks that Christopher had bragged about not two days ago lay on the ground with the throwing stones, broken among their killers, a sad testament to the dangers of a false sense of security.

"It doesn't matter where the water is, as long as it's inside the walls," I said, my mouth speeding along without conscious connection to my head. "Send everyone below to fetch water however they can—buckets, baskets, whatever it takes. Get the women out of the mess hall. Go!" I barked at the soldiers who had been eavesdropping. Several of them scrambled to their feet and down the ladders.

If it were possible, the stones came more frequently while I paced the eastern wall, yearning to help with the water—to do anything useful—but knowing I could not leave the ramparts in case the Morroks had ladders. After two agonizing minutes, an army of women bearing buckets, bowls, and even thick cloths filled with water appeared at the base of the ladders. A few more soldiers slung themselves halfway down the ladders to begin an assembly line of passing the buckets up to us. However, before the first drop of our water spilled over the wall, the sound of liquid replaced the knocking of stones outside.

Bewildered, everyone froze midmove. One of my soldiers—a man named David, who had a wife and two children back at the Outpost—stuck his head through the parapets to investigate. A second later, he fell backward, an arrow through his skull.

"Damn it," I swore. Snatching a shield from the nearest man, I stuck it over the parapets to block any more arrows as I squinted down at the wall. I hardly needed to have looked. The smell alone betrayed the liquid. Oil.

"Get the water up here, now!" I screamed, retreating to the safety of the ramparts. Everyone hastened to comply, but no Human was quicker than a flaming arrow.

We all heard the thud—so insignificant compared to the pounding we had lived through for the past two days, but this sound carried with it more dread than a thousand stones could instill. Less than a moment after the thud rose the crackle of flames. Then fire—moving faster and faster until it snaked its way to the tip of every liquid trail the oil had carved into the now-vulnerable wall.

I imagined it all in my head but saw only the smoke. The smoke was barely visible against the backdrop of a midnight forest, but still my soldiers stood transfixed with horror. Before I could master myself enough to spur the water assembly line along again, one of the few holding a bucket dumped it almost blindly over the top of the parapets. Encouraged, the rest threw themselves into their respective tasks as if the last minute's events had never occurred.

Even as we fought the initial fire, the Morroks proved that they weren't finished with their siege. From what should have been an impossible angle, the Morroks shot arrows from the forest through the parapets. Despite the narrowness of the gaps, many arrows found targets, so crowded were we on the ramparts. Although every instinct in me ruled against it, I ordered more than half the soldiers to leave the wall and the other half to douse their torches so the Morrok archers would have fewer targets.

However, once the last torch was extinguished, it became painfully apparent that the fire was winning our struggle. The breeze, which had begun as an idle observation upon coming outside, became an ally to the Morroks as it coaxed ferocity out of the flames and wafted the ashen remains from our wall to smother us with its taste. Although the fire itself had not climbed to the parapets, its glow illuminated the surrounding trees as if threatening to invade them as well. More arrows—these raining down from the sky and landing on the ramparts, on houses, on the dirt within the settlement walls—claimed the lives of soldiers and water-bearing women alike. My mind finally noticed that I was coughing and sweating and that my eyes were watering against smoke and ash.

"Lieutenant, we need to get everyone off the wall," Christopher said. His face was black with streaks of sweat forging through the ash, giving him stripes that looked like war paint. "The fire is going to start eating through the wood. The wall's thick, but not thick enough."

I heard the urgency in his voice but couldn't accept its message: We had to surrender the wall. I gazed through the haze of smoke that had invited itself all throughout the village. The occupants of the northern and southern walls were inching ever further from where their ramparts met the eastern wall. Panicked shouts from those around me prevailed even over the roar of the flames. How could the settlement have yielded so quickly?

"Get everyone off the wall, and form lines parallel to it," I said.

Soon my orders were passed along the wall in tones nearing hysteria. In a last desperate act, the soldiers dumped their buckets over the parapets before fleeing to the ladders or to the other walls.

"Lieutenant, why are we forming lines? The wall is burning on their side. They couldn't possibly cross," Christopher said.

"Just do it," I said through clenched teeth. After checking that we were the last two left, we raced back to solid ground to the gathering of coughing and bewildered soldiers.

"Lieutenant, the western wall!" I heard over the murmurs of those around me.

"Tell them to shut their mouths so they can hear orders, and form those lines," I barked at Christopher. Without pausing to find who had shouted, I hurried back across the town. As I neared the western wall, the reason for alarm became obvious. The bombardment of the eastern wall had been like children skipping pebbles compared to what was now happening to the western wall. Not only had the Morroks taken a battering ram against the gates, but they also had begun a direct assault to break the bricks from the walls. Considering the Morroks' height and strength, I shuddered to think of the size and effectiveness of their weapons against the wall.

"Archers, slingers!" I bellowed even as I mounted the ladder to reach the ramparts.

"Taken care of, Lieutenant!" Scott shouted from somewhere down the wall.

When I reached the ramparts, I found the people there in a state of cramped chaos. The two lines of soldiers who had stood so calmly in their rows not twenty minutes ago now crowded every inch of the wall and dared not rise above a hunch. They seemed to have a system already; soldiers were paired in twos or threes so that as one shot an arrow or slung a stone, the other prepared his own missile to take the first one's place. Scott squeezed his way through the pairs and dragged me down closer to the ground.

"They have arrows trained on every gap in the parapets," he said in a rush. "The trees are far enough back that they can't shoot over the wall, but more than one arrow has already found its way into a man's chest."

"Are the arrows and stones slowing them at all? How are the doors holding?" My heart seized within me as I thought of Levina.

"I'm not sure if our arrows are doing much good. The hammering hasn't slowed—I don't know if they're sending new men out when one falls or if we're just not hitting them. . . . The doors are starting to give."

"Damn it, damn it, damn it," I growled. I was out of ideas. I was a fool. The Morroks had been battering the walls for forty-eight hours, and I had done nothing. This was my reward.

"Lieutenant, what are we doing?" Scott demanded.

"Keep at it," I murmured with as much confidence as I could muster. "Keep your hand-to-hand weapons close in case they change tactics, and I'll call for water for when the bricks give. The eastern wall is burning as we speak."

Turning my back on Scott's distress, I crawled back to the ladders yet again, already calling for the women who had thought their duty that night was over.

With surprising speed, the women flooded from the mess hall again and assembled at the base of the western wall without a trace of fear in their eyes. I nodded to them, expressing my confidence in their leadership, and raced again toward the eastern wall.

"It's burning very slowly," Christopher said as soon as I reached the silent lines of soldiers watching their town collapse like an animal too stubborn—or perhaps too afraid—to acknowledge its fatal wound. "But wouldn't these soldiers better serve the western wall? I hear the gates are about to—"

"Don't question me again," I snapped. "I know the Morroks."

"The gates!" someone shouted from the northern wall.

My legs were carrying me that way before my mind registered those two simple words. How many times had I circled the settlement? Climbed the walls? Where had I gone wrong?

All sense of organization had fled those guarding the settlement gates. What had been prim stacks of wooden boards ready to bar across the door's joints were now scattered splinters of failed locks. Instead, the guards now threw their own bodies against the doors as the Morroks continued to batter. With each monstrous blow, the door gave a little more, and half the people pressing against it flew backward, earning cuts and bruises before they ever drew a sword. It was clear that the Morroks were going to win this struggle, and I wanted to be prepared.

"Call down the melee fighters from the northern and southern walls," I ordered the two soldiers nearest me, both of whom bore signs of having worked as Human door bars for some time. After a moment's confusion, one ran in each direction, calling the command before them.

Within the minute, soldiers poured from either side of the settlement and clustered around my upheld sword. When it seemed that most of them had arrived, I raised my voice over the bombardment outside and the shouts inside. "In a few moments, I am going to allow the doors to give. Your job is simple: Keep the Morroks contained and away from the mess hall. Officers, form a ring around the door."

As soon as I lowered my sword, the officers sprang to life, organizing roughly a fourth of our available fighters into a tight semicircle around the doors. I hurried among the original gate guards and ordered them to ease slowly off their desperate task and ready their own hand-to-hand weapons. To my relief, Levina appeared next to me, her sword already drawn. We barely glanced at each other before we quickly positioned ourselves back to back—the greatest display of care that we could show each other on the battlefield.

About half the original gate guards had fallen back when the door finally yielded to the Morroks. The battering ram—made from a portion of a single mighty tree—carried its bearers several feet past the threshold and over several of my men. It took the Morroks only a moment to realize their victory, and in that moment, dozens of other Morroks that had been waiting outside spread the doors wide, eager for real bloodshed.

More than a year of training together paid off for Levina and me as we slaughtered a Morrok within moments of the battle beginning. Our companions weren't as lucky. Our ring around the door swelled and nearly broke as the Morroks threw themselves at us, their gigantic weapons held high. For every one we cut down, two more shoved their way through the gates, stepping over splintered wood, broken weapons, and fallen bodies. We wouldn't have been able to contain them if it hadn't been for Scott and Caleb, who gathered the remaining fighters from the northern and southern walls after only ten minutes of the gates giving.

I lost all sense of time after that. If mortal combat could ever be called relief, this was the time. After days of worrying about and anticipating this clash of arms, my mind was released from its burden, and my body eagerly took up its task. Levina and I complemented each other in every move we made. We maneuvered through the battle with ease as bodies of friends and enemies alike pressed so closely together in that small ring around the gates that I could hardly swing my sword behind me without striking someone.

After some time, Caleb made his way close to me and signaled for us to move away from where the fighting was fiercest. Over the clanging weapons and shouting men, he reported, "They put out their own fire on the eastern wall, and they've been climbing over."

"Isn't Christopher there with some men?" I asked.

"Yes, but his soldiers are having to chase the Morroks down one by one. They're losing. At first, the Morroks were trying to break into houses, but now they seem to have figured out that the women and children are in the mess hall, so they're heading there as they are able."

"All right. What about the western wall?"

"Not sure. I think they're all coming through the gates now."

"Okay. There's nothing we can do now but try and keep them at bay here."

"Yes, sir."

The fighting continued until dawn. My muscles had gone beyond the pain of exhaustion into numbness as the bodies around me continued to pile up. More and more of my men were having to break off from the main battle to chase down Morroks that escaped through the line. But even with these losses, the ring held and even closed in around the gate, forcing the Morroks back almost outside the gate. We were, at least at this wall, winning.

The sun had almost fully risen when I ordered Scott, his entire face splattered with blood, to lead a small group to help Christopher. Yet even after they left, we continued to press the Morroks further back until, to my own shock, I called for men to begin closing the gates.

Weapons were tossed aside for a bizarre contest of strength. As many men as could put their hands on the doors pushed against them with all their might as the Morroks, still vying to squeeze through the entrance, did the same to the other side. The Morroks trapped inside turned their attention from penetrating further into the village to taking down our men facing the gates, but our remaining fighters formed a new ring around the defenseless pushers.

Then, suddenly, with a last heave on our side, the doors locked into place.

"Archers, to the walls!" I screamed over the cries of victory. "Rain arrows on them until they're too battered to push. Until then, hold the doors. Whatever it takes, hold the doors!"

The Morroks left inside bolted away from the gates toward the eastern wall. Rallying the people nearest me, I led the way to track them down.

Within half an hour, the village was ours again. The doors were bolted shut again nearly as securely as they had been at the beginning of the battle. Our archers quickly routed the Morroks pushing against the gates and forced them to retreat into the forest. Christopher saved the half-burnt eastern wall by stationing archers every few yards along its inner base. Each one held his bow angled so that at the first sign of a Morrok climbing, he could shoot it before it invaded.

When all this news reached me, I sheathed my sword for the first time in hours and sighed in temporary relief.

"I need a body count," I told Christopher.

"Very well. I'll send one of my men and one of yours to try and account for everyone—"

"No, not of Humans," I said. "At least not yet. I need to know how many Morroks are still out there."

"Right, I'll start that right away. And we have sentries set up again, correct? Anything I need to do about that?"

"It's taken care of for now. Go ahead with the count."

"Yes, sir."

I sighed again and leaned against a nearby house. The street was lined with three dead Morroks that Levina and I had defeated not twenty minutes before. Unable to bear the sight of them, I looked to the sky. It was as clear a day as I had ever seen. Hardly one cloud shaded us from the sun. Every drop of blood was laid bare.

Out of the corner of my eye, I saw Levina staring at me. I realized I hadn't really looked at her in all our time of fighting or the brief embrace of victory we had shared before I was bombarded with reports about the status of the walls. Now that I did gaze at her fully, I saw that she looked exactly like I felt—torn, battered, and tired beyond description. Except she didn't lean against a wall or look relieved at all. Instead, she stood upright, holding herself and staring at me as if I had just threatened her life.

I pushed myself from the house and put an arm around her shoulders. "What's wrong?"

She didn't move into my embrace. "Orestes, you were . . . you were amazing."

"Well, so were you. We did great. It felt right—natural how we worked together."

"No, Orestes," she whispered. She didn't exactly move away but still did not draw near. "I was just trying to keep up with you. I—I did nothing. I just followed. Do you realize—didn't you see? They were avoiding you by the end. They were actually giving you space—they wouldn't come near you."

"That's ridiculous," I said uncomfortably. "Morroks aren't afraid of anything."

She finally rested her head on my chest. "There are only Eight whom the Morroks fear."

"Lieutenant," a voice called from the end of the street. Levina and I broke apart, the moment lost.

"Yes?" I asked as the owner of the voice drew near. It was a young man from Settlement Four whose name I didn't know.

"Christopher sent me to tell you that they found the bodies of eighty-one Morroks."

"Eighty-one?" Levina and I both repeated incredulously.

The young man stepped back as if afraid he had upset us. "Yes, sir . . . my lady."

"Nicolas said there were about two hundred surrounding the village before the battle, right?" I asked Levina. She nodded mutely. "We need to find someone who was on the western wall at the end of the battle. Surely we couldn't have pushed the gate shut against more than a hundred Morroks."

I turned to walk away, but the messenger said, "Wait, sir, I was one of the archers on the western wall."

I moved toward him eagerly, and he took another step back before continuing. "There were only twenty or thirty Morroks left outside the gate when we shut it. We picked off a few, but the rest retreated into the forest."

"Could you see any in the forest from where you were standing?"

"No, sir," the messenger replied.

"All right, thanks. You can go back to whatever you were doing."

"That leaves a hundred Morroks unaccounted for at any point in the battle," Levina said.

I grabbed her hand. "Let's find Scott and Caleb."

*

"I'll go," Scott said immediately.

A chorus of emphatic noes followed his offer. I, Levina, Caleb, Scott, Christopher, and a couple of his men had gathered in someone's house far from the noise of the infirmary and fortification of the doors. We had cleaned the large plate of food put before us within moments, but none of us had slept or changed out of our bloody clothes. However, Scott seemed distinctly worse off than the rest of us; it was clear he had been cut several times, and the blood he had failed to wash off made him look like he shouldn't have been able to sit upright.

"Tramping off into the forest is the last thing you need to do," Levina said to Scott in her most maternal voice. "We need someone who is light and quick and who can move through the canopy."

"She's right," I said before she could go on to nag him about visiting the infirmary. "Silence is key. We just have to know if the hundred that didn't attack is still near the village. If they fled, I don't want to stay holed up in here wondering what to do long enough for another force to come."

"Is Nicolas healthy?" Caleb asked.

"Our scout?" Scott asked. Caleb nodded. "Yes, I saw him running around the infirmary earlier. To help, of course, not because he was hurt."

Levina caught and held my direct gaze for the first time since the battle had ended. "Orestes, don't ask him to do it."

"Someone has to go, Levina, and he's our best option."

"I know. I just mean let Caleb or me ask him. Nicholas wouldn't be able to say no to you, even if he thought he couldn't do it. You can be intimidating."

I was tempted to suggest that she was projecting whatever was bothering her about me onto Nicolas, but I refrained. "Go ahead and ask him then. Send word if he agrees."

Levina rose and left without a word.

After a few minutes of catching up on the number of dead and injured, Levina sent for us to meet her on the northern wall. We made it there with only a few people stopping us for questions or reports they felt couldn't wait.

The streets were mostly clear of bodies, but blood and broken weapons still spotted the ground. The children still weren't allowed to leave the mess hall, but the nonfighting women had already worked miracles refortifying the gates and bringing fresh food and weapon supplies out of storage.

When we ascended the wall, Levina and Nicolas were already deep in conversation. Nicolas was holding a thick rope and looking smaller than ever.

Levina looked up at our approach. "We figured we'd lower him by rope since this wall is closest to the tree line—in case they're watching for someone to leave the town."

"Good idea," Christopher said. He took the rope from Nicolas, and Caleb helped him fasten it to the parapets.

"Anything particular I need to know, Lieutenant?" Nicolas asked, his voice strained.

"No, just do a sweep of the town's perimeter. Particularly check around where their original camp was for signs of desertion. And when you come back, make sure not to come too near the eastern wall. Our archers there are shooting at any movement without discrimination."

"Yes, sir. I'll be back quickly."

Once Nicolas had disappeared into the trees, I couldn't sit still to wait for his return. I paced the ramparts as best I could among all the sentries, stumbling occasionally as if I were drunk. I felt myself falling asleep as I walked, and everything around me slipped more and more out of focus as I fought to stay awake. On my third or fourth lap, Levina appeared next to me and inserted herself under my arm like a crutch.

After twenty minutes of anxiety, we heard calls for the gates to be opened. Levina and I rushed to the western wall and watched as Nicolas dashed across the clearing, completely exposed under the bright sun.

"They're dead," he called out when he saw me jump atop the parapets to yell at him. "Every one of them. I counted—more than a hundred, all dead in the camp."

"Well, get in here before whatever killed them kills you," I called back.

Christopher, Scott, and Caleb were already at the gate helping the guards pry the bars away to let Nicolas inside. The guards cast Nicolas withering glares for forcing them to destroy all their work from the last couple hours, but he, flushed with the excitement of bearing good news, paid them no heed.

"I never thought I'd see something like that," he told us in a rush. "It looks like they killed each other. Their camp was still there, but it was in shambles like there was a big battle. All the Morroks were bloody and cut apart, and some had arrows and daggers in them, so it's not like they all ate something bad or got sick or something. And obviously they hadn't been dead very long, you know. The only strange part was some of the weapons I saw. They were real small and thin, not anything like Morroks or even most Humans would carry. Oh, and there were a lot of big feathers everywhere, but other than that, nothing was—"

As soon as he had said "feathers," Levina and I locked eyes in mutual revelation. "It has to be," I said, and Levina let out a shriek of joy. Perhaps because we were so tired, Levina and I shamelessly jumped around in celebration for a moment, hugging and laughing for the first time in days.

"I thought they'd never help us after what happened with Sylvia, but now they've saved us!" Levina shouted.

"Hopefully, hopefully," I said, trying to pull myself back together. "They might have had their own motivation for—oh hell, it had to have been for us! We have to find a way to contact them right away."

"Sorry, but what the hell are you two talking about?" Scott asked. Everyone around us was regarding us like an insane relative; they thought us ridiculous, but they were obligated to us nonetheless.

"It's the best news we've had in a while, maybe ever," I replied, unable to wipe the smile from my face. "Levina and I are going to get cleaned up quickly, and then we're going out to the forest to meet what could be a war-altering ally."

Chapter Twenty-Two
New Year's Feast

"HOW ARE WE GOING to get their attention?" Levina panted ten minutes later as we jogged into the forest, just the two of us, recklessly, armed only with swords.

"Yell, scream, I don't know. They'll only let us see them if they want us to."

"What if we speak in their tongue? That'll get their attention."

"Oh? And since when do you know Serenial tongue?" I teased.

"Sylvia taught me a few words," Levina said defensively. "I might be able to piece together something. Let's see. . . ."

As Levina tried to work out how to say "I am Orestes. I mean you no harm. I wish to speak to you," we pulled each other along to where Nicolas told us the Morrok camp was. For a brief moment, it felt like one of our first days in Serenity Valley, like we had snuck away from camp for a moment just to enjoy the forest and like we were not really concerned about Morroks leaping out at us.

That moment disappeared when we stumbled upon the Morrok camp. The remains of the Morroks were not like those we had killed at the settlement. At the settlement, their wounds were numerous and obvious; their bodies were mangled and their limbs cut off. But the Morroks in the forest had been killed with minute precision. There was very little blood, and their bodies were all whole. Most had only one or two arrows protruding from their necks or left breasts; the rest had nothing but very neat slashes across their throats. If I had not known better, I would have thought them sleeping. It was the closest I had ever come to feeling pity for them.

"I guess the Serenial cleaned up their dead already," I said as I found the strength to move my legs again.

Levina seemed unwilling to join me as I wove through the dead Morroks, crouching every once in a while to inspect their wounds or a fallen weapon.

Instead, she backed into the nearest tree and murmured to herself, continuing to work on her Serenial translation.

A strong voice from above us made us both jump and gasp. "Who are you?"

Recovering quickly, I turned my gaze to the canopy. "Lieutenant Orestes of Warrior Peak. I know who you are; we've met your kind in the west, and we are close friends with Sylvia, if you know that name."

The canopy rattled for a few moments until an opening appeared, showering leaves and twigs on us. Levina ran to join me as a lone Serenial let itself through the hole, glided down to the forest floor, and landed lightly in front of us. It struck me anew how small and brittle the Serenial were. Sylvia must have been unnaturally large for her kind because the one who stood in front of us, who was also a woman, could not have been more than four and a half feet tall. Her skin and hair were as light as ever—almost translucent—while her feathers were a brilliant red-gold. The wrinkles on her face told me she was well into her forties, and the décor of her clothes told me she was a leader, if not a chieftain.

"Yes, I know that name," the woman said. "Sylvia is my sister. And I also knew your name before you said it. Every adult Serenial has been drilled to recognize you."

I smirked, mostly to hide my unease. "Then why did you ask?"

"In case you were just a remarkable lookalike, in which case you would have run off thinking you were hearing voices. You—the real you—are said to have more fortitude than that."

As I considered her, Fallon's words from a few weeks ago came to mind. He had said that the Morroks and Serenial had made me an entity in the war for whatever reason, but I never expected that I would become part of Serenial education.

"I am aware," I said, "that the Serenial have kept track of me for most of my time in the forest, but I am confused about . . . well, about . . ." Unable to come up with the words to describe it, I trailed off and gestured at the graveyard of Morroks surrounding us. When the Serenial only stared, Levina picked up my speech.

"When we encountered your people in the west, they made it clear to us that they viewed the Morroks as a problem we Humans are responsible to resolve. Plus, Orestes—and Sylvia too, for that matter—did not part well with the Serenial in that part of the country. So you can imagine our surprise that you would do all this to protect us."

"Yes, we heard about Sylvia's . . . departure," the woman replied almost dismissively. "I am afraid that our brothers in the west have not yet been forced out of old prejudices against Humans. We in the eastern and central Valley have learned to think otherwise."

"What do you mean?" I asked.

"Well, you must understand what my people thought when Humans first came to Serenity Valley," the Serenial said. She stood rigidly as she talked, with no outward mannerisms or gestures whatsoever. Her sword hung on her waist while her arms remained firmly crossed. "You see, no Serenial ventures outside the forest. It is just not done. So we knew nothing of Humans or Warrior Peak, and we saw little of Morroks until they crossed the desert boundary. When they—the Morroks—first began to explore, my people tried to contact them, and the Morroks, as they are wont to do, killed my people on the spot and for a time proceeded to try and root us out of the trees."

"But you must have seen the difference between Morroks and Humans when we started to come," Levina said.

"Not really," the woman replied. "Neither of you have wings, so for all we knew, Humans were just Morrok children. For that reason, we hardly tried to contact them, at least not at first. Why would we risk it?

"This was years ago, of course, before anyone alive today had been born, and truly, it has taken most of that time for us to be sure of how to treat Humans. We observed that they fought against the Morroks as fiercely as we did, but when we eventually tried to speak to them, they too raised swords to us, though now we realize it was out of fear. For just as we were, for a time, baffled by Serenial without wings, so too your people must be by Humans with wings."

Levina and I nodded, remembering all too well our first sight of Serenial descending from the canopy.

"So the Serenial we met in the west still distrust Humans because of this," I said. "But you fight the Morroks—though apparently without Humans knowing. The few who have seen Sylvia at the Outpost were quite surprised to learn about your people's existence."

"Yes. We track the Morroks' movements around the forest as closely as we have tracked yours. Whenever we can gather a militia large enough, we try to pick off the groups we see, especially if we notice that they are moving toward Human villages. We are not always successful, though."

"We would be so much more effective if we worked together," I said, my heart suddenly racing. "If you could just convince your leaders, I know we could work everything out so that—"

"I am one of our leaders, and the rest are already listening to this conversation," the Serenial said, her eyes flickering upward. Levina and I followed her gaze a little uneasily. "And we already agree with you. We are ready to try exposing ourselves to Humans again. My sister joining with your friend in marriage and then befriending your group has encouraged us in many ways."

"Oh, please tell her that," Levina said. "She so wanted her relationship with Ritter to do just this. It would mean so much to her—she's pregnant, you know. That child could be a symbol for this alliance and our—"

"Later, Levina," I said, resting a hand on her shoulder and trying not to laugh. "I'm glad you contacted me, um—what's your name?"

"Aderyn."

"Aderyn. And since you say that you track the Morroks' movements—could you tell me if there have been any major attacks in the far west? Two of our settlements were supposed to meet and follow us eastward."

"I know the group. We have protected them as best we can. They should reach the lake very soon," Aderyn said.

I exhaled in relief. "Thank you." Fallon and I had spent many sleepless nights speculating the fates of Settlements Six and Eleven. "Anyway, like I said, I'm glad you contacted me, but if we want to make this alliance official, I hope your leaders will come to the Outpost, where my general is."

"We already had intentions of doing that," Aderyn said. "There are no Morrok forces left within miles of this settlement, but we have noticed a raised level of activity in the tower on the western side of the lake. We had hoped to speak with you to assess if your people were ready to see ours so that we could begin to fight together."

"Nothing would make my people happier," I said as evenly as I could. Out of the corner of my eye, I saw Levina looking as if she wanted to jump up and down again. "However, considering all the injured and small children among us, it will take my group here a few weeks to travel back to the Outpost."

"We will protect you while you recover and then while you journey back to the lake. But I would like to travel ahead to begin negotiations in case something happens at the tower. Would this be wise?"

"If you're careful," I said. "Walk—don't fly—up to the front gates during the daylight and ask for General Mark, Colonel Fallon, or even Sylvia. Tell the gate sentries that Lieutenant Orestes sent you. You shouldn't have trouble."

"Very well," Aderyn said. Her wings unfurled abruptly, causing Levina and me to flinch. "Warn your fellow Humans about our existence because we may need to contact you again without waiting for you to wander outside the town. If not, know that you are still protected. Good-bye, Orestes . . . Lady Orestes."

With that, the Serenial half flew, half climbed back into the canopy, leaving a few swinging branches in her wake.

Levina and I stood, unmoving, for a moment, straining to hear any additional signs of the Serenial, but to no avail. Then, after one last look at the slaughter around us, we sprinted back to the settlement.

*

The next few days passed in a blur. Between long bouts of deep sleep, we did everything we could to patch up the injured and ready ourselves for travel. Even the citizens of Settlement Four were anxious to leave their home for the relative safety of the Outpost. True to Aderyn's word, the Serenial flew in and out of the settlement without a care, but their foreign appearance was the biggest delay in our preparations as my people stopped to gawk at their wings from the time they landed to the time they took off again.

The night before we planned to leave, I was fortunate enough to be on the sleep rotation for a full eight hours. I wasn't surprised to find my bedroom empty; Levina and I had ended up on entirely different schedules soon after our meeting with Aderyn. All our belongings were packed and near the door, and the bed was even made, as if Levina wanted to appear tidy to anyone who might one day stumble upon the abandoned settlement. Only Levina's diary remained unpacked as it lay open on the desk, probably to let the ink dry.

In spite of myself, I glanced at the little book and marveled at how many pages she had filled. Levina had never told me not to read it, and I couldn't help but notice that my name appeared several times in her latest entry:

The past few days have been so unbelievably eventful that I could fill the rest of this diary describing them. I won't have time to record everything fully until we are safely back at the Outpost, but I had to write this before I lose the gravity of what I am feeling and later justify it away into nothing.

Orestes has, once again, baffled me beyond recognition. As I read over my earlier writings, it's becoming more and more clear to me that there are two Oresteses, one of whom I know very little about. The first Orestes is the one I love. He is the one who is transparent in an almost childlike way. He is frank and sincere about his strengths and his passions, and he genuinely enjoys meeting other people and encouraging them. I know that this Orestes loves me, although he has never said it directly. I've never put much stock in the power of eyes to speak, but even from our days at Warrior Peak, the way he looks at me has told me that he loves me.

The other Orestes, however, is the one who cannot say the word 'love,' no matter how much his face shows it and his heart feels it. That is the Orestes I don't understand. That is the Orestes I was with when the battle began a few nights ago.

I've watched Orestes fight a hundred times, a thousand times even. I've watched him duel Acules, Ritter, all his peers at Warrior Peak, half the forest Warriors we've come across, and I've dueled him myself countless times. But last night was the first time I've seen him really, truly fight since the rogue Morrok he slaughtered at the end-of-year tournament of 325.

I did not recognize the man who wove his way through the battle with unchecked passion. I know that my horror at the violence should have outweighed my awe, but Orestes—this other Orestes—was captivating. His power was both beautiful and terrible to witness; even the Morroks, who tower two feet above any of us, seemed rattled by his flawless display of might. I've never been in a real battle like that before, and besides the overwhelming fear, the one thing that I remember is this sense of powerlessness, like I had no control over what was going to happen to myself or others. But Orestes seemed to have full mastery over it all. He was fighting and ordering what to do across the town and protecting me all at the same time without once breaking his stride.

Although this other Orestes is little better than a stranger to me, I felt so safe with him, almost addictingly safe. Yet for all the control Orestes has over a battle, I can't help but wonder how much control he has over himself. Maybe it was something in his eyes again, but something about him during the battle made me wonder more than once what state we would be in if Orestes somehow forgot he was on our side. But even with that irrational fear, I can't help but desire that power to be nearby, and I depend on the chance that this Orestes is as good-hearted as the one I know and love.

I love my Orestes, and I depend on him as much as any lover depends on her partner, but this new need for the other Orestes—the one I don't know and am quite frankly a little frightened of—is disturbing to me. I know that when I marry Orestes, I will marry all of him, but how will I know when this other side is going to come out? It seems to be connected with fighting or perhaps just with the Morroks. Maybe it's something I'll never understand, if there's any explanation to be had. It doesn't seem right, though, that I won't ever know Orestes—all of Orestes—like Glynis knows Fallon or my grandmother knows my grandfather. Or maybe one person just can't know everything about another, whether they're married or not. Ah, well, I'm wasting pages now, and there are things to attend to if we're going to leave the settlement in the morning.

I tried reading the passage again, but mostly I had to keep myself from tearing the book apart. I hated when Levina made me feel like this—like I was a monster and she was the victim of my cruel secrets. The first time she had confronted me with it—after the tournament of 325—I had resented her for being the first person besides myself to point out my Morrok traits. Since then, Cassandra had said the same, but even when she did, she didn't leave me with such a feeling of self-loathing.

After several minutes of me fuming and staying as far away from the diary as possible, Levina herself came in. Closing the door behind her, she smiled and sighed as if the sight of me gave her more pleasure than anything in the world. She took my face in her hands and kissed me sweetly before sitting next to me on the bed.

"I love you," I blurted. The words sounded hollow to me, but at the same time, my insides inflated with unbidden excitement.

Levina's eyes shined with tears and disbelief. "I love you too."

In that moment, I decided I could be Levina's Orestes if that was what she wanted. As long as I didn't read her diary anymore and as long as I avoided her after I did what I had to do in battle, we would both be happy. It seemed like a small price to pay for a woman who was willing to marry a man she feared and only half loved.

*

After more than two weeks of painstaking travel, the trees finally gave way to the vast lake of the central Valley. The morning of our arrival, we found the Outpost in a state of organized chaos because the refugees of Settlements Six and Eleven had arrived only the day before and were still living on the training grounds as they waited for housing assignments. Levina and I barely took two steps into the gates before we were barraged with greetings from old friends. I remembered everyone's name who came up to me, but in all the confusion, I struggled to recall every family member I ought to have asked about. Within five minutes, Levina had a crowd of children surrounding her and asking her to tell them stories. As I debated whether to help her or to watch her struggle, Fallon finally caught up with me. I was prepared for him to drag me off to meetings immediately, but instead, he clapped me on the shoulder.

"Chieftain Aderyn told me about your performance at Settlement Four. You did very well."

"Um, th-thanks . . . thank you, Fallon."

"Don't pretend to be so surprised. Now stow your belongings and meet me at the fort in twenty minutes. We have much to discuss."

Satisfied, I mock saluted him and hurried through the crowded streets to my house. As I jogged, I saw groups of Serenial roaming around the settlement, often accompanied by a Human who seemed to be giving them a tour. I was pleased to see that most Humans were hardly giving Serenial a passing glance, which demonstrated a level of comfort I hadn't expected, even after nearly three weeks of alliance. What did disturb me, however, was the fact that the Serenial did a double take every time I came within fifteen feet of them. It took me a moment every time to remember that Aderyn had said all Serenial were taught to recognize me, but no amount of time could acclimate me to that knowledge.

I thought arriving at my house would be a relief from all the staring, but there was no solace to be found in the madness of that building. As I walked up the street, I saw a line of people protruding from one of the houses, and as I neared, realized with dread that the house was mine. Angry looks and biting protests followed me as I marched past the line and through the front door without a word.

Inside I found that the line led to Glynis's room. The looks and protests grew exponentially more indignant as I inserted myself into the room, where a dozen people clamored around Glynis herself. When she saw me, she gasped and pushed through the people with strength I didn't know she had. Trying not to laugh at the full-grown man she had nearly knocked off his feet, I embraced her and kissed her on the cheek. I didn't realize until that moment how much I had missed her over the past month.

"Oh, Orestes, I know the Serenial told us you were safe weeks ago, but I just couldn't sleep well until I saw you for myself!" she said.

She pushed me away from her and observed me from head to toe as if looking for any scratch or bruise. "You do look well. Where is Levina? You did take care of her, didn't you? She was so excited to go with you. I know she probably didn't tell you that, but it meant so much to her to—"

"She's fine, Glynis. Better than fine, actually. We're, uh—well, we decided we're getting married—"

"Married!" Glynis exclaimed. "Married! Oh, finally, how wonderful! You can do it tonight! At the feast! Oh, it would be perfect, I know it would!"

"Wait, slow down—what feast?"

"The one I'm in charge of. That's why all these people are here—to ask questions about their duties and such. We've had so little time to prepare for such a great event! We're celebrating our alliance with the Serenial, Settlements Six and Eleven arriving, and, most importantly, your victory at Settlement Four. Already there are requests for speeches, public announcements for new babies, formal toasts for birthdays and anniversaries—a wedding would fit in perfectly!"

The dozen people in the room and the countless more outside had been listening to every word of the conversation, but they didn't seem to be sharing in the joy of our reunion. Instead, their irritability had grown so that the moment I didn't respond, both men and women drew in impatient breaths to call attention back to themselves and their hectic tasks. Before they could explode, I said, "Will you excuse us for a moment?" and ushered everyone out the door.

"What about the tower?" I whispered once the door was closed. "How can you be planning a party that will most likely intoxicate three-fourths of the Outpost when we've got the tower to consider?"

Glynis tilted her head in confusion. "Tower? Oh! The Morrok tower—well, 'fortress' is what they've been calling it. Fallon's talked of nothing else. Aderyn told us that her people had noticed a large group of Morroks coming down from the desert to the fortress and that several of the little groups wandering around the forest were reporting back to the fortress. So, naturally, they thought the Morroks were amassing forces for some attack, but once that big group from the desert arrived—well, most of them just turned around and left, and the rest went back to whatever they were doing. Aderyn said it looked like an escort of some sort, but who knows? All the Morroks are so much alike—how could we know if one's more important than the other?"

"Yes, it was probably nothing," I lied. I hoped Fallon would have a better plan of action than just assuming that such a gathering at the tower—however brief—was nothing more than coincidence. "Well, I have meetings to attend. I'll be back soon, I hope, but if not, I'll see you at the feast. Good luck with all the planning and—"

"What about your wedding?" Glynis asked. Her eyes shone with the anticipation of a hopeless romantic.

"I, uh . . ." I tried desperately to remember the conventional Warrior Peak waiting period between an engagement and a wedding, and I realized with a jolt that it was usually very short—only as long as it took to apply for housing and to hire an official from the Inventory division to perform the ceremony. I hadn't really worried about *when* Levina and I would marry, just that we would.

"Ask Levina when she comes home," I said. Levina was the more practical of the two of us, and her idea of practicality did not involve impulsiveness such as this.

The next few hours passed in a haze of conversation. The meeting room in the fort was crammed not only with the Outpost leaders, but also with those of Settlements Four, Six, and Eleven and those of the Serenial. In spite of this new diversity, nearly every face around the table was familiar to me, and I was happy to give my account of the past month's events in minute detail. Once I finished, I demanded a more official update on the tower, but they told me the same as what Glynis had—that the threat seemed to have passed.

Aderyn and Fallon also filled me in on their meetings from the past few weeks. I wasn't completely behind, however, as Serenial messengers had traveled back and forth several times between the Outpost and my traveling group to keep me informed of the less secretive matters the council had discussed. Mostly I learned about the Serenials' network of communication that spanned more than a third of the forest and that enabled them to track Morrok movements with great efficiency. Aderyn told us that thousands of Morroks were in Serenity Valley but that most of them were in small groups that roamed the forest, apparently for the sole purpose of terrorizing any group of Serenial or Humans they caught unawares. The Serenial had worked tirelessly to prevent this from happening, but in spite of their efforts, they had lost several lives.

The windowless room kept us ignorant of the time until one of Glynis's messengers called through the door that it was nearing evening and the feast was about to begin. After the usual lamentation about having no natural light, General Mark apologized and promised our meetings would be "more efficient" from then on. And so, feeling like we hadn't accomplished anything, we trudged out of the fort and into the fading sunlight.

The streets around the fort were deserted, but we could hear the multitude of voices and see the collection of torches coming all the way from the training grounds. When we came into view of the grounds, cheers erupted before we could enter.

"It's because they won't serve the food until I give the go-ahead," Mark shouted in my ear as he waved to the crowd. I laughed and began to drift away from the council in search of Levina, but Mark and Fallon both grabbed my arm.

"Like it or not, you're the hero of the day," Fallon said as he guided me after Mark, who was ascending a makeshift raised platform in the middle of the mass of people.

When I joined Mark, I was momentarily shocked by the scope of the gathering. At least two thousand Humans and Serenial were crammed in the training grounds and along the ramparts above. Large crowds didn't intimidate me, but after nearly a year of living with only a dozen people, I had forgotten what it was like to be among so many. In fact, the only other times I had seen such a great number were at the end-of-year tournaments at Warrior Peak.

Nostalgia threatened to overtake me, but then Mark began to speak.

"My friends, as this year draws to a close, so also does our old outlook on the world around us. Before this time, we lived as ones not in control of our fate. We have allowed the Morroks to attack us and to destroy us little by little, but no more.

"I will not be so arrogant as to say that this change in attitude comes solely from some arbitrary resolution on my part. Indeed, this change is made possible by events we all have seen unfold in just this past month. And because we have all been witnesses to these events and because we are all only feigning politeness as we wait for this meal, I will give only brief welcomes to those who have transformed the face of the new year.

"First to Settlements Six and Eleven, who have traveled months on end to join us here at the Outpost." Hundreds of voices shouted their approval.

"Next to the people of Settlement Four, who fought heroically for their place among us." Hundreds more joined the din and roared all the louder when Mark bowed to Christopher and me.

"Last to the Serenial, who are our new allies and friends. Nothing I can say will express how grateful we already are for your aid in this fight against the Morroks. Welcome."

Even if every Human there had hated the Serenial, the momentum of the applause was unstoppable at that point. Mark bellowed something about the feast beginning, but his work was finished. He stepped back and smirked at me.

"You know how to handle them!" I yelled as the crowd surged toward the mess halls.

"Exciting a crowd is the easiest part of my job," he replied. "Glynis has had this place in a frenzy for days looking forward to this thing. All I have to do is smile and sound important!"

"I'll keep that philosophy in mind next time I'm sharpening my sword for battle."

"Laugh all you like, but just wait—you'll have to make speeches later. Then you'll want my tips."

I rolled my eyes and hopped off the platform, happy to be swept along toward the mess halls. When Scott and Caleb found me in the madness, they each miraculously already had a goblet of ale in both hands. I accepted one gratefully as I was barraged by people to meet and remeet. There were still many people from Settlements Six and Eleven to catch up with, and perfect strangers somehow knew me enough to congratulate me about Settlement Four and the Serenial. The Serenial themselves also sought me out, though none of those conversations lasted long; most of them were more like Aderyn than Sylvia, speaking with no expression or warmth so that I felt awkward every time.

True to Mark's promise, I was called on for speeches throughout the night, everything from recounting our battle at Settlement Four to announcing a couple's wedding anniversary. Within the first hour, the feast had spread from the mess halls to every corner of the Outpost, and so my speeches were, in truth, me climbing on the nearest chair and shouting to those close enough to hear and sober enough to appreciate my words. After a few hours, my voice was sore from such labors and from introducing Scott and Caleb to every available woman from Settlements Six and Eleven.

During one of my brief moments of relative peace, a dark-haired woman appeared at my elbow and murmured, "Congratulations on your victory, Lieutenant."

My automatic "thank you" was halfway out of my mouth before I realized the woman was Cassandra. She was completely changed from the woman I had carried out of the Morrok's camp a month and a half before. Her hair was trimmed and swept partly on top of her head with tiny decorative pins woven throughout. Her dress was actually sewn to fit her and was made of some delicate, dark green material. Even her face was painted—or perhaps I had never seen her with her skin completely healed from the Morroks' abuse. She looked so healthy and so pretty that I had the urge to embrace her, but I refrained.

"Oh, Cassandra—thanks, but no, it wasn't my victory. I mean, we wouldn't have made it without the Serenial, and even then, I had very little to do with how well—"

"Save your humility for the stage," she said. She grinned before I could think to be offended. "That just seems to be the proper way to greet you tonight."

"I wish it weren't," I said. "I never knew my name would get lost to a title."

"You mean you never thought it would this early in life," she said. "Weren't you set to claw your way up the rankings at Warrior Peak? Top of your class and all?"

I laughed. "Yes, but ambition of that sort seems foolish now. I'm not sure if it was the Morroks or the forest that made it so."

"They are terribly tangled together now, aren't they? All the same, I wouldn't shy away from your title or your victory. I've never seen ambition as a negative thing, especially when you have an end goal as noble as yours."

"Even if my ambition drives me to act as I normally wouldn't?" I asked, thinking of Levina's diary in spite of my efforts to forget it.

"If you're willing to make the sacrifice, I see no room for shame."

I laughed again. "How ruthless of you."

She grinned. "Yet somehow I manage to sleep at night. Anyway, we shouldn't be talking like this—this *is* a party after all. Go back to your friends; I just wanted to see the hero up close before he ascended to the stars with the rest of the immortal bodies."

"Be optimistic; there may be other opportunities to kiss my feet as the night goes on," I said airily. She turned to leave. I wanted to pat her shoulder or give her some other reassuring gesture but suddenly felt too awkward to do so. Instead, I said, "Cassandra, in all seriousness, you look well. I hope you feel the same."

She nodded and continued on her way. I had, again, come as far as I was allowed into her world and couldn't hope to go further.

Scott and Caleb approached me as soon as Cassandra left. "Damn, Orestes, you weren't lying about her," Caleb said as they stared shamelessly at Cassandra's retreating form.

I felt a wave of protectiveness rise up inside me, but I also remembered what Frank, the late leader of Settlement One, had said about Cassandra—that she had always been social and popular with men before her kidnapping.

"Yes, she is beautiful," I murmured.

"Well, I think we need to introduce ourselves. See you later," Scott slurred. The two of them stumbled off in her direction.

Left to myself, I set out to find Levina again. I had seen her a few times throughout the night, but she was always surrounded by a group of women from some of the settlements. Luckily this time I found her only with Sylvia. The two of them were huddled together in the corner of the farthest mess hall, which was littered with the discarded remnants of the feast. When they caught sight of me, Sylvia, now five months heavy with her baby, burst into laughter, and Levina, blushing, jumped up to meet me.

"Talking about me?" I asked as I kissed Levina. I tasted wine on her breath. Sylvia attempted to rise to greet me as well, but before she could, I embraced her and slid onto the bench across from them.

"How are you?" I asked Sylvia. "I asked Ritter, but he rattled on too long for me to get a clear answer."

Sylvia smiled. "I'm doing wonderfully, in spite of my husband's incessant worrying. I am a little bigger than I should be at this point, but no matter. Now that you've reunited me with my people, especially my sister, I am greatly comforted, and I have already spoken to several midwives of both races. I'm not concerned."

"And you shouldn't be," Levina said bracingly. Sylvia smiled even more broadly at her and after a moment began to laugh again. Levina's flushed cheeks returned as well.

"How much have you been drinking?" I asked.

"Sylvia not at all, and I had just half a glass," Levina said defensively. She looked at me suspiciously. "What about you?"

"Not much either. Glynis pesters me for speeches every half hour, so I have to be aware of myself."

"Oh, so you've talked to Glynis?" Levina asked, her voice tensing.

"Why?"

"Excuse us for just a moment, Sylvia," Levina said as she swung her legs out from under the table. Sylvia laughed yet again as I joined Levina a few feet away from the mess halls. "Did she, uh—did Glynis talk to you about the, um . . . the wedding?"

"Which one? I know of a couple that were supposed to happen tonight, but I think I might have missed them. I wish I hadn't, though, because I think I knew one of the—"

"No, dear, ours," Levina said. She twisted handfuls of her dress nervously.

"Ours? Oh, yes, well—she mentioned it to me before the feast, but I told her to ask you. Did you tell her yes?" I asked, more surprised than anything.

"Well, yes," Levina replied, distressed. "It's so hard to say no to her—I mean, you know that—that's why you sent her to me. And we never really talked about it, so I wasn't sure, and you were in council all day, and I didn't know what to do. Besides, I think now is a good time." Her face reddened yet again. She had never been a good liar.

"Any particular reason?" I prodded.

"No," she insisted, not looking me in the eye. "I just thought—well, we don't have to now, of course, but I thought we should soon before I start to . . . I just thought now would be a good time."

"I think now is a good time too." I lifted her head up to make her look at me. "I really do."

She kissed me and brought my hands to her stomach. "Let's find Glynis."

Chapter Twenty-Three
Immunity

Year 327

THE MONTHS FOLLOWING OUR JOURNEY to Settlement Four were the busiest and yet most exciting of my life. Within weeks of our alliance with the Serenial, we were in contact with the remaining three settlements to the far east. On foot, it would have taken us months to find them and bring them back to the Outpost, but with the Serenials' wings and protection, they were able to arrive safely at the lake in half the time. Like Settlements Six and Eleven, they had been largely ignorant of the Morroks, and the Serenial had to spend days convincing them not only that the Morroks existed, but also that they, the Serenial, were there on behalf of other forest Warriors and meant them no harm.

Once Settlements Three, Seven, and Ten arrived, housing all but disappeared, and we spent weeks obstructing the former training grounds with new lodging for them. Other new projects sprang up as well, the chief among them being the Serenial teaching Humans how to move in the canopy. With the Serenials' ability to track the Morroks from the trees, we were able to send men through the canopy to ambush any small groups they found wandering around the forest. For the Morroks continued to circulate in a wide radius around the lake as if they were scouting for something. This unsettled me, but as long as they weren't amassing at the fortress, I rested easy at night.

Although the Morrok numbers were large, we were working on guarding the border between the forest and the desert to prevent them from communicating, just as they were doing to us by separating us from Warrior Peak. We still had not had contact with the Peak, because every Serenial who had attempted to fly through the desert either had been shot down or had to land due to exhaustion, where they met a similar fate. All the same, we hoped that once we had control of the northern border of the forest, we would be able to lead a large force through the desert to combine with Warrior Peak's army.

My part in all this was balanced between talking and fighting. I continued to attend Outpost councils and was even invited to a few meetings among local Serenial chieftains. General Mark valued my opinions more and more because, as the youngest member of the council by decades, I was out in the forest the most. He wanted to give me a higher title, but I had led so many people under the name *lieutenant* that I told him it would be too difficult to change. I also led or helped to lead several ambushes every month if the Morroks were near enough to the Outpost. Once I became accustomed to being a leader in battle, I enjoyed perfecting our attacks and melding our strategies together with the Serenials' fighting style.

I never strayed too far from the Outpost, though. This was only partly due to council meetings, but mostly it was because I wanted to be near my new family. For just shy of nine months after our wedding, Levina had delivered our first child, a girl. We named her Jamie, after Fallon's great-uncle James, one of the heroes of the Laconic Warrior story that the General had told me two years ago.

Many people joked about me having a girl, saying they were sure that I—the great war hero—would have a son, but I only laughed and said that Jamie was far better—and bigger—than any boy we would ever have. The midwives who assisted Levina all said that they had never delivered a larger child, and later they told me that it was a miracle Levina had made it through unscathed. This haunted me sometimes when I was left to my own thoughts, but I could never stay sad for too long. For although Jamie had my hair and eye color, when I looked at her, all I saw was Levina, and that was enough for me.

However, not everyone was as fortunate as Levina and I. Not long after the turn of the year, Sylvia lost the child she had been carrying for more than five months. I wasn't at the Outpost when it happened, but our family felt the devastation of it for months afterward. Sylvia could hardly leave her bed for weeks, and to distract himself, Ritter took on as many duties as he could around the Outpost, although he performed all of them terribly. After a month of this, they left the Outpost entirely and joined the Serenial who guarded the northern border of the forest. Since then, we had received a few letters from them that sounded progressively more cheerful, but Levina said she wouldn't be convinced of their recovery unless she saw them for herself. Secretly I doubted we would meet them again for many months, perhaps not until after the war was over.

About two months after Jamie was born, we were expecting another letter from Ritter, but the messengers from the north arrived without any word from him. Even though I wouldn't admit it aloud, I had been putting off a trip to a Serenial tribe on the other side of the lake to wait for that letter. Now that it hadn't come, I began the painful process of leaving my wife and daughter.

After dinner at the mess hall, I rushed home to avoid being obligated into any evening social activities. Once safely inside, I pulled an old cloth sack from under my bed and set about packing several clean tunics even though the trip would be short. An unfortunate consequence of being in a place of leadership was that people expected me to appear clean and dignified whether I had been tramping through the forest or sitting in council meetings all day.

Not long after I finished packing, I recognized Levina's footfall on the stairs. As soon as she opened the door, I said, "What are you doing here? We agreed."

"I know," she said, waving a hand in surrender. In her other arm, she cradled Jamie. Levina had changed very little since Jamie was born. Physically she was heavier because she hadn't picked up a sword since giving birth, and she never let her hair down anymore. Instead, she spent her time educating Humans and Serenial alike about Morroks and their history because she insisted that half of people's fear over the Morroks sprang from simple ignorance. As much as I loved to hear Levina get herself worked up over the importance of her job, there was nothing I liked better than watching her with Jamie, whether she was dressing and rocking her to sleep at home or hauling her around the Outpost on one hip as she worked and greeted people throughout the day.

Now she laid Jamie in her cradle at the foot of our bed and held up her hands in mock surrender. "I know I promised to stay away, but I couldn't help it."

"We said good-bye this morning, and we weren't supposed to eat dinner together—supposed to pretend I'd left already so I could leave right away and be on time—"

"I know!" she repeated.

Jamie hiccupped in her cradle, and we both paused to gaze at her for a moment. She was awake but didn't make another noise, and she looked back at us with better concentration than I had found in some grown men. I put a hand on Levina's shoulder, but she jumped away from me and pressed herself against the wall opposite me.

"I don't want to delay you," she said. "I just wanted to see you one more time. I tried to find you at dinner, but—"

"I looked for you too," I admitted, grinning. "I walked around the damn mess hall ten times. Didn't get a bite to eat. . . ."

Levina laughed. "So are you ready?"

"Yes," I said. I slung my bag over my back and picked up my sword. "If I leave now, I should make it by dawn."

"I don't know why they can't come to you," she said for the thousandth time, "or send messengers. There's no reason to make you go."

"It promotes good relations," I replied, also for the thousandth time. "There's nothing like meeting someone in person, and many Serenial still aren't used to dealing with Humans directly instead of just watching us."

"I know."

We stared at each other for a long moment before I gave up and pulled her toward me. "I need you to come with me to these things."

"I will," she whispered. "When Jamie's a little older, I'll get back in shape, and I'll go everywhere with you. Okay?"

"Okay."

"Okay. I should go. You need to get there by dawn."

"Yes," I said, feeling a slight twinge of guilt. It was true that I was due to arrive at the Serenial village by dawn, but not tomorrow's dawn. I had two days before I was supposed to meet the Serenial, but no one knew my plans for the next day, least of all Levina. The twinge in my stomach threatened to become a pain as I thought of what could happen if I went through with my plan. Levina couldn't know.

After a while, Levina and I let go of each other. She went to the cradle to retrieve Jamie, but I waved her off. "I want to say good-bye to her. I'll give her to Glynis or someone on my way out."

"Okay," she replied. She kissed me quickly and said, "Be safe," as if I wouldn't have been otherwise.

"Two weeks," I said as she closed the door behind her. I sighed and tied my sword around my waist so I could pick up Jamie. Her eyes began to droop as I rocked her. In a world where I was supposed to be a war hero and an army officer, Jamie was the only person who had no qualms about interrupting or ignoring me, and I loved her for that.

"It's not really going to be two weeks," I confided to her. "I should be back in eleven or twelve days, but if I tell your mother that, she'll pull all her hair out at dawn on the eleventh day wondering why I'm not back. Besides, I like to surprise her when I get back 'early.' Soon enough, I'll get to surprise you too."

Wary of the setting sun, I padded outside, trying not to jostle Jamie along the way. To my relief, I ran into Glynis halfway down the street. She was happy to take the baby and even happier to have a last opportunity to tell me to be careful.

"You and Levina tell me that more times than I care to count," I said in mock exasperation.

"That's because it's a selfish request," Glynis replied seriously. "If you're not careful, we're the ones left behind, and that is a terrible fate to push on someone, least of all your wife. I've been telling Fallon to be careful for years, and he's never once listened to me."

I laughed and kissed her and Jamie one more time. We parted ways, and when I glanced back a few moments later, Glynis waved, but for once she didn't smile.

*

Without question, the great lake was the most populous area in Serenity Valley—whether by Serenial, Humans, or Morroks, it didn't matter. The immeasurable gathering of fresh water attracted us all, but that night, I cursed its size more than I ever had before. At Warrior Peak, *boat* was a foreign word because the mountain rivers were littered with sharp drops and turns that would make such travel suicidal. Yet in spite of spending generations beside this calm lake, the forest Warriors had ventured to create only a few shaky rafts. I knew about more sophisticated boats because of Aldis's stories and the sketches she had drawn for me when I told her I didn't believe her.

And so that night, boatless, I walked around the very edge of the lake, not bothering to take cover in the trees. Because the Morrok fortress stood along the lake's shore, albeit on the opposite side of the Outpost, the lake itself had become our most direct territorial dispute. Most of the skirmishes I had led within the past year were struggles to keep the Morroks as far from the Outpost as possible, though none of us dared come within a hundred feet of the fortress itself.

If I hadn't had to keep a decent appearance, I would have swum for a while to break the monotony of walking. With all my new responsibilities, I hadn't had time to swim for months. At first, I didn't mind so much for myself as for the time I lost spending with Cassandra, but she turned out not to need me as much as I thought she did. After the feast toward the end of 326, Cassandra had rapidly come out of her shell. It started with Scott and Caleb, who, taken with her appearance, had followed her around for weeks. To Levina's amusement, Cassandra hadn't paid them any attention until they gradually lost interest. Caleb had since married a woman from Settlement Eleven, and Scott was on his way to doing the same with a woman from Settlement Three.

Cassandra too had moved on to an arguably better life. After winning Scott and Caleb's affection for a while, she gained some of the old confidence that Frank, the leader of Cassandra's old settlement, had told me about before he died. Now Cassandra always had one man or another in tow, and she hardly spent the night at our house anymore. We sometimes didn't see her for days at a time, which wouldn't have bothered me so much if I didn't know she was probably with a different man every few weeks. Levina didn't seem too concerned, but she had never quite taken to Cassandra and was probably just glad to have her out of the house. With Ritter and Sylvia up north and Cassandra out all the time, Jamie, Levina, and I had the second floor all to ourselves, which was a rare privilege with housing as tight as it was.

It was still a few hours before dawn when I reached the point around the lake where I was supposed to reenter the trees. The Serenial village I was visiting was close by, but the real reason most people took refuge in the canopy at this point was that the Morrok fortress was now within seeing distance.

As I looked at it now, the plan that had been in the back of my mind for a year now pushed its way to my active thoughts. It wasn't so much as a plan, really, as a question—a test. It had been fourteen years since Acules rescued me from the Facility in Tyrclopia, but I still remembered the day quite clearly. I remembered Acules telling me that Dirth had let him go, and yet the General had told him that the Morroks would be angry because he took me.

But why would Dirth let him go? Aldis had also told me stories about Zachaes and Xander moving about freely in the Facility and that Zachaes had even rescued some children. It didn't make sense unless they were all connected somehow—Zachaes, Xander, and Acules. At the moment, I couldn't guess what that connection might be, but I wanted to know if I was a part of it.

I hesitated before I started toward the fortress as Glynis's words from the night before rang in my ears. "Be careful," she had said. This certainly wasn't careful, and I had Jamie and Levina to consider now. But I also had a feeling that if I didn't go now, I never would, and I couldn't go my whole life without knowing.

With each step I took toward the fortress, a growing sense of defiance welled up inside me and started to drown out the fear and self-loathing that I always carried with me in the presence of Morroks. I had panicked three years ago when I had actively pursued the Morroks of the Gravel Lands, but not this time. I didn't want to be pursued anymore. I wanted answers.

I reached the fortress without seeing a single Morrok. The fortress itself was really just a tower, eight stories high at most, with a four-story square wall surrounding it. All of it was made of stone, though it was hard to tell what kind; the walls were painted solid black, as if to ensure that the fortress stood out among the green of the trees and the blue of the lake. I found a small door hidden among the stones, and with a deep breath, I pushed it open.

The courtyard around the tower was deserted as well. In fact, I felt as if I had entered a real desert. Outside the fortress, healthy grass and other plants surrounded the lake, but inside, all the grass was either dead or torn up, making the ground brown and muddy. There was no evidence that anything lived there—no food, no clothing, not even a broken weapon. I had wondered if I would find young Morrok trainees, but perhaps they were all in the desert to the north.

Grasping my sword handle, I proceeded toward the tower, which had a much more distinctive entrance of two twelve-foot-tall wooden doors. I pushed these open as well and wasn't terribly surprised to find that it was empty inside.

The entrance hall, if that was what it was, was at least two stories tall and looked like it included the entire area of the tower. The interior was strangely dim in spite of the early morning light, and it took me a moment to realize that the great room was lit only by candles; no windows punctured the thick walls. The space had some crude furniture—long wooden tables and several chairs that were slightly larger than I had ever encountered. Perhaps this was where the Morroks ate. None of the chairs were very close to each other, as if their occupants didn't want anything to do with each other. I imagined that even if the room had been full of hungry Morroks, there would still be silence.

I had taken only a few steps inside when I heard movement at the other end of the room. It was only then that I noticed an archway that led to a wide spiral staircase. I considered running, but it sounded like only one pair of feet descending. Instead, I checked again that I was alone and that the doors remained open. Then I backed against a wall and waited.

When the owner of the feet arrived, my mind froze completely. For some wild reason, I had half expected it to be Dirth, but it wasn't. In fact, this . . . man, monster, whatever it was . . . was the most Humanlike Morrok I had ever seen. He was tall like any Morrok, and his features were just as sharp and pointed as ever, but his skin was all evenly pale and didn't seem stretched across his skull. I couldn't begin to tell how old he was or if he was a leader of some kind. He wore layers of frayed and torn cloaks just like the rest of them, concealing whatever weapons he might or might not have had.

"Hello, Orestes," he said, almost pleasantly. His voice wasn't as low and hoarse as most Morroks' were. In fact, it was perfectly even and almost Human.

I didn't reply. He continued to cross the distance between us but stopped ten feet short of me. He drew a chair to him and sat down in the middle of the aisle between tables. Somehow the unadorned chair now seemed much more like a throne.

"Relax your sword hand. There is no one else here, save a few lookouts who alerted me to your presence."

"If there's no one here, why are all the doors unlocked?"

"Very good question," he said as if I had passed some sort of test. He was studying me very carefully, almost calculatingly, without a trace of fear or dislike. "You of all people should know that intangible fear is a powerful tool. Your people are so terrified of me that they won't dare come within an archer's range of my fortress. Why, then, would I lock my doors?"

I said nothing. So he was a leader—perhaps *the* leader, at least around the lake. The familiarity with which he spoke to me was as alarming as his leadership status, but I decided not to question it yet. Still, the way he spoke about fear reminded me of something I had heard before, but I couldn't quite place when or where. . . .

"I must say," he continued, "I am surprised it has taken you this long to come here. Your predecessors were much more curious."

"My predecessors? Like Acules?"

"Yes, among others. But I suppose being cooped up in Warrior Peak has kept you ignorant of our presence on this side of the mountain, correct?"

"It did for a while."

"I thought as much, or else I imagine you would have come to the Gravel

Lands long before I had to start baiting you."

"Baiting me?" I repeated.

"Yes. First Aldis, but no one connected her murder to the Morroks—they thought it was an accident, I suppose. Then Acules came to Warrior Peak, and I let that man—Todd, I believe—report our existence. I thought that would be enough, but you did nothing more than skirt through the Gravel Lands one day. I finally had a boy killed during one of your tournaments, and that set your war in motion and got you to come out of the mountains."

"So it was—all of that, all the threats and murders—they really were because of me?" I asked. I was having a hard time breathing. I wanted to sit down but couldn't bring myself to look that weak in front of him.

"Oh yes, I had to get your attention somehow. Unfortunately, Warrior Peak's walls were more formidable than I had ever thought. I never was able to send more than one spy. Given that, I couldn't manage to get to anyone close to you, or you might have sought us out directly long ago. But that is in the past. You are here now." His voice had a hint of pride in it.

"Why . . . why do you care where I am or what I'm doing? We're on different sides. You should just want me dead."

"You ought to know by now that being enemies isn't that simple," the Morrok replied. "It took you a while not to feel guilty for killing Morroks, correct? As harsh as my training procedures are, you were one of us for several years, and you cannot forget that."

"It doesn't matter. I didn't take the serum, so I'm nothing like you," I said. My voice had risen almost to a shout, and I now wondered just how far away his lookouts were.

"Are you quite positive you did not drink any? I hear you broke the vial the day of your escape, and one cannot always control where liquid trickles."

I said nothing. Even if I tried to deny that I thought like a Morrok, I could never rid myself of the fear that I carried the serum with me every moment of my life.

The Morrok chuckled. "Ah, Orestes, it makes no difference whether or not a drop or two runs in your veins. Do you not remember what I have told you?

What effect do you think the serum really has, besides the change in our physical appearance? I win my army's loyalty through my training—a training that was instilled in you at a very early age. I let you go to see what you would accomplish without my help, but you will never truly escape my influence."

Quite suddenly, a memory fourteen years old surfaced in my mind—Dirth's very last words to me before he left: *No matter what happens today, you are under my control, under Lernuc's control. You will never do anything he won't be pleased by. Kill me, kill Humans, kill Morroks—prove your power the only way you know how, and we will have won.*

Was this Lernuc? Surely Lernuc would look like a Morrok—a super Morrok, like Dirth—eight feet tall, huge muscles, fanged teeth, claw-like hands. He wouldn't look like a Human. Only a weak draught of serum would produce such a Morrok.

"So you don't care what side I fight on," I said. I struggled to control my breathing.

"Not particularly. Your success is what interests me."

That sounded uncomfortably like something a father or a mentor would say, and those were the last roles I wanted a Morrok to play in my life. I cast about desperately for something to say and could only come back to his apparent care for my survival. "All this time, you've been killing people around me, but you haven't wanted me dead?"

"Oh, I never attempted to protect you, if that's what you mean. You and Acules are the first of a group of most interesting people whose destinies could tip the balance of our little struggle."

"What group of people?"

"Did you not receive the message I left you at Settlement Eleven? 'There are only Eight whom the Morroks fear.'"

I remembered the night we found the message—and the kidnappings that went along with it—with another jolt of guilt.

"So Acules and I," I said, "and who else?"

"I don't know," he said. His ignorance didn't seem to distress him; in fact, he sounded almost excited as he continued. "They may not exist yet, but I'm working on ways of testing before they grow old enough to hold a sword. By then, it is obvious that they are of the Eight but perhaps too late to gain as desirable a measure of control over them as I have over you."

Suppressing the urge to argue his last point, I plodded forward with another question. "How do you know Acules and I are part of this group?"

This question actually made him pause for a moment. He frowned, and if he had been a more frivolous person, I would have expected him to start pacing or tapping his foot. He didn't do either, but when he spoke again, he did so quite slowly and deliberately. "Morroks fear you—for reasons you do not know but that are well-deserved—and I doubt I need to emphasize to you how rare that is among Humans and even among fellow Morroks. That is why you may fight for either side. Against the Morroks, you experience success because they know you are more powerful than they. However, should you choose to fight among Morroks, they will follow you without question because they, as you said once yourself, are motivated solely by fear."

"When did I ever say that to—but wait, are you offering to let me lead Morroks?" I asked incredulously.

"The option has always been there," he replied as if surprised I had to ask. "It seems foolish to me for you to remain a lieutenant among weak Humans when you could be second-in-command in my elite army, but I suppose you have your reasons."

The absurdity of his statements nearly made me burst, but I saw the futility of my words before I began to speak. This Morrok spoke rationally—almost *too* rationally, with no concern about the horrors of what he called "his training" and about the terror he caused both to Humans and to his own kind. I had always imagined all Morrok leaders to be like Dirth—hateful and frightening inside and out—but this one was eerily calm and calculating with an alarmingly loose sense of loyalty, as if it didn't matter who won or who didn't, who lived or who died.

The Morrok rose to his feet, and I pressed myself further against the wall, my hand going back to my sword. He didn't seem to notice.

"Well, Orestes, now that I have seen you, I must leave for Tyrclopia. I recommend that you go back to the Outpost, though I imagine the battle will be over by the time you reach it."

"Battle?"

He laughed. "You and your scouts know very well that I keep my soldiers within half a day's journey from the lake. Surely you didn't think that I was always going to keep them near my fortress, which, as you have seen, is quite safe from attack?"

I felt my mind seizing up even though I knew it was too late for thought. It was true that most of the Morroks in the forest were near the lake, but they had always stayed in small groups—never enough for us to be alarmed. We had always worried about them gathering at the fortress but never converging on the Outpost. . . .

"You were just waiting for me to leave," I said as I moved toward the door.

"Perhaps. But take heart—what difference will one man make in a battle?"

He smiled, this time rather maliciously.

Trusting the Morrok's word that I would meet no obstacle on the way, I turned my back on him and ran out of the fortress. Before I left, I could have sworn I heard him call, "Farewell, Orestes!"

Chapter Twenty-Four
Fallon's Penance

ALTHOUGH I WAS RUNNING AT FULL SPEED, the journey back to the Outpost seemed to take hours longer than the journey away. The whole time, I replayed in my mind the battle procedures at the Outpost. We had done settlement-wide drills to see how long it took to get everyone barricaded inside. Seven minutes if we had a considerable number of people in the fields.

Seven minutes. Surely the Serenial would have noticed the Morroks heading toward the Outpost in time for everyone to get inside. And once they were inside, I was fairly confident in our walls and very confident in our leadership. I had seen all our tactics and planned some of them myself. But as I started to imagine my friends putting those tactics into practice, I felt a pain in my chest that threatened to stop me in my tracks. And then there was Levina and Jamie. . . . I ran faster.

As the hours passed, I was bombarded with Serenial messengers bearing news about the battle. The first had been sent just after Mark, Fallon, and the Serenial leaders realized that the pockets of Morroks were all closing in on the Outpost. The next confirmed that the battle had begun. The third didn't realize anyone else had come and told me about the beginning all over again. Each of them jogged next to me long enough to deliver their news, and then they flew off again, glancing back helplessly at me as if they wished I could fly as well.

By the time I rounded Settlements One and Eight, I knew the general story of the battle and was fairly sure it was over, just as the Morrok had said. The Morroks had tried battering the main gates, of course, and they had also tried to climb the outer walls with ladders—a tactic we had anticipated and prepared for long ago.

From what the Serenial told me, our preparations had paid off—at least for a while. Months ago, we had lined the ramparts with flint and oil for burning

Morrok ladders, and we also used metal rods to help push the flaming ladders off our walls. During the battle, they had carried out this plan well, but gaps in our ranks inevitably sprang up, allowing a few Morroks to infiltrate the Outpost. Most of them were killed, but a few had run through the town and then escaped back over the walls, after which the Morroks retreated abruptly.

This was not nearly enough detail to sate my anxiety, but it prepared me enough not to panic when I reached the Outpost and found a small pile of Morrok bodies outside the walls. To my relief, no officers were outside to slow my journey. Ignoring hails from others, I continued at my breakneck pace inside, looking only for Levina.

Moving inside the walls was difficult because it seemed that everyone was still too energized from the battle to remain indoors, and so I had to contend with hundreds of people no matter what street I turned down. No one realized that I hadn't been home for the battle and kept me asking for any news or updates. They sounded nervous. I kept asking about Levina, but no one had seen her.

Before long, I ran into Caleb and Scott along a row of houses near the fort. If the rest of the Outpost seemed crowded, it was nothing compared to this area. The fort both housed the infirmary and acted as a shelter for those who could not fight, and so the doors were blocked with nonfighters trying to leave and those outside trying to find out about their loved ones' injuries. Both Caleb and Scott had several cuts and burns, which told me they had been in the heart of the action on the walls.

"Orestes, why are you back? Aren't you supposed to be across the lake?" Scott asked as we moved toward the mess halls, where it was quieter.

"Yes, but the Serenial caught up with me, so I turned back," I lied. "Where's Levina?"

"She's fine," Caleb said. "I saw her after the battle, and she had only a few bumps. I bet she's trying to get through that chaos to get Jamie out of the fort."

"Good," I said, relaxing a little. If I couldn't see her for myself, hearing this from a friend was the next best thing. "Were you two waiting to see anyone inside?"

"No, we're just trying to hear if there's anything new to report," Scott said.

"Everyone's been asking for news," I said. "I don't understand why everyone's so concerned. The Morroks left, didn't they?"

"That's the thing. We can't figure out why they stopped attacking. From where we were on the eastern wall there," Caleb said, jerking his thumb toward the wall closest to the fort, "we were losing, to tell you the truth."

"We heard the eastern wall got hit the worst," Scott said. "All the same, it wouldn't have made any difference how badly the rest of the walls were doing because we were close to being overrun. It's not good having two-story houses backed up against a three-story wall like that. The Morroks were climbing over the parapets and jumping down on roofs in two seconds."

"And then they just stopped?"

Caleb nodded incredulously. "Yes. I saw a few of them climb back up the inner wall and then go back to the forest, and soon after that, new ones stopped coming up the ladders. Those inside kept going toward the main gate, but we hunted them all down. Then the ones battering outside just sort of walked off. . . . It was really strange, even stranger than the battle at Settlement Four."

"But that battle stopped only because all the Morroks were dead," I said. "This time, they just gave up."

"Which Morroks don't do," Caleb said.

"Right," I agreed. "And if they were trying to open the main gate, why were most of them attacking the eastern wall? They're on opposite sides of the Outpost."

Before we could come up with an explanation, I felt a tap on my shoulder. Hoping it was Levina, I whipped around, but it was Cassandra who stood behind me. A deep purple bruise obscured half her face, reminiscent of the injuries she had had when I first found her held captive among Morroks.

"Your presence is no longer a secret," she said with a wry smile. "The council is already in the fort, and they're asking for you."

I said good-bye to Scott and Caleb and followed Cassandra back toward the crowd. "Are you okay?" I asked her.

"I'm fine. This bruise is about all that happened to me, and it looks worse than it is. I was on the ground chasing down the ones that got over the wall. The people on the ramparts got the worst of it."

"Well, I'm glad you're not hurt," I said as sincerely as I could when I had one man elbowing me and another treading on my foot. We weren't making very good progress through the mass of people. "Listen, I'm going to have to pull rank if I want to make it through here before sundown, so . . ."

"I understand. I need to get some fresh air anyway. Levina's okay, by the way."

"I heard. Thanks, Cassandra."

"My pleasure, Lieutenant."

After watching Cassandra disappear down the street, I gathered my voice and began to shout that I was on important business and had to get inside the fort. As people looked around at the noise, they recognized me and made a path right to the door.

Inside the fort was, if possible, worse than outside. I couldn't move a foot past the doorway, so tightly were people packed in the entrance room. I kept shouting, and somehow people squeezed aside enough to let me shuffle sideways toward the council room.

When I opened the door, all the faces in the room looked up warily as if bracing themselves for another pointless interruption. I noticed immediately that a face was missing from among them.

"What happened to Fallon?" I asked.

Mark rose hastily from his seat, strode over to me, and put an arm around my shoulder. "Orestes, I wanted to be the one to tell you. Something happened—"

"What happened to Fallon?" I repeated, my voice rising uncontrollably.

"Not Fallon. He's with Glynis right now in the infirmary. She . . ." He didn't finish.

I mumbled something between "thank you" and "okay" to Mark as I pushed my way out of the room again. The few feet to the infirmary didn't give me time to prepare myself. I heard children everywhere in the offices nearby and thought vaguely of Jamie. I would get her after I saw that Glynis was okay. We would get her together. . . .

The infirmary was uncrowded and very quiet. Unlike with the nonfighters, we had made plans long ago to ensure that the fort's infirmary would not be overcrowded after a battle. We had designated several houses throughout the Outpost to act as secondary infirmaries so the injured wouldn't have to be moved far from where they fell. Glynis must have been close to the fort when she was struck. Maybe she had been trying to get inside so she wouldn't have to fight. She was getting older. Fallon was too.

I found them near the door. Glynis was lying on a low, flat table, and it was clear that she had been dead for some time. Even in the candlelight, the paleness of her skin shocked me, and her body seemed somehow smaller, almost deflated. She didn't look like the same woman, not without a warm smile and her bustling movements.

Fallon knelt by her, holding her hand. He had his fair share of blood and scratches, but he had done nothing to help his injuries. Before I could think of what to say, he spoke.

"I'm leaving," he said in a low voice, so that no one else in the room could hear.

"Leaving?"

"I'm going after the Morroks that killed her, and I will not come back until I have repaid them in kind."

"Fallon," I said incredulously, "you know you can't track Morroks. You know how hard it is to tell them apart. You'll never be able to find which ones—"

"I am a selfish man, Orestes," Fallon interrupted. "I always have been, even in marriage. Especially in marriage." He stood. "I never asked her opinion on the decisions I made for us, but she always went along with them. This is where it led her."

"It's not your fault. There's no way you could've—"

"It's not about blame or fault. I have to do something for her, and avenging her is my last chance."

I didn't know what to say. Fallon was always so practical, so focused and in tune with what needed to be done and who ought to do it. He took on challenges but knew his limits. What could I say to change his mind when his mind was so different from what I knew?

"You can still honor her," I said. I felt tears in my eyes, and my throat was beginning to ache. "Give her a good burial. Make sure everyone knows how kind and loving she was."

"I have to do this, Orestes," he said. He started to go on but then stopped himself. But I understood all the same. He wasn't coming back. He was choosing an impossible task to occupy the remainder of his life, which, in this new reality, would probably be very short.

"Good luck," I whispered.

He smiled a little. "Two last pieces of advice because I am your father. One: In my absence, people will look to you. Because I was their only connection to Warrior Peak for so long, the forest Warriors have given me more credit than I deserve, and that burden will now fall fully on your shoulders. Let them think of you as more than you are; it will give them hope."

I nodded. He was sounding a bit more like the old Fallon.

"Two," he continued, "protect Levina however you can. I can't pretend I figured out how to do this for my wife, but I . . ." He looked down at Glynis, shaking his head. "I promise it is valuable enough to make the effort."

I nodded again. I wished Levina were with me now. I didn't know what it was to miss my parents or to be apart from them in any capacity. I felt very young.

Fallon embraced me, and I couldn't keep myself from crying. I couldn't think of anything to say other than further pleadings for him to stay, and so when we broke apart, all I did was nod. He kissed Glynis one last time and strode out of the infirmary.

I sat with Glynis for a while, trying to gather myself. I couldn't stop looking at her, couldn't stop thinking about our last conversation, about her sadness. The more memories that came to mind, the more I wanted to join Fallon in his hunt. But I knew I couldn't. As much as I wanted to fight the

Morroks directly, I was now saddled with leadership of an army and with a family of my own. I had to stay where I was, and I never thought that that would feel like a burden as long as I lived among Humans.

After a time, I left the fort to find Levina. While I had been with Glynis, someone had restored some order to the fort; the interior still held dozens and dozens of children, but their parents were now lined up outside waiting to retrieve them in an orderly fashion. I found Levina in line near the door, but when she saw the expression on my face, she left immediately and followed me to the deserted mess halls.

Levina sobbed uncontrollably when I told her about Glynis, and it took me a while to talk her out of running after Fallon and trying to force him to come home. Even as we grieved, whenever people spotted me, they came up to ask questions. At the sight of our tearstained faces, their curiosity quickly gave way to panic, but neither Levina nor I could bring ourselves to explain. When a crowd started to form around us, we agreed to retrieve Jamie and go home as quickly as possible. There would be plenty of time for others' problems later.

As before, the crowd parted to allow me into the fort ahead of the rest. Most of the children had been ushered into offices, but the sound of their cries could be heard even over the noise outside. It had been hours since some of them had seen their parents, and the anxiety of separation was taking its toll on both sides.

When we found Ruby, the woman in charge of babies and toddlers, she looked as frantic as if the battle were still going on. "Jamie?" she repeated distractedly when I asked where she was. "Haven't seen her in a while. Didn't someone already pick her up? No, that was a James, maybe. Hold on a moment." She walked away, consulting a long list of names.

"We'll get Jamie and everything will be okay," I said numbly, gripping Levina's shoulders. She nodded, her eyes glazed.

Ruby came bustling back a few minutes later with her list still in hand but without Jamie. "I don't have her checked off, but she's not here. One of my helpers must've given her to someone without telling me. I saw Abby here earlier. She lives in your house, right?"

"She was probably just checking in at the infirmary," I muttered to Levina. Abby had been trained as a healer at Warrior Peak and had continued that profession ever since we arrived at the Outpost.

As we bade Ruby good-bye, I couldn't stem the panic rising in me. Morroks had been within the Outpost walls, and now no one could find my daughter.

"You took Jamie to the fort, right?" I asked Levina as we broke into a run toward home.

"Of course. I took her myself, and I didn't tell anyone to pick her up for me," Levina replied, her voice strained.

When we reached home, we found Cyrus, Joanne, Holt, Abby, Jacob, and Cara all there—the last remnants of our group from Warrior Peak. They were surprised to see me and asked about Fallon and Glynis, but I found that I couldn't explain what had happened, especially not why Fallon was gone.

"Did any of you take Jamie out of the fort?" I asked after several failed attempts at answering their questions.

One by one, they shook their heads. Levina and I exchanged terrified glances and tore out of the house again.

We dropped all pretenses after that. With increasing hysteria, we stopped every person we came across as we ran aimlessly through the Outpost. I was dimly aware that I was spreading panic where I should have been containing it, but I didn't care. My mind was beginning to form conclusions that I couldn't bear, not now—not ever. Scott and Caleb had said that a few Morroks had made it back over the wall, and then the attacks had stopped. It took only one Morrok to carry a baby. What if the attack stopped because they had gotten what they wanted?

"What difference will one man make in a battle?" the Morrok had asked me. A hell of a difference if the one man was a father. . . .

We were the only parents missing a child. We ran around the Outpost for hours, long enough for the postbattle census to be completed. Jamie was the only person missing. I knew Morroks kidnapped children, but this was too pointed to ignore. They had waited until I left the Outpost. But how could they have entered the packed fort without anyone noticing?

Levina and I hadn't spoken to each other since we left the fort. We had followed each other blindly, and now she took the lead, running out of the Outpost entirely. Night had fallen, but she plowed into the trees without a torch. The canopy blocked out most moonlight and starlight so that I was forced to follow the sound of Levina's crashing movements for several minutes before I grabbed her arm.

"Levina, I think—I think she's—"

"This is your fault!" she screamed, so loudly and so shrilly that I was sure Morroks within five miles could hear.

I couldn't even ask "what" before she continued, her voice out of control. "It's because you weren't here. I've been waiting for it to happen. Every time you leave, I just wait for it, and here it is—it happened—"

"What the hell are you talking about?"

"The Morroks!" she shrieked. "They act differently when you're around! I don't know why, but they do. And as soon as you leave, look what happens! My daughter is gone!"

I stared into the darkness where I thought Levina was, wondering if the trees obscured hearing as well as vision. "Levina, how could you—how dare you blame me for any of this? If I have to tell you how much I love Jamie, then you've completely lost your—"

"This has nothing to do with your feelings," she spat. "I've watched it happen since the day I met you. Aldis killed inside Warrior Peak's walls. Conrad killed right in front of us. The Serenial capturing us and demanding to know why Morroks are following us—you—around the forest. Todd. Glynis. And now . . ."

"And now what?" I asked, fighting to keep my voice steady. Everything the Morrok had said to me half a day ago seemed infinitely worse coming out of Levina's mouth.

"Now whatever mark you have on you has lost me my child, and damn it, Orestes, I want to know why."

I froze, all the usual defenses coming to mind. Levina couldn't know about me growing up in the Facility. She couldn't know that I had talked to Morroks—not then, not yesterday, not ever. She couldn't know that I had ever thought like them, acted like them, moved like them. I hated myself for it, and surely she would too.

"I don't know why they follow me," I lied, defeated. "I wish I did, and I wish I knew how to stop them, but I don't know why they do it."

"Yes, you do. I know you've always hidden something from me, but I overlooked it. I thought that you must have had your reasons for staying quiet, that you would tell me in time, or that it didn't matter for me to know. Apparently it did matter. I know now that you're involved with the Morroks somehow, and if I had known sooner . . ."

"You'd have done what?" I snapped. "Stayed at Warrior Peak? Not married me?"

She didn't say anything. I felt my insides shutting down and disappearing as the silence lengthened. Aldis, Conrad, Todd, Glynis, Fallon, Jamie, Levina—four of them dead, two of them moving further and further away from me as I stood there talking, one of them slipping away before my eyes. Was this what the Morrok at the fortress had wanted?

After a while, Levina spoke again. "You know, I talked to all the Serenial who flew to you around the lake so I could make sure you were safe and on the way. I talked to the very first one—the one who left as soon as we realized there was going to be an attack. He went straight to you, not the Serenial village you were going to, and he said you had already started back to the Outpost. Why is that, Orestes? How did you know to come back?"

I opened my mouth to speak, but no cover-up came to me. I thought vaguely about telling her the truth—everything from the Facility in Tyrclopia to the Morrok I had met in the Valley fortress—but it was too late. I said nothing.

"I guess I'll have to use my imagination on that one too," she said. I heard her moving away, back toward the Outpost.

Something about the nastiness in her voice—whether because I had never heard it before or because it was directed at me—suddenly made me care very little about her feelings at that moment. "Off to write in your diary?" I called after her.

Her footsteps stopped. "What do you care?"

"Well, I know if I had any secrets, I wouldn't record them in a book anyone can read."

"What the hell does that mean?" she asked, her tone distinctly less confident.

Relishing my newfound power, I forced a mocking laugh. "If you think I'm so involved with the Morroks, why do you feel so *safe* around me, even though there are two *sides* of me, even though you'll never know the *whole* me?"

A horrible, pregnant silence followed in which I only half regretted what I said. I waited for Levina's counter—waited to see if I had gone too far—but no protest came. Instead, I heard her turn away again.

I took a few steps toward her. "Wait."

"Stay away from me," she said, her voice surprisingly strong for being full of tears.

"Look, I don't like you very much right now either, but you can't walk away. What about Jamie?"

There was another pause. I could make out her silhouette just a few feet in front of me. Her shoulders rose and fell dramatically as her breathing became more erratic.

"You tell me, Orestes," she murmured. "Can you get her back?"

"No, I can't," I whispered.

"Then I guess we're finished here." The rustle of leaves marked her footsteps until she was gone.

I started to run after her but stopped after a few steps. I started to run west toward the fortress but stopped just as quickly, knowing it was fruitless. Instead, I stripped off my weapons, threw them farther into the trees, and collapsed to the forest floor, unable to act and unable to comprehend the new lot that had been set before me.

Chapter Twenty-Five
One of the Eight

THE DAYS AFTER THE BATTLE were very dark for the Outpost. I missed the immediate aftermath because for a day—or maybe two—after my fight with Levina, I staggered aimlessly north, searching for any Morroks that might have had Jamie. I didn't stop to eat or sleep, and I took no precautions to hide myself from Morroks or Serenial. Eventually a Serenial tribe did find me collapsed on the forest floor, and they convinced me that the Morroks heading toward the desert had long outstripped me. I asked them if they had found Fallon, but the last they had heard, he was traveling east pursuing a group of four Morroks. I asked them to bury his body if they ever discovered it.

When I returned to the Outpost, Mark informed me that my absence had been poor for morale. As confirmation spread of Fallon's disappearance, people didn't automatically transfer their trust to me like Fallon had predicted; I heard panicked whispers in the mess halls about the possibility of us being cut off from Warrior Peak for good now and the council dissolving without someone like Fallon, who had known each of the settlement leaders for years, to unite them. I made some speeches with Mark and the other leaders, telling the people truthfully that the attack could have been much worse, that we had done well, and that we had plans for any future incidents.

But no matter how confident I appeared or sounded in front of a crowd, everyone from the oldest man to the smallest child knew that I had lost both my parents and my baby in one night. And so, rather than looking to me for courage, they looked at me with pity.

Normally, such pity would have annoyed me, but I found that I was detached from any emotion besides a dull ache in my stomach that I could ignore only if I were immersed in work. I took on tasks that were completely irrelevant to my role as a leader, everything from replacing flint for fire on the ramparts to hauling wood from the forest to repair the front gates. I remembered that after Sylvia miscarried, Ritter had taken on any physical task and avoided home until he was so tired he could fall asleep immediately. Now I understood why.

In fact, I found myself missing Ritter now more than ever. Although Scott and Caleb brought me and Levina food when we avoided the mess hall and acted as my bodyguards when I didn't want to answer questions throughout the day, I couldn't talk to them the way I could to Ritter. They didn't know about my past and didn't know and love Fallon, Glynis, and Levina like Ritter did.

Even though she didn't say it, I knew that Levina wanted to talk to Sylvia for many of the same reasons as I wanted to talk to Ritter. As my wife, Fallon's daughter-in-law, and an active worker in her own right, she led far too public a life not to have several friends, but she wasn't nearly as close to these women as she was to Sylvia. While I busied myself talking to people all day about trivial details, she stayed at home most of the time, though doing what I did not know.

Levina and I hadn't spoken much since I returned from my rambling journey north. She didn't even ask where I had gone. Instead, her diary disappeared from immediate sight, and we both had trouble looking each other in the eye.

Far worse than whatever argument Levina and I could have, there was now a hole in our family that Jamie had left, and neither of us was coping very well. When Ritter and Sylvia lost their baby, they had managed to lean on each other as they grieved, but Levina and I were drifting apart by the day. For both of us, everything about the other reminded us of Jamie, and our unspoken solution was to avoid each other as much as possible. When we met around the Outpost, we spoke very little, and whenever I did come home, we didn't last long in the same bed. Inevitably, one of us would make some excuse and take one of the empty rooms left by our disintegrating family.

I couldn't decide if it would have been easier not to know Jamie's fate. I wasn't sure if Levina had ever deduced that the children that the Morroks kidnapped became Morroks themselves, but even her knowing that Jamie was alive with only Morroks to care for her was enough to keep her up at night.

I, however, knew exactly what was in store for Jamie. There was no doubt in my mind that the Morroks had taken her to the Gravel Lands to start her training. Her first couple years—the ones in which she could not walk, hold a weapon, or feed herself—would not be too terrible as long as she didn't get sick. Although the Morroks' nurturing side was limited, they did keep babies sheltered from the elements and fed regularly. After those first few years, however, was where my memories of the Morroks began—the ones in which I, along with my peers, were left to fight each other for food and territory with the occasional interference from brutal trainers who supplied us with weapons and beat us with their own swords when our technique was wrong. I couldn't bear imagining Jamie getting to that point, and it became my new life's goal to prevent that image from becoming reality.

Whether my thoughts were transparent or my line of thinking was not uncommon, Mark regarded my input in council meetings with great suspicion over the next few weeks. At first I thought he was anticipating my grief to interfere with my decisions, but he revealed his real concern one day in a council meeting when the subject turned, yet again, to contemplating an offensive movement against the Morroks.

"I know we haven't discussed this in a while," I said, "but I feel that we've lost sight of our ultimate goal in the midst of all that's been going on in the forest."

"That goal being?" one of the other men asked politely. Since I had come back, the other officers had been very cordial in their every address to me and hesitant to ask anything of me. With Fallon gone, I had wondered if they would discount me as his lackey, but thanks to Fallon's insistence that I distance myself from my role as his son, they continued to ask for my opinions and treat me as a fellow commanding officer in spite of my young age.

"Reconnecting with Warrior Peak," I said. "The Serenial are already gathering at the northern border of the forest to keep the Morroks out, but that can only last for so long. The Morroks are a growing people, and so containing them rather than purging them will only cause problems for future generations. We aren't making any progress picking off small groups that are wandering around the forest. We need to go to the source—the Gravel Lands—and going there is our best chance to contact Warrior Peak."

It was nothing they hadn't heard before, but the mood of the cramped, windowless room changed immediately. Some of the men leaned forward and murmured to their neighbors. A few, however, exchanged knowing glances with Mark, who cleared his throat.

"Now, Orestes," he said, "I know how . . . recent events . . . might inspire you to suggest moving forward, but we have to be realistic."

"What does 'realistic' mean?" I asked.

"As much as we all know and respect Warrior Peak's power, you have to understand that just as it is your childhood home, so is the forest most of ours," Mark said. Many of the others nodded. "Although everyone is shaken up right now, they feel safe at the Outpost, and more importantly, they feel at home. It's going to be difficult to rouse people to war when we've been able to live in relative peace thus far."

"We are their commanding officers, and they will go to war when we declare it," I said, far more passionately than I meant to. I had to resist the urge to rise to my feet, and the stuffy room suddenly felt suffocating.

"This isn't Warrior Peak," Mark said evenly. "Not everyone here is a soldier, and it will take more than a few persuasive speeches to move them to war."

"So we're just going to wait for a tragedy to convince them?" I said. "Are we going to wait for their mothers to be killed and their children taken away in the night?"

No one spoke. A few men shifted in their chairs. Just as Mark was clearing his throat, there was a knock on the door.

"Come in," Mark called.

A young Serenial man strode into the room. His tan feathers were ruffled and his dark eyes drooping. He was clutching a bundle of letters.

He dropped the bundle in the middle of the table. "Letters from the north. And I was told to give this directly to you." He drew a single letter from his vest pocket and handed it to me. "It seems to be of some importance, so I encourage you to read it soon. My superiors hoped that I would bear your reply when I return."

"When are you going back?" I asked.

"I would like to rest for a day or two, and then I will be ready."

"Then let me find you lodging in one of the—" Mark began.

"Thank you, but I would prefer sleeping in the trees."

After a few murmured thank-yous and good-byes, the Serenial left. Without a word, I opened my letter and was surprised to see that this supposedly important letter was from Ritter. I couldn't help but grin, however, as I read through his rambling words and barely legible writing.

Orestes,

Thanks for your last letter. Sylvia and I are both doing well. We're with a militia traveling east, where we've seen a lot of Morroks sneaking in and out of the forest. The border's so big, we're having a rough time keeping the whole thing covered like we want to, even with all the Serenial we have coming from the south to help. It's strange being the only Human around here. Sometimes I feel so much like a Serenial, I forget I can't fly (Sylvia says she's already preparing the letter telling you I've broken my neck.)

I know I've told you this before, but it's just so strange being able to see the mountains again, even from a distance. Like I said, we're moving east, so we're getting further away from Warrior Peak, but I can't help looking over to it every time I get the chance. I wonder what they think happened to us? I'd give anything to be able to find out what's going on there.

I know we don't usually talk business in our letters (hell, who am I kidding, I'm not ranked high enough to talk business with you at all), but the Serenial have been leaning on me to run this idea past you, one Human to another. The place I told you about, where the Morroks keep coming in and out of the forest—well, we have reason to believe there are Humans in that area. Strange, right? I told the Serenial it's impossible because there were only ever twelve settlements, and none of them are in the northeastern part of the Valley, but a few Serenial swear they got close enough to see a couple Humans before they got a bunch of arrows shot at them. Apparently the Serenial have never been able to get very close to the area, even before the Morroks really started to invade the forest. The Serenial think if you send a group of Humans up here, whoever's in there will let them in and talk to them. We're not asking for an army or anything—just a small group to investigate what's going on.

Well, the messenger who's taking this letter is waiting on me, so I'll end this now. Tell Levina and Jamie we miss them. And think about sending that group, will you? I need all the credit I can get with all the in-laws I have up here.

Ritter

I let out a small laugh as I finished the letter. Perhaps my companions had expected to hear dire news because some of them had stood and were casting each other alarmed glances. Once I had summarized the important parts of the letter, the tension that had filled the room before the Serenial's arrival eased considerably, and we were able to put together a list of people we thought could be entrusted with such a diplomatic mission. Soon after, we dismissed for the day.

I was surprised, as always, to find that evening had fallen by the time I made it outside. With a twinge of sorrow, I remembered at Warrior Peak when Fallon would come home from work every day exhausted and complaining that he had accomplished nothing. At the time, I thought he was absurd to think that talking all day long would ever get anything done, but now I understood how it felt to plan for hours and leave the table feeling both accomplished and frustrated.

I wandered around the Outpost for a little while looking for something to do, but to no avail. Since I had no desire to eat, there was nothing left for me to do but go home.

When I arrived on the second floor landing, I hesitated before choosing a door. The evening sun was still drifting through the hallway window, so I couldn't justify going to sleep yet. Still, I wasn't sure I could handle another failed conversation with Levina. I heard papers rustling on the other side of our bedroom door, so I knew she was in there, alone, though not waiting for me. Maybe she was writing in her diary.

I still had Ritter's letter in my pocket. Perhaps that would be enough. With a deep breath, I opened the door.

Levina was poring over some papers she had spread all over the bed. They looked like census records, and I was reminded vividly of the first time I had ever met her, when she was copying a census on the tiers of the end-of-year tournament. She had been shy then but at least willing to talk to me. Now she barely looked up as I entered the room.

"Letter came from Ritter just now," I muttered. I tossed the letter on top of her papers. "Sylvia didn't write anything this time, but there it is."

She looked at it and set it aside so fast that I thought at first that she hadn't read it at all. I busied myself for a few minutes with changing shirts and putting away my sword before taking up the letter again.

"So what do you think of this?" I asked, flapping the letter in the still air.

She looked up. "I don't know. I guess I agree with Ritter; it doesn't make sense that there are Humans outside the Outpost. Unless they're escapees from the Morrok training—"

She stopped as we both flinched.

"So are you sending the group?" she asked in a falsely light tone, as if to make up for her last comment.

"I think so," I replied. Grateful for a safe topic, I sat down in a chair facing her. "I think Scott or Caleb should lead. Mark and the others want someone older, but those two have been traveling the forest even more than I have, and they've been doing well leading the militias lately."

"It would be a good opportunity for them."

We lapsed into silence again. Levina's gaze drifted to her papers.

"I wish I could go myself," I said.

"Mm-hmm."

I sat there for a few minutes, watching her, and then rose and left without a word.

It was dark by the time I reached the shore of the lake. The sentries at the outer doors had let me out and closed the doors behind me without comment. I had come out here the past few nights when I couldn't sleep, and although it didn't make me feel any better, it was quickly becoming habit.

I always walked west, though I tried to pretend that I wasn't heading toward the fortress. I didn't think Jamie was there, and I had a feeling that I wouldn't be greeted as hospitably as I had been last time. Still, I kept going toward it, kept reliving the night before the battle. If I hadn't left a day early, if I hadn't been so curious and reckless, maybe I could have changed what happened during the battle. Or maybe the battle wouldn't have happened at all.

What I couldn't figure out, though, was how the Morrok at the fortress could find out I had left the Outpost and get word for his army to attack within the time it took me just to walk to the fortress. Morroks' legs were long, but even a Serenial's wings would have a hard time traveling that distance in so short a time.

I had just passed Settlement One when I first noticed three figures walking toward me. It was a clear night, but they were so far away that I couldn't tell who—or what—they were.

For a moment, everything in me wanted them to be Morroks—wanted to run at them and attack them until my sword arm fell off. But I kept my head enough to dart toward the trees and hide just far enough in the tree line to wait for them to pass.

Soon after I crouched down, an odd chill fell over me, so quickly and so intensely that my breathing constricted and goose bumps rose all over my arms. I had felt chills in the forest before, especially when I was alone, but only once had it been this intense. I remembered the night at Settlement Six, not long after we had been in the forest, when the cold came and a voice spoke, though I had never known its source. So when it spoke now, I wasn't as shocked as perhaps I should have been.

"Hello again, Orestes."

"What do you want?" I asked as I backed against a tree. Although the owner of the voice hadn't hurt me last time and although I wasn't entirely sure it could, I didn't want to expose myself unnecessarily.

"I have an offer for you," it said. The voice had the same evenness to it that the Morrok in the fortress had, but there was still a raspy, whispering quality to it that made me question, in my wildest fears, if the voice had a body.

"I don't want to hear your offer," I replied, squinting in the direction I had last heard the voice. Since we weren't deep into the forest, it was lighter here than it had been the last time. Still, I saw no silhouette.

"I think you will," the voice said. "I know where your daughter is."

In spite of myself, I let hope swell within me. Jamie . . .

"I know where she is too," I said. "In the Gravel Lands."

"But where in the Gravel Lands?"

I said nothing.

"I thought so. If you knew where to look and if you knew you wouldn't be killed within seconds of entering the desert, you would have gone after her by now. But you can't. Therefore, as I said, my offer will interest you."

"You can tell me your offer if you want, but I don't trust you."

"Of course," the voice said. It was now coming from the opposite direction. "I wonder, however, why you think we took only her when we could have had any number of children from your pathetic fort."

I was reminded forcefully of the night of the battle when Levina shouted at me and blamed me for Jamie's kidnapping. Even then, I had agreed with her, but I couldn't bring myself to say it aloud, not then and not now.

But as the silence lengthened, I knew the voice wouldn't go on unless I admitted it. "Fine," I said. "It's because of me. That damn Morrok at the fortress told me that he hurt people close to me to draw me out, so here I am, childless and talking to you. Just tell me what the hell you want from me and let me have my daughter back."

"Are you positive that you want her back?" the voice asked.

The sound was jumping from side to side with each reply. I focused on a tree directly in front of me to keep from appearing frantic in my efforts to keep up with it.

"Of course I want her back."

"Think, Orestes! If I give her to you, she will probably survive this war you are orchestrating, and after that, she will be with you whether you go back to Warrior Peak or remain in the forest. Because you are her father, she will be well-trained in war and well-respected by many Humans—Humans who, as you and I both know, she is already far superior to. Like you, she will receive a high rank in the military; she will have her own battles, and she will die in one of these battles because she is a Human."

"We all die eventually."

"But if she remains with me," the voice continued as if I had said nothing, "she will be more than Human. She will be honored among Morroks and lead them at the right hand of Lernuc himself. And if she obeys Lernuc and Dirth, she will outlive any Human ever born. She will follow them to victory in this war, something you will never truly achieve such as you are now."

"You already told me—no, the Morrok at the fortress already offered the same to me. I don't want to lead any of you, and I certainly don't want that for my daughter. Give her to me!" I shouted, no longer able to conceal my desperation.

"Very well," the voice said, its volume rising as well. "You are sentencing her to a life of obscurity and loneliness among people to whom you yourself have never belonged and among whom she will find the same. You'll have her for a few years, and that will content you and keep your mind free of guilt for the duration of your short life. Never mind the consequences you will not live to see! Never mind all the people who will die because her defiance, like yours, will delay Lernuc and Dirth from reaching their goal. You know," it continued, humor coloring its tone, "you are far more selfish than I thought. Positively Morrok-like, wouldn't you say?"

"Just give her to me!"

"I will," the voice said coldly. "It won't be now, and it might not be for some years, but you will see her again."

"What's the difference if you're going to let her go? Why not now?"

"Haven't you figured it out? We have to see if she's one of you—one of the Eight."

Suddenly I heard crashing foliage close by. With a jolt, I remembered the three figures that had driven me into the trees to begin with. My shouting must have attracted them. I drew my sword to fight.

"Farewell, Orestes," the voice whispered as the footfalls came near.

I didn't wait for the figures to find me. Deciding that it would be better to confront whatever approached in the light, I darted toward the lake.

My worst fears were confirmed as I emerged from the trees, three Morroks close behind me. For a second, I considered climbing into the canopy, where the Morroks could not follow, but fear of exposing my back kept me on the ground. I looked to the lake but knew I could never tread water long enough to outlast a Morrok that desired my blood. I stopped running and turned to face them.

The Morroks continued at full speed, the three of them shoulder to shoulder with their weapons raised. The one on the left, which bore an ax, also had a small shield, which I would need if I wanted to fight more than one at a time. Without pausing to think, I hurled my dagger at the center one. The blade buried itself into the Morrok's stomach, and although the Morrok didn't fall over, it did break away from the other two to clutch at its new injury.

The remaining Morroks fell upon me, their arms as strong as ever. I met the first's sword with my own and narrowly avoided the other's ax. The ax-bearer's momentum threw it off-balance for just a moment—just long enough for me to kick out at its shield hand.

There was an awful crunch as the Morrok's fingers crushed between the point of my boot and the metal of the shield. The Morrok howled and shook the shield off its injured hand as I twisted away from the sword-bearer. I drew the sword-bearer toward the fallen shield and landed a lucky blow to its thigh as we came upon it. Taking advantage of the Morrok's pain, I grabbed the shield just in time to meet the ax-bearer's angry retaliation for its crushed hand.

The third Morrok had managed to extract my dagger and was heading toward us. I bolted farther away, toward the lake, and noted that the sword-bearer could only hobble with its thigh sliced as it was. Before the third Morrok could catch up, I beat the ax-bearer's weapon to the ground with my new shield and sliced the Morrok's good arm at the elbow. I ran my sword through its stomach and turned to meet the Morrok that now bore my dagger in addition to its own sword.

The Morrok with my dagger didn't last long. Because it was weakened by its stomach injury, I was able to strike it down quickly and focus my attention on the last Morrok. This one managed to lay a few blows on me before it too fell with the others.

I stood by the lake's shore for a moment, a little amazed at what I had done, and then stumbled into the water. I floated on my back like Cassandra had taught me and let the Morroks' blood and my own seep away from me and form a dark circle around where I lay.

Killing those Morroks didn't have the effect I thought it would. After weeks of lamenting the battle I missed, I thought fighting Morroks again would make me feel productive, like I was a part of the war in some way other than talking to old men. But to have Jamie dangled in front of me and torn away again was a feeling no victory in battle could cure.

What had the voice meant by needing to see if Jamie was one of the Eight? I remembered the Morrok in the tower telling me that he was trying to figure out how to test children before they grew up, but what did that mean for Jamie? What if his tests were painful or took years? I thought of Jamie's soft skin and thin blonde hair and started to cry so hard that I could barely swim back to the lake's shore.

I shouldn't have gotten my hopes up, not even for a moment. The Morroks couldn't be trusted, much less ones I hadn't exactly seen. I forced my breathing to even and washed my face in the water. Then I stood, trudged over to one of the Morrok corpses, and ripped my dagger from its grasp. The *L* etched in the blade shone brightly in the moonlight.

As I set off for the Outpost, I tried to ignore the irony of Lernuc's dagger being the weapon that gave me the most confidence and most success against his followers.

*

Late that night, long after I had thrown away my bloody clothes and fallen asleep in Ritter and Sylvia's old room, I awoke to the sound of the bedroom door opening. I barely had time to sit up before Levina had tiptoed inside and sat next to me, closer than she had in weeks. My heart quickened as I felt her weight against my side.

"I want to go," she whispered as she stared at the wall.

"Go where?"

"North, to investigate the Humans that Ritter wrote about."

I sat up straighter and rubbed my eyes, trying to make sense of what she was saying. "Levina, I can't go. I have to stay here and convince these idiots to go to war, and traipsing to the border is the last thing—"

"I know you can't go."

I rubbed my eyes harder and scooted away from her. "What is this? Do you want to get away from the Outpost? Away from me? See Sylvia and Ritter? What?"

She scooted farther onto the bed and grasped my hands. "It's not you," she said, an odd longing in her voice. "I just need to do this. I want to help. I'm sick of sitting around the Outpost. When we were traveling through the forest, I always felt like we were really *doing* something, but here . . ."

"You can't get her back, you know," I snapped. I suddenly wanted to hurt her, perhaps because she was leaving, perhaps because she was sounding like her old self when I could not do the same, or perhaps because she was getting closer to doing exactly what I had wanted to do from the moment we discovered Jamie was gone.

Whatever my motivation, the pain I intended settled in immediately. She didn't let go of my hands, but tears sprang from her eyes. I watched the moonlight reflecting in them as they trickled down her face.

"I know," she whispered.

"You can't leave," I said, my voice breaking. "Things aren't right between us, and I . . . I won't—I won't know if you're safe. If it really means that much to you, I'll go with you—to hell with everything else—someone else can take care of it. . . ."

Levina released my hands and crawled next to me, her tears turning into sobs. "You know that's not true. They need you here—Fallon knew it, and in time, the rest will too. And I want to . . . I have to do this on my own. I love you, but please don't try to stop me."

I tried to kiss her, but she responded awkwardly, feebly for only a moment before we both turned away. We held each other without speaking, without looking at each other or acknowledging each other except as someone to cling to as we waited for sleep to come.

After a while, Levina's grip slackened and her breathing quieted. I lay awake until the sun began to rise, all the time wishing she had never left her own bed.

Chapter Twenty-Six
Hollow Victories

LEVINA LEFT TWO DAYS LATER with Scott, a council member named Ethan, and a middle-aged woman named Julia who helped the council with all our speeches. Besides Scott, who had been chosen for his sword arm, all the Humans in the group were known for their knowledge of Morroks and their skills in persuasion and diplomacy.

They left early in the morning, so the number of people who saw them off was very small, consisting only of spouses and the council. We agreed it was better that way because the general public might have been alarmed to hear that there might be strange, violent Humans in the northern forest.

Scott's betrothed sobbed throughout the farewells, which gave the entire mission a rather foreboding feel, as if we were sending them to their deaths. Levina was tearful as well, but she was just as determined as the night she told me she was leaving. She kissed me once, briefly, promised to write, and left without a backward glance.

Weeks passed. Bereft of my wife, my parents, and my closest friends, I filled my time reconnecting with the acquaintances I had accumulated ever since entering the forest. My surface motivation—and what I allowed Mark to believe my only motivation—was simple loneliness, but, as I quickly discovered, people were keen on discussing any upper-level matter that, without me, they could only speculate about. Naturally, I chose to discuss the possibility of attacking the Gravel Lands, which, contrary to Mark's earlier assertions, people seemed very open to attempting. Like Levina and I, they were tired of not acting, and my late-night conversations with them only increased their fervor. After nearly a month of this, I had had breakfast, lunch, or dinner with more than a third of the Outpost's population, and every day I saw more people muttering and casting dark glances when the other members of the council walked by.

It was near that month mark after Levina left that I heard the first real news of her progress in the northeast. On my way to dinner with my host couple from Settlement Six, I found Sylvia's sister Aderyn. As an important chieftain among the central Valley tribes, she was no stranger to the Outpost; in fact, she was one of the few Serenial whom most everyone at the Outpost could distinguish from the rest. Still, I never expected to hear news of Levina from her.

"Aderyn," I called just as her wings disappeared around the corner as she strode toward the fort. It had taken a while to explain to the Serenial why it was alarming for them to swoop down anywhere they wanted in the Outpost, but in the end, they agreed to use the front gates and walk the rest of the way.

Aderyn doubled back and met me halfway down the street.

"Is council not in session?" she asked.

"No. It's shocking, I know, but we do leave that room occasionally."

"Well, I suppose it's most important that I speak with you anyway," she said, apparently oblivious to my sarcasm. "Could we speak indoors?"

"Of course, we can go to my house." If Aderyn was requesting to go inside, I knew it must have been important because the Serenial hated our buildings; they said that they were too closed in, almost suffocating.

I understood why they felt that way once Aderyn and I had squeezed our way into the spare room on the second floor of my house. Although there was little furniture, the room suddenly seemed very small as she ruffled her enormous wings.

Once I had procured a stool for Aderyn, I sat down opposite her, awaiting an explanation.

"A messenger from the northeast came to my village last night, exhausted from a week of hard travel. He told me his tidings before I sent him to rest."

"And?" I prompted, unable to stomach her pause.

"Your people reached the desired area about eleven days ago."

"Are they all safe?"

"We know they were safe eleven days ago," Aderyn said.

"Your messenger left them a week ago." I stood up and began to pace.

"What happened between them arriving and your messenger leaving? Were they hurt? Did they find the Humans?"

"As of the time of my messenger's departure, we do not know what is inhabiting that area. We do not believe that your people are dead, but they have not returned since they entered the area."

"So they—they were allowed to enter?" I asked, trying to keep my voice calm. "I was told that Serenial have been shot at for coming too near—whether on the ground or in the canopy—but no one ever saw by whom or what."

"Yes, they crossed the invisible line without incident, and we have not had contact since, at least not that I know of."

I nodded.

In an odd display of emotion, Aderyn pursed her lips and patted my arm once. "That is all I know, Lieutenant. I wish I could have brought better news, but as it is . . ."

"I understand. Thanks, Aderyn."

Aderyn now stood as well. "Where can I find General Mark? I wish to tell him of this as well, among other things."

"In the fort, I'm sure," I said. I watched her face closely for signs of what the "other things" were, but even though she revealed nothing, I had a good guess as to what they were. As much as I liked Aderyn and suspected she liked me, our relationship with the Serenial was becoming strained. Ever since the attack on the Outpost, we had sent very few Humans to help the Serenial monitoring the Morroks' movements throughout the forest. The Morroks were becoming better at detecting and shooting Serenial moving in the canopy, and so they were experiencing many losses. That, coupled with the fact that the Serenial were guarding the northern border alone, was creating a feeling of resentment from many Serenial, and personally, I couldn't blame them.

Deciding to let Mark handle that subject, I instead asked Aderyn, "Did your messenger bring any letters from any of my people or from Ritter?"

Aderyn gazed at me with distinct pity. "If Levina wrote to you, her letters did not come with this messenger. I will contact you the moment I hear more."

I murmured another thanks as Aderyn left the room. It took several minutes of sitting perfectly still and breathing very slowly to quell the desire to set off for the northern border right then. I didn't think that Levina was dead, and beyond that, I had to trust Scott, Ritter, and the Serenial to protect her. I hated that that task fell to anyone other than me, but Levina hadn't really left me a choice in the matter.

After a time, I remembered that I was supposed to have dinner with Richard and Victoria. Heaving myself to my feet, I made my way to the mess halls, determined to go through the motions no matter how I felt.

Richard and Victoria were much like I had left them at Settlement Six, though with a new toughness undoubtedly instilled by their months of travel to the Outpost. They had enough tact to sidestep questions about my family and instead filled the time talking about their own children, who were still quite young. I found it very difficult to share in their happiness and was grateful when the subject turned to the war.

"So, Orestes," Richard said as we were finishing our food, "what do you make of the attack two months ago? I mean, the Outpost gets attacked, and then nothing. . . . There hasn't been anything happening, has there?"

"Just the normal skirmishes," I said. "Nothing that will make a difference."

"Won't make a difference?" Richard echoed. A few other dinner stragglers had already begun to listen in. "Why not?"

"Well," I said, perhaps more loudly than I needed to, "suffice it to say, Morrok numbers are growing faster than we can pick them off in the forest, even with the Serenials' help. The Valley's just too big, and the longer we wait, the more time the Morroks have to spread through the forest until they outnumber us."

A stunned silence followed as everyone glanced at each other. They weren't used to hearing such negative predictions from anyone on the council.

"But what does that mean for us, Orestes?" Victoria asked. "Is it hopeless?"

"Of course not," I said. "We just have to make some steps forward without letting much more time pass."

"That's really specific," Richard scoffed.

I laughed. "Well, if you want to know the truth, I think we need to get back to Warrior Peak, but we haven't had any luck sneaking through the Gravel Lands, whether by land or by air. The Morroks have almost complete control over the desert."

"There must be something else we can do," said a man I didn't know. A sizeable group had formed on both sides of Richard and Victoria. They were staring unblinkingly at me.

"There is," I said. "I think if we could just make one concentrated offensive on the desert, we could really—"

"Orestes, may I speak to you?" a voice behind me interrupted. I looked around to see Mark standing there, his jaw clenched and his face splotched red all the way to his cropped hair. A few feet away, Aderyn had exited the fort and was taking flight from the middle of the Outpost; the people standing near her jumped in alarm as she rose jerkily into the air.

I swung my legs around the bench to face Mark. "Did Aderyn tell you about Levina and the others?"

"Yes, in addition to reminding me just how many of her people have died this week," he said heatedly. "But that's not why I want to talk to you. Would you please come to the fort with me?"

I bade my audience good-bye and followed Mark out of the mess halls. As soon as we were out of earshot, Mark spoke again, the anger in his voice increasing with each sentence.

"I honestly wouldn't have expected this of you, Orestes. I know you don't agree with me about attacking the desert, but really, warmongering to half the Outpost—publicly contradicting the rest of the council . . . I thought you knew more about leadership, being a lieutenant at Warrior Peak."

I stopped short of entering the fort and let out a humorless laugh. "Mark, I didn't even graduate from military school. Fallon gave me that title so you'd pay attention to me, but if I haven't done enough to gain your respect by now, I don't think there's much more we have to say to each other."

"You—well—I mean, of course a title doesn't make a difference," he stammered, not quite meeting my eyes, "but the fact remains that you've been put in this position, and now you're confusing people with your—"

"The people I've talked to aren't confused. They just don't agree with you."

"Only because you prod them into agreeing with you instead! I was listening to you before I interrupted, and you were using your influence to manipulate them into thinking your plan is the only reasonable solution."

"These are grown people. A few words from me aren't going to sway them so easily."

Mark shook his head. "Orestes, I know you want to act. I know you've suffered much in the past few months, but decisions such as these cannot be dictated by emotion or circumstance or anything other than—"

"This isn't just some stupid whim!" I shouted. The crowd from dinner and other passersby had stopped to listen, and this time I didn't care how I sounded to them. "Fallon, Glynis, Levina, and I—all twelve of us who left Warrior Peak—we came to the forest to warn you, to prepare you, to do whatever it took to save you from Morroks. Twelve people out of hundreds of thousands came to help you! We sacrificed everything—comfort, protection, respect, and three of us sacrificed our lives—because we believed so passionately in uniting our people against the Morroks. No, Mark, this isn't emotion or circumstance. We left Warrior Peak because the General and the War Council wouldn't do anything to help you, and now here I am with another general and council who won't act, and if going behind your back is what it takes to change that, then so be it."

Mark didn't say anything. No one did. With nothing more to say myself, I stared at Mark until he murmured something about not wanting to undermine my sacrifices and about continuing this conversation later.

Unable to bear the stares of the crowd, I kept my eyes focused forward and marched away, leaving the silence behind me.

*

That night I found myself, yet again, on the shore of the lake. There were no Morroks, nor had there been since the night Levina told me she was leaving. Still, I wandered around the edge of the water, searching for some solitude that I couldn't find in the house where Fallon, Glynis, Levina, and Jamie used to sleep.

I made it only about a third of the way to the Morrok fortress before fatigue started to wear on me. Turning on the spot, I began to retrace my footsteps. I hadn't traveled very far before I heard splashing in the distance. I unsheathed my sword and jogged toward it.

I found a small blanket and a woman's cloak and boots piled neatly a few feet away from the water. Squinting through the darkness, I could see a head bobbing a great distance from shore, too far for me to recognize the face.

"Who's out there?" I called.

The head didn't reply. Instead, it disappeared underwater, and I saw ripples coming toward me. After several moments, it was Cassandra who surfaced at about half the distance she had been.

I sheathed my sword. "What are you doing out here?"

"The same as you, I imagine," she said. "Join me."

I couldn't tell if it was a question or a command, but either way, I kicked off my boots, unbuckled my sword belt, and waded into the water. Cassandra was already moving farther out again, and I felt a momentary thrill of fear as I tried to remember the last time I had gone deeper than where my feet could touch ground. Still, not to be outdone, I kicked after her, enjoying the resistance of the water against my movements.

I followed Cassandra around the water for a long time. We said nothing to each other so that I nearly forgot that someone else was there except for her dark hair swirling atop the moonlit water.

I tired more quickly than Cassandra but felt no need to compete with her. After swimming back to shore, I flopped into the grass and watched her dive and resurface for several more minutes before wading out herself. She sat a careful distance from me and grabbed her blanket. After wrapping herself in it, she glanced over at me. "Aren't you cold?"

"Yes," I said, suddenly realizing that my skin was covered with goose bumps. "I don't mind, though. I think I needed that swim."

"Long day?"

"Sort of. Aderyn came to the Outpost, which is always cause for alarm on some level, and Mark and I had a—well—disagreement."

"So the duel on top of the fort I heard about was fairly accurate?"

"Give or take a few missing limbs."

She laughed. I realized I had never heard her laugh before and was surprised at how delicate and warm it was compared to her strong speaking voice. I couldn't help but smile.

"So what are you really doing out here?" I asked.

"I come out here when I can't sleep. Usually I'm on the other side of the lake, though . . . as far away from Settlement One as I can get."

I remembered the night we had first found Settlement One—how Cassandra had wandered through her deserted old home as if in a trance. It was the place where she had lost her family and been kidnapped by Morroks; I couldn't blame her for giving it a wide berth.

"I thought I had worked up the nerve to go inside tonight," she continued, "but when I got there, I just kept walking and ended up here."

I nodded. I wanted to tell her I knew exactly how she felt, but instead I said, "You shouldn't walk around alone at night. Do you ever take your"—I paused for a moment, trying to find the right word for the men with whom she spent her nights—"friends with you?"

She smirked. "First of all, I never walk alone." She lifted the corner of her cloak to reveal the hilt of her curved sword. "And second, I don't have nearly as many 'friends' as you think I do, and the ones I do have I could probably beat in a duel any day of the week."

"Sorry, I didn't mean to imply . . ."

"It's okay, I know what everyone says about me. Did Levina tell you I was with someone new every night?"

"Well, no, not exactly. I'm sure she didn't mean anything by it—I mean, it's your choice, but—"

She laughed again. "It's okay, Orestes. I know she doesn't like me."

"Doesn't like—of course she does, she just . . ."

"Doesn't like me," Cassandra repeated. "You don't have to make excuses for her. I don't know why people think it's so wrong not to like someone. I don't like Levina either."

"Oh," I said, more thrown off than ever.

"Does that make you like me less?"

I opened my mouth and closed it, trying to figure out what the right answer was. Cassandra's tone was casual as she wrung out her hair and her dress, making me think that it wasn't a trap after all.

"Yes," I said finally.

"See? No harm done. Neither of us keeled over or lost a limb or turned Morrok."

Forcing myself to laugh, I let my gaze drift to the water again. I didn't want to think about Levina or the Morroks just then. I carried them with me all the time, and I wished I could escape them, even for a moment, without feeling guilty for wishing it.

Out of the corner of my eye, I saw Cassandra uncurling her legs out from under her blanket. Even in the moonlight, I noticed that she had lost the paleness that had marked her long stint under the canopy with the Morroks. But no amount of color could cover the scars.

"So why are *you* out here?" she asked, her tone still light.

"I couldn't sleep."

"And the quickest way to the Morroks is to follow this shore."

I looked around at her so quickly that my neck cricked. "What do you know about that?"

"I'm afraid, Lieutenant, that people care far more about your nighttime wanderings than they do about mine."

"But I never go that far. Do people think I'm going to the fortress?"

"I'm also afraid that you are in the presence of a woman who knows how very interested in you the Morroks are. I always assumed that you're just as intrigued by them as they are by you. Hell, they abused me and dragged me around this country for months, and I've thought a thousand times about going to that fortress to find out why—or even to get revenge."

I wanted to look away from her but found that I couldn't. Again I found myself understanding and agreeing with everything she said. I even felt my passion rising with hers, but now she was getting too close to asking about my involvement with the Morroks. My heart was pounding, but not the way it did when I was nervous that Levina was going to ask me a question I didn't want to answer; instead, I felt myself wanting to tell Cassandra why I wanted to go to the fortress, just as she had shared with me.

"Cassandra, I . . . there's something I've never told . . ."

When I didn't continue, she nodded. "Believe me, I don't like to talk about the specifics of my captivity; actually, I never discuss it with people who don't already know about it. I always thought the Morroks did something similar to you, except you got away somehow and now they're trying to get you back."

"It's not exactly like that. I wasn't really a victim like you. It was more like . . . do you know where Morroks come from?"

She cocked an eyebrow. "No. I mean, they're just another race like Humans or Serenial, right?"

"No, that's what most people think, but it's not true. Even if Morroks do have children, they come out as Humans or whatever race the parents were before they transformed."

"Transformed?"

"There are no Morroks that are younger than thirteen years old," I began awkwardly. Cassandra's look of concern deepened as I tried to gather my thoughts. "You see, Morroks will take children—any children, Human, Serenial, whatever—and they'll train them to fight their whole childhood until they're thirteen. Then there's this tournament, and whoever wins gets the serum."

"The what?"

"Serum. It's what makes you a Morrok."

I stared at her helplessly, wishing I could make her understand all the pain behind the cold facts, but she just stared back, also helpless, perhaps wanting to understand just as badly.

"What does this have to do with you?" she asked finally.

"I was one of those children," I said, my heart pounding. "I grew up in the Morrok Facility until someone rescued me when I was five years old. But I still remember so much, and I think . . . sometimes I worry that I—that my parents were . . . not Humans."

This time I did look away, afraid that I had told her too much. I couldn't believe I had said any of that out loud, and the longer the silence stretched, the more I wished I never had.

"I don't see why that should make any difference," Cassandra said, her tone so upbeat and bracing that I looked back at her. She was staring at me even more intently than the people at the mess hall earlier. "You are what you make of yourself. The first few years of your life—even your blood—don't determine what kind of person you'll be."

I felt my heart lift a little, but at the same time, I thought she must not have understood me.

"But the tournament," I continued, "and all our training—they made us do things—hurt each other . . . little kids, you know, slashing at each other with real knives. And we didn't know it was wrong. Even after I came to Warrior Peak, it took me a while to learn it was wrong. . . . And every time I fight," I said, my voice shaking now that we were at the heart of the matter, "I get that same feeling—that horrible, yet amazing thrill you get when you're dominating someone so completely that his life is in your hands. . . ."

Cassandra reached a slender hand toward my arm, but she stopped short, instead letting it fall on the grass between us. I watched the blades poke between her pale, scarless fingers.

"Orestes, that isn't a sign of being a Morrok," she said. "It's a sign of being Human, but most people will never admit that feeling aloud. We all have that urge to conquer, even to kill. As much as we repress it otherwise, we can't help but feel the urge rise to the surface in battle when we're given the power to end life without suffering rejection from society."

My heart swelled in my chest, and I wondered all of a sudden why I had never shared this with anyone before. Yes, I had touched on my feelings of isolation with my parents, the General, and Acules—the people who already knew why I was isolated—but none of them had ever reassured me like this. They always made me think my feelings were wrong and unnatural, but maybe they were just afraid to admit that they felt the same way.

"Thanks, Cassandra," I murmured. I reached over to squeeze her hand, but even as I did, I knew it was a mistake. If we had had any innocence between us before, it was lost as we touched for the first time since I had carried her, bruised and unconscious, away from the Morrok camp.

A shiver that had nothing to do with the cold raced up my arm as Cassandra gripped my hand in return. Neither of us let go, and I quickly found myself not being satisfied with this touch alone. A few moments later—though I couldn't say how it started—our lips had met, and Cassandra was leaning into me with an intensity I had never felt before.

Somewhere in the back of my mind, I knew I should have jumped up and run without a glance backward. Yet all the loneliness Levina had saddled me with since she left the Outpost and even before that kept me where I was, and for better or worse, I got my wish and thought of Levina no more that night.

*

It was nearly dawn by the time I made it back to the house. Cassandra had walked mutely beside me, and we were careful not even to glance at each other the whole journey. When we reached the Outpost, she didn't come inside and instead planted herself, yet again, by the lake's shore just outside the walls. I didn't say good-bye or try to persuade her to come inside.

When I arrived at home, I was surprised to find Mark leaning against the door of my house. He looked almost as exhausted as I was, and I wondered if he had been waiting for me all night.

"Well, I must admit, even if I don't like the way you went about it, you sure rallied the Outpost better than I've ever been able to," he said.

I didn't reply. Further Human contact was the last thing I wanted at that moment, and my only hope of not shouting at Mark was to keep quiet.

"Between your little speech at dinner and Aderyn returning with a number of Serenial chieftains in the middle of the night demanding that we fight alongside them, the council and I have decided to change our strategy."

"So I can't campaign behind your back, but the council can meet without me even being in the vicinity."

Apparently taking my response for sarcasm, Mark grinned. "Just accept your victory humbly. We won't have time for 'I told you so' when we start planning the attack in a few hours."

Knowing this information should have made me happy, I forced myself to smile and shake Mark's hand. I babbled for a few minutes about looking forward to the meeting until Mark seemed satisfied, and then I excused myself and hurried inside. When I reached my bed, I tried desperately to fall asleep, to dream, to find any way to escape what I had just done.

Chapter Twenty-Seven
The Laconic Warriors Again

THE YEAR 327 WAS RAPIDLY DRAWING to a close, but the war was, at last, underway. After just a week of planning, the entire Outpost was mobilized. The storage buildings were emptied, and all the food, weapons, clothes, tents, flint, and other supplies were laid out in the streets for inventory and disbursement. Clerks from the fort offices walked up and down the lines of goods for days, making notes and figuring out how to reallocate the mass of supplies to our newly reorganized fighting divisions.

The council had appointed a slew of new officers to lead our army north in manageable shifts. Everyone in the Outpost was thrilled to learn who they would be traveling and fighting alongside in the coming weeks, and I often saw whole divisions eating dinner together even after a full day of training. Although many people lamented abandoning their homes, leaving still felt far enough away that they were swept up in the romance of our great offensive move, which, as far as they were concerned, could not fail.

That uplifted feeling was punctured slightly when we started to move the nonfighters into the trees. Fearful that the Morroks would realize what we were planning to do and then attack the Outpost before we could reach the desert, we had made a deal with the Serenial to keep our children, elderly, and untrained women in the canopy and so out of the Morroks' reach while we traveled north. As families began to part ways, morale weakened considerably as fathers, husbands, sons, and daughters wandered out of their houses at night, lonely and yielding to fear without anyone to comfort or encourage them.

This fear, coupled with simple boredom as the fighters waited to leave, led to restlessness within the Outpost three weeks after we had begun preparations. With the last of the nonfighters moved safely into the canopy, all that was left in the settlement was a large number of men and women who were living day to day under the possibility of having to be packed and ready to leave at a moment's notice. At that point, all we were waiting for was the return of the Serenial messenger we had sent our first day of planning, who was to notify the Serenial at the northern border of our intentions and return with their approval.

Our plan was to move our fighters through the canopy all the way to the Gravel Lands, but we were sure that it wouldn't take long for the Morroks to realize that thousands of Humans had joined the Serenial and for them to begin finding ways to attack us. The Serenial at the northern border were responsible for keeping the Morroks in the forest from alerting the Morroks in the desert of our presence. Hopefully the Morroks in the forest would remain scattered enough so as not to pose an immediate threat to us, but if the desert Morroks found out about our movement, they would have too much time to make strategies of their own in preparation for our attack. Because we still had no idea how many Morroks were in the Gravel Lands, we were relying rather heavily on our element of surprise.

As much as we believed in our plan, our fighters were still on edge, and so when a Serenial messenger—conspicuously a messenger because of his larger-than-average wings, good for traveling—flew up to the Outpost around that three-week mark, people dropped what they were doing and started scrambling for equipment even though the council had given no order. It was only when I came to investigate and recognized the messenger that I was able to restore some calm.

"He's not from the north," I said to those still clamoring around the Serenial as he made his way toward the fort. "It's personal business. Go back to dinner."

I escorted the Serenial the rest of the way to the fort and invited him into an abandoned office. The Serenial, called Aether, cast me an irritated glance as he crammed his wings inside and I shut the door behind him.

"Is she okay?" I asked without greeting. I hardly felt inhospitable, though; Aether didn't know Human tongue very well, so I had learned to keep our conversations succinct.

"I lost her trail," Aether replied, not looking at me. His face was drawn with guilt and shame, and if we had spoken the same language, I knew he would have been giving me several excuses. As it was, he said nothing more.

I told myself that I wasn't showing my frustration at the news out of politeness to Aether, but deep down, I knew there was no frustration at all; in fact, a small, guilt-ridden part of me was relieved that he had failed. Two days ago, Cassandra had disappeared completely from the Outpost. Ever since the night we had spent together, I had seen even less of her than usual, and when I did, we barely spoke. And although at first I thought I was imagining it, there was no denying the malicious smile she gave me whenever our paths crossed.

Once I realized Cassandra wasn't among the nonfighters in the canopy, I had sent Aether to search the surrounding area and had combed all of Settlement One myself. Now that we had both lost our leads, I hadn't the faintest idea of where to look for her. I remembered our mutual desire to infiltrate the Morrok fortress, but even if I thought she were there, I doubted I could help her at this point.

After a few minutes of indecision, I dismissed Aether, telling him that he didn't have to track Cassandra anymore but that he should keep an eye open just in case. I couldn't help but feel that, by giving up my search, I had somehow sentenced her to death, though I tried to reassure myself that I had done all I could. Surely being responsible for an army of two thousand was enough for one man to worry about without the additional burden of a single missing woman.

When I left the fort several minutes later, wondering how I could do something productive in a settlement already too well-prepared, I heard a commotion similar to what Aether's arrival had caused. I hadn't taken two steps away from the fort before the source of the noise rounded the corner. Half the council was ushering an exhausted Serenial messenger toward the fort with a small crowd in tow.

"Find the general!" several of the council members shouted at the crowd as we filed inside our cramped meeting room.

The Serenial stopped short of the doorway of the meeting room. "My message is simple. The chieftains of the north approve of your plan and await your coming. I have already alerted Chieftain Aderyn; her forces are gathering along the northern border of the lake as we speak. I must leave to join them."

"Very well, you may leave," one of the older men said. "I'll tell Mark, and the rest of you can alert the fighters. As soon as night falls, we will enter the trees."

We all murmured our assent, but I had no intention of spreading the word—at least not until I had spoken to the Serenial messenger myself.

I sprinted out of the fort and elbowed my way through the crowd, scanning the skies for a winged figure. Seeing none, I continued to the front gates, where I found him ready to take flight.

"Wait," I panted. "Any news from the party we sent eight weeks ago?"

The messenger cocked his eyebrow at me. I tried to gather my breath enough to elaborate, but then a look of comprehension came over him.

"I was not told anything official, but I did hear some gossip about crashes and a large fire to the east about a week ago. The Human married to one of our people nearly got himself tied up because he was making such a scene about going to investigate."

"No one went to check on them?" I asked. The rush of affection I felt for Ritter was immediately eclipsed by the acute panic that always came with news of Levina.

"No. Your council said that your first priority is this offensive, and the Serenial agree. Not a man can be spared, Lieutenant, especially for only four Humans."

Not trusting myself to reply, I watched the messenger ascend and disappear toward the north. After a time, the shouting and scrambling within the Outpost brought me back to my senses, and I rushed back inside to prepare for travel.

*

By midnight, we had reached the Serenial gathered by the north shore of the lake. Even more remarkable than having two thousand Humans assembled was the sight of an equal number of Serenial perched in the canopy, their many-colored feathers stretching as far as the eye could see. We had been able to leave the Outpost without incident, but it became clear soon after that we had underestimated how much noise we would make traveling through the canopy. Everyone had been practicing walking through the trees, but having us all move together was straining the branches unlike they had ever felt when they had had only lightweight Serenial as their burden. Luckily no one fell, but if any Morroks were looking skyward, they probably would have seen a foot slip through the canopy every once in a while.

In spite of the noise, we continued forward. The Serenial had spread us out to distribute the weight more evenly, but it hardly mattered anymore if the Morroks heard us; it was too late to turn back.

We traveled for two days, thousands of us. Between our supplies and the Serenials' knowledge of plants, we never went hungry, but sleep was hard to come by because none of the leaders wanted to stay in one spot for too long in case Morroks with arrows passed under us and heard voices. We had scouts coming and going constantly, and they all reported the same thing: that the small groups of Morroks throughout the forest were banding together and closing the gap between us more quickly than we could hope to move.

The third morning after we left the Outpost, Aderyn woke me halfway through my allotted six hours of sleep to tell me that a few groups of Morroks had reached the southernmost fringes of our group. I grabbed my sword and went with her through our entire makeshift camp, listening to the heavy gaits of the Morroks below. The canopy was thicker here, so we were confident that the Morroks wouldn't see the branches move under us, but we couldn't mask our sound unless we left the area two by two. Many of the Morroks carried bows and arrows taller than Serenial, but they made no move to use them—at least not yet.

By the time morning came, more than a hundred Morroks were milling around below us. Although we outnumbered them twenty to one and they couldn't climb into the canopy, their presence froze everyone in place. Many did not dare whisper or even lean to the side to reach their swords. The

Outpost council and the Serenial chieftains sidled together to confer and agreed that it was better to act now than to risk exposing our position when we left or to wait for more Morroks to arrive.

As silently as possible, we distributed every bow we had. Ten minutes of painstaking positioning passed in which we assigned every archer to a Morrok target below. Never having practiced much with a bow, I gripped my sword hilt pointlessly as the rest waited for Aderyn's signal.

After one last glance at the archers nearest her, Aderyn threw back her head and let out a wild, birdlike screech that made me start even though I knew it was coming. Even before the sound died on her lips, there came the *whoosh* of hundreds of arrows being released, followed closely by the screams and grunts of their victims.

Injured or not, each Morrok grabbed its bow and nocked an arrow within seconds. Our archers barely had time to grasp at their quivers before a hundred thick arrows broke their way through the canopy with devastating accuracy.

Time seemed to suspend for a few moments as Mark and I gazed at each other across the canopy in shock and fear. We had considered the possibility of the Morroks' arrows reaching the canopy, but we had never fathomed that they could penetrate it or that the Morroks would be able to aim that well with so many branches blocking us from their sight.

"Fire again!" Mark shouted over the groans of pain and shock from Serenial and Humans alike.

Still shaken, our archers fumbled with the second volley, striking less than half the number as they did before. The Morroks' next round didn't suffer at all, however, and more of our archers were pierced before they could move from their shooting position.

I darted through the archers lying on the canopy and grabbed Mark's shoulder. "Shouldn't we move to the forest floor? We can't just sit here and watch our archers die."

"You mean *you* can't sit here," Mark snapped. "I know it's hard to watch, but you of all people have to keep—"

Mark's words were drowned out by the sounds of crashing foliage as hundreds of our fighters rushed past us, stomping on unattended bows and tripping over the injured archers. Billows of smoke rising through the canopy marked the area they had deserted.

"Fire arrows from the east and the south!" an officer shouted at us as he ran past to check the north side of our gathering.

Hundreds of people had now converged to the center of our loose formation, where I stood with Aderyn and Mark. Even over the shouts and the increased crackling of flames, I could hear the tree branches groaning under our weight. The smoke had reached us now, and I couldn't turn around without knocking into someone else equally blinded from the dark mass. I closed my eyes and tried to breathe through my shirt, but there was no escape from the heat.

"They're herding us together!" Aderyn shouted as we saw flames from the north and west as well. She let out another screech, and nearly every Serenial rose as one from the canopy and hovered just above the top of the trees. Only a few stayed on the canopy, their swords poised down toward the branches as if ready to cut through.

"Get your fighters out of the canopy! We will follow," Aderyn barked at Mark and me before taking off herself.

Mark nodded, and we both began shouting the orders to anyone who could hear. We hardly needed to have told them, however; the rush of air that had accompanied the Serenial's ascent was agitating the fire more than ever so that we had nowhere else to go.

Those closest to the tree trunks were the first victims. The moment they broke through the canopy, they exposed themselves, defenseless, to more of the Morroks' arrows. Still, panicked by the spreading ring of fire, people rushed at the bases of the trees, trampling each other and pushing each other out of the canopy. The Serenial on the canopy were yet more violent, batting at Humans with their swords to clear a circle where hundreds had been standing not a minute before. At Aderyn's piercing screech, they hacked at the canopy, breaking branches and vines until they no longer supported even the Serenials' slight weight. The ones in the air rose a few feet higher and then began to pelt through the canopy like living arrows, their small, curved swords flashing in the sudden flood of sunlight.

The Serenial, with their peculiar dive-and-jab fighting strategy, held the Morroks at bay as the Humans, including myself, descended to the forest floor. Glad to be able to breathe and use my sword, I threw myself off my tree onto the nearest Morrok and severed its bow cleanly in two.

I wanted to lose myself in the fighting, but cries from above kept me so distracted that I nearly lost my sword arm more than once. The fire continued to spread at an alarming rate, more quickly than the rest of the army could climb down the trees. A few Morroks continued to shoot arrows into the canopy, following the sounds of Humans burning and Serenial attempting to find a clear spot through the fire.

On the ground, a battle that, according to numbers, should have been easily slanted toward us was slipping the other way. Our rout from the canopy had so shaken my people that they were running wildly through the melee, foolishly challenging Morroks one on one.

I abandoned my own duels to help Mark and the officers urge everyone to fight in groups as we had drilled countless times back at the Outpost. Even this didn't last long, though. Above us, the fire had reached a terrible climax, and ash and flaming branches began to rain down, scattering Human, Serenial, and Morrok alike. The canopy was burning away, but instead of sunlight beaming down on us, smoke obscured both our vision and our breathing so that I was too afraid to swing my sword lest I hit a friend.

Over the chaos, I heard Aderyn screech the same command she had made not ten minutes before. The Serenial rose yet again, and I heard, as if from a great distance, Human voices shouting to flee northward.

Coughing and shielding my head with my arms, I sprinted blindly away from the battle with no real idea of which way north was. Whether they recognized me or not, several Humans followed me with their shirts covering their mouths and their weapons forgotten at their sides. As soon as we were clear of the smoke, I scrambled into the nearest tree to check the position of the sun and then led those with me north through the canopy.

When we found where the Serenial had landed, we were far out of reach of the fire, but I could have sworn I still heard the screams. More people were arriving by the minute, but we were still nowhere near the two thousand Humans we had left the Outpost with.

"How are we going to help the ones left behind?" I asked Aderyn the moment I found her.

"I have scouts with arrows circling the perimeter, helping where they can."

"But there are people trapped in the flames. We have to do some—"

"There is nothing to do," Aderyn snapped. "The fire will burn out on its own eventually. We need to move before the Morroks rally together again. There are hundreds of additional troops moving toward us as we speak, so we must not waste time."

But time was already against us. Perhaps because they had been prepared for the fire, the Morroks were outstripping Humans as they fled from the battle, and they were picking them off faster than Aderyn's archers could protect them. Soon Aderyn and Mark were ordering us back to the forest floor to take up the fight again.

Spurred by an unknown number of our companions' deaths, we came at the Morroks with new ferocity. But no matter how well we did, it seemed that there was always a fresh group to take one fallen Morrok's place. As I watched familiar faces get struck down one by one, I could barely keep focused. I didn't fall into the usual mindless, angry rhythm that I had described to Cassandra three weeks ago; instead, I cared more than ever, and I had never fought worse.

As the battle wore on, the smoke drifted all the way to our new battlefield, blocking the sun and casting us into further darkness. I found myself buffeted further and further to the edge of the battle, to the point that I could climb back in the canopy without fear of being struck in the back. Although I hated the thought of leaving a battle still in progress, I finished off the two Morroks nearest me and clambered up a tree as quickly as I could to see how everyone else was doing. I was about to make my way back to the heart of the battle when I caught the sound of my name.

"Where is Orestes?"

The voice was low and grunting, clearly a Morrok, and it came from even further away from the battle. I crouched down and separated a few branches so I could see below me. Two Morroks, both of them particularly tall and both of them wearing comparatively well-kept cloaks, stood under me, apparently in deep discussion. The one that had just spoken seemed out of breath, as if it had just arrived from traveling.

"He's somewhere in the battle," the second replied. "We can't subdue him, not with the numbers we have here."

"It doesn't matter. Our orders were to keep the three groups separated—nothing about Orestes yet."

"Have you kept the traitors from contacting the birds? We've kept this group contained."

"The traitors are being taken care of," the first Morrok snapped, as if the other Morrok had been rude to ask. "I admit that they are closer to Orestes than is desirable, but we are matching them well with the few I have been allotted."

"If you say so," the second Morrok said. "I must return to direct the incoming groups."

Without another word, it left the first Morrok standing there, muttering mockingly under its breath. "'Direct the incoming groups.' Lernuc doesn't trust you to direct anyone; it's just because Orestes is here. . . ."

Then it set out at a jog toward the east, away from the battle.

I sat on my heels undecided for about five seconds before following it. The Morroks wanted to keep three groups separated. Of course there were those of us from the Outpost and the Serenial stationed in the north, but who was the third? It didn't sound like the Serenial were being attacked; the Morroks just wanted to keep us and the third group from sending messengers to them. But the third group—what had the Morroks called them? The traitors? That didn't make sense; no Morrok was capable of rebelling, much less joining our side. . . .

After just a mile or two of travel, the sounds of another battle reached my ears. The Morrok I had been following sped forward into the fray, but I slowed down and crouched again peek through the branches at the scene below.

This battle was considerably smaller than the one I had left. The Morrok leader hadn't been exaggerating when it said it had only a few fighters allotted to it; the Morroks were outnumbered at least three to one. No Serenial were involved, and I didn't recognize any of the Humans that I saw, though I did note that most of them were women. All of them were pale as if they had lived their whole lives under the canopy, and none of their clothes or weapons bore the symbol of Warrior Peak. Surely it couldn't be . . .

My stomach tightened and a yell escaped me as I saw Scott dart through my narrow range of vision, his hair matted and his sword bloody. But he was alive.

I tried to stand up so quickly that I fell flat on my face again, the branches scraping my arms and cheeks. Not bothering to try again, I scrambled on my hands and knees to the nearest tree trunk and dropped to the forest floor.

I was more distracted than ever as I entered this battle, but this time, the distraction didn't hamper me. I knew I was receiving strange looks from the other Humans, perhaps because they didn't recognize me but more likely because I was moving through the battle with little regard for whether or not I was killing the Morroks as I pushed past them. The Morroks too were reacting; I thought I heard my name more than once.

If I thought the Humans had the upper hand before I joined the battle, fighting among them proved I had underestimated them. They fought with rare intensity and skill against Morroks, even more so than some of the Warriors from the lake settlements who had known about the Morroks for years.

The battle dissolved soon after I joined. The Morroks fled to the battle in the west, and the Humans only halfheartedly pursued them. By then, my presence had become conspicuous among a group who apparently all knew each other. I scanned each face with increasing desperation until a tall man with wild gray hair grabbed me roughly by the forearm and forced me to look at him.

"Are you Orestes?" he demanded.

I shook out of his grip. "Yes. Who are—"

"You're the one who knows my wife. How is she? How is Lexa?"

"Lexa?" I repeated, bewildered. For a moment, I had no idea what he was talking about. I knew the name—her dark, tired face even flashed through my mind—but the hunger in his eyes was so alarming that I couldn't think of why I knew her or how this man with an eighteen-inch beard standing on end could possibly be her husband.

"Xander, should we follow them?" a pale woman nearby asked.

"Of course, Orestes's group may need help," the wild man said, not taking his eyes from me.

"Xander!" I said incredulously, my mind finally loosening. "From Aldis's stories! I mean, you're real, of course—you knew Acules and all them. But you . . . you disappeared. Lexa told me you led an army into the desert and died."

"Lexa told you? When? When was the last time you saw her? Your wife told me you've been gone from Warrior Peak for some months, but—"

"My wife?" I repeated, my voice becoming quite as strangled as his. "Where is she?"

"She's fine—she's around here somewhere, but you must tell me—"

"Orestes!"

First I saw Xander's eyes widen as he stumbled backward—perhaps to the ground, perhaps just to the side; I couldn't tell either way, because the next thing I saw was Levina's face as she leaped toward me, throwing her arms around my neck. I responded automatically, lifting her off the ground, both shocked and thrilled anew by the familiarity of her touch. Secure in my arms, she drew back and brought her hands to my face, tracing a finger along a thin new scar on my jaw that I hadn't really noticed before that moment. Levina's face was different as well—older somehow, thinner—and her hair, once so long and full, now barely hung to her chin. She saw me staring at it and blushed.

"It . . . it just got to be more trouble than it was worth," she whispered.

I nodded, unable to speak. Even though I had been looking for her from the moment I saw Scott, I couldn't believe she was with me, alive and safe and smiling. Kissing her and holding her didn't seem enough to explain what I felt, and for some reason, my heart ached now more than it ever had while she was gone.

Xander coughed, and we both looked around to where he stood, still indignant at being knocked aside by a woman a foot shorter than he was. Levina winked at me and wriggled back to the ground. I wiped my eyes quickly as she took Xander's arm and brought him back to where I stood.

"Orestes knew Lexa at Warrior Peak," Levina said patiently. I had a feeling she had explained this to Xander before. "He was close to Aldis because she worked as a blacksmith at the school, and after she died, Orestes visited Lexa a few times."

"She's alive and well, and she still thinks of you," I said, looking Xander directly in the eye. Now more than ever, I knew that that was what he needed to hear.

I thought for a moment that Xander was going to lose his composure as well, but just as quickly, he snapped back to an attitude of military austerity surprising for a man of his wild appearance.

"Right. Now, as you heard, I sent my people to join yours. We will travel with you to join the bird people in the north and then have our war."

With that, he strode westward, his head held high.

"Who the hell is this guy?" I whispered to Levina as we hastened to keep up with the remainder of Xander's people.

"Exactly who he says he is—Lexa's husband, the one who disappeared in the desert all those years ago."

"So all these people," I said, waving ahead of us, "are the remnants of his army? They've just lived at the edge of the forest for all these years, holed up and shooting at Serenial?"

"Oh, it's much worse than that," she murmured, so low that I had to lean down close to her as we walked. Everything in me wanted to stop with her and let the rest go ahead, but the battle still going on kept us both trudging forward, however reluctantly.

"Don't make me sound too bad, Levina," Xander called over his shoulder.

Levina laughed—something I hadn't heard her do since Jamie was captured.

"He'll sound bad no matter how I tell it—they all will, but keep an open mind. Parts of it are, well . . ."

She glanced around at those jogging near us and lowered her voice again. "Now keep in mind that I didn't know any of this until recently; we had no idea where these people were from until a few days ago, but I'll tell their story chronologically for your sake. It starts back a long time ago with the Laconic Warriors."

"The Laconic Warriors?"

"Hush, let me finish," she said, though the corners of her mouth twitched. "Yes, the Laconic Warriors. You know that after Caden and his brother"—noting her reluctance to say "James," I reached for her hand in support—"helped destroy the Laconic division, most of the Laconics who weren't killed in that awful battle fled the mountains instead of facing Warrior Peak justice.

"Most of them stuck together and decided to head for the forest because—I mean, you know, most of the mountains are uninhabitable, and the desert . . . well, you can guess what they found in the desert."

"But how powerful were the Morroks at that point in time?" I asked. "They weren't in the forest yet, were they?"

"I don't think so. But they've always had a good hold on the central Gravel Lands. For their own insane reasons, they let our settlers through the desert in later years, but they approached the Laconic Warriors—I think because they knew somehow that they weren't under Warrior Peak's protection."

"Approached?" I repeated. "Don't you mean attacked?"

"No, I mean approached. They made a deal with the Laconic Warriors. The Morroks agreed to let them live peacefully at the edge of the forest as long as the Warriors handed over their babies every five years."

"They—they agreed to that?" I gasped, not bothering to keep my voice down. Several of Xander's people looked around.

"It gets worse," Levina said. "They would take most every child under five—I guess because by the time you're four or five, it's too hard to change from how you've been raised so far—"

"I don't think that's true," I said.

Levina cocked an eyebrow at me but continued without comment. "Well, that's how it happened. And the Morroks would take mostly boys, so the Laconics' village quickly became dominated by women. And because having as many babies as possible was the priority, you can imagine—men had multiple partners . . . whatever it took to give the Morroks as many children as they demanded."

"Okay, but that still doesn't explain Xander. He's from Tyrclopia and wasn't even alive when the Laconics rebelled."

"They went on like this for generations, mothers willingly giving up their children to the Morroks, just handing them over freely, putting up no fight whatsoever—"

This time it was Levina's voice that had risen uncontrollably. I didn't think I was imagining that most of those who turned to glare were women.

"Anyway," Levina said after taking several calming breaths, "they went on like that for years, right up to Xander's attempted attack on the Morrok camp. Xander only ever managed to gather a couple hundred, so they stood no chance. Once they saw just how many Morroks there were, Xander had enough sense to flee, and they ended up wandering around the desert and the northern border of the forest for months, trying to figure out how to get back to Warrior Peak without attracting Morrok attention. But the Morroks were much more powerful by that time, and they finally drove Xander and his people completely into the forest. By chance, they came across the Laconic Warriors, who introduced them to their society."

"But surely Xander didn't—I mean, there's no way he could agree to that. He was in all of Aldis's stories. He and his brother, Zachaes, were Tyrclopia's leaders against Morroks, and he was the only one at Warrior Peak who considered the Morroks a threat because he knew—he *knows*—what they're capable of."

"I know," Levina said. "I'm not defending him, but just think of his situation—separated from his wife, away from his homeland, with people he'd known only a few years at most, wandering around the wilderness for months, feeling responsible for leading all those people from safety. Can't you see why he might've given in, just for some rest and security?"

"No," I said, "not to that."

"Well, it happened all the same. Xander eventually became the leader of their society, and they gave up all hope of going home. They knew about Serenial and kept them away out of fear. They even knew that other Humans were in the forest, but I think they were so closed off and so resigned to their way of life that they didn't ever think of rebelling."

"But they let you in."

"Yes, they let us in," she said. "No Humans had ever directly approached them before, and they were curious about what was happening at Warrior Peak and in the rest of the forest. I honestly don't think they were going to let us go for fear that we would expose them."

"So what did you do?"

Levina grinned. "We kept telling them what they wanted to hear. We had story time after dinner, just like you and I used to do for the children at Settlement Six, remember? Among the four of us, we had tales from all over the forest and from Warrior Peak. They were fascinated. Even though they'd all been away from it for so long, it's still their history, you know? And I won't pretend that we didn't drop some anti-Morrok propaganda here and there throughout the stories—"

I laughed. "Here and there my ass." I thought suddenly of the night I had first kissed Levina, of how she had fluttered around her room, ranting about how she believed so strongly in working against the Morroks that nothing would stop her from coming to Serenity Valley to help its people against them.

"Finally," Levina plunged on now, grinning more broadly than ever, "about two weeks ago, we were running short on ideas, and the leaders—including Xander, though I didn't know who he was at that time—were becoming unhappy with the ideas we were planting. People were starting to ask why they couldn't come with us to the Outpost. Plus, the five-year mark was coming up, so it was almost time for them to give up their children again. There was talk of refusing.

"It got to be my night to speak. Now, like I said, we didn't know who these people were at this point, and I'd run out of stories I'd read in the Inventory division's old papers, so that night, I thought of you and told the story of the Laconic Warriors."

"You used my stories as a last resort?" I teased.

She started to protest, saying the Laconic Warriors had nothing to do with the Morroks, but I waved her off and told her to keep going.

"Anyway, yes, the Laconic Warriors. And of course, most of them knew at least parts of their own history, and they got restless and upset when I started describing the Laconics in a poor light, so I stopped telling the story, even though I didn't know why it was affecting them the way it was.

"But the night was still young, and all I had left were Aldis's stories about Tyrclopia. I didn't think any of them would know what Tyrclopia was, but the stories were all about Morroks, so I thought they might still work. But the moment I started saying names—Acules, Zachaes, Lexa, all of them—Xander lost control. He jumped to his feet and ordered me to come with him, alone. Scott was so upset that he nearly had to be knocked out, but he couldn't stop hundreds of Xander's people, so I went with Xander.

"And you know what happened?" Levina said, shaking her head. "The moment Xander and I got inside his hut, he started bawling. That grown, very hairy, frighteningly large man cried right in front of me and told me who he was and what he'd done—how he'd gone from the man in those stories, fighting Morroks alongside his wife and brother, to the man he was right then, hiding and scared and surrendering children he once would've rescued. The change was almost instantaneous. He told me he'd do anything to get back to Lexa, and I told him that the only way to do it was to help you storm the Gravel Lands.

"Once we had Xander on our side, it was easy to get the rest to agree to fight with us. To tell you the truth, they were a little *too* enthusiastic; they insisted on tearing apart their huts and burning anything they wouldn't need for the trip south. I thought for sure it would draw the Morroks' attention, but thankfully it didn't, though I'm sure the Serenial noticed. Anyway, we sent the children to the Serenial, and we were on our way to the Outpost when the

Morroks attacked and . . . oh my."

We had reached the site of the first battle. Although the fighting seemed to be over, the smoke still hung heavy in the air, and the smell of charred wood and burned hair and flesh wafted steadily from the south. It was still midmorning, but the most I could see beyond the group I had traveled with were silhouettes of figures moving in the distance. Xander's people had stopped short and drawn their weapons. Seizing Levina's hand, I unsheathed my own sword and marched forward.

"Who's there?" one of the silhouettes called.

I relaxed and put my sword away. "It's Mark."

Mark's stocky form solidified, but he kept his sword raised as he looked around at all the unfamiliar faces. Then his gaze fell to Levina and me, and he did a double take.

"Levina!" he exclaimed, embracing her. "Then that means . . ."

Levina broke away from me and brought Xander forward. "General, I present you an army about four hundred strong, headed by Xander, a man who probably knows more about Morroks than anyone else present. I would give equal credit to the three others you sent me with, but I believe they all ran ahead to assist with this battle."

"Yes, it did end rather abruptly," Mark said, sounding dazed. "There seemed to be an upsurge of men on our side, and the Morroks retreated. We're rallying a few miles north in the canopy. I thought the smoke was playing tricks on my eyes and keeping me from recognizing my fellow Humans, but I suppose that our rescuers were your men, Xander."

Xander nodded. He was scrutinizing Mark as if he doubted a man so much shorter and younger than he was could lead thousands in battle. Mark smiled pleasantly back, waiting for the verdict of his inspection from a man who couldn't have looked less like a fellow leader. Levina and I caught each other's eye and had to look away to keep from laughing.

"I need to be updated on our plans," Xander said gruffly.

Mark spread his arms invitingly, directing us northward. "If you would like to join us, our council is convening with the Serenial shortly. Are you coming,

Orestes?"

"No," I said. The question had probably been rhetorical, but at the moment, I didn't care much about how we were going to incorporate Xander's troops with our own or how many Morroks we speculated were still in the forest. Levina looked like she was going to protest, but I continued, speaking to the group at large but looking only at her, "I'm sure you'll agree that Levina and I have contributed enough for today. We'll catch up with you in time for you to brief me on the council's decisions."

Mark nodded, and without another word, he, Xander, and the rest of Xander's people disappeared into the haze of smoke. Levina and I retreated several yards eastward and climbed into the canopy.

I cradled her head in my hands and leaned in to kiss her, but she grabbed both my shoulders and held me firmly at arm's length. Her entire body was trembling, but her face was set.

"There are many things I want to say to you, and I'm sure you have some as well, but most of those things can wait," she said, her voice as unsteady as the rest of her body. "One thing we have to decide now, though, is what we are going to do when we reach the Gravel Lands."

I knew exactly what she was asking me, and now that we were together again, I knew the answer as well.

"We're going to find Jamie," I said. "We'll kill as many Morroks as we can along the way, but we're not leaving until we find our daughter and rescue her from those horrible monsters."

For the first time in my life, I honestly believed that that was possible, and even though I knew that the feeling might not last, I was content to live in hope for a while with the one person who I knew would always share it.

Chapter Twenty-Eight
Alec's New Name

It was a harrowing task to trek through the Gravel Lands after two years of living under the protection of Serenity Valley's canopy. Weighed down with armor and weapons, we had little to shield us from the sun's direct rays as we moved blindly forward, both hoping and dreading to see any sign of the Morroks.

The flat terrain gave us the advantage of being able to see for miles around us, and so far it presented us no disadvantage. For even if we had been marching in winding hills, there would be no hiding our numbers. With Xander's men included, I had been proud of our Human gathering of nearly two and a half thousand, but as soon as we had reached the northern border of the forest, we realized our forces were dwarfed by those of the Serenial. The last estimate before we left the forest had put their number at twelve thousand fighters, gathered from all over the country in the past few months. Aderyn said that, given more time, thousands more would have come, but we couldn't give the Morroks any more time to strategize than we already had. Within hours of our arrival at the border, we had organized and set off, prepared to meet whatever awaited us in the desert.

We were nearing midmorning on our second day in the desert when we started to see signs of life, but none of my companions would have noticed if I hadn't pointed them out. For all around us, I saw marks, not of Morroks, but of children—rocks piled as headrests or in patterns like play battle formations. Our army, which was far ahead of the small contingent I was leading, had long ago stamped out any Morrok footprints, but I was confident that we were getting close. Our main army was moving in a wide convex arc toward Warrior Peak, counting on its breadth to ensure that we would stumble across the Morrok camp if the Serenial couldn't locate it from above. I found the Morroks' absence thus far alarming because before today no Serenial had been able to set foot in the desert for months, much less lead an army into it. I hoped that even if the Morroks had gathered at their camp, they wouldn't have special defenses ready before we arrived.

Of course, for all I knew, the main army could already have been fighting and we just hadn't caught up. My group consisted of thirty of the best fighters from all over the country—the Outpost, Xander's people, and several Serenial from all different villages. True to my word to Levina, I had asked Mark to lead this group, which had a single mission: to find where the Morroks kept the children and rescue as many as we could.

Xander and I couldn't decide what we thought the children might do once we started to attack the Morroks. We had warned everyone that they might try to fight us, in which case we were going to disarm them and cause as little harm as possible as we rescued them against their will. Personally, I thought the Morroks would move the children away from the battle because if we were successful, those children would be the Morroks' best hope of rebuilding their army.

In light of my prediction, the council had assembled my group with the most elite fighters in anticipation of the Morroks defending their children with great zeal. I didn't know anyone under my command except for Levina, who had proven her worth in the most surprising way just hours before we entered the desert.

I had told Mark and the council all along that Levina was coming with me no matter what troop I led, but when I took over such a specialized group, Mark had felt the need to intercede.

"I understand the desire to stay together and protect her, I really do," he had told us after pulling us aside from a brief but joyous reunion Ritter and Sylvia. "And I won't deny that the rest of the council suspects your ulterior motives in seeking the captured children. I vouched for you on that account, Orestes, but it's something of an insult for Levina to be in this group as well; the others consider their place under you as an honor for their fighting skills, and it undermines the prestige when you start including your own people over others whom the Serenial have recommended."

I paused before I spoke, conscious of the ramifications of Mark's dilemma. As far as the Serenial were concerned, he was ultimately the voice and leader of all Humans, and so every move he made was crucial to us staying in the Serenials' good graces, especially after having left them to defend the northern border alone for all these months. Not many chieftains besides Aderyn had interacted with Humans, so our inactivity was their first impression of us, and Mark and I had been doing our best to overcome that impression in the few short days leading up to the battle. My taking over such a specialized group, populated mostly with Serenial, had already raised some eyebrows, and I understood how it might have looked to the Serenial for me to include my wife in the group instead of opening her spot for another Serenial fighter.

Before I could begin to enumerate any of these sympathies to Mark, it was Levina who took the initiative to reply.

"Stand up," she said.

Mark and I both looked at her, bewildered, as she stood and drew her sword. We were in the canopy with thousands of people milling around us, but Levina looked only at Mark.

"Stand up," she repeated.

I shrugged at Mark and scooted as far away as I could as he rose slowly to his feet.

"Levina, I didn't mean to offend—"

But his words were cut off by his own yelp as Levina slashed her sword within inches of his chest. He reached for his sword and warded off her next few blows with increasing alarm showing on his face.

I knew Mark didn't want to fight back, but even if he had, I wasn't sure he would have been successful. More than once, I thought about interceding, but Levina continued to attack him with ferocity I wouldn't have believed if I hadn't witnessed it. She kept at him for a full five minutes, drawing several scandalized onlookers, until she batted the sword from his hands and got close enough to slap him full across the face.

"No man's ego will stand in the way of me finding my daughter," she hissed. "I have been patient thus far only because my husband told me it was impossible to reach her. But now I have my chance, and no one—Morrok, Human, or Serenial—will take it from me."

And she had stalked away, leaving the general stunned and humiliated just hours before he was to lead thousands in battle. Mark stayed long enough to tell me that he would report Levina's fighting merit to the Serenial, and since then, he had not spoken to Levina or me.

Levina had remained in this crazed mood ever since, barely talking to me as we trudged through the desert. Before her confrontation with Mark, however, we had spent five wonderful days constantly in each other's company. Although much of our time was given to preparation for the battle, we couldn't help but smile whenever we looked at each other.

Levina had a never-ending supply of stories to share with me about her travels and her interactions with Xander's people. Although horrified at their warped attitudes, she had formed friendships by throwing herself into the work of the village, which centered largely on caring for children. She said that the women gave birth so often that she couldn't help but learn some skills as a midwife. And once born, the children were taken away to be raised by "the whole community," as they put it, so that no one would become too attached to any one child in case the Morroks chose to take him or her.

"It's so sad to watch the mothers almost try to forget which baby is theirs," she had said with a sigh.

I nodded, trying my best not to let my mind wander to Jamie. Would we recognize our baby after being separated from her for months?

"I've been talking too much," Levina said, thankfully steering us away from that line of thought. "Tell me what happened back at the Outpost. You haven't said much about what you did while I was gone."

I told her about my dinners with all our old friends, about council meetings, and about preparing to travel north. Even as I spoke, I dreaded that she would guess where I had gone when I couldn't sleep at night or, worse, that she would ask me where Cassandra was. Since Levina and I had found each other, I had been doing my best to forget that Cassandra had ever existed, though I knew I was being childish to do so. Still, I could not bring myself to tell Levina what had happened between me and her; since Cassandra was gone, the only result would be Levina feeling hurt and betrayed, and that was the last thing I wanted to bring on her after the few precious days we had just spent together. It was all I could do to keep my guilt under the surface, and I mollified my own conscience by telling myself there would be time to fix everything after the battle.

Now that we were in the desert, it was clear that the time for battle was approaching quickly as we began to hear shouting in the distance. Before we could exchange too many exclamations, our scout flew into view and landed among us. He was sweating profusely.

"We found the camp. It is almost directly south of Warrior Peak, so luckily the thickest part of our army found it first, but we are nowhere near penetrating their walls. There are thousands of Morroks inside and out. I did not hear the official estimate, but I am afraid we might be outnumbered. No sign of children outside."

"What about the groups moving toward Warrior Peak?" another Serenial asked.

The scout shook his head. "Almost all dead. Although no one has been able to figure out where they are hiding, apparently there are Morrok archers scattered throughout the desert; they have been shooting down dozens of our people since morning. And the Morroks have formed a defensive line stretching out from either side of their camp to keep us away from the mountains."

"Keep moving," I ordered because we had unconsciously slowed our pace while we listened. "What does the camp look like?"

"We are not sure about the interior because we cannot fly high enough to see without being shot," the scout said between sharp puffs of breath. "The shape of the settlement is not very structured, but there is a thick stone wall surrounding the whole thing. It is a huge camp, far bigger than your Outpost, but the wall is not very tall, especially considering the Morroks' height."

"Lieutenant, may we fly? We weren't built for running," a female Serenial near me panted. I wondered vaguely how much the Serenials' wings weighed them down in this heat. Many of them had complained about sand getting in their feathers, but I had assumed this was out of vanity.

"Of course, but stay low, and don't get too far ahead of us," I said.

The Serenial sprang, midsprint, from the ground and unfurled their wings. A cloud of dust rose with them, causing us Humans to cough and tear up. We proceeded running in this manner, the Serenial hovering over us like a great cloud, for nearly fifteen minutes before we encountered the back of our army.

Our troops were so thick that I could see the Morroks only over several hundred heads. True to our scout's report, I saw a rough wall in the distance, clearly made from the desert's rocks with such sloppiness that I wondered if the Morroks had just thrown it together in the days leading up to our attack.

But far more concerning than the mystery of the wall was the battle that unfolded before it. Even from my poor position, I could see that the fight was in early stages, with the front lines still slamming against one another, trying to gain ground.

It was remarkable to watch the three races work around each other. The Serenial were as peculiar to me as ever as they flew just feet off the ground but navigated through the mass of bodies as if they were moving on solid ground. Probably for the first time in their lives, the Morroks had to look up to fight, and although I had no wings myself, I cringed empathetically every time a Morrok slashed over its head at the Serenials' largest and most vulnerable appendage. I couldn't get a very good glimpse of the Humans fighting, but as far as I could tell, they were using the Morroks' skyward distraction to their advantage, slashing at the monsters in ways that I would have called unfair if this had been an end-of-year tournament at Warrior Peak.

"What is our plan, Lieutenant?" one of the Serenial asked, breaking me out of my reverie.

I scanned the battle line again, wishing I had a better idea of what was going on. "Find a weakness in their defense and break through it," I said. Several of them began to draw their weapons.

Levina touched my arm to get my attention. "Not that I entirely disagree, but I thought the purpose of us coming after the main army was to wait until they've distracted the Morroks enough for us to sneak in."

"If that's all the council wanted from us, then they shouldn't have put me in charge of thirty people who know how good they are at killing Morroks."

She grinned and drew her sword. I pointed toward the army's right flank, where the fighting seemed to be lightest, and set off at a run again.

To keep us together, I led my group around the back of our army until we reached the edge of our troops. The fight had developed more than I had predicted at first; the Morroks had penetrated far into our ranks, and I could only hope that we had gained similar ground toward the wall. When we arrived at the eastern border of the fighting, we were a considerable distance from the camp, but the line of Morroks still reached farther than the eye could see. We couldn't outflank them.

"Let's join in," I said to the others. "We'll work our way to the center, close to the wall. Try to stick together."

Without another word, we clustered into a loose formation and moved toward the fighting.

Perhaps it was because the Morrok forces were thinner where we were or perhaps it was because we were supposed to be the best fighters in the country, but either way, we moved through the battle almost as quickly as we had walked around it. We felled Morrok after Morrok with only light injuries on our side. The wall, which seemed to form a rough circle around the buildings of the camp, loomed ever closer, and now that my view was better, I could see that the first of our numbers had reached the stones.

I had focused most of my attention to the front of our formation, but when I heard a cry of pain behind me, I couldn't help but look around. The first of our group had been struck, a male Serenial whose right wing was so battered that his naturally brown feathers were now caked red with blood. Before any of us could try to help him to his feet, a Morrok with a spear impaled him through the chest.

My moment of hesitation cost me dearly. I had barely worked up a feeling of sadness when something flat and metal collided with the side of my head.

Everything went black for a moment, but I fought for consciousness enough to enjoy the full impact of crashing to the ground and being stepped on by two different people, friendly or not I could not tell. I curled up as quickly as I could to prevent further injury while I felt the side of my head. My hand was bloody when I drew it away, but the cut wasn't deep and my vision was almost normal again. I scrambled to my feet and snatched up my sword. In the short time I had been on the ground, my group had moved away, lost to me in the confusion of battle. No Morrok stood over me, so I assumed I had been hit by a stray shield or spear butt rather than as part of a direct attack. My jaw and ear ached terribly, but I did my best to ignore the sting as I started to fight again, keeping my eyes peeled for Levina and the rest of my contingent.

As worried as I was about finding my group again, I felt much freer being on my own. I moved through the battle with new clarity, stepping in duels where others weren't doing well and taking on fresh Morroks at my own pace. In a very short time, I found myself within feet of the wall, where I was surprised to find no gate or door of any kind.

I decided to circle the wall to search for an entrance, which seemed to be everyone's new objective now that we had reached the camp. I continued to help others in their duels, but I was finding fewer and fewer unattached Morroks to fight myself. Their numbers weren't diminishing, however; indeed, there seemed to be more and more of them pouring from the opposite side of the camp. It wasn't until two Morroks turned pointedly away from me and ran deeper into the battle that I understood: There were only Eight whom the Morroks feared, and this was what it meant to be one of the Eight.

With new boldness, I worked my way around to the western wall, where the Morroks nearly outnumbered the Humans and Serenial. To my surprise, I found myself fighting next to Aether, the scout I had sent to find Cassandra before we left the Outpost only a week and a half ago.

"Lieutenant, have you heard? We circled the entire wall, and there is no gate. I have been trying to locate someone to tell."

"I'm not the one to tell," I shouted over the clangs of metal around us. "You need to find Mark or Aderyn or one of your other chieftains. They're in charge of the main army. I'm not sure what their strategy is right now."

"I will find them, Lieutenant," he said, leaping into flight. Alarmed, I glanced at the Morrok archers on top of the stone wall, but Aether was so deft in his movements that he hardly attracted any attention to himself in spite of his great wings.

No gate. . . . That was very disturbing. Perhaps day to day the Morroks used ladders, but how did they get the children in and out? We must have missed something.

As much success as we had had so far, we now were losing as the minutes dragged on. The Morroks pushed us back toward the southern edge of their wall as their numbers increased seemingly out of nowhere. But for every wave they sent, we were able to rally and push forward again so that we alternated between gaining and losing ground every twenty minutes.

In one of our advances, I found myself near the very front of our troops, again on the western side of the wall. We were closer to the northern curve than ever, and it was here that I noticed that new Morroks were joining the battle from this side of the camp. Could Aether have missed spotting a door somewhere?

I called to half a dozen people fighting nearest me, five Serenial and one Human, none of whom I had ever met. They huddled around me at the base of the wall and kept looking over their shoulders at the duels dancing around us.

"Are you ready to take a risk?" I asked them.

They all nodded, though some of them paled.

"I need you to cause a distraction so I can run north to see how they're leaving the camp. I don't know what it'll take to get their attention, but do you think you can do it?"

"We'll handle it, Lieutenant," the Human said immediately. The Serenial nodded again and huddled closer to the Human to hear his plan.

I fought my way as far north as I could, hugging the wall to let the shade hide me from the archers atop the ramparts. After a few minutes of fighting, I was worried I had strayed too far and would miss the diversion, but I was proven wrong seconds after the thought came to mind.

There were audible gasps from all three races as the five Serenial rose as one into the air, all of them lifting the Human among them. The Human had a bow and was shooting arrows so quickly that I wasn't sure how he had time to aim. The archers on the ramparts immediately turned their own arrows on them, and the Morroks below started hurling their weapons upward, apparently infuriated by their inability to reach them.

Seizing my chance, I bolted along the wall, past the fighting and past the archers, so far that the noise of battle faded from immediate attention. Every so often, a few Morroks ran past me, but none of them noticed me sidling along the base of the wall.

After a few minutes, I rounded the curve enough to see three rickety ladders leaned against the outer wall. No Morroks were in sight.

I knew it was impossible to sneak in using those ladders; for all I knew, there could have been fifty Morroks standing on the other side of the wall. But another possibility struck me with such force that I actually gasped aloud; with all the Morroks fighting behind me, my way was clear to Warrior Peak.

I didn't pause to consider. I started running.

My rising heart rate had little to do with my strenuous movements. Even as I sprinted north without a backward glance, I couldn't accept the fact that I was not only fleeing a battle, but also moving farther and farther away from Levina and Jamie. But I had no choice. Maybe we could win the battle without Warrior Peak, but I doubted we could go on like this for long, not with unknown numbers inside that camp and not with hundreds of Morroks still milling around Serenity Valley just waiting for us to fail in the desert.

I didn't know how long I ran, and I never had the courage to lift my eyes to the mountain, knowing that the closer I got to it meant I had less of a chance to be able to help my wife and daughter. The heat had increased so much that I could hardly breathe as I ran. I waited for numbness to set in as my legs began to ache from fighting the heat, from the greaves rubbing against my shins, and even from my own indecision about turning back. My eyes produced a constant stream of moisture, trying to wash away all the grit I kicked up as I ran. But even my unbidden tears could not distract me from the Morrok that appeared, quite literally, out of the ground a few yards in front of me.

If I hadn't been running for so long, the shock might have stopped me, but as it was, I continued to barrel toward the Morrok, drawing my sword as I went. The Morrok had a bow in its hands, but before it could reach for an arrow or a close-range weapon, I stabbed it through the stomach with all the force of my legs' long labor behind the thrust.

I skidded to a stop to see what I had accomplished. The Morrok took a heavy step toward me before it fell over, gasping and cradling its middle as blood poured from it. I slit its throat to alleviate any further suffering and then stepped over it to investigate where it had come from.

A lantern lay next to a small hole in the ground, barely wide enough for a Morrok to fit into. I dropped to my hands and knees and squinted into the darkness. Like at the camp, there was a ladder here too, but this one led straight underground and was made of metal, ready for constant use. The ladder didn't seem to reach down very far; in fact, I could see a flat rock landing just a couple yards down with tunnels branching off in all directions.

The temptation to explore this apparent underground network nearly rivaled my urge to go back to the battle, but I knew I had to keep moving. As I set off again, several things dimly began to fall into place—how the Morroks had been surprising our scouts all day, why the Morrok camp didn't have gates, and perhaps (I dared to hope) where the children were hidden.

I didn't run into any more tunnel entrances for several minutes, maybe hours. It was nearing evening. I couldn't imagine how many hours I had been away from the battle. Finally, for the first time in my journey, I looked up and saw that I was very near the old rings used in the boys' and girls' end-of-year tournaments.

When I reached Warrior Peak's gates, I found myself noticing all the differences in my home rather than the familiar things. The rings had nearly faded from the ground; the gates had more locks on them than ever; and countless more parapets and guards now sat atop the wall that embraced the foot of the mountain. Still, the golden-brown face of the mountain, glowing in the evening sun, nearly made me forget why I was there.

"Who is that?" one of the guards shouted down to me. "Be advised that you have a dozen arrows pointed at you."

"I'm Orestes," I called, my voice sounding wild and panicked even to my own ears. "I'm a citizen of Warrior Peak, and I've been in Serenity—"

One of the great doors creaked open, drowning out my words. A heavily armed older man I recognized as one of Fallon's many acquaintances hurried out to meet me.

"Are any of the other twelve with you?" he asked.

It took me a moment to realize that he was referring to the group with whom I had originally set out from Warrior Peak. "No, I'm alone, but I really must speak to the General immediately. There's a battle—"

"No, you're to go straight to the Elder," the man said, ushering me inside. Two young officers heaved the door closed behind us. "I trust you know your way. I have other things to attend to."

Before I could argue, he disappeared from my side and ran back to the outer wall.

I continued up the mountain on my own, drinking in the faces and houses as much as I could as I passed them at top speed. The Elder. . . . I never thought I would be disappointed at the chance to speak to the leader of our nation, but the whole trip here, I had been counting on speaking to Alec—the General, Fallon's cousin, the man who had taken me from Tyrclopia. Even if we had disagreed with the past, I knew he would understand now that we had to take action. He hadn't wanted to send tens of thousands to Serenity Valley to meet an unknown threat, but I had numbers and stories for him now, not to mention a chance to destroy the Morroks' base in the Gravel Lands.

The sun was beginning to set when I passed my old house. It appeared to have been reassigned to another family, as I could see candles flickering in the windows. I was surprised by the longing that welled up in me as I plowed on toward the military school. How could they give away our house?

The kids I found practicing in the military school training grounds also surprised me by how young they all looked. Some faces still looked familiar, but I couldn't believe I had ever trained among any of them. Their biggest care right now was probably preparing for the end-of-year tournament. Had I ever cared about winning that silly game?

When I reached the General's level, I paused for the first time. I wanted more than anything to speak to the General, but right on cue, one of the guards approached me to crush my hopes. He was one of the many who remembered me from my days of stealing up here for the General to question me about my progress and about anything he considered potentially Morrok-like behavior.

"Orestes, correct?" the guard asked.

I nodded and opened my mouth to speak, but like Fallon's acquaintance, the guard hurried away from me, into the General's cave. Left with no alternative, I continued up to the Elder's level.

Remembering my first experience with the Elder's guards, I fully expected to be tackled the moment I reached the top of the ladder, but when I straightened up, they merely surrounded me in an uncomfortably tight circle. I would have backed away, but my only alternative was down the ladder again.

"Orestes?" the guard facing me asked.

Truly bewildered this time, I blurted an intelligent, "Uh-huh," and they all moved away from me except for the one who had spoken. He pulled me toward the tiny, rotting wooden door protruding from the side of the mountain and knocked sharply on it four times.

"You may enter now," he told me before slinking back into the shadows to await his next victim.

Unable to keep my hand steady, I fumbled with the latch for a few moments before I was able to push the door open and enter.

Compared to the rest of Warrior Peak, the Elder's cave was laughably primitive. The cavern was enormous, yes, but it had none of the expert carving and tunneling of the General's cave and no real attempt to make it feel less like a cave—no paintings, no wood or cloth covering the ground, no room divisions, and almost no furniture. Most of the adornment was on the walls; weapons of all kinds hung on pegs, almost covering numerous yellowed and peeling maps and battle strategies.

The only source of light was a fireplace whose chimney disappeared high into the twenty-foot ceiling. Two stuffed chairs sat in front of it, and it was between these that I saw Alec himself standing, looking twenty years older than when I last left him. He wore a long, embroidered robe that I never would have imagined him even touching after years of wearing only generic military uniforms.

He smiled at my shock and waved me into one of the chairs. I stumbled across the rocky floor and collapsed where he had pointed, too dumbfounded to argue. When he took the remaining chair, he said nothing but only continued smiling politely, as if waiting for me to speak first.

"General, there's a battle going on," I said finally. "I left it hours ago, and I know if you would just send the Army, even the Militia, we would have a chance. You have to—"

"I have to do nothing," he said, sounding amused. "I am the Elder, and I am marked by issuing few direct orders to my people."

"Sir, you can't seriously mean—"

"Fortunately," he continued, "I issued one of those rare orders one year ago as soon as I took this office. And that order was to send out all available Warriors the moment Orestes or someone representing him came to our gates."

As always, others seeming to anticipate my movements better than I did unnerved me a little, but I had to assume that, as Elder, Alec had gained whatever wisdom that was foretold to come with the office. I had never fully embraced the mysteries surrounding the Elder until this moment; but now the change that had come over Alec was too complete to ignore. I had never seen him smile before, I had never seen him wear anything but an official military uniform, and we had never gone this long without one of us yelling. But he was different now. Maybe I was too.

"So you . . . so they know where to go, sir?" I asked, determined to stay on task. "You know where the Morrok camp is?"

"Of course. You don't think that we did nothing once you and Fallon left, do you? Just because I chose not to go as far as Serenity Valley does not mean I did not comb the desert quite well."

"Why didn't you attack before now?" I burst, losing some of my sense of awe to anger. "You have tens of thousands at your disposal, and I've had to work for two years to scrape together two and a half thousand Humans. And even then, if we didn't have the Serenial, we'd all be dead for even leaving the trees, much less—"

"So you did get the Serenial to ally with you? Excellent work."

I was aware that my mouth was hanging open, but I did not have the pride to close it. Until Ritter had stumbled upon Sylvia, no Warrior had ever even heard of Serenial, and yet here Alec sat, never having set foot in Serenity Valley, congratulating me as if I had passed some test he had given me to see if I could persuade the Serenial to join us. And what was more, he had done nothing with this knowledge to help any of his people.

He leaned forward across the arm of his chair. "Don't be angry with me, Orestes. How could I hope to be successful without knowing you were in the battle? I knew you would succeed in contacting Warrior Peak if you were planning to storm the Facility yourself, and receiving that contact was my cue to send out my Warriors."

"I wish all of you would stop saying things like that about me!" I shouted, thinking of the Morrok at the fortress by the lake. I wanted to stand but contented myself in gripping the arms of my chair until the fabric ripped a little. "Why couldn't you have been more practical? I'm only one man. I don't care who the hell I am; I can't compare to the thousands you've had behind these walls doing nothing to help us all this time—all these years we've been fighting and barely hanging on."

"Orestes, do you know who the Eight are?"

"How do you know about that?" I said quickly, as if he had caught me in the middle of a crime.

"First, let me make it clear that I am not the man you knew as a boy," Alec said, the old edge creeping back into his voice. "Before the former Elder died, he spent weeks imparting to me knowledge as old as Warrior Peak itself. It is rare that anyone besides the General comes to see me because most who once knew me cannot accept that I do not belong to myself anymore. I recognize neither the name Alec nor any of the accomplishments or relationships he made in his life. Therefore, speak to me as if I have been living for three hundred years, and do not be surprised that I know about more than my own cavern."

"Yes, sir," I murmured.

"Good. Now, do you know who the Eight are?"

"I know that they are the only ones that the Morroks are afraid of," I said. "And I know that I am one of them, along with the Tyrclopian Acules."

"So Lernuc explained it to you?"

"Lernuc?" I repeated. "No, I would never . . . I don't know who Lernuc is. I just talked to some Morrok in the forest once or twice and to another Morrok in the fortress by the lake once."

"I imagine it was Lernuc in one form or another in all those instances. But there is more to the Eight than he probably told you. The Eight are believed to be the only ones who can defeat the Morroks for good. Yes, I can send my thousands to overrun the Gravel Lands Facility, but what good would that have done without you there to ensure us our chance at true victory?"

"Did you know all this when you let me go with Fallon to Serenity Valley?" I asked. "Wouldn't it have been easier to keep me here and send me into the desert with the Army two years ago?"

"As General, I did not know who you were," the Elder replied. "The former Elder told me years ago, when I took you from Tyrclopia, that you could turn out to be very important, but he didn't tell me why. None of us knew if you were one of the Eight, though Lernuc tried very hard to find out by drawing you out of Warrior Peak and pitting you against his followers to see how they reacted to you. After you left for the forest, my predecessor and I noted that the Morroks were preparing for war more than ever, which led us to believe that Lernuc thought you a real threat. When I understood the full meaning of your position, I kept my Warriors out of as much trouble as possible while we waited for you to come."

I closed my eyes against the irritation welling up in me. Although I knew Warrior Peak was already mobilizing, my anxiety at leaving the battle behind had not gone away, and the Elder's cryptic statements were only increasing my desire to return to it. "If I'm really that important, then shouldn't I be getting back to the battle?"

"By all means, your aid is essential, but unfortunately, both Lernuc and Dirth are in Tyrclopia, and so we cannot accomplish as much as I might've hoped. We can, however, save Serenity Valley from a generation or two of real strife. I believe you'll agree that that is a worthy cause?"

"Yes," I said immediately. I could seek out Lernuc and Dirth any day, but right now all the thousands of friends and allies I had made over the past two years apparently depended on me to some extent, and I would help them with everything I had.

I started to rise from my chair but hesitated as a question came to mind.

"Sir, what made Lernuc even suspect that I was one of the Eight? It's not like he heard I was a good fighter and then started to worry about me. I mean, Dirth had a guard outside my door when I was just a baby."

The Elder gazed at me for a long moment as if trying to decide whether or not to answer. Finally he asked, "Orestes, do you have a child?"

"I—I did . . . I mean, I do. I do. I have a daughter. Her name is Jamie, but a few months ago, the Morroks—" I looked away from the Elder as my throat began to tighten. I had never had to explain what happened to Jamie before. Everyone at the Outpost knew, and they were tactful enough not to ask Levina and me about it.

"The Morroks took Jamie because she shares your blood," the Elder said gently. "That is why they suspect her of being one of the Eight."

"Then whose blood do I share? Is it because of my blood that they've been after me all these years?"

"It's because of your bloodline that this entire war exists—exists, has existed, and will exist until the Eight put an end to it. I cannot tell you all you'd like to know, Orestes—not when there is a battle at hand. I hope you will not resent me for that."

But he had already answered my question. If my bloodline was the cause of this war, then surely that meant that I had born of Morroks. I had always suspected it, but having it confirmed only made me feel worse.

Not sure how to reply to the Elder's last words, I stood and walked toward the door. It was only when I was about to leave that I said, "I don't know if you know, sir, but Fallon and Glynis died a few months ago."

I couldn't see the Elder's expression as he remained staring at the fire, but he didn't speak for so long after I said it that I nearly left again.

"I thought Fallon might give his life for his cause," he said just as I had grasped the door latch.

"We found the Laconic Warriors, though," I said, feeling that I ought to bring good news as well. "From the story you told me about your grandfather and his brother—Caden and James. They're fighting with us right now."

The Elder laughed. "Legend meets legend. I would expect nothing less."

He said nothing more, but I felt that we had both left many things unsaid. He knew everything I had ever wondered about myself and my past, and I apparently was the key to his success against the Morroks. Still, I felt so inferior to him, whether he smiled or yelled, whether he wore robes or tunics.

"Good-bye, sir," I said after a time.

"Good luck, Orestes. I have given up my name for the greater good, but you must cling to yours in order for us to survive."

For a brief moment, I thought back to how having my own name used to be my one source of strength as I grew up in the Morrok Facility. None of the other trainees knew the names their parents had given them, and so they forgot that they were different from everyone else and had unique lives to give them joy and worth. I had worked my whole life to guard myself against the Morroks in any way I could, but they had given me my name, and even outside the Facility, it seemed that my name—Orestes, one of the Eight—was all I had ever needed to survive.

Chapter Twenty-Nine
A Human Morrok

I HAD SEEN MANY AMAZING EVENTS in my life—several in just the past week—but nothing quite as amazing as Warrior Peak marching out to battle. By the time I left the Elder's, evening had given way to night, but no darkness could hide the thousands of bodies that filled the streets as they streamed down the mountain and into the desert. I let myself get swept up in the crowds, though I couldn't have been more out of place in the swarm of clean-cut uniforms, newly sharpened weapons, and unscarred skin.

The troops must have started moving from the moment I entered Warrior Peak because when I reached the Gravel Lands, whole divisions had already formed and were marching southward, almost far away enough now to be out of sight. With no one to report to, I broke away from the crowds and started to run again.

The cool night air, coupled with the fact that I had untold thousands accompanying me, made the journey south pass much more quickly. I wove in and out of troops, my battered appearance earning curious glances along the way, but I didn't care. The vision I had had from the moment I heard that Morroks were on this side of the mountain was finally coming true, and nothing could diminish my happiness.

Before long, we came across the Morrok I had killed that afternoon. I cursed my own forgetfulness and called over the nearest officer to tell him about the tunnels. He followed me to the hole from which the Morrok had come and squinted down it.

"Do you know where it leads?" he asked.

"No, I didn't go down there myself," I said. "I just wanted you to be aware that they can take us by surprise, though this exit doesn't seem to be wide enough for more than one at a time to pop out."

The officer crouched down and lit the Morrok's lantern that still lay nearby. After a moment of consideration, he started to call over one of his subordinates to tell him to climb down, but I held up a hand.

"Let me. I want to see them for myself anyway."

He nodded and handed me the lantern. I swung my legs onto the ladder and descended quickly, wary of having my back exposed to any Morroks hidden in the tunnels below. After just a few moments of climbing, my feet rested on solid ground again, and I peered down the tunnel nearest me. It was so narrow that only one person at a time could fit inside; it was, however, tall enough for a Morrok to walk upright. There were four of these tunnels, leading directly north, south, east, and west.

"What do you see?" the officer called.

"Nothing and no one," I said, glancing upward. He looked to be no farther away from me than if he had been atop one of the old settlement's walls.

I climbed up again and set down the lantern without letting it blow out.

"It's no good to us," I said to the officer. "The tunnels are only wide enough for one, so even if we sent men down in a line, they'd have to fight Morroks one on one if they found any, and we know that won't end well."

The officer nodded gravely and thanked me for my help. As soon as his division had marched away, I grabbed the lantern again and climbed back into the earth.

As I entered the southern tunnel, I suddenly understood what it was like for the Serenial to come into Human buildings. Although there were caves throughout Warrior Peak, I had never been in a space so confining and so far from natural air and light. I tried to focus on the lantern that I held in front of me rather than the darkness that enveloped each step behind and before me, and I tried to enjoy the foot and a half of space above me rather than think about the walls that threatened to scrape against both my arms if I didn't keep my elbows reined in.

Although I didn't run into any Morroks, every once in a while I passed an exit to the surface just like the one I had used to enter the tunnels. There was always a metal ladder leading straight up to the surface of the desert with some camouflage to cover the hole, such as a thick net or small boulder. At the bottom of each of these entrances, there were again four tunnels leading in the cardinal directions, which made me think that the tunnels were laid out in a grid, though I didn't keep track of how far apart the entrances were spaced.

As little as I had kept track of time on the way to Warrior Peak, I now had no way of judging the time even if I wanted to. Every time I passed a tunnel entrance, all I saw was a starry sky above. It occurred to me that the tunnel I was traveling through might take me past the Morrok camp completely, but I hoped that the sounds of thousands running and fighting above would carry down to me.

After a while, I noticed that my tunnel was beginning to widen slightly. By the time it was big enough for four men to stand comfortably shoulder to shoulder, I saw a dot of light ahead. Another lantern. Drawing my sword, I sped up toward it, determined to silence whoever it was before he or she could figure out that I wasn't supposed to be there.

Two Morroks with one light between them were strolling toward me. Because of the dim light and their false sense of security, I was able to strike down one before they even realized I was not one of them. The other got as far as unsheathing its sword before I plunged my own into its chest. It struck clumsily at me, grazing my arm, before it stumbled against the wall and slid to the floor. Thankfully, neither of them had enough strength to shout before they died. I extinguished their lantern and kept moving.

I met a few more pairs like this, and although I was able to dispose of them just as quietly, I sensed that my time of remaining undetected was limited. The tunnel was wider than ever, and I saw a bright light ahead, brighter than any single lantern could produce.

I thought about backtracking to the last exit I had passed, but curiosity drove me forward. When I drew near the light, I extinguished my own lantern and slowed my footsteps to make less noise. Even at a distance, I could tell that the lighted area was yet another exit to the surface, but it was different than most I had seen; although no Morroks were present, lit lanterns hung on pegs around the cavern walls, and multiple ladders were bolted to the walls between the wide tunnels. But perhaps the most distinguishing features were two large crates attached to a pulley system leading up to the surface. The crates were the perfect size to hold two babies apiece.

Hardly daring to breathe, I crept into the circle of light and glanced upward, expecting to see the usual patch of night sky. Instead, I saw only darkness, but not as if the hole were covered with another boulder; rather, it was as if a building was surrounding the opening.

I crossed the distance to the nearest ladder in three quick steps and was at the top rung within seconds. Peering over the top edge, I saw that I was inside a hut that was barely wide enough to enclose the tunnel entrance. In fact, I imagined if someone coming inside the hut didn't know what he would find on the other side of the door, he would fall straight down to the tunnels below.

Luckily for me, this meant that there were no Morroks milling around inside the hut, and so I was able to pull myself out and circle around to the door in peace. I pressed my ear to the wall, but I hardly needed to do so to hear the chaos that was ensuing outside. From the sound of it, the battle was still going on and had reached the interior of the Morrok camp, if that was indeed where I was. I couldn't begin to guess which side had the upper hand, but at least the fighting would give me cover when I went outside.

When I opened the door, I found I was only partially right. Although the vast majority of Morroks were occupied with what looked to be mostly Serenial, four were stationed just outside the hut as if to guard the entrance.

Even though it was night, there was no way to hide in the open air as I had in the tunnel's darkness. I was able to strike only one of the guards before all of them realized that it was not a Morrok that had come from the tunnels.

I raised my sword, ready to take on all four myself, but thankfully, I didn't have to. Six Serenial descended near me, and together we made quick work of the Morroks. Unfortunately, the entrance to the tunnels seemed to be a point of great interest to the Morroks, and so several more were quick to take the other guards' place.

"What's been happening the last few hours?" I called to my Serenial companions as we continued to duel.

"Most of our army has been routed," one of them replied. "Around evening, Morroks arrived from the forest and attacked from behind. We were scattered in all directions, but a female Human convinced a great number of my people to swarm the Morrok archers and fly over the wall."

I dearly hoped I knew who that female Human was. "And how have you been doing in here?"

"Tolerably well because so many Morroks are off chasing the rest of our army," the Serenial said. "Right now, we are interested in getting to a barrack they have heavily guarded about two rows over. They seem to want to create a path between it and this hut, which you have kindly drawn more attention to."

I was so impressed with a Serenial having a sense of humor, albeit disdainful, that I couldn't be offended. I chanced a look around and saw what he meant by "barrack" and "rows"; besides the hut, the entire camp was filled with lines of long, low buildings made of the same stones as the outer wall. Even the path the Serenial had spoken of was hard to miss. Although the battle seemed to spread throughout the camp, the fighting was densest in a lane between two barracks very close to the tunnel entrance.

Before long, a dozen more Serenial had joined us to gain control over the hut, and I felt confident enough to slip away toward the barrack that the Morroks were so interested in protecting. Even though it was, like the Serenial had said, only two rows over, I had never had so much trouble weaving through a battle. So many bodies were squeezed between the buildings that I brought out my dagger because I was concerned that my sword's wide swing would cut a Serenial's wing.

I didn't see any other Humans as I moved, but the Serenial were certainly getting their revenge after a day of being shot out of the sky by Morrok archers. Under the cover of the night sky, they sprinted and flew along the tops of the barracks, shooting or diving into the fight at random and scattering the Morroks with deadly success. It was impossible to say who was winning, but as long as we stood firm until Warrior Peak arrived, I wasn't worried, even in the heart of enemy territory.

The first Human I found in the battle was one of Xander's men who had been part of my original thirty fighters. Elated, I pushed forward until, finally, I found Levina fighting on the front lines close to the disputed barrack.

"There you are!" she screamed as I fell in next to her and a Serenial, who were handling one Morrok on their own.

"Warrior Peak is on the move," I told her.

The Serenial dealt a well-placed blow that sent the Morrok staggering away, fatally wounded.

"Good, because I would've killed you if you'd left the battle for anything less," she snapped as we moved on to the next Morrok.

"How did you know I left?"

"Nearly everyone in the battle heard about your spectacular escape. Five Serenial carrying one Human. They all died, but everyone heard it was part of some secret plan of Lieutenant Orestes."

I flinched at the news. Obviously everyone here knew death was a possibility, but I hated to think that those five had died because of something I had asked of them.

"The battle was nearly even until the Morroks came from the forest," Levina continued. "By the time that happened, our contingent was close to getting over the wall, but then our army started to scatter. Still, I couldn't let us get pushed away when we'd worked so hard. So I called together all the Serenial on the west side of the wall, and we flew up and attacked the archers all at once and got inside."

"*We* flew?" I repeated.

"I took a leaf out of your book and had a few Serenial carry me. It cost us a lot in the initial strike, but you see how far we've gotten. I'm almost positive they have the children in there because they've been trying to keep us away from this building ever since we came over the wall."

"They're trying to take them underground and away from here," I said. I explained briefly about the tunnels I had found.

We continued to fight for several minutes, just feet from the door of the barrack, but we were unable to get any closer. Morroks were pouring back into the camp by the minute, and I couldn't figure out why until I noticed a sharp, successive banging of metal in the distance that had been lost on my ears among the hundreds of clashing swords and spears.

"I think it's a bell or gong or something," Levina said. "Maybe it tells them to come inside?"

"I don't think so. I wonder if—"

But my question was answered before I could finish. To the north rose a war cry of thousands of voices, deep and resounding as if it were a rolling thunderclap from above. Even the Morroks fighting us paused, as if torn between staying here and going to investigate this new threat.

The next leg of the battle passed in an anxious daze as we listened to Warrior Peak's divisions marching nearer. Little by little, the Morroks fighting us peeled off toward the northern wall, and we were able to push right up to the door of the barrack. As the strongest among a group of Serenial, I was the one to bash the lock while Levina and the Serenial protected me. My hands were shaking so badly that I could barely control the butt of my sword as I worked. Just a little longer and I would get to hold Jamie again. . . .

The latch finally broke, and the door swung open before me. There were so many people pushing behind me that I was thrust into the room before my eyes could adjust to the total darkness of the barrack. Both Morroks and Serenial streamed into the room, still battling fiercely, but I couldn't break my gaze from the hundreds of eyes staring at me from every corner and every bunk in the room.

Children of all ages, from infant to early teen, huddled on rows of bunk beds, all of them eerily still and quiet as the fight grew around them. Barely clothed and already scarred, they weren't exactly unhealthy—it was in the Morroks' interest to keep their trainees somewhat robust—but they were still smaller and their faces more drawn than any child of Warrior Peak. In a brief moment of clarity, I finally saw the difference between me and them, and that was simply that I lived with hope, while they hardly cared to move as swords and bodies came within inches of striking them.

Still trembling in anticipation, I pulled myself onto the nearest bed and shouted over the battle, "Serenial, forget the fight. Grab the children and fly! Take them to Warrior Peak, to the forest—anywhere to get them out of the desert."

It was only after my proclamation that the children finally acted. Some, mostly the older ones, resisted the Serenials' hold, but others ran to the bird people and nearly tripped them as they struggled to slip toward the door carrying their loads. I leaped down from the bed and grabbed Levina's hand, drawing her farther into the building. Most of the infants, dozens of them, had been squeezed between and under two bunk beds at the end of the barrack farthest from the door. Morroks and Serenial alike followed us, for the Morroks were now also grabbing as many children as they could, most likely to take them to the tunnels and out of our reach for good.

Levina and I inserted ourselves between the babies and all our pursuers. I drew my sword and began to strike at any Morrok that came within range, and Levina started grabbing babies, two at a time, and handing them off to Serenial to take. Their shrill wails added a new octave to the clangs and grunts of the battle, but Levina remained stoic and efficient in getting them to safe hands. She did, however, check each face before she gave a baby away.

This went on for several minutes, and in spite of our limited perspective, I got the distinct impression that the battle as a whole was turning our way. Human voices now joined Serenial and Morrok within the walls of the camp. But this hardly meant that fewer Morroks came to fight over the children; if anything, their numbers in the barrack increased. I wondered, with mingled elation and fear, if the Morroks had decided to flee their camp and were trying to take as many as children as they could with them.

Before long, there were fewer than twenty babies left. Levina had cuts and bruises all along her back and her arms from handing off the children without defending herself. My heart sank as I quickly surveyed the remaining infants. In spite of all the ones we had saved, our efforts would be in vain unless we found Jamie.

And then the last one was gone, and the Morroks took off after the Serenial cradling the children close to them as they ran. Levina grabbed my arm, her eyes bulging, the unspoken question hanging between us: Where was Jamie?

A Serenial skidded to a halt in front of us. "Are you Lieutenant Orestes?"

"Yes," I said.

"You are wanted outside. We are doing very well, but your mountain people want to talk to the Valley leaders, and they say you're essential to the meeting. If you cannot find one of your mountain people's ladders, then my people will lift you over the wall."

"Thank you," I said, though I had barely paid attention to his instructions.

As soon as he had gone, I turned back to Levina. "Do you think they might've hidden them anywhere else? Were they guarding any other building when you got in here?"

She shook her head. I glanced around the room, which was emptying as quickly as it had filled.

"Let's not give up hope," I continued. "Maybe one of the Serenial got her. And even if she is in another building, we'll be able to find her because it sounds like the Morroks are abandoning this place."

Levina drew her sword. "Let's keep searching then."

I drew mine as well and took a few steps out from between the bunks.

No sooner had I done so than I felt the flat of a sword blade slam across my shoulder blades and spine. I collapsed to the floor immediately, too shocked and pained to move. A large foot from somewhere to my side flipped me over so I could see my attacker. Judging from the strength of the blow, I expected to see a Morrok, but instead a beautiful Human woman with flowing black hair stood over me, dangling her curved sword over my chest.

"Hold the girl," Cassandra barked, and the Morrok feet that had flipped me stepped back toward the bunks. I heard Levina struggle for a moment and then whimper in pain. "And take his weapons." A second Morrok ripped the sword from my hands and the dagger from my belt.

Cassandra sneered down at me. "Did you honestly think we would keep Jamie here once we'd heard you were in the desert?"

"We?" I repeated, bewildered. For a few wild moments, I tried to imagine how Cassandra might have been captured again after leaving the Outpost and then dragged up to the desert against her will. But there were no bruises on her this time, and the Morroks had taken her orders.

"You didn't figure it out after I left the Outpost?" she asked, sounding sincerely incredulous. "You Humans are far too trusting! Or no, I suppose your guilt would keep you from suspecting ill of me. Guilt from breaking a vow of fidelity—again, trust strikes you ill!"

Cassandra glanced over to Levina and laughed. "Yes, girl, your faithful husband waited about a month after you left to sleep with me. Did you know that? But don't be too angry with him. It did take you leaving the Outpost entirely to get him to go through with it finally."

The shock of being hit and the hesitancy over attacking Cassandra both wore off very quickly during that speech. She seemed to have only two Morroks with her, and it would be all too easy to trip her, take her sword, and continue from there.

As if reading my mind, Cassandra turned her attention back to me and said, "And don't think of trying to disarm me, you twit. If anything were to cause my fingers to slip"—she let go of the sword with all but her thumb and index finger—"this would fall straight into your chest."

"Who the hell are you?" I asked, trying to muster some authority in my voice but failing as it cracked like a pubescent boy's.

"Who the hell am I?" she repeated. "Why, Orestes, I'm just like you. Born of Morroks but never took the serum. It's rare for people like us to be born at all, but not to go through regular training and not to take the serum? It's nearly unprecedented."

"But *you* still work for them," I snapped. "Without the serum, you would still work for those evil monsters."

"Of course. You think just because my body is Human that I am trustworthy. Did you learn nothing from your precious Laconic Warriors? But I have done much more than merely work for the 'evil monsters.' It was one thing for you—one of the Eight—to be allowed to live, but why am I still here? Why would the Morroks keep a Human female in their midst, when so few girls ever survive training?"

She seemed to want me to guess, but I refused to let her play with me. She laughed again, low and derisive, so unlike the laugh I had once thought was hers.

"When I was born here, not long after you were born in Tyrclopia, Lernuc saw the vision of our union almost immediately. Who better for you to produce the next of the Eight than with another person of full Morrok blood?

"Many thought the idea had been foiled when you were taken so unexpectedly from the Facility, but Lernuc's plans are not so limited. He ordered me to remain Human and to be trained differently from my peers—indeed to become more Human than any of them had ever been. Our union would still take place, but now that you were to be Human, so soft and so prone to emotions and attachments, I had to learn how to interact with Humans—how to endear them to me and how to get what I wanted out of them without raising suspicion."

"But you grew up in Settlement One," I said. "The leader—Frank—knew you as a girl after you came from Settlement Nine. We talked about you at the Outpost."

"That's why I poisoned him so soon after I learned that he was still alive," she said. "He told you that I was an orphan from Settlement Nine, but what he didn't know was that I had never once set foot there. Lernuc had it destroyed to make my orphanhood seem plausible. So a Settlement One family pitied me and took me into their home, and Frank even gave me the job of council recorder. Among Humans, a young, pretty girl raises no eyebrows if she overhears important tactics, because what could she possibly do with such information? And so I was able to monitor whether or not the leaders told Fallon's messengers about the Morroks; if they did, we had them killed, but if not, they were allowed back to Warrior Peak so we would not be revealed until the proper time.

"But as you neared adulthood, Lernuc wanted you to leave Warrior Peak, and who better to check on your progress than I? We crossed paths once or twice—my hair was blonde like yours then, don't you remember?—but as long as I didn't tell you my name, you wouldn't remember me. I found out who was close to you and planned their deaths to get you angry and frightened enough to leave the mountain. First the old blacksmith—what was her name?"

"Aldis," I said through gritted teeth.

"Right, Zachaes's wife. It was a pleasure to lead a Morrok through the Peak to dispose of that traitor's spouse. But after her, I had limitations. I couldn't go after your parents because they were going to lead you into the forest; I knew Fallon's name from my time at Settlement One, and when I heard he was your father, my hands were tied there. Hard as I tried, I never could get to Ritter or Levina, and I didn't dare try to harm Acules, so I had to settle for one of your classmates during that school tournament. After that, all it took was a few petty threats and letting you see a Morrok within Warrior Peak's walls, and you were finally in the forest."

"If you have the authority to coordinate all these Morroks, then why were you bruised and tied in a sack when I found you in the forest?" I asked, desperate to find a flaw or imperfection in her plan.

Her nose wrinkled. "I allowed them to do that to me. What better way for you to find me than as a pathetic wretch who'd been kidnapped and tortured by Morroks for months on end? Like Settlement Nine, we destroyed Settlement One so I could join you without anyone catching me in a lie and thus instilling doubt in you that I was anything more than an innocent girl. No one who had any sense would really believe that Morroks would keep a Human woman alive for no reason, but I knew your gallantry would produce a lasting bond between us, not to mention make you think that I *understood* you, that I more than anyone knew how *horrible* Morroks were."

She paused simply to laugh again, disdainful and pitiless. "I noticed almost too late that you were traveling with someone who'd seen me before—Todd, the messenger who came to Settlement One and whom the Morroks allowed to live so he could report our existence in the desert. I had my companions take care of him while you saved me.

"After that, my way was easy. Ironically enough, considering our blood, I am a beautiful woman, just as you are a beautiful man, and so the matter of attracting you wasn't my obstacle. Rather, it was getting you to look away from this inferior woman. I considered trying to kill her again, but I'd seen men lose wives at Settlement One; they wouldn't look at another woman for *months*, even *years*, so I decided to bide my time and wait for you two to fall apart on your own. Then I would be the loving voice of comfort for the poor, misunderstood husband."

"I was weak because I felt sorry for myself and because I missed Jamie," I said, fully aware that I was defending myself to Levina as well. "It wasn't Levina's fault."

"Ah yes, Jamie," Cassandra said. "I'm glad you mentioned her. In the midst of all this, Lernuc asked another task of me—stealing your child. While you were off whining to Lernuc, I had my companions stage an attack on the Outpost, and it was all too easy for me to deliver her to them. I believe Glynis saw me with the child, and her thick head might have pieced it all together if I hadn't had a Morrok silence her. Regardless, to my delight, Jamie's disappearance unhinged your foolish wife and depressed you so much that a bearded woman could've caught your attention as long as she listened to your pathetic ruminations.

"Pathetic," she repeated. "I don't know why Lernuc is so threatened by you. If he'd watched you as closely as I have over the years, he certainly wouldn't be."

"You did all this work—all the murders, all the deception—just to sleep with me?" I said. "I would call that pathetic as well."

She laughed yet again, more wildly than ever. "Sleep with you? What do I care about sex, especially with you? No, you stupid man, did you not listen to the beginning of my story? A child! Lernuc wanted our child! And here it is." She cupped her free hand under her still-flat stomach. "As you know, two Morroks conceive nearly every time they mate, but I waited around the Outpost for a few weeks after our union just to make sure. Then I was finally free to leave you insufferable Humans and to enjoy the glory I have achieved among my people."

"Then why did you take Jamie?" Levina asked, speaking up for the first time. Her voice was unsteady but free of tears. "If you were so confident in Orestes's weakness for you, why did you have to take my daughter?"

Cassandra's smile faded. "I admit it was a precautionary measure in case I failed to seduce Orestes. But now that I have succeeded, Lernuc has the opportunity to watch both children grow together and compare their behavior. Then, when it becomes clear if they are of the Eight, he will be prepared to act should one of them try to rebel like you."

"He told me he'd give Jamie back," I said, rising a little from the floor in spite of myself. Cassandra tightened her grip on her sword and brought it closer to my chest.

"And Lernuc keeps his promises," Cassandra snapped. "I just wanted to see your face when I told you that for the next thirteen years, your children will be pitted against one another in every way imaginable. They will be raised just as Dirth was raised and as it was intended for you and Acules to be raised. The two of you were mistakes that will not be repeated. You will see your daughter again, Orestes, but I just hope you recognize her after she's taken the serum."

With one last laugh, she gestured to the Morroks, and the three of them jogged out of the building.

I jumped to my feet and scrambled for my sword and dagger, but they were gone. Undeterred, I sprinted to the door and looked out. With the Warriors now inside the walls, so many people were fighting that I couldn't begin to pick Cassandra out of the crowd. For a fleeting moment, I considered joining the battle, weaponless as I was, but I forced myself to turn back inside the barrack.

Levina had come out from between the bunk beds and had her hand on the sword that I had made for her back at Warrior Peak. She kept walking forward, toward the door, not looking at me. I strode toward her to block her path. When I drew near, she raised a hand, and I was sure for a moment that she was going to hit me.

She didn't. Instead, she pushed my shoulder without real force as she squeezed past me and left the barrack. I scrambled after her, determined to protect her wherever she went, for whatever that was worth to her now.

PART III: TYRCLOPIA

Chapter Thirty
Building a Home

Year 328

THE BATTLE LASTED FOR TWO FULL DAYS and weeks longer if one counted the zealots who chased the Morroks through the desert, into the trees, among the mountains, and inside their own tunnels. Warrior Peak sent the Militia to do an extensive sweep of the Gravel Lands, and when they found only a few Morroks, we agreed that enough were still at large to form another Facility. But that was a problem for another time, perhaps another generation, because we suspected that most of them had fled beyond the mountain range, and that was not within our current military's strength to defend.

Still, it was hard to fear Morroks now that we could travel freely between Warrior Peak and the Outpost. Because the walls and buildings of the Gravel Lands Facility were made of rock, we weren't immediately concerned about dismantling it, but there was already a road nearby that hundreds of Humans and Serenial used to tramp between the mountains and the forest daily. As stories spread of the mystery and adventure that the forest offered, several citizens of the Peak who had never known anything but mountains were eager to visit Serenity Valley. Likewise, many of the forest Warriors, including my friends Scott and Caleb, were entranced by the grandeur of such a large city as Warrior Peak. The Inventory and Domestic Affairs divisions were overwhelmed by the number of people applying for houses, which, as citizens of Warrior Peak, the foresters had every right to own.

Like the forest Warriors wanting to move to Warrior Peak, I too was homeless since my parents' house had been reassigned more than a year ago. I didn't really want to live there anyway, not with Fallon and Glynis gone. In fact, I found much about being back at Warrior Peak somewhat empty. As I reacquainted myself with the different sections of the mountain, I couldn't help but think about how exciting it would have been to show Jamie each level and building, and grief nearly overwhelmed me when I realized I might not ever have the chance. And although I called the mountain my home, many of the faces here now looked stranger to me than those from the forest. Ritter and Sylvia had remained in the forest in spite of a few vague promises in their letters that they would visit. Cyrus, Jacob, Holt, and their wives had moved back to Warrior Peak, but seeing them often brought me more pain than pleasure as they reminisced about Fallon and Glynis. In the end, I stayed with Xander and Lexa, who hardly minded having me since I spent most of my days up at the General's level giving accounts for what had happened during my years in the forest.

Levina, on the other hand, was living with her grandparents. I had seen her three times in the past two weeks since the battle—once when she visited Lexa and Xander and twice when she had been called to the General's level to answer some questions and give her perspective on some events. Each time, I had literally chased her down afterward, but all she said, very quietly so that no one else could hear, was, "I don't want to talk to you right now, and I want you to leave me alone for a while. Good-bye."

I saw her for the fourth time two and a half weeks after the battle. I had been up late the night before with Mark as we tried to piece together what was going on in Serenity Valley through different letters and conversations we had had with Serenial messengers. Mark was in an odd position now that we were back in contact with Warrior Peak; he couldn't call himself a general anymore, but he was still undeniably the leader of the Outpost. The Serenial had delivered messages to him, not the War Council, ever since he arrived at Warrior Peak, and he and I had pored over every scrap of news in between our summons to speak to the War Council generals. Recently, we had been going through our scattered census records, trying to account for everyone who had entered the battle, but it was tiresome and heartbreaking work. In fact, when he knocked at Xander and Lexa's door early that morning, I was ready to tell him I didn't want to do any work until he mentioned that we were going to see

Levina as well.

"The General wants to meet with the three of us in private," Mark said as we made our way up the mountain. Although I had seen the new General almost every day since I had come back to the Peak, it was still difficult not to think of Alec whenever someone mentioned the General. I had hoped that Alec—rather, the Elder—would speak to me again once the battle was over, but he had not invited me up to his level; and now that he was Elder, I could not demand an audience without his consent.

"You should get Levina," I told Mark as we reached the top of her grandparents' street. "She won't come if I knock." I had learned this lesson after a week of nasty looks from her grandparents when they answered the door to tell me Levina wasn't available to talk.

Mark nodded without comment and continued forward alone. When he returned a couple minutes later, Levina in tow, he proceeded to walk several feet ahead of us. I couldn't help but notice how pretty she looked in her pale blue dress, so different from the forest Warriors' earth tones, and with her hair and skin finally free of leaves and dirt.

"Did Mark tell you where we're going?" I asked her.

She didn't even look at me. "Yes."

"I don't know what he wants, but maybe after it's over, we can go somewhere and talk, just for a little—"

"Orestes, I am angry with you," she said calmly. "Understand that it's not because your parents are Morroks or because Lernuc has pursued you all these years or even because I have suffered due to these things. Although I don't understand everything Cassandra said that day, it is quite clear that you have made decisions, independent of your Morrok background, that have forever hurt our marriage and our family. It is for those decisions that I am angry with you, and I don't know when I'm going to stop being angry."

"Levina, I want to help you understand what Cassandra said—explain all the things I've been too ashamed to tell you all these—"

"No," she said with finality. "It's too late for that."

With that, she sped up to walk with Mark, and we continued the rest of the way in silence.

The General invited us to meet with him in the council room, which had lost much of its mysticism and secrecy in the past weeks with so many people needing to give accounts to the War Council. I had laughed the first time I walked into the council room at the Peak because it was hardly different from the stuffy, unadorned room we used for council back at the Outpost. There were no windows, and the only furniture was a hand-carved dark wooden table with matching chairs. A detailed map of the Peak hung along the longest wall, and a few shelves' worth of papers from the Inventory division sat gathering dust in the corner.

The General was a familiar face to Levina and me because he had been general of the Training division all throughout our time in school. Secretly, I wondered why he had been elected because he was quite old—much older than Alec; it might turn out to be one of the few times in history in which an Elder would outlive a General.

"Thank you for coming so promptly," the General said as we sat down. The room had only eight chairs—one for the General, six for the generals of the divisions, and one I could only assume had belonged to the general of the Laconic Warriors. "I know you have been anxious to hear what is to be done about our presence in Serenity Valley. As you know, the Serenial have allowed us to repopulate our settlements, but we have been deliberating how to maintain leadership over the forest Warriors. The council had almost reached a decision about this, but then the Elder summoned me. It turns out he had some opinions about Serenity Valley's place in Warrior Peak society."

At the mention of the Elder, I sat up straighter. It was difficult to tell, but I got the impression that the General didn't necessarily agree with what he was about to say, as he hesitated for a long moment before continuing.

"The Elder believes that it is good for us to remain in the forest as long as the natives approve of our presence, which, judging by their continual visits to the two of you, they do. Furthermore, the Elder does not think that the Intelligence division is large enough to handle overseeing all Warrior activity in Serenity Valley.

"Therefore," he continued, "he has recommended the creation of a new division—one to replace the old scars that have finally healed now that the descendants of the Laconic Warriors have returned to our numbers. This division will be the Foreign Relations division, and its primary work will be in Serenial Valley since our presence in Tyrclopia is very limited. The general of Foreign Relations will sit on this council, live on this level, and have the same authority as any War Council general. The question now is which of you it will be."

Mark and I glanced at each other, surprised, both by the news of this division and by the dilemma that had been laid before us. I had never had much desire for power, but a seat on the War Council was not something I could walk away from, especially when it could do so much good for Serenity Valley.

"I won't pretend the council doesn't have a preference," the General continued before Mark or I could say anything. "We have strong objections to such a young man, especially one who has not even graduated military school, being thrust into our midst. However, we cannot contradict the extreme confidence the Elder has in you, Orestes, though we don't know his reasons."

I opened my mouth to speak, but this time it was Mark who cut me off.

"Let me make this very simple," he said. "I cannot bear to be away from the Outpost any longer. I will take any title or any position in any division to be able to live there again, preferably with the War Council's approval."

"If that is your choice, then you cannot be a War Council general," the General said. "Given the nature of this division, we are not opposed to the Foreign Relations general traveling fairly often, but he must call Warrior Peak home."

All eyes now turned to me. I wished more than ever that Fallon were still alive; if he had been, there would be no question about who should be Foreign Relations general. This had been his job all along, except he hadn't had a seat on the War Council. And if he had been on the council, this whole war might have been averted, and I might not have lost so many people I loved.

I turned my back to the other two men and looked at Levina. "I wish Fallon were here."

Her eyes flickered past me to the other men, and then she leaned closer so that only I could hear. "I think this is right. Think of it: You are one of the only people alive who loves Warrior Peak and Serenity Valley passionately enough to call them both home. You are Fallon's son, and so you've heard and shared his vision for Serenity Valley since you were a boy. And you are one of the very few people whom the Morroks fear, and if they are ever a threat again, you'll be able to work directly with the council to stop them. They're fools if they think age is a disadvantage; this is a new division, and giving it to an old man who will die in a few years will only disrupt its creation and growth."

I laughed softly. "Would you be in my division?"

She sighed as if irritated that I had asked. "Yes."

"Thank you, Levina," I said, squeezing her hand. She squeezed mine once in return and drew it away quickly.

"I'll do it," I said to the General. "I'll need a lot of help. I don't know where to begin with setting up offices and duties, and I'll need your advice on who to appoint as officers, but I'm ready to learn. All I ask for now is that Mark lead the Outpost—as general, colonel, whatever the proper title is. He's the only one I trust to do it."

"Very well," the General said, his face impassive. "I will send word to the Elder and the council. Until we make some of the decisions you mentioned, your position won't be official. You will, of course, have input on matters concerning your division, and given your housing situation, you and your wife may move up here as soon as you like. And Mark, you are free to go back to the Outpost. We will be in contact very soon, and I'm sure your general will keep you informed. You are all dismissed."

We waited until we were down to the military school level before we all burst with excitement, drawing alarmed looks from the students as Levina and I embraced Mark and Mark and I congratulated each other at the top of our voices.

"I can't wait until Aderyn hears this," Mark said. "She used to ask me all the time why our mountain brothers wouldn't help us. I don't think the Serenial ever believed us about how powerful Warrior Peak was until they joined the battle! Now we'll never have to worry about being abandoned again."

"Never," I said, grinning broadly.

Mark excused himself to see if there was a Serenial messenger at the Peak with whom to share the news. Now without a buffer, Levina and I kept our gazes focused on the training grounds where we had spent so many afternoons together.

"I am happy for you, Orestes," she said stiffly.

"Thank you. But I was serious back there. I want to know if you're going to help me. You love both places just as much as I do, and you and your diary probably know Serenity Valley geography better than any Human."

"Of course I'll be in your division," she said in the same exasperated tone she had used earlier. "But I don't want you to think it's magically going to reconcile us. I would've joined the division no matter who was in charge."

"Naturally," I said. All my excitement shrank and knotted in the pit of my stomach. "Are you—will you move to the General's level with me?"

She sighed again. "I don't know, Orestes."

Deciding not to push her further, I made an excuse about wanting to see the Foreign Relations cave for myself and turned back to the ladder leading up to the General's level. However, once Levina had left, I walked through the school training grounds until I reached Aldis's old blacksmith shop. It had not been opened since I had left it two years ago. Dull, forgotten blades littered dusty tables and the grimy floor. Bags of coal lined the walls, untouched, and a single giant cobweb spanned the distance between the furnace and the bellows. The last time I had been here was my last day at Warrior Peak, when I had been scrambling to pack my gear and finish my sword before we left for the forest. It amused me to think that probably everything I had taken with me that day was now lost somewhere in Serenity Valley.

Wondering if I still remembered how to make a sword, I started a fire in the furnace and looked around the room for old scraps of metal to melt down. Cassandra had taken my old weapons from me, but I couldn't let that anger me, not when the Morroks had taken so many more important things. Besides, I probably needed a new sword anyway.

*

In spite of the General saying that my new title and office wouldn't be official for some time, word of the new division spread throughout the entire Peak and into the forest within days. The general of the Inventory division informed me that a wave of people were clamoring to transfer, and the general of the Training division said that all his graduating students were curious about the opportunities Foreign Relations held for them. I, of course, didn't know the answers to any of these questions, and I was glad for the seclusion that the General's level offered me.

Living in a cave was, however, a sharp contrast to the open environment I had enjoyed in Serenity Valley. The Foreign Relations cave itself, having been unoccupied for generations, had been a moldy, rodent-infested wreck before the Domestic Affairs division cleaned it and the Inventory division supplied it with furniture. But even after the cave became inhabitable, it was still strange to have only seven families as my neighbors instead of the thousands surrounding me at the Outpost. And as the exoticness of the mountain faded, Mark, Scott, Caleb, and most of the forest Warriors trickled back to Serenity Valley, leaving me without any close friends.

The most important thing missing, of course, was Levina, who, as far as I could tell, still couldn't decide if she lived with me or not. She would come up to the General's level for any dinner or meeting we were both invited to, but she hardly ever stayed the night there, and if she did, she slept in another room. She talked to others pleasantly enough but brushed me off if I tried to engage her. My only insight into her line of thinking was that she told me she didn't want me to have to deal with questions about our marriage when I had so many other issues to handle.

About two weeks after my meeting with the General, the most pressing decision I had to make was what to do about the children we had rescued from the Morrok Facility. There were about a hundred and fifty in all, their ages ranging from infancy to about eight years old. Right now, they were scattered all throughout Warrior Peak and the northern border of Serenity Valley. Some of them had been taken into individual homes, and others were being looked after in groups. No matter where they were, however, none of the adults around them could understand how to combat their aggressive and isolated behavior.

I passed along as many tips as I could to adoptive parents at the Peak, but the council and I agreed that it was best to gather the children together at the Peak to educate them and monitor their progress as their grew, especially the older ones. Although I would have loved to lead the project myself, I knew I didn't have the time. Luckily, the council agreed with my decision to give the responsibility to Xander and Lexa. All that was left was for me to ask them.

Lexa was already smiling when she opened the door to let me in their home. Ever since Xander had come back, she had taken to wearing bright colors against her dark skin, and her every movement had a jaunt to it, as if she were suddenly twenty years younger.

"I'm cooking!" she said as she ushered me inside. "I haven't cooked in years. I hardly ever knew how, but who cares? Xander eats it."

Xander himself was sitting in the front room. He too looked much better than he had when we first met; his hair was cut and combed so that he didn't look so crazed at first sight, and, like the rest of us, he now wore clothes free of holes and the smell of leaves.

Xander stood to shake my hand warmly, and Lexa kissed us both before she left for the kitchen. She had done this quite often before I moved out, and I thought for sure she would have lost some enthusiasm over the past few weeks. I didn't mind her affection, but I didn't feel like I deserved her gratitude when Levina was the real reason for Xander had returned. I knew Levina visited Xander and Lexa as well, so I could only imagine Lexa's behavior toward her.

"I have a feeling this is a business visit," Xander said once Lexa had left the room.

"How did you know?"

He chuckled. "Well, you requested dinner via a War Council messenger."

I grimaced. "Sorry about that. I hate doing that, but the other generals give me strange looks when I say I'll do things like that for myself. I'm not ready to tell them to get over themselves yet."

"I understand."

I glanced at the door through which Lexa had disappeared. "I should probably tell you part of my proposal before Lexa come back."

"Why?" Xander asked.

"Well, part of the reason I thought you might want to take on this project is because of your time in the forest, and I didn't know if Lexa knew about . . ."

"About me handing children over to Morroks?" Xander said, unabashed. "She knows about it. How could I not tell her?"

"Oh," I said, surprised. "But wasn't she . . . I mean, she must've been mad or shocked or . . ."

He sighed. "She was disappointed in me. Hell, I was disappointed enough for the both of us, but she forgave me. We've been married for more than twenty-five years, and she has stayed with me this long, even when she thought I was dead."

I must have still looked confused because Xander laughed. Lexa swept back into the room and perched on the arm of Xander's chair. When I explained the idea to them, they glanced at each other and said they would have to think about it.

Although our meals were usually loud and full of laughter, we ate almost in silence that night as we all thought about my offer. Immediately after the last bite, Lexa whisked my plate away, and Xander joined her in the other room to wash off the dishes.

While they talked, I looked around the room a bit more. Where it used to be bare and unadorned, it was now decorated with flowers, more furniture, and even some paintings. I remembered with a dull pang that Glynis used to keep our house decorated like this. Perhaps Levina would have done the same if she stayed at my new home for more than one night at a time.

After a few minutes, Lexa and Xander returned.

"We'll do it," Xander said.

"Wonderful!" I jumped to my feet to shake Xander's hand again and embrace Lexa. I started to talk about some of the logistics—details from council meetings, ideas for possible locations for the school itself, and so on—but Lexa interrupted.

"There'll be time for that later. We want to talk to you about something as well. Sit."

A little unsettled, I resumed my seat.

"We think you need to get away from Warrior Peak for a little while," she continued. "You've suffered many losses in the past few years, and everyone here knows your face, your story, and your title so well that you can't get any relief from that pain."

"Well, I'm not going to get away from that in Serenity Valley," I said.

"I agree," Lexa replied. "We think it might be good for you to go to Tyrclopia, even for just a few days. You can tell the generals it's something for Foreign Relations."

"Go to Tyrclopia?" I repeated. For all the times I had heard about it, whether in stories or in others' recollections, I had never thought about going there myself. Even though it had been years since I had found out that the country was real, I still always thought of it as an imaginary place from Aldis's story.

"And make sure Levina goes with you," Xander added.

I scoffed.

"Just promise us you'll ask her," Lexa said.

"I'll try," I said just to appease them. "But what about you two? Your sons are still there! Acules said they are alive and healthy. Don't you want to see them?"

Lexa smiled sadly. "Yes, we do, but it's not as simple as that. The journey over the mountain isn't as easy for us anymore, and our sons are grown by now. We don't want to disrupt their lives, especially since we didn't leave in a very honorable manner. What they must think of us I cannot imagine."

"You can't let that stop you," I said. "Acules didn't bear a grudge, and I'm sure Matthew and Jonathan won't either. If I had parents like you, I'd want to meet them. And I know if I had the chance to see my daughter again . . ."

An awkward silence fell.

"I appreciate it, Orestes—I really do," Lexa said. "But we've decided. However, if you go, I do hope you'll tell Acules that Xander is still alive."

"I will," I said. "If I go."

After that, the conversation lightened considerably, and we were able to spend a few hours enjoying each other's company. By the time I left their house, I felt more uplifted than I had in days.

On the way back to the General's cave, I passed Levina's house and remembered my promise to Lexa. I didn't want to ruin my good mood, especially since I wasn't seriously considering going to Tyrclopia, but it was too difficult to walk by Levina without saying something, even if I didn't ask about Tyrclopia.

Because it was so late, I bypassed the front door and snuck around to the side of the house. I thought of the night we first kissed when I had slid through her window without announcing myself, but this time, I restrained myself to rapping on the window frame. Her room was dark, but I kept knocking until I heard her on the other side of the heavy curtains.

"What?" she hissed.

Suddenly without anything to say, I cleared my throat and blurted the only thing that came to mind: "I just thought you should know that I'm going to Tyrclopia for a few days, so I won't be around if you go up to the General's level. I know how much you love visiting."

She didn't speak for so long that I was thinking about walking away. Then thankfully she broke her silence.

"When are you leaving?"

"I—I don't know. The day after tomorrow maybe. I haven't brought it up to the General yet."

"Could I come too?"

If I had been undecided before, I knew at that moment that I loved Tyrclopia as much as any man could love a piece of land.

"Of course," I said, unable to contain my excitement. "I'll let you know the details as soon as I decide. Do you have anything going on you need to be here for?"

"Nothing I can't rearrange," she replied. I was pleased to hear some eagerness in her voice as well.

"Okay then. Good night, Levina."

"Good night, Orestes."

The rest of the walk up to the mountain passed quickly. I didn't think about any of the council meetings I might miss while I was gone or any of the people who would be upset when I turned down dinner invitations. Instead, I had the carefree feeling Aldis's stories had always given me, and I laughed to myself as I mused that if Tyrclopia always gave me this bliss, Warrior Peak would be lucky for me to come back at all.

Chapter Thirty-One
Line in the Sand

TYRCLOPIA WAS JUST AS ALDIS had always described it. Even from the top of Warrior Peak's mountain, farther up than even the Elder's cave, we could not see for any great length, but I imagined to myself that I could spot the desert in the west, the farmlands in the east, the forest and ocean in the north, and, somewhere in the middle, Acules's house.

Xander had instructed Levina and me to climb straight up Warrior Peak and straight down the other side of the mountain, at whose foot sat a village called Highland. He had warned us that the other side of the mountain was completely unsettled except for this village, but even so, the climb was not difficult. Even without ladders and steps and carved paths, Warrior Peak's opposite face was kind to Humans, providing many gentle inclines and footholds, almost as if inviting Tyrclopia to visit the other side. In fact, by the time we reached Highland, I couldn't understand why Acules was the only Tyrclopian who had ever bothered to explore the mountain.

Highland was easily the largest flat settlement I had ever seen. Built snuggly on a great plateau at the very bottom of the mountain, it was nothing to Warrior Peak, but none of the Peak's many levels could compete with the one continuous city that Highland was. In that way, it reminded me of the Outpost, but the similarities stopped there. Highland was much bigger than the Outpost but had none of the Outpost's organization, as the streets wound in every direction and pushed the buildings into eccentric positions. Highland was also more populated than the Outpost had ever been; the streets were a constant din, and stretching one's arms was never an option. Tyrclopia's government didn't seem to provide its people with anything, because street after street was filled with merchants in booths and outside shops haggling and bartering their wares, everything from fine jewelry and clothes to basic bread and fruit.

Levina and I clung to each other's hands simply for survival as people of all ages and both sexes pushed past us, apparently intent on reaching their destinations in as little time as possible. We tried to find an uncrowded street so we could snag someone to ask about Acules, but there seemed to be no such thing as a quiet place in the town. Finally we chose one of the packed streets and started pushing our way through.

Everyone we asked knew exactly who Acules was and where he lived, but no one gave us clearer directions than "a couple hours north of here." Finally, on the fourth street we tried, a woman running a grain stand gave a nod of recognition.

"Acules's son came by my booth just a moment ago. I'm sure he wouldn't mind showing you the way." She pointed a little farther down the street. "He's barely in his teens, but he's tall for his age. He's wearing a gray tunic if I remember right."

After thanking her, we hurried in the direction she had indicated and found a gangly boy in a gray tunic lingering outside a blacksmith shop. He was looking at the smith's products with distinct disdain.

"Are you Acules's son?" I asked him.

His disdain remained as he turned and scrutinized us from head to toe. "Yes, I'm Lance. Who are you?"

"Orestes, and this is my wife, Levina. We knew your father at Warrior Peak."

I thought that this would be all the explanation he needed, but his expression didn't change.

"Warrior Peak," I repeated. "He stayed there for a few years . . . came in the year 323, left in 325. . . ."

"Oh right. That's the place he went when he missed Asgerd's first word. And first step, come to think of it," Lance said. I remembered that Asgerd was the name of Acules's other son. "He's back at the house. Do you want me to take you there?"

"Please," Levina said.

"Okay. Follow me."

Following him was easier said than done as we tried to keep an eye on his bobbing head through the crowd. After a few more minutes of struggling, the noise died down, and we found that we were at the town gates, which were thrown wide open to a winding path leading down the plateau. Lance didn't spare a glance at the structure, but I couldn't help but sweep my eyes quickly over the gate and locks, wondering how they would hold up under an attack.

"He doesn't look very much like Acules," Levina said to me as we walked a few paces behind the boy down the dirt path.

"He doesn't?" I looked a little closer at the back of Lance's head. He did have Acules's light brown hair and perhaps his height, but there must have been something in his face that Levina didn't find familiar.

"No, Asgerd's the one who looks like Dad, not me. Everyone says so," Lance said over his shoulder. There was a trace of bitterness in his voice.

The end of the dirt path led us to a grassy field that stretched farther than we could see. There seemed to be no other structures and no distinguishing landmarks to help guide travelers.

Lance had turned aside to an open wooden building at the edge of the path, and he now returned leading a large, four-footed animal. I realized with a start that this was the same kind of beast Acules had used to get us away from the Facility all those years ago. Levina jumped back when she saw it, and I was obliged to join her as I saw how big it still was in spite of my own growth.

Lance didn't seem to notice our shock. "He can't hold all three of us, but I could walk him if you'd like to sit on him, ma'am."

Levina looked only more flustered at being addressed as "ma'am." "You don't mean people get on top of that thing, do you?"

Lance cocked an eyebrow at us. "Of course. Haven't you ever seen a horse before?" When neither of us reacted, Lance took a few steps toward us so that the beast was within arm's length. "Go on and pat him. He's tame."

Shrugging at Levina, I reached out and ran my hand across the animal's side. The hair was coarse and sweaty in spite of how soft it looked, but the feel did at least go along with the terrible smell of the thing. Levina refused to touch it, and so, without further introductions, we set off into the open field.

Because Lance didn't seem to know who we were, I wasn't sure what to say to him as we walked. Eventually, once she had stopped looking sideways at the horse as if afraid it would pounce suddenly, Levina started asking him questions about his life—how old he was, what kind of sword he used, who his siblings were, and so on. I only half listened to their conversation as the bliss of being in a country where no one knew my name washed over me.

After a couple hours, a building came into view. It was large for a house, built almost like a fort, and it rose defiantly out of an otherwise bare landscape. Standing two stories high, it had a flat roof with thick guard rails, and several narrow windows spotted the second floor. The timber of the outer walls was broad and free of spots or signs of decay, and each of the four corners was reinforced with additional wood, which made it look as if lookout towers could be added any day. A single chimney rose out of the side of the house and seemed to be shared with a small, one-story shack built next to the house. Even at a distance, we could see several figures scurrying around the front of the structure.

"People always come from the farmlands or Highland to train," Lance said. "Matthew and Jonathan are always around to give tips, of course, but really they all just hang around waiting to see if Dad will come out."

True to Lance's word, we found that nearly all the people outside the house—most of them young men—were dueling or drilling in weapon techniques. None of them had the precision of Warrior Peak cadets, but they were no worse than many of the fighters at the Outpost.

Lance called for his father a few times before disappearing behind the house to tie up the horse. As soon as he was out of sight, the door of the shack beside the main house opened. Judging by the smell of smoke and metal and by the way the wooden walls were discolored and distressed, I guessed it was a blacksmith forge.

Out of the forge stepped Acules, his face and hands marred with soot but his figure as tall and impressive as ever. Several of the young men looked around hopefully but didn't stop their training; if anything, they redoubled their efforts. Acules ignored them, but, spotting us, he left the threshold of the forge and wiped his hands absently on his shirt. He stopped a few feet short of us and eyed my belt.

"That is a terrible sword," he said to me.

I grinned. "I had a better one, but I lost it. I made this one a few weeks ago, but I hadn't been near a forge for a while, so I guess I'm out of practice."

"Hello, Acules," Levina said, stepping forward to embrace him. He smiled at her and said hello back, but he kept his eye on my sword.

"No, really, look at this," he said, drawing it out of my scabbard. He strode over to the house and slammed the sword against one of the thick corners. The blade cracked a little as it shifted off the handle. "Terrible. If it can't handle a wall, how the hell is it going to go through a Morrok?"

I laughed. "Fine, if I'm such an awful blacksmith, you can make me a new sword."

"All right, but you should watch me so you know what metals I used and where the balance—"

Acules's diatribe was cut off as the door to the main house flew open and a dark-skinned woman who reminded me very much of Lexa poked her head outside. Acules thrust the sword back into my hands immediately.

"Damn it, Acules, I told you to keep your little students away from my house," she snapped at him.

"My wife, Jade," Acules said, apparently unfazed by her reprimand.

When Jade saw Levina and me, she strode outside herself and looked us up and down just like Lance had.

"I don't recognize either of you. Are you from Highland?" she demanded. I got the impression that always talked like this.

"They're friends from one of my trips," Acules said before Levina or I could speak. "Orestes and Levina. You are married by now, aren't you?"

Levina laughed a little at his bluntness. "Yes."

"From one of your trips," Jade repeated, not looking overly pleased. "Very well. Come on inside. You can meet the boys."

We followed her into the house. It turned out that most of the building was made up of the large central room, big enough to hold scores of people, with at least a dozen doors branching off the side and back walls. Against the wall facing the blacksmith forge was a fireplace, not currently lit, with several stuffed chairs and couches surrounding it. Four boys sat in this area; two of them were about sixteen and had identical dark skin and light hair. The next youngest had equally dark skin and black hair, and the last was about six years old and had a pale complexion and Acules's brown hair.

Jade waved at one of the dozen doors leading off the main room. "I'll fix up one of the bedrooms for you later. Anyway, the twins are Matthew and Jonathan, the dark-haired one is my son Donahue, and the little one is Asgerd."

"I'm *not* little," Asgerd snapped. Levina laughed, but I was distracted by the way Asgerd and Donahue seemed to be playing. They both sat on the floor with several toy figurines laid out before them, but not scattered like one would expect from children; instead, they were arranged in what was unmistakably a battle formation, at whose head was not the older boy, but Asgerd.

My fascination at this was broken when I realized Levina had left my side to give Matthew and Jonathan each a hug. I tried my best not to laugh. I had told Levina about Xander and Lexa not wanting us to say anything about them to their sons, but I supposed the boys looked too much like their parents for her to resist. Matthew and Jonathan seemed confused, but not altogether displeased, at winning an older woman's attention.

I felt drawn to the twins as well, but for different reasons. I couldn't remember what they had looked like as babies, but just knowing that the two of them were the ones who had been dropped in my cell that fateful day in the Morrok Facility brought back memories so vivid that I could barely focus on the conversation around me. Levina squinted questioningly at me when she caught me staring at the boys, but I just shrugged and asked what we had been talking about.

Once we acclimated to Jade's harshness and fell back into rhythm with Acules's bluntness, Levina and I spent a restful afternoon with their family, talking and touring their house and even trying to ride one of their horses. The one place we didn't explore was Acules's blacksmith shop, simply because its owner seemed too distressed at the thought of having so many people in it at once.

By the time evening fell, the last of the duelers had left for home, and we were back in the main room of the house. Asgerd and Donahue had gone to bed, and Lance was fighting to stay awake as he listened to us talk. Once Levina and Jade started to dominate the conversation, Acules rose from his seat and sidled out of the room. After a moment's pause, I followed.

I thought he might have gone to his forge, but I found him leaning against the side of the house, looking up at the stars.

"Xander's alive," I said.

"I always thought there was a chance," Acules replied. "He lived his whole life here and Dirth didn't come after him, so it seemed odd that he'd be killed the first time he actually defied them, even on the other side of the mountain."

I leaned on the wall next to him and glanced upward as well. "I don't know how much you've told Matthew and Jonathan about him and Lexa, but they wanted me to pass that message along to you in case you want to tell them."

"You came all the way here just to deliver a message? Don't you have lackeys for that by now?"

I laughed. "I do, actually, but that's not why I came. I didn't really know why until I got here."

He turned away from the stars to look at me. "You want to go to the Facility."

"Yes," I replied. I hadn't realized my desire until just then, after being among Acules, Matthew, and Jonathan, after seeing a horse again, and after walking through the field and the mountain through which Alec had once carried me. As much as I loved Warrior Peak and Serenity Valley, they didn't hold one thing that was a part of me, no matter how much I had looked for it in the fortress on the lake and the camp in the desert; they didn't hold that damn tower, and I had to go back to it at least once more.

"I'll have Lance take you to the desert in the morning," Acules said. "You'll know your way beyond that, trust me."

"Thank you."

I let several minutes pass as we listened to the talk and laughter from within and enjoyed the cool night air. I wanted to tell Acules about everything I had done and accomplished since he left Warrior Peak, and I wanted to hear from him what the Morroks were doing in Tyrclopia. But I couldn't think of how to discuss any of that before I knew the most important matter that lay between us.

"Do you know about us?" I asked him. "You and me. How the Morroks . . . how we're different with the Morroks than any other Human."

He didn't speak for a long time, and his next words came slowly. "I know we're connected. And it's just like I told you back at Warrior Peak: We know a hell of a lot about Morroks, and that will forever give us an edge over them."

"But there's more to it than that. There's this—I don't know—prophecy or prediction or something that makes us even more unique than just being kids who were rescued from the Facility—"

"I don't put much stock in prophecy," Acules said. "No one has to do anything he doesn't want to because of something someone else said. We're good at killing Morroks, but that doesn't mean we have to do it."

"But we can."

"And we choose to, and that's enough for me. So hold on to your prophecies. I don't need to hear them."

Although I wanted to argue further, I didn't think it would help, and so I kept my silence. After a time, Acules left me and crossed to his forge. He returned bearing an old but sturdy sword. "Just in case," he said.

*

Lance and I arrived at the edge of the desert early the next morning. I had barely slept the night before in anticipation of this journey. My pacing around outside late into the night had saved Levina and me from the awkwardness of having to share a bed, but it hadn't helped to calm my nerves at all.

As Lance and I rode on the horse through the plains, I felt a little foolish clinging to a twelve-year-old boy, but it was all that kept me from falling off the beast. Lance accepted my ignorance with only a small grin, which I thought was very mature of him.

As the grass started to give way to sand, Lance drew the horse to a halt. "I can take you closer if you promise not to tell Dad."

"What do you mean?"

"He doesn't think I know where you're going, and he definitely doesn't know that I know where it is." He stuck his chin out as if daring me to scold him.

"It'll be our secret then," I said.

He kicked the horse's side again, and we plunged into the perpetual sand storm that forever separated this desert from being anything like the Gravel Lands.

My anxiety rose with each gallop the horse took. The sand muting the sky's color, the total lack of water or other signs of life, the uneven landscape of dunes and valleys—all these things took me back to my first years of childhood, and coming back only reinforced the misery of the memories. Lance had thought to bring a skin filled with water, but we emptied it quickly, and our eyes were soon rubbed red and raw from trying to keep them clear of grit.

Finally I spotted the tower in the distance. Just the tip was visible at first, but as we rode, more and more of it seemed to rise up over the sand until we were at the very edge of the dune, looking down at the great black needle. It was just as large and jagged as I remembered it.

"I don't really want to hang around here, but I'll wait for you at the edge of the desert," Lance said, his voice unsteady. "Just walk straight east. It's not the shortest way back home, but you won't get lost."

I thanked him and fumbled off the horse.

As Lance galloped away, I squinted down into the dune. Morroks dotted the level below, and several children were there too since it was daytime. With a deep breath, I started down the dune, half walking and half sliding until I reached the bottom. I had to trust that my name was still worth something at least here in Tyrclopia.

The Morroks nearest to where I landed reacted as I would have expected them to—drawn weapons and threatening advances—but I did not move to fight them. Instead, I walked steadily forward, staring each of them in the eye until they turned away. I heard my name whispered once or twice as I entered the tower itself.

As familiar as the desert was, it was nothing to the memories that flooded me as I walked through the tower doors. Even though I had been so young when Acules rescued me, I still remembered what each door on the first floor led to—where the Morroks ate, where the infants slept, where the training weapons were kept. But most importantly, I knew where the stairs were, and I began to climb.

I paused about halfway up when I reached the level of my old room. I left the stairway and padded through the narrow corridors until I found the door with the lock.

It looked as if the Morroks hadn't touched the room since the day I left it, except that they had disposed of my guard's dead body. The door still stood open, the lock hanging off it. I stepped over the threshold and glanced up at my window, which was still a little too high for me to see out of. Now fully grown, I could not hope to lay flat on the floor at any angle, and I wondered how I had ever survived in such a small space, especially when Dirth had visited.

Once I found the stairs again, I continued upward, my heart beating quickly and my hand on my borrowed sword. I encountered very few Morroks on the way, and those I did meet treated me just as the ones at the base of the tower had. By the time I reached the top, I knew I had passed hundreds, if not thousands, of children who were trapped just like I had once been, but I had a feeling that I would not receive similar amnesty if I tried to open one of their doors.

On the top landing was a single door without a lock. I pushed it open and was not surprised to find Dirth sitting on the opposite end of the room, as if waiting for me.

As I walked toward him, I couldn't help but be reminded of the Elder's cave. The room was very large, encompassing the circumference of the tower, but it was poorly lit and sparsely furnished, and there was no shortage of weapons piled along the walls. But Dirth did not sit on a stuffed armchair like the Elder. Instead, like Lernuc in the Serenity Valley fortress, he sat on a hard chair in the middle of the room. This chair, however, was truly a throne—carved from stone with harsh, spiked patterns that matched the jagged outer walls of the tower itself.

I stopped in front of Dirth just short of striking distance. Even sitting, he was taller than I was, but just barely. His face was exactly as I remembered it—stretched and haggard and angular, not helped at all by the crooked smile he was giving me now. What surprised me, though, was that his face did not horrify or frighten me like it used to. If anything, I felt calm after the anxiety-ridden climb I had just made.

"So you have returned," he said.

"Yes, but only to say one thing."

"What, that you hate me? That you're swearing revenge on me? I've heard it all before, so do try to make your speech more interesting if you must speak."

I ignored his taunts. "I know that I am a Morrok. I know that I might've swallowed a drop or two of the serum the day Acules rescued me, and I know my parents are Morroks."

"I'm not your father, boy," Dirth sneered. "Have you been worrying about that all these years? No, I have two sons, but one of them is long dead, and the other I hear you recently disrupted from doing the first useful thing in his life."

"What do you mean?" I asked, temporarily distracted.

"Zachaes and Xander," Dirth replied. "Why else would I allow them to enter my Facility unharmed? However, when Zachaes was foolish enough to try to keep Acules from me, I had him killed. And Lernuc has kept me informed about my other, weaker son—about how he has been leader of those who have supplied us with children in Serenity Valley for generations now. That is, he was doing so until you interfered."

"It doesn't matter now. He might have strayed for a while, but Xander has chosen his side. And if both of your sons can defy you in such a way, then it is that much easier for me to do the same."

"You are still stubborn," Dirth said, flexing his claw-like fingers. For a moment, I was afraid he might rise from his seat, but his face merely fixed into a scowl. "Stubborn and foolish. So you think you can turn your back from this completely?"

"I can, and I have, a long time ago. I don't know why you and Lernuc ever thought I could be on your side. There is nothing appealing about this life. All you have to offer is a promised dominance that you have yet to exercise. I was afraid for the longest time that I was like you, but that time is over. This is the last time I walk into any of your settlements with a sheathed blade. If, like your sons, it is my bloodline that allows me inside these walls, I now reject that privilege. We are enemies, and after today, if I have the chance, I will kill you or any of your followers, not to glorify your training but to stop you from terrorizing my people any more than you already have."

I expected Dirth to treat my proclamation with the contempt and sarcasm he had shown thus far, but instead, he looked angrier than ever, and perhaps—if I wasn't mistaken—a little threatened.

"Dominance that we have yet to exercise? Just wait, boy. Our blood and our serum will preserve our army to terrorize many of your generations yet to come. You may have chosen to fight against us, and you may be one of our first real threats besides Acules, but remember that there are six of you still out there. We will not make mistakes with them."

I laughed. "You have already failed twice, and yet you still expect to succeed with the same brutal, underhanded tactics that repulsed Acules and me. I have chosen to side with Humans, and I assure you that if any of my children are one of the Eight, they will do the same."

"Lofty words for a man who doesn't know where either of his children is."

"That won't last forever," I said quietly. Turning my back to him, I began to walk toward the stairs.

"They are not here!" Dirth called. "And if you try to 'rescue' any of the others, I will kill you myself!"

Blocking out his threats, I descended the stairs as quickly as I could. The Morroks didn't know of my defiance yet, but I knew that wouldn't last for long.

By the time I reached the foot of the tower, I heard shouts following me from every level of the building. Resisting the urge to look back, I sprinted toward the dune and, like so many years before, scrambled on my hands and knees until I reached the top.

I was only mildly surprised to find Lance there, still sitting atop the horse.

He grabbed my outstretched arm to pull me up. "I thought you might tick them off, so I came back," he explained. The Morroks breached the dune only seconds after I was on the horse, but Lance dug his heels into its side, and we sped off without them landing a single blow.

Even as we fled the tower without a single attempt to fight back, I couldn't help but feel victorious in my own way, and I was glad to turn my back on Dirth for good.

*

Gray clouds were starting to obscure the afternoon sun by the time Lance and I arrived back at Acules's house. No men were outside training today, and it seemed as if most of Acules's family was gone as well. Levina was sitting outside the house about where Acules and I had stood last night, but she jumped to her feet when she saw Lance and me ride up.

Lance disappeared to tie up the horse before the rain began, and Levina ran to where I had jumped off. She threw her arms around me but just as quickly pushed me back, causing sand to shower down on us both as it loosened from my hair and the folds of my tunic.

"Acules told me where you went! Thank goodness you're all right, but really, Orestes, what a huge risk just to peek at a tower that will never affect us—that we'll never have to worry about attacking or being attacked from—"

"That tower does affect me," I told her, and she fell silent immediately. "At least it did until today. I didn't go just to look. I went inside because I had to finish something that started fifteen years ago, before I came to Warrior Peak."

She gazed up at me in disbelief, but I knew she was willing to hear me now that I was, at last, willing to tell.

"And did you finish it?" she whispered.

"Yes," I murmured, just as softly.

She took my hand and smiled at me for the first time in weeks.

"Would you—would you mind if I told you about it?" I asked her.

"I'd like that," she said.

And together we walked inside, ready to start the next journey of our lives, whatever it would bring.

Author's Note

Thank you for reading *A Warrior's Legacy: Orestes*! If you enjoyed the book, please consider leaving a review at Amazon.com or your favorite online retailer.

To find out about upcoming releases in the *A Warrior's Legacy* series, sign up for my mailing list at JEBell.net.

I love connecting with readers, so please feel free to contact me via my website (www.JEBell.net) or the following social media sites:

www.facebook.com/awarriorslegacy
www.twitter.com/JenniferBell211

Made in the USA
Lexington, KY
02 August 2014